# FRENCHMEN AND LONG KNIVES

*Patriots of the American Revolution Series Book Three*

©2017

## Geoff Baggett

**Cocked Hat Publishing**

ISBN: 0997383356
ISBN 13: 9780997383355

*Dedicated to my wife, Kimberly Gremore Baggett, and her father, the late Charles Hunter Gremore. I wish that he had lived long enough to read my story about his ancestor. Pierre Grimard captured my heart and my interest the first time that I stood in front of his headstone at the Old Cathedral Catholic Church in Vincennes, Indiana. Dedicated also to my wife's aunt, the late Sue Gremore Gibson, who worked diligently for many "pre-internet" years to discover the rich history of the Grimard/Gremore family in America. It has been a joy to explore and research their French ancestry.*

*With special thanks to Kim Baggett, Ronella Stagner, Steve Mallory, Debbie Mallory, and Dennis Adams for their generosity, expertise, editing, proofreading, and input.*

Cover Photography:  Kimberly Baggett

Cover Design by Natasha Snow - natashasnow.com

# PART I

*The New World*
*1769*

# 1

## THE VOYAGE BEGINS

*March 28, 1769*

A massive wave slammed against the hull on the starboard side of the ship. The roar of the merciless, powerful water was deafening. The timbers of the ship screamed in protest at the force thrown against them and the vessel tilted precariously to port, leaning almost thirty degrees. Screams of fear erupted from throughout the ship and carried across the decks above. In the midst of the howling wind and rain, Pierre Grimard heard the ship's captain barking furious orders to his crew. The men of the vessel were waging a desperate battle to save their ship. It seemed to Pierre that they were losing the battle.

The sudden lurch of the ship's hull had tossed Pierre out of his tiny lower-tier bunk and deposited him in a soaked, bruised heap on top of Antoine Alexis, his Austrian friend, business partner, and bunk-mate. He, too, had been thrown from his upper bunk along the starboard wall. The sudden angling of the ship caused the invasive rain and sea water inside their cabin to pool almost two feet deep in the corner where the port wall met the deck. Clothing, papers, bottles, refuse, and vomit floated in the unimaginably filthy water.

Pierre gagged as he attempted awkwardly to scramble to his feet and remove himself from the sickening pool. He heaved and vomited the remaining contents of his stomach into the putrid sea-water soup and then wiped his mouth.

"Antoine! I am so sorry, my friend. I did not intend to land on top of you in such a violent manner, but as you see the choice was not mine."

There was no response from the body that lay beside him.

Pierre called his name excitedly, "Antoine?"

There was still no response. A narrow beam of light penetrated through a crack in the deck above Pierre's head, illuminating their dark cabin with a dull, gray glow. Pierre gasped when he saw Antoine floating, face-down, in the knee-deep water along the port wall.

Just as he lurched to grab his friend the ship dipped into the trough of another great wave and suddenly righted itself. Antoine's limp body floated awkwardly toward the center of the room. Pierre, holding on to the railing of the bottom bunk with his right hand, grasped Antoine's collar with his left hand and pulled the man toward him. The ship bobbed violently as it rode to the crest of what must have been another thirty-foot wave. Still, Pierre clung tightly to the clothing of his friend. He somehow managed to roll him over onto his back and lift him up onto the lower level bunk.

Pierre examined Antoine for injuries. There was a rather large bruise on his forehead and a bloody gash on his scalp just above his left eye. The lad had taken a serious blow to the skull. Pierre leaned forward and placed his ear over Antoine's mouth. His friend was not breathing. Another wave slammed the ship. More water poured into the opening above and added to the volume that floated around Pierre's feet.

Panicked, Pierre rolled Antoine onto his belly, climbed into the bunk beside him, and then straddled his back. The ship continued to sway and roll in the violent waves. Pierre had to brace himself by planting his left foot against the corner of the bunk and pressing the top of his head against the ropes and thin mattress of the bunk above him. He vigorously pounded Antoine's back. He knew of no other way to clear the water from his lungs. He beat the boy with his fists and in the calmer moments between waves leaned forward and pressed the lower part of Antoine's back with both hands in an effort to clear his airway.

Pierre began to weep. He was heartbroken by the possibility that his friend … his one and only friend … was dead. And what a pitiful, pointless death it would be! Drowned in a only few inches of water inside of his own cabin! Still, Pierre continued to pound Antoine's back as he attempted to force the foul water from his lungs.

Pierre was only moments from giving up when Antoine suddenly jerked and emerged into consciousness. The stricken lad gagged and coughed a geyser of foul water from his mouth. Pierre cried out in relief and rolled Antoine onto his back. Once again Antoine coughed, expelling more water. There was also thick mucus tainted with blood. He pushed Pierre away and rolled over onto his right side, coughing even more. When it seemed that his lungs were finally clear Antoine rolled once again onto his back.

Pierre howled with delight. He slapped Antoine's cheek playfully, then lifted his friend's head to his chest and hugged him tightly. His tears of terror converted into tears of joy.

"Wha … what happened, Pierre?"

Pierre gently released his friend and allowed him to lie back onto the thin, lumpy mattress.

"You took a blow to the head and damned near drowned in six inches of water, you dumb Austrian. I thought that I had lost you. You were not breathing at all."

"So you saved my life, then?" asked Antoine.

"I am afraid so, *mon ami*. You owe me." Pierre grinned and punched his friend in the shoulder.

Another tremendous wave slammed the ship, this time from the port side. The powerful explosion against the hull tossed both of the men to the right, rolling them against the starboard wall. It took several seconds for the ship to right itself again and deposit Pierre and Antoine back onto the mattress.

Pierre noticed that Antoine did not look well, at all. His face was extremely pale, and his teeth began to chatter violently. Pierre shivered as he realized how cold and numb his own limbs felt. Both of the men were soaked to the bone. Antoine was beginning to turn blue and seemed on the edge of passing out again.

"You are having a rigor," declared Pierre. "I have to get you warm and keep you in this bunk. You must not go into the water again."

Pierre spotted a length of rope dangling from a nail in the port wall. Taking advantage of a relative moment of calm in the storm, he darted to the nail and retrieved the rope. He also grabbed two thin wool blankets from his own bunk above.

"Wha … wha … what are you doing?" Antoine mumbled through his trembling, clicking teeth.

"I am going to lash us into this bunk and get you warm. Scoot over against the wall and cover up with these blankets. I must work the knots."

Pierre sat on the edge of the bunk and began to tie the rope to the bunk frame. He worked the length of rope back and forth, forming a loose zig-zag pattern across his and Antoine's legs. He burrowed beneath the blankets, as well, and then continued to weave the rope. Once he reached mid-way of their chests he yanked the rope taut and tied it to the post of the bunk near his head.

"There!" Pierre proclaimed. "We will not be tossed from this bunk again, no matter how big the waves become. Now scoot closer. We must use the heat of one another's bodies to stay warm."

"I … I'm from Austria, re … remem … b … ber? I've h … heard about you F … F … French fellows. So, d… d … don't go get… getting any ideas." He managed to chuckle even as Pierre gave him a good-natured jab in the belly.

"Don't worry, Antoine. I'm not one of those pale-skinned wig-wearers from Paris. Besides, you're not my type, anyway. You stink from all of that rancid cheese that you eat every day."

Antoine laughed again. Then there was silence … a violent silence pierced by winds, waves, and screams from the decks above.

"Just think warm thoughts, Antoine," encouraged Pierre. "Think about how warm it will be up on that deck in the sunshine tomorrow. Try to imagine how wonderfully warm New Orleans is going to be."

Antoine closed his eyes and scooted closer to Pierre. Quietly, slowly, he felt the warmth creeping back into his body. Soon the chattering of his teeth stopped.

But the storm did not relent. The cool waters of the Atlantic raged. Water poured through the overhead hatches as waves pounded the upper deck. Water seeped through cracks in the boards. It sloshed around several inches deep in the floor on every deck of the ship, soaking the feet of the men who strained to keep the frigate *Auguste* afloat. It flooded the forecastle and cargo hold. The timbers of the ship continuously creaked and groaned under the howling winds and waves of the massive storm.

"We're going to die on this ship, aren't we, Pierre?"

"No, Antoine. We are not going to die on this ship. I will not have it. We have far too many plans and far too many Creole maidens to woo in New Orleans."

Antoine laughed lightly as he drifted off into a deep sleep. Pierre listened to his friend's steady breathing. As he lay there in the stormy darkness he remembered back to that day in La Rochelle when he secured his position with the company and earned his passage to New Orleans. Finally, despite the storm that raged around him and threatened to claim his very life, he succumbed to the sleep of exhaustion.

*Six Weeks Earlier*

Pierre sweated nervously as he waited in the stuffy, smelly office. He tugged at his shirt collar and chastised himself as he thought,

"Pierre Grimard, how can you be sweating so profusely in the middle of winter?"

Cold, damp February lay beyond the other side of the rickety door, but the roaring fire in the poorly-drawing stone fireplace made the tiny office feel and smell like a smokehouse. Pierre coughed to clear the soot from his throat. He was tired, hungry, bored, and thanks to the ample heat, growing more and more sleepy as each minute passed. He shook his head and stomped his feet in an effort to revive himself and stay awake. He did not want to appear lazy when *Monsieur* Henri Daubaret made his appearance ... *if* he ever made his appearance.

Beyond the ample heat, Pierre was anxious and sweating because his entire life and all of his dreams were hanging in the balance. He was rapidly running out of travel options. He wanted desperately to go to America, where he dreamed of striking out on his own and making a name for himself in the New World. But no one seemed willing to take him on as a ship's hand. He had already made the rounds at the port and offered his labor to over two dozen shipping companies and ship's captains, but to no avail. There was not much demand for destitute, inexperienced young men from the inland grape country on board any of the privateers docked in La Rochelle, France.

He stole a glance through the cheap, milky glass of the office window at the row of frigates tied off at the docks of the harbor. Their huge masts jutted high into the air. Their decks were like a beehive of activity as sailors and dock workers moved about loading and unloading cargo and performing their duties.

How Pierre longed to be one of those men! He did not want to indenture himself in order to reach America, but he had resolved himself to the fact that it might, indeed, come to that. After all, he was only twenty years old. He was young, adventurous, and unmarried. He could afford to invest five or six years in servitude. Anything was better than going back home.

Pierre could not bear the thought of returning to his father's house and vineyards in Germignac with his crushed pride, empty pockets, and travel bag in hand. No ... he had no intention of playing the role of the Prodigal Son. He was going to New Orleans or Montreal even if he had to sell himself into indentured servitude or row a bateau to get there! But, realistically, the dubious *Monsieur* Daubaret was his final and only option.

As Pierre looked around the mysterious man's office he was less than impressed. He shifted his weight in the rickety, uncomfortable chair and examined the decor of the room. The curtains that flanked the lone window in the room were drab and threadbare. There was a large desk in front of the rear wall that was covered with a scattered bee's nest of documents, candles, rolls of ribbon, and quill pens. A rather smoky oil lamp burned in the corner. An ancient portrait hung behind the desk, presumably an ancestor of the proprietor. A map of the Americas hung on the wall to the right of the fireplace.

The room reeked of mildew, wood and oil smoke, stale sweat, and fish. An incessant and annoyingly loud ticking emanating from the direction of the fireplace served to heighten Pierre's anxiety. He glanced at the source of the sound. It was a small clock perched on the far-right corner of the mantle, well away from the billowing clouds of smoke that escaped the front of the fireplace. The clock, if it could be trusted, read a quarter before five. It was almost time for close of business in La Rochelle.

"He's not coming!" Pierre exhaled aloud. "I cannot believe it! What shall I do?"

Quite suddenly the door opened and swung inward on its leather hinges. A pale-skinned, thin man dressed in a suit of brown breeches, weskit, and jaccoat walked rapidly into the room. His arms were full of parcels of various shapes and sizes, which he unceremoniously dumped on top of his already-cluttered desk. Several of the parcels rolled off of the top of the mountain of clutter and tumbled into the floor.  The man hummed a tune as he removed his brown fur-felt cocked hat and hung it on a peg behind his desk.  He was startled when he noticed Pierre sitting in the chair along the far wall.  The man literally jumped into the air.  His humming ceased abruptly.

"Good Lord, *Monsieur,* you gave me a fright!  Who are you and what are you doing lurking in the shadows in my office?"

Pierre stood and bowed to his host, "*Bonjour, Monsieur* Daubaret.  I am Pierre Grimard of the village of Germignac.  We had an appointment at 4:00 regarding a possible position."

The man slapped a single hand over his forehead in frustration. "*Monsieur* Grimard!  A thousand apologies!  Your appointment completely slipped my mind.  I was engaged in business at the customs house and lost all track of time.  Please, please forgive me for my oversight.  Of course … the position.  I am desperate to fill it, but am having trouble finding anyone with qualifications in this city full of smelly seamen."

Pierre's face registered confusion.  He thought that he was applying for a seagoing job.

*Monsieur* Daubaret saw the look of distress upon Pierre's face. "Come, come, Pierre … may I call you Pierre?"

Pierre nodded in the affirmative.

"Come, and bring your chair over to my desk.  Sit with me.  We have much to discuss."

The man moved swiftly to his desk and removed as much of the clutter as he could, piling papers and boxes on the floor beside his feet.

"Now, *Monsieur* Grimard, I assume that you brought papers of introduction."

"*Oui, Monsieur.* Of course.  I have a letter from my bishop at the diocese, the Right Reverend Germain du Chastergner de la Chasteigneraye.  He is familiar with my family and circumstance."

Pierre reached into the satchel and retrieved the church letter for the businessman, who scanned it quickly and handed it back to him.

"You would be wise to hold on to that document, young man. You will need it in America for introduction to the church or in your negotiations for a future bride."

Pierre's eyes widened at the mention of a wife. *Monsieur* Daubaret chuckled at the young man's reaction.

"No doubt, Pierre, you will want to secure a bride before your trip upriver to the Illinois Country. There are no women to be had on the frontier except for the Indian savages. You'll want a good French girl from New Orleans."

"Illinois Country? New Orleans?" exclaimed Pierre. "I thought you were hiring sailors!"

*Monsieur* Daubaret threw back his head and laughed enthusiastically. "Sailors? I think not! I can find sailors by the hundreds in this massive port. No, I am in search of a man with merchant skills, experience in sales and shipping, and the ability to read or write. I assumed that you possess such skills."

"*Oui, Monsieur* Daubaret. I have worked in the office of my family's business for several years. I practically ran the operation over the past year, except for production."

"And what is your family's business?"

"Cognac, sir. It is the lifeblood of our region. My father owns vast vineyards and an impressive distillery."

"And you have kept books, shipped finished product, handled currency and notes of debt, and dealt directly with customers?"

"*Oui.* That was the essence of my work."

"Excellent! You are hired, young man!"

Pierre smiled. "I am most grateful, *Monsieur* Daubaret, but perhaps you could tell me a bit more about the position. Thus far, all you have mentioned are destinations."

"Oh, my goodness! Please forgive me, Pierre. I was so excited to find a candidate that I forgot to describe the details of the work. To understand our business, you must first understand the context of current politics in the Americas."

"I must confess that I am somewhat ignorant of such matters, *Monsieur* Daubaret. I merely wish to cross the sea and find opportunity and independence in America."

"Very well, then. Allow me to explain." He stood and invited Pierre to join him in front of the map on the office wall. "France, as a result of the outcome of the Seven Years War, ceded the Louisiana Territory to Spain in the Treaty of Fontainebleau in 1762." He pointed to the area on the west side of the Mississippi River. "Likewise, we lost the areas east of the river in the Illinois Country to the English." He indicated the area on the map to the east of the Mississippi.

"Though we have lost vast amounts of territory, we are still able to have some lucrative commerce through the port of New Orleans. My partners in this venture are two entrepreneurs in America. One is Gilbert Antoine de St. Maxent, a French military officer in New Orleans. The other is Pierre Laclède, a businessman in the village of St. Louis, located on the western side of the Mississippi River ... directly across from the Illinois Country. They have formed the *Maxent, Laclède, and Company* for the purpose of importing Frenchmen, slaves, and goods to gain a monopoly of the Indian trade in Illinois. For now, the Spanish are allowing us to bring in ships full of men and goods ... food, munitions, and various merchandise necessary for Indian trade. We do not know when this door of opportunity will close, so we intend to take advantage of it for as long as we can."

"So, your role in this enterprise is to provide the goods and men?" asked Pierre.

"Exactly. Goods for trade. Men to manage and develop the trade. I am an importer and exporter. Though I receive some goods from Louisiana, my most lucrative portion is found in the exports bound for Louisiana and Illinois."

"And what would my role be in such an enterprise?"

"I need you to accompany and supervise my next load of cargo to New Orleans and then negotiate its sale and transfer. You will be my company's merchant and representative. You will sell eighty percent of the goods to brokers in New Orleans and insure the transfer of the funds to my partners there. You will then book passage up the Mississippi River, with the additional twenty percent in hard trade goods, and help establish and maintain commerce in that area. We expect that the goods you ship downriver for export to France will help make us all rich someday!"

"Why do you not make the journey and handle such important business yourself?" asked Pierre.

*Monsieur* Daubaret grinned and shook his head. "No, no, Pierre. Travel over those treacherous seas is not for me. The journey will likely take fifty days or more. The conditions on board ship are dreadful, if not unbearable at times. The journey is fraught with peril and danger ... disease, storms, even pirates. Those who die during passage are simply cast overboard. And God help you if the bloody flux or the pox break out while you are on board."

The businessman shivered as he thought about the horrors of sea travel. After a quick moment of reflection, he continued his discourse. "Some ships do not even survive the journey and perish in the deep. No, Pierre, such adventures are for young men like yourself, not for old businessmen like me." He could see the look of consternation forming on Pierre's naive face. He smiled reassuringly. "So, with all of that in mind, are you still interested?"

Pierre stared numbly at the map on the wall. He knew that travel across the Atlantic was treacherous, but he had never before heard it described in such vivid detail.

He breathed in deeply. "What would be my reimbursement for this endeavor?"

*Monsieur* Daubaret turned back toward his desk. "You will, of course, receive free passage to New Orleans. I will provide you with fifty livres in gold and silver as a salary for your travel time. You will also receive one per cent of the total sale of the product at market as your personal commission."

Pierre was intrigued. "What do you anticipate the total sale to be?"

"Eighty per cent of my last load fetched over 40,000 livres in gold."

Pierre's eyes widened. His mind reeled. "That would be at least 400 livres commission for me!"

The merchant smiled. "Not a bad payday for two months of travel, eh Pierre?"

"No, sir! Most excellent, in fact!"

"It would be to your advantage to negotiate the highest price possible to increase your share of the profit. Good for you and good for our enterprise. Of course, you may receive a portion of payment in sugar or furs. I would recommend negotiating your personal commission in coin. All commodities will be forwarded to France through my partners in New Orleans."

"What is the cargo that I will supervise en route?" inquired Pierre.

"Muskets, flints, gunpowder, iron tools, farm implements, axes, medicinals, wine, rum, cognac, textiles, beads, and ribbon … things that will useful for Indian trade." The businessman leaned back in his chair and interlocked his fingers across his belly. "Well, Pierre? What do you think? Do you want the position?"

Pierre jumped to his feet and extended his hand to *Monsieur* Daubaret. *"Absolument, Monsieur!* Where do I sign?"

Daubaret grinned as he produced a document from his desk. "I will draw up the contract this evening. If you will return tomorrow morning after breakfast we will sign the papers and then you will be off to Louisiana!"

"That sounds wonderful. I will secure lodging for the night. But tell me, when does the ship depart, *Monsieur* Daubaret?"

"One week from tomorrow. Our ship, the *Auguste,* is currently being outfitted, scraped and painted. Careening and ballasting begin in two days. The cargo will be loaded in the final three days leading up to the launch. You will need to find lodging for the next four nights. You will be able to stay on board the ship for those three nights prior to departure. You will need to inventory all of the cargo as it is brought on board. How are you set for cash?"

Pierre shook his head. "I have very little, I'm afraid. I spent most of my savings here in La Rochelle over this past month as I was seeking employment."

*Monsieur* Daubaret nodded his understanding. "I suspected as much. I will pay you an advance of ten livres now. You will receive the remainder on the day of departure. Does that sound fair to you?"

"*Oui, Monsieur. Absolument, Monsieur.* You are most generous."

The older gentleman reached into the pocket of his jaccoat and remove a handful of coins. He counted ten livres in gold and handed the coins to Pierre.

"*Merci, Monsieur* Daubaret. I will see you in the morning."

"Excellent, young Pierre. I look forward to it. Please come around eleven o'clock. I've already hired a young Austrian who will be your assistant. He is educated, but you have much more business experience. I am placing you in charge."

"I will be here promptly, sir."

Pierre spun and walked toward the door. He placed his black cocked hat on his head as he stepped out into the frigid air. He could barely contain his excitement. His education and experience in business were taking him to New Orleans!

*March 30, 1769 - The Day After the Storm*

Pierre awakened to the sound of hollow, distant shouts. Sunlight poured into the cabin through the hatch and in between the planks of the deck. He heard laughter and the sound of men singing a song on the forward deck. The ship bobbed gently in the modest swells of the Atlantic. The storm had passed.

Pierre was a bit disoriented. He wondered what day it was and how long he had been asleep. He attempted to sit up but the ropes across his body prevented his rising. Suddenly he remembered the events of the storm and Antoine's injury. He gave his friend a jab in the side with his elbow. Antoine answered with a snort and then began to stir. He, too, attempted to rise from the bunk.

"What happened, Pierre?"

"The storm has passed. You hit your head and almost drowned. Do you remember?"

"Yes, but how long have I been sleeping?"

"I do not know, Antoine. I have been sleeping, as well. We will have to go topside and check on the condition of the ship. Surely someone has some information."

Pierre quickly untied the ropes and released them both from their life-saving restraints. Antoine climbed the ladder first so that Pierre could assist him. They emerged into the brilliant, warm sunshine of morning. Captain Jean-Luc de Laurent was standing at mid-deck and supervising the feverish work ongoing all around him. He spied the two young men emerging from below.

"Ah! *Messieurs* Grimard and Alexis! *Bonjour*, gentlemen. I trust that our little storm has left you none the worse for wear." He grinned broadly.

"You call that a *little* storm?" challenged Antoine. "It felt like the end of the world to me!"

"*Oui*, Antoine. A little storm, indeed. I have experienced and survived much worse during my many years on the sea. Though it appears that you suffered some injury during the night."

"He cracked his skull on the bunk when a big wave tossed us around and then he tried his best to drown in the ankle-deep water that covered the floor of our cabin," explained Pierre.

The captain nodded. "An all-too-familiar story, I am afraid. Many a good man has been incapacitated and drowned in storm water aboard ship. You are fortunate that Pierre was there to help you."

"Indeed, I was!" proclaimed Antoine. "He fished me out of the water and then beat it out of my lungs. It seems that I owe my life to Pierre."

"Well, perhaps you can repay him that great debt someday," affirmed the commander.

Pierre attempted to change the subject. "What day is it, Captain? I'm afraid we have lost track of time."

The captain chuckled. "It is mid-morning on Friday, March 22."

Pierre glanced at Antoine, who stared back at him wide-eyed. They had lashed themselves to the bed and gone to sleep before sundown on the previous day and slept for almost eighteen hours! Antoine shook his head in disbelief.

Pierre questioned further, "Did the ship suffer any significant damage or losses?"

"Unfortunately, we did, Pierre. We lost five men. Three were washed overboard in the storm, one was accidentally hanged when trying to retrieve a line, and another lost his balance and slammed his head into a cannon. Quite unfortunate."

"When will the funerals be?" asked Antoine.

"We hold no such services, young man. The two remaining dead men were cast into the sea at first light. Their friends said a few words over their bodies. They each died a noble sailor's death. They will be remembered over cups of rum this evening, but we will not mourn them as you may be accustomed to doing. It is different, I know, but it is our way. You are, of course, welcome to join us."

"What about the ship?" pressed Pierre.

"We have much water in the holds. It is barely above the ballast. Since we stored the liquor barrels on the bottom I do not believe any of the dry goods have been affected. We will, of course, bail and pump the water out of the forecastle and holds. We will also have to remove the water from all of the other decks. It will take us two or three days to get the ship dried out. We will work however long it takes to do so."

"That is good," proclaimed Pierre. "The cargo is our mission. We must protect its condition."

The captain nodded. "Indeed. But there is one other little problem." He pointed upward. "The main mast is in good shape, but the top of the forward mast is snapped and the rear mast is cracked. We will have to put ashore someplace, anchor, and make the necessary repairs. It may take several days, perhaps even a few weeks, depending upon the availability of timber."

Pierre began to calculate the days in his mind. He reasoned that a couple of weeks for drying out and making repairs would not do irreparable harm to his plans. It might even be quite fun to explore a tropical island!

"Then, it will take several days for the repairs?" asked Antoine.

"No ... it will take several days to find an island," the captain stated flatly.

"Why must it take that long? Aren't we closer to land than that? After almost four weeks I thought that we would be well into the southern islands by now."

"We may be. I simply do not know."

"You do not know?" exclaimed Pierre.

"No, Pierre. The storm may have blown us hundreds of miles off course. I will not know our relative position until tonight when I can see the North Star and use the sextant to determine our latitude."

"So, Captain, what you're telling me is that we're lost," clarified Pierre.

"*Oui*, Pierre. For now, until darkness falls, we are lost."

# 2

## CAYMAN BRAC

*April 3, 1769 - Four Days After the Storm*

"Land! I see land! Due north! It is definitely land!"

The excited declaration voiced by the lookout in the crow's nest electrified the crew of the ship. The men began to chatter excitedly, dance, and sing in celebration. Some climbed the ropes and riggings in an effort to view the shoreline. Pierre and Antoine ran forward to the bow and strained to catch a glimpse of their salvation.

The *Auguste* had been limping along to the northwest for three and a half days under partial sails and dull winds. The captain's reckoning of their position on the evening after the storm confirmed his worst fears. They were, indeed, significantly off course to the south. He determined that their best bet was to point the ship northward and hope that they would find an island. Depending on how far west they had progressed, it was possible that they may find their way to the shores of Hispaniola on their present course.

But this was not Hispaniola. It was far too small. Minutes after the lookout spotted the land mass, Pierre and Antoine could make out the western and eastern ends of the island. It could be no more than a few miles in length.

Moments later Pierre heard the lookout call down another word … a term that was unfamiliar to him. The man shouted, "Brac!"

At the mention of this word the celebration among the sailors ceased. Their songs and dancing transformed into worried looks and mumbling.

Antoine looked curiously at Pierre. "What do you think this means, Pierre?"

"Let us go speak to the captain and find out."

They turned from their spot along the railing on the bow and began to make their way through the mass of humanity, crates, and ropes that littered the crowded deck.

Captain de Laurent was busy barking orders to the pilot. "Yeoman, adjust course five degrees to port! Take us around the western end, nice and easy. Maintain safe distance from shore." He yelled down toward the deck, "Ready the launch! Lieutenant Bourreau, prepare your landing party!"

"Aye, Captain!" shouted a deep voice from the starboard side of the deck.

Pierre and Antoine bounded up the narrow steps onto the captain's quarterdeck.

The captain smiled broadly at them both. "Were you lads getting a bit worried, perhaps?"

"No, Captain," responded Antoine. "We have the utmost confidence in your seamanship."

"Where are we, Captain?" inquired Pierre, his gaze still focused on the island in front of them.

"Well, we are a bit further west than I anticipated, approximately eighty degrees longitude," responded the Captain.

"What does that mean?" asked Pierre, confused.

"It means, young Pierre, that we are due south of Cuba, the largest island in the Caribbean."

"That island doesn't appear to be very large," quipped Antoine.

"That is not Cuba, son. That is Cayman Brac."

"Cayman Brac? We heard some men say that word, 'Brac,' but did not know what it meant. How do you know this is Cayman Brac?" inquired Pierre.

"There is no mistaking the landscape. The island is roughly fifteen miles long. Its entire southern rim is marked by a high limestone bluff. Can you see how tall the island appears to be?"

Both men stared at the land mass and then nodded in response.

"This is, without doubt, Cayman Brac. We will sail around the western end and put in on a shallow bay on the northwest side. There is fresh water on this island, as well as ample small game. You gentlemen wouldn't mind a little meat, would you?"

Antoine licked his lips and smiled. He responded, "Wouldn't I? I haven't tasted fresh meat in over a month."

The captain chuckled. "Antoine, you shall have your fill this night. I hope you like the taste of iguana."

"What is iguana?" asked Antoine.

"An unusually large lizard."

Antoine made a disgusted, bitter face in response, causing the captain to laugh enthusiastically.

"Trust me, Antoine. You will like it. But we must remain vigilant while on the island and make haste with our repairs and foraging. It is not safe to stay here for long."

"Not safe? Why?" asked Antoine. "Are the natives violent?"

"No, son. Cayman Brac is a frequent place of respite and hideout for local pirates."

Both Pierre and Antoine exclaimed, "Pirates?"

At the sound of that word, anxious heads popped to attention and men all around them began to scan the horizon.

The captain called out, "There is no need for alarm, gentlemen. I was just explaining to our passengers about the circumstance and history of Cayman Brac."

The men grunted their understanding and returned to their duties. Some of them cast looks of disgust toward their two passengers.

The captain smiled and lowered his voice. "Try not to say that word too loudly up on deck, gentlemen. It elicits some unpleasant responses from the crew."

"Yes, sir," they responded with some measure of shame.

"Now, fellows, go and fetch your weapons and pack a small bag. I'm sending you to the island with the shore party."

⚬

Antoine and Pierre accompanied a small group of men whose mission was to find fresh water. There were four well-armed seamen escorting them. All six men carried jugs and bladders of various sizes for hauling fresh water back to the beach. At least three other similar parties had been dispatched in various directions from their landing point. All carried water jugs and muskets for hunting. Pierre and Antoine carried pistols tucked into their leather belts.

"Is the water far?" Antoine asked one of the rough, old, greasy-looking sailors.

"Not far, *Monsieur*. Only about four hundred yards off of the beach. That's how it was the last time I was on the Brac. There are several spring-fed pools relatively close by. You'd just better hope that these water holes have not gone dry."

Antoine asked innocently, "What if they have?"

"Humph!" responded the sailor. "Then we'll be hauling water over a half-mile instead of just a few hundred yards. You might even get a blister on those tender, pale hands of yours."

The other sailors chuckled at Antoine's expense. It appeared that he and Pierre were the victims of some ongoing humor and derision aboard ship.

Pierre made a note of the comment and chose, for the moment, to ignore it. He was too focused on the landscape that surrounded him. He was completely mesmerized by the sights that greeted him on the lush island. He had never seen such a tall canopy of trees. And everything was so amazingly green! The ground was literally covered with the large reptiles that the captain had mentioned ... iguanas.

The trees that surrounded them were filled with the most amazing birds. They were huge, green animals with white faces and scarlet feathers beneath their eyes. Surely these were parrots ... the amazingly colorful birds of the tropics that he had only read about in books!

Pierre gasped when he saw one of the sailors point his ancient musket toward a cluster of the birds in a nearby tree. He challenged the man, "What are you doing? Those birds are magnificent creatures. Surely you are not going to shoot one."

"*Non, Monsieur.* I am not going to shoot just one. We are going to shoot dozens of them. Our muskets are packed with buckshot."

Antoine protested, "But the captain said that we would be eating the iguanas tonight!"

The four sailors burst into raucous laughter. Clearly, Pierre and Antoine had borne the brunt of yet another sailor's joke.

"You gentlemen can eat those nasty lizards if you prefer," retorted the sailor, "but we prefer these tender, tasty parrots."

He raised his musket and began to take aim.

"But they are so exquisitely beautiful!" protested Pierre.

"*Oui.* And they taste exactly like chicken when roasted over a fire."

The other three armed men grunted and nodded in enthusiastic agreement.

Antoine grinned at Pierre. "Roasted chicken does sound delicious, does it not?"

Pierre's mouth began to water. It had been several long weeks since he had enjoyed a fresh meal. For weeks he, like the others on board, had survived on ship's biscuits, salted fish and pork, and tepid tea. He was lost within a delicious memory of his last real meal back in France when the first sailor fired his musket. Pierre jumped involuntarily. Three other shots erupted in rapid succession. At least a dozen of the birds fell to the ground. Soon other shots erupted in the distance both to their right and left. Obviously, the other scavenging parties had found trees full of parrots, as well.

"It sounds like there will be a lot of feather-plucking on the beach this afternoon," quipped one of the seamen. "Now there's a task that even you fine gentleman can accomplish."

"Great," thought Pierre. "Another derogatory dig." He was beginning to get angry at the disrespect on display by the crew. He tried to dismiss the offense from his mind and focus on the ongoing task of hunting parrots.

Amazingly, it seemed that the innocent birds were so unaccustomed to being hunted that most of the surviving ones did not make any effort to move from their resting places in the lower limbs of the trees. The sailors calmly reloaded their muskets, aimed at nearby branches that were thick with the beautiful parrots, and fired again. Several more birds fell dead or flopped injured onto the ground.

One of the sailors then quickly spread out a piece of canvas that was approximately ten feet square and then the men began to collect their birds. They trapped the ones that were still alive and smacked their heads against nearby tree trunks and then callously tossed them onto the canvas along with the dead birds. When the men were finished, there were twenty-seven of the plump critters collected on the square of cloth. One of the men pulled the corners of the cloth together, tied the bundle closed, and began walking back toward camp.

He called over his shoulder to one of his friends, "Adam, I will see you back on the beach."

"*Oui, mon ami.* Try to have those birds picked and cleaned before we return, eh?" replied the tanned, leathery sailor.

"Let us keep moving," urged Henri. "Jacques will take the birds back to the beach and begin cleaning them for us. We must find the water."

Less than a half-hour later the men discovered what they were looking for in a tiny jungle clearing. It was a small, spring-fed pool, located beneath a limestone overhang. The pool was no more than fifteen feet across and rippling with crystal-clear water. An almost imperceptible overflow of water leaked into a narrow rivulet that wandered off into the trees to the west. The color of the pool was astounding. It was a deep azure blue in the center, but slowly converted to a hazy green along the edges. The water was absolutely clear. Pierre could see the fine rocks that lined the bottom.

The three remaining sailors dropped down on their bellies beside the water and plunged their faces into it.

Antoine asked, "Are you sure that it is fresh?"

Henri lifted his smiling face from the water. "*Oui.* Fresh, delicious, and cold!"

Pierre and Antoine dropped onto their bellies and joined them. The water was amazingly cold and refreshingly sweet. All of the men drank until they thought they would be sick. They rolled over onto their backs in the shallow grass and reveled in their satisfied thirst. Pierre was so relaxed that he dozed off momentarily as the parrots squawked overhead and the dancing rays of sunlight warmed his body.

Henri's voice jerked him and the others from their all-too-brief naps.

"Come, men, let us fill our jugs. We must return with the water and make our report to the captain."

"This is only twelve to fifteen gallons at most. Surely this meager amount of water will not last long, even with other groups out searching for more," commented Pierre.

"You are correct, *Monsieur.* This is just enough to serve us for the evening. But now that we know the status of the water supply we will return in the morning with more men and larger barrels to collect enough for the remainder of our journey."

Pierre nodded in response. He knelt down and began to fill the jugs and water bladders that were assigned to him. He glanced around the clearing as the water slowly filled his first jug and noticed a dark mound of weed-covered debris to his right. It seemed very much out of place. He popped the cork into his newly-filled bottle and laid it aside to investigate.

As he walked near the mound he discovered that it was a burn pile. He poked through the mound of refuse and discovered pieces of flat wood from crates, iron trash and nails, broken glass, and bones of various shapes and sizes.

He called out, "Henri! Take a look at this."

The sailor sealed the water jug that he was filling and joined Pierre near the edge of the clearing. He looked at the pile and nodded grimly.

"It is an old campfire or refuse pile."

"How old is it, do you think?" asked Pierre.

Henri moved some of the trash with his foot. "Only a few months, I am thinking. Others have been here relatively recently."

"Others?" asked Antoine, joining them beside the curious pile.

"Pirates, *Monsieur*," Henri responded matter-of-factly. "They stop here often for water, food, and rest. But it appears that none have been here in recent days."

"And that's good news?" asked Antoine.

"I hope so. Or it could mean that we are due for a visit." Henri grinned.

𝕽

The men of the *Auguste* enjoyed a lively evening on the beach beside warm fires. Roasted parrot was, indeed, the table fare for the evening. Pierre was shocked at how much he enjoyed it. He believed, however, that the flavor was more similar to that of pigeon than chicken. He devoured an entire bird on his own. A scant few of the sailors killed and roasted some meat from the tails of the iguanas. Both Pierre and Antoine tried small bites of the bitter, tough flesh, but politely refused more and returned to picking the tiny pieces of meat from the carcasses of their tasty birds.

Unfortunately, it was too early in the year for any of the local fruits to be ripe. The sailors lamented the fact that there were no mangoes, guineps, or ju plums to sweeten their meal. So they settled for rum instead. The captain ordered a barrel to be brought from the ship and the liquid refreshment flowed freely throughout the evening, as did the singing, storytelling, and dancing.

Pierre and Antoine joined in the contagious revelry that continued into the late hours of the night. Men slept in the open wherever the rum led them to fall. Pierre wisely chose to restrain his drinking just a bit. He was still in control of his faculties when he eventually stretched out near one of the smaller campfires. When the coolness of night set in he used a canvas tarp as a blanket. He quickly drifted off into a deep, satisfying sleep.

Pierre awakened the next morning to a buzz of activity in the makeshift camp. About a dozen men were busy cutting a straight, thin tree near the outer edge of the nearby forest. Others were busy cleaning up camp refuse and organizing supplies on the beach. Two groups of men rolled large barrels from a beached launch. They were the water-collecting crews, headed for the inland springs.

It took several minutes for Pierre to locate Antoine. He lay in a contorted pose behind a large log, still clasping his rum cup in his hand. An unpleasant puddle of vomit lay congealed near his open mouth. The young man was not as accustomed to such great volumes of rum as were his sailing compatriots. While the seamen were already up and hard at work, Antoine remained in a rum-induced unconscious state.

Pierre left his friend as he lay and went in search of the captain. He wanted to see if he might be needed for a particular task or assignment. He soon located Captain de Laurent near the tree line where he was supervising the cutting crew.

"Ah! *Bonjour, Monsieur* Grimard. I trust that you had an interesting evening." He smiled devilishly. "Do you still hear the thunder of rum in that skull of yours this morning?"

"No, Captain. I feel fine. I was restrained in my consumption of your wicked juice."

"And where is Antoine? Did he drink and act responsibly, as well?"

Pierre grinned. "I'm afraid not, Captain. He tried to keep up with your crewmen, I think, but fell short of their level of expertise. He is passed out behind yonder log on the beach."

The captain laughed enthusiastically. "Well, let the boy sleep it off. He will have an epic headache later. Perhaps he will learn a valuable lesson, no?"

"Indeed," replied Pierre.

The captain turned and faced the tree cutting crew. The tree was already felled. Men were busy hacking off limbs and cleaning up the trunk.

"How will you repair the mast, Captain?" inquired Pierre. "It looks to be a monumental task."

"It's not quite as difficult as you may think, Pierre. As you know, we made temporary repairs to the rear mast as we worked our way northward."

"*Oui.* I observed your men winding the rope around the mast and covering the crack."

"Exactly. We packed the crack with a crude glue and applied several pegs in critical locations. The final wrap of rope served to lash the entire structure tightly together. It is not a long-term fix. It is merely a patch. But, barring any future cataclysmic weather events, it should serve us well until we reach New Orleans and secure permanent repairs."

"And the broken forward mast?"

"It requires a slightly different sort of repair. The mast snapped completely through approximately one-fourth of the distance from the top. We need the upper portion of the mast to be in place to properly deploy the sails and riggings. So we will cut three narrow lengths of this tree, float them out to the ship, wrestle them on board, and then lash them onto the broken mast at the point of the break. It is called 'fishing' the mast. It is much the same as applying a splint to a broken arm."

"And that will work, you think?"

"It should work quite nicely," replied the captain. "The ship's carpenter has made this exact repair several times in his many years at sea. It will not be pretty, by any means, and I would not set sail for France with a makeshift mast. But it should suffice until we reach New Orleans and put into dock for a professional replacement."

"How long will the repair take?"

"I'm confident that the carpenter will have the mast sufficiently fished by mid-afternoon. Once the timber is aboard it will not take long."

"It sounds fascinating. How can I be of assistance?"

"We will handle the repairs of our ship, Pierre. Even I am planning to stay ashore for now and allow the carpenter to do his work in peace." The captain grinned broadly. "He is in charge of the *Auguste* right now."

"Very well, then. What shall I do?"

"I would recommend that you enjoy your time on this beautiful island. Explore to your heart's content. You might enjoy a trek southward to the limestone bluffs. It is not even a half-mile from our location. Just mark your trail and try not to get lost. Whatever you do, don't wander off to the east. This island is almost fifteen miles long, and we have scarce little time to be searching for you."

"I will make every effort not to get lost, Captain de Laurent. I promise."

"Very well. Enjoy your excursion. And take this with you." The captain reached into his pocket and took out his telescoping spyglass. "Survey the waters to the south and east. Let me know if you see anything unusual, or any other vessels of any kind. But make sure you are back by mid-afternoon. We make sail at sundown."

"Aye aye, Captain," replied Pierre, throwing him an awkward salute.

Captain de Laurent chuckled and gave him a dismissive wave and then returned to his supervision of the crew of makeshift lumberjacks.

Pierre returned to the camp on the beach where he downed a quick breakfast comprised of two ship's biscuits and a cup of hot tea. He stuffed some more of the horrid wafers of rock-hard bread into his haversack, grabbed a canteen of water, and headed off into the jungle toward the southern edge of the island.

Almost an hour into his leisurely cross-island hike, Pierre emerged from the canopy of trees onto the high bluff overlooking the vast Caribbean Sea. The bluff appeared to continue endlessly toward the east. Looking to the right it appeared that there was a small cut in the cliff just a couple hundred yards to the west. He decided to make his way to the cut, hoping to find a good location to drop a line and perhaps catch some fish. He reached the spot in a matter of minutes. Peering over the side he spied a narrow, but manageable, path down the side to a small, dark pool surrounded by stone.

"Now this holds promise!" he proclaimed out loud. "A spot that is sheltered and easy for fishing!"

He slowly made his way down the pathway and examined the small pool. It was basically a tiny twenty-foot diameter pond, currently cut off from the sea by the low tide. The water lines on the rocks proved that once high tide moved in the entire pool would be covered with an additional foot of water.

Pierre walked around the sandy edges of the pond and tried to see signs of life below, but the water was too dark and murky.

"Oh, well," he thought. "There's only one way to find out if there are fish in here."

He reached into his haversack and took out a small leather pouch. It was a handsome fishing kit and a valued gift from his cousin and close friend, Rémi Grimard. Inside one flap of the pouch were two beautifully shaped iron fish hooks and several pieces of flat lead. Inside the other flap was a lengthy coil of fine fishing line. Pierre dug deep and pulled out a wine cork from the bottom of his haversack. He had saved the cork for just such an occasion.

He quickly threaded and tied the line on one hook and then tied on the cork. For bait he collected several limpets from nearby rocks and pulled the soft meat from the shells. Once he was satisfied that the bait was secure he tossed the line toward the center of the tidal pool. He waited for several minutes, but there was no response to his bait.

Being impatient, Pierre retrieved his line and pulled the cork about a foot higher in an effort to lower his bait deeper into the water. Once again, he cast his bait as far as he could toward the center of the pool. On his second attempt, he did not have to wait at all. His cork disappeared almost immediately. Pierre let out a gleeful shriek and began retrieving his line. On his hook was a small, flat, smooth-skinned silver fish that weighed about a half-pound. The fish was extremely strong and active and fought valiantly in an effort to avoid being caught. Pierre carefully removed the fish and placed it in a cleft in the rocks behind him.

He repeated the process and less than five minutes later had another fish on the hook, this one a bit larger than the first.

"Shall I try once more?" Pierre asked out loud to the pool at his feet. He proclaimed rather magnanimously, "I think I shall."

He tossed his hook into the water, baited with a large glob of limpet meat. And, like before, the cork plunged violently below the surface. He quickly retrieved a third fish that was comparable in size to the second one.

"I think that is enough, Pierre. Now let us have a feast!"

Pierre whipped out his folding knife and skillfully gutted the fish. Afterwards he rinsed them in the salty water. In order to make his catch easier to carry he threaded a section of line through the gills and mouths of the three fish to form a stringer. He then began his climb up the narrow trail toward the top of the bluff. He located a shady, comfortable spot at the edge of the trees, whipped out his fire-starting kit, and set about making a small fire.

A little less than an hour later the fish were cooked all the way through and falling off of skin and bone. Pierre laid the steaming fish on large leaves from a nearby plant, removed his fork from his haversack, and enjoyed devouring the flaky, succulent flesh. He seasoned them lightly with a dusting of salt and some crushed pepper that he carried in a small spice tin. After his fresh, delicious seafood meal he reclined onto a mound of soft grass, covered his face with his cocked hat, and relaxed. Insects droned among the flowers near his head. Sea birds squawked and called as they hovered over the warm water. Sleep came to Pierre effortlessly and quickly.

҂

Pierre awoke with a start. He was thoroughly disoriented and, due to his very deep and comforting sleep, had almost managed to forget where he was. He glanced quickly at the sun.

"It's almost mid-afternoon!" he exclaimed.

He reached into his pouch and pulled out his brass compass and sundial. He lined up the needle with magnetic north and then flipped up the arm of the dial. It read half past 2:00. There were just under three hours of sunlight left. It was definitely time to head back to the beach.

Pierre stood and stretched. He coughed a bit from the smoke that drifted into his face from his cooking fire. He kicked sandy dirt onto the remaining coals and took a quick drink of water as he checked the area to make sure that he had not forgotten any of his personal belongings. Satisfied that his property was collected and secure, Pierre turned to begin his return trip into the dense forest of the Cayman Brac jungle.

But then something on the water caught his eye ... a dark speck on the horizon far to the southeast.

Pierre rubbed his eyes to make sure that it was not his imagination. He looked again, and the speck was still there. He strained to make out the shape, but it appeared to be many miles away and well beyond his range of vision.

Quickly he thought, "The captain's spyglass!" He feverishly dug through the mass of items in his haversack until he felt the smooth brass cylinder. He extended the barrel of the spyglass and lifted the ocular to his right eye. It took him a moment to focus the instrument and find his tiny target with the telescope.

When the object in question came into view it sent a violent shudder down his spine. It was a dark, weathered, battle-scarred ship. There were numerous holes from cannon balls in the smoke-stained hull. The deck was brimming with cannons. Numerous closed cannon ports dotted the side of the ship just below the main deck. A plain black flag flew from the center mast. Men dressed in ragged red and black clothes populated the deck and dangled from the masts and riggings. All of those men were armed with pistols and swords.

They were pirates! And they were heading west along the southern edge of Cayman Brac. In an hour or less they would be able to cut off the escape of the *Auguste.*

A sudden twinkle of light from the area of the quarterdeck flashed in Pierre's scope. He whipped the device toward the direction of the flash. Terror filled his heart when he saw a man who was clad in black, quite obviously the captain of the vessel, staring back at him through his own large spyglass. The pirate lowered his scope and smiled devilishly, then turned and barked orders at his men.

Pierre took a quick look at his smoldering fire. It was still belching a wisp of thin, white smoke that wafted high into the sky.

"*Mon Dieu!* I have been discovered! I must alert the captain and crew!"

Pierre spun around and ran into the woods. He stuffed the spyglass into his haversack as he ran. The young man was oblivious to logs, obstacles, and barriers. He leapt over huge rocks. He climbed steep grades by holding on to saplings and trees. He clawed his way through dense patches of vines and bushes.

Pierre fell twice during his mad run. The first time he landed in a narrow wash littered with rocks and seashell fragments. They slashed his wrists and hands, ripped the knees of his breeches, and tore the front of his weskit. The second time he fell he landed flat on his face in the dank, black earth of the jungle. Tiny fragments of sticks and rocks punctured his forehead and right cheek. Blood ran freely into his eyes. His hands and knees had bleeding cuts, as well. But still he ran. His legs churned the ground as his lungs billowed in a futile effort to extract more oxygen from the humid air.

To his great relief and amazement, less than a half-hour later he saw the edge of the woods. The clear northern sky shined brightly beyond the tree line. Pierre burst onto the open beach about a hundred yards to the east of the *Auguste's* camp. He ran feverishly toward a cluster of sailors on the beach.

Pierre shouted as he ran, "Alarm! Alarm!"

Heads began to turn. The men watched him curiously as he approached. Pierre quickly reached the sailors.

One of the men exclaimed, "What are you shouting for? And what happened to you, *Monsieur* Grimard? You are a battered, bloody mess."

Pierre stopped and leaned forward, resting his hands on his knees. It took him a moment to compose himself and catch his breath. He hissed a single, dramatic word ... "Pirates!"

The sailor's eyes widened. The other men who were standing nearby became very distraught and animated. They moved closer to Pierre to hear his report.

"Pirates, you say? Where?" inquired the sailor.

"South of the island, moving due west under full sail."

The sailor looked to his left toward the western tip of the island. "Then they will be rounding the western end soon."

Pierre nodded. "In an hour or less, I would imagine. And their captain saw me on the bluff."

"Are you certain?"

Pierre nodded. "Captain de Laurent loaned me his spyglass. We looked right into one another's eyes. The man saw me."

The sailors groaned.

"Where is Captain de Laurent?" inquired Pierre.

"On board the *Auguste*," replied the sailor. "The repairs are complete. We are loading the last of our tools and supplies into the launch and preparing to leave. We were instructed to wait for you."

"Well, now you have me, and to hell with the tools and supplies. We have to get on board and get underway right now! There are at least a hundred men and dozens of cannons on that pirate ship!"

The sailor nodded. "Into the launch men! Abandon the materiel." He turned to a nearby sailor. "Andre, signal the captain. Emergency evacuation!"

# 3

## BATTLE AT SEA

The mid-afternoon sun unleashed a flesh-baking heat upon the stifling deck of the *Auguste*. Captain de Laurent and the crew worked feverishly to coax the ship toward full speed. All of the sails were fully deployed, and they strained to capture every movement of the wind, but the ship's speed was frustratingly slow in developing. A whisper of wind was blowing toward the northwest, but it was severely diminished on the leeward side of the island. The high, forested bluffs on the southern side of Cayman Brac served to scatter and deflect the prevailing winds out of the southeast.

The captain turned to Pierre. "You are convinced that they were pirates?"

"*Oui, mon capitaine.* The ship carried the scars of many battles. The deck was practically littered with guns. The men were slovenly in appearance and fully armed with pistols and blades. And she flew a plain, black flag."

The captain frowned grimly. "The black flag of submission. As long as ships comply with their demands and surrender their cargo, the officers and crew will remain unharmed. But if any resistance is offered, they will hoist the red flag of blood."

Antoine's eyes widened in fear. Pierre looked into the tired eyes of the captain and subtly nodded his understanding.

"Were you spotted?" asked the captain.

Pierre stared at the stained wood of the deck and nodded in shame. "I had a small fire for cooking fish. I have no doubt that they saw the smoke. Anyhow, the captain saw me through his spyglass."

"He saw you?" exclaimed the captain. "Are you certain?"

"Yes, sir." Pierre paused. "Captain, we looked directly into one another's eyes. The man smiled right at me!"

Captain de Laurent covered his eyes and groaned. "Then we are discovered, indeed. Tell me, Pierre, do you believe the ship was at full speed?"

"It appeared so to me, Captain. I am no expert, but its sails were fully deployed and it appeared to be under a decent wind and moving fast."

"And how long ago did you see them?"

Pierre glanced at the sun and attempted to reckon the time. "I'm not sure, sir. But it's been close to an hour, I think."

"How far to the east?"

"They were well past the eastern end of the island, I think … maybe five miles off shore."

Both men stared at the western tip of the island. "That means they were less than an hour and a half from circumnavigating the island. If they were under full sail they would, no doubt, have to drop speed significantly in order to round the tip of the Brac and attempt to cut us off and come ashore. Otherwise, they would shoot right past the end of the island and miss their opportunity. They cannot, after all, turn her around and sail back into the wind." He glanced once again at Pierre. "You say she displayed several guns?"

"Yes, sir. I counted maybe twenty on the deck. And there were several firing holes on the starboard side."

"She sounds unusually large for a pirate vessel. We have only fifteen pieces for our defense, all eighteen pounders, except for our long nine to the aft." The captain sighed. "Perhaps they are not expecting us to already be underway. We may be able to escape without combat."

"What are you saying, Captain?" inquired Antoine, who had joined Pierre on the Captain's quarterdeck.

"I am saying that if we can reach full speed as the pirate vessel is lowering sail and slowing down to make its turn, it may be just the opportunity that we need to make our timely escape. The current prevailing winds will take us all the way to port in New Orleans. Hopefully, the pirate vessel is not as well-rigged as the *Auguste*. We must try to outrun her in the open water. We do not stand a chance in an all-out, broadside fight." He glanced at the sun. "We have less than three hours of daylight left. If we can keep out of range of any forward cannons until sundown then we can make our escape into the darkness."

Pierre's spirits began to lift. Perhaps they would, indeed, escape this pirate menace!

The captain looked upward and inspected their sails, which seemed to be somewhat listless in the light winds. He slammed his fist in frustration on a nearby railing.

The captain declared, "Gentlemen, we must get clear of this island! It is shielding us from the precious winds that we need to reach maximum speed in order to escape."

He glanced once again at the western edge of the island, which was less than a half-mile from their current position. His mind was churning. He closed his eyes and his left thumb moved quickly over the tips of his four fingers as he performed calculations in his head.

The captain opened his eyes and belched out his order, "Helm, twenty degrees to port. Hold the wind, but take us more toward the tip of the island."

"*Oui, mon Capitaine,*" responded the pilot. He began to spin the wheel to his left and soon found the course that his captain had ordered.

"But, sir! That will take us closer to the path of the pirate vessel!" protested Antoine.

"Yes, son, but it will also get us clear of those bluffs and high trees much faster. We can stumble and limp along in these weak winds for the next hour, or we can make for the vigorous ones that await us off the western tip of Cayman Brac. We can be at full sail and top speed in a matter of minutes."

The captain called down to the deck below, "Prepare for closed quarters! Ready the port cannons! Ready the aft cannon! Let's give our pirate friends a little surprise should they make a sudden appearance!"

The men on deck jumped into action. Five-man crews darted toward each of the seven artillery pieces mounted on the port side of the vessel. They stacked small piles of shot and powder cartridges beside the cannons. Men began to lower buckets on ropes and haul seawater up onto the deck for swabbing the cannons and for fighting fires. Other men closed and secured various doors, hatches, and ports. They were preparing for the possibility of being boarded.

As Pierre observed the actions of the men manning the cannons he noted that they all seemed a bit awkward at the preparation of the weapons. They obviously knew how to prime and load the artillery pieces, but it was equally obvious that there were not very proficient at the task. It took several minutes to load the powder charges and projectiles and then spike the powder and insert fuses into the vent holes.

"Your crew does not have the look of artillerymen, Captain," commented Pierre respectfully.

"No, Pierre. Though we have drilled with the weapons and fired them on occasion, these men have never fired a shot in defense or in anger. They are able seamen, but unproven warriors. I hope that even after this day they remain so."

"So, you still plan to outrun them … that is your primary goal?"

"*Oui*, Pierre."

"How might they attack?" inquired Antoine.

"If they engage us they will attempt to get close enough to hail us and demand our surrender. If we do not immediately lower our sails they will, no doubt, fire a warning shot."

"And if we refuse … if we flee or fight back?" asked Antoine.

"Then she will attempt to overtake us and get alongside and rake our decks with swivel guns and cannon fire. Their captain will not wish to sink us. He wants our cargo far too badly. Instead, he will simply try to kill as many of the crew as possible."

"And then?" asked Antoine, swallowing hard.

"They will attempt to board us as rapidly as possible and take the ship. Unless we surrender before then, the combat will be hand-to-hand."

"I assume that we would stand little chance at that point," remarked Pierre.

"No. Little chance at all," verified the Captain. "But thanks to you, Pierre, we have a little bit of warning. We have a running start. And if we get a fair shot at the pirate vessel, then I am going to take it. Perhaps we will get lucky, no? Maybe wing them just a little … slow them down just a bit." The captain grinned enthusiastically.

"I pray so," affirmed Pierre. "Meanwhile, what else can we do?"

"Arm yourselves and pray, young Pierre," replied the captain. "For now, we must wait. We are at the mercy of the wind. Meanwhile, once you have secured firearms and blades, I would appreciate it if you and Antoine would return to the quarterdeck and remain here near me and at the ready. If some of my men are wounded or killed by their cannon fire, I will be forced to assign you duties that you most definitely did not sign up for."

Pierre nodded grimly. "Of course, *mon Capitaine*. We serve at your pleasure."

The men all fixed their gaze upon the western tip of Cayman Brac, now less than a quarter mile away.

※

Ten minutes later the *Auguste* was less than a hundred yards from the westernmost end of Cayman Brac. The tension was building dramatically.

Pierre remained silent and stood well behind the captain. He had a single pistol tucked into his belt alongside a discolored, stubby sword. He held a Charleville musket across his chest, already primed and loaded. Antoine was similarly armed.

"We are almost there!" Antoine uttered excitedly.

The entire ship hovered on a razor-sharp edge. Several men darted about the deck in an effort to make final preparations. The boatswain issued appropriate orders to the sailors as he readied them for battle. The men manning the cannons leaned over the ship's rail as they attempted the impossible … to see through the island that blocked their view to the south. Some of the men chattered and spoke to one another, though not many. Several clutched rosaries in their right hands and prayed.

Then a loud voice from the lookout who clung to the high timber of the main mast broke the subdued, fearsome silence.

"*Mon Capitaine*! I see a mast and black flag! Sixty degrees to port, four hundred yards beyond the island!"

The captain yelled upward to the lookout, "And her sails?"

The lookout took a moment to get a better view of the ship and confirm his sighting. He finally responded, "Main sail and topsail are furled!"

The captain raised a celebratory fist into the air. "That's it! She's slowing down!"

He leaned over the rail and barked his orders, "Cannoneers, check your primers and prepare to fire! Gentlemen, we are only going to get one volley. I want to see and hear iron crushing timber! Do you understand me?"

The shouts of the men echoed from the deck below, "*Oui, mon Capitaine!*"

The *Auguste* was moving a mere five degrees north of a due westerly heading. Up ahead Pierre could see the radical difference in the surface of the sea. The protected waters on the northern rim of Cayman Brac were almost still. But just beyond the tip of the island those same seas roiled and churned in the stout winds out of the

41

southeast. Those were the lifesaving winds that Captain de Laurent was striving for.

They were less than a hundred yards from those windswept waters when the captain gave his next commands.

"Helm! Turn twenty degrees to port! Gentlemen, prepare to fire on my command! Remember that these thieves plan to steal our cargo and our lives! Make them pay for their treachery!"

The ship cantered slightly to the left. Pierre feared that it might strike the island, or perhaps the shallow sandbar that lay in a bowed line beyond its tip. But the captain had expertly reckoned their position and placed them on a perfect heading. In less than a minute they would clear the island and present a broadside view to the oncoming pirate vessel.

Pierre and Antoine held their breaths in anticipation. The sudden appearance of the dark hull of the pirate vessel above the western dunes caused them to gasp. It appeared to them that they were on a collision course. The large sails of the pirate vessel were, indeed, lowered and furled. The black ship eased along in a slow arc, preparing to allow their forward momentum to carry them around the tip of Cayman Brac. They had absolutely no idea of the welcome that Captain de Laurent had prepared for them.

Suddenly the *Auguste* was clear of the island. The spiked bow of the pirate vessel loomed at a range of a mere one hundred yards and ninety degrees to port.

The captain performed the complex ciphers in his mind as he tried to account for the wind and the speeds of both ships. He feared that the men might become excited and fire too soon. He looked below and saw that mates stood beside all seven primed and loaded cannons, each one holding his slow match at the ready in preparation to fire.

The captain urged his men, "Hold! Hold! Not yet! Just a little further! Wait!" Then suddenly he screamed, "Fire!"

Three of the cannons exploded in unison and lurched backwards in their tracks. The ship gave a small shudder in response. Three others fired after a short delay of about a half-second, causing the ship to shudder once again. The seventh and final cannon malfunctioned and failed to fire altogether. The deafening explosions of the six cannons rocked the ship and covered the deck with a white shroud of billowing, acrid smoke. The concussions of the weapons made the wooden joints of the vessel creak and pop in protest.

Quite suddenly the smoke cleared from the deck of the *Auguste* as a vigorous and refreshing wind swept across the ship. The waiting sails billowed and popped taut as they harnessed the incredible power of the steady wind, causing the ship to give a mighty lurch forward.

The captain bellowed, "Helm! Forty-five degrees to starboard! Turn full with the wind!"

The pilot offered no verbal response. He simply spun the wheel to his right and eyed the ship's compass, finally stopping once the ship was on a steady northwesterly heading. The ship began to pick up speed until it was soon slicing through the waves. The two repaired masts were working perfectly. The *Auguste* was capturing the wind and soon sailing at top speed.

Pierre was mesmerized by the activity all around him. The sailors were no longer manning the cannons on the deck. They ran hither and yon, securing various lines and expertly lashing the sails into their perfect positions. They secured loose items and equipment and made sure that the decks were clear of obstructions and hazards. Truly, they were an expert and admirable crew.

Once the ship was secure and moving at top speed all attention focused upon the pirate ship that loomed behind them. It was coasting past the end of the island. Black smoke billowed from just beyond the bow on the starboard side. At least one of the cannons had registered a hit! The ship continued its forward momentum toward due north. She was a damaged vessel, no doubt manned by a slightly dazed and confused crew.

The men of the *Auguste* cheered and danced with joy. Pierre and Antoine hugged one another and joined in the seafaring celebration. The glee lasted for several minutes.

The captain smiled in response to the joy of his men, but in his wisdom he knew that the fight was far from over. It was only a matter of time before the pirates attempted to follow and capture the French merchant ship. He took several steps toward the rear of the quarterdeck so that he might see over the stern of the ship and check the condition of the pirate vessel. It was still drifting northward, but the crew seemed to be working feverishly to deploy their sails.

He returned to the quarterdeck and bellowed, "All right, men! Let's get to work! I want top speed. Do not waste a single breeze. Check every line and rigging. We have to put as much distance as we can between ourselves and that black behemoth. Cannon crews, see to your guns. And clear that unfired cannon! I do not want any accidental explosions or discharges."

Suddenly splashes began to erupt in the water on the starboard side of the ship. A few seconds later the dull boom of distant cannon fire reached the decks of the *Auguste*. The pirate vessel had fired a volley from its port-side cannons. The shots fell harmlessly into the water about fifty yards off of the starboard side of the fleeing *Auguste*.

The captain gave a taunting laugh and shouted to his men, "We've given her a sting that she'll not soon forget, gentlemen. Let's pick up the pace! She'll be coming after us in a matter of minutes!"

The captain's declaration proved to be prophetic. Moments later the sails of the pirate ship were unfurled as the vessel labored to turn with the wind. Even as the enemy ship attempted its maneuver, the *Auguste* continued its northwesterly course and steadily increased its distance from Cayman Brac and the pursuing pirates.

"She is raising a red flag!" screeched the lookout.

The captain stole another glance at the enemy ship. He shouted to the men below, "Gentlemen, she's coming about, and she wants our blood! The chase is on!"

The bow of the pirate vessel slowly turned toward the northwest. As it attempted the maneuver of turning with the wind several plumes of white smoke belched from her port side, just as that side was angling toward the *Auguste.*

"Another volley!" shouted the lookout from high upon the main mast. "She has the angle this time!"

Moments later there was another dull splash in the water on the starboard side. Then another. And then another. Each succeeding cannon ball inched its way closer and closer to the Auguste. The fourth round landed directly beside the ship and splashed a great geyser of water onto the gun deck.

But the fifth projectile, against all odds of distance, movement, and wind, struck the vessel amidships. Pierre had traced the high arc of the ball in the air and watched, mesmerized, as the dark, smoke-trailing sphere struck wood and metal. When it hit the ship Pierre thought, "What an odd sound ..." It reminded him of the sharp ringing of a large axe striking against a log.

But the dull crack of metal against wood lasted for only a split second. The cannon ball landed at the base of the fourth cannon from the stern on the port side ... the gun that had suffered a misfire in the volley. Amazingly, the round exploded among the pile of powder charges stacked beside that cannon.

The resulting secondary explosion was enormously deafening. The concussion of the blast caused the entire ship to shudder. It blasted a deadly wave of flame, splinters, and metal shrapnel in every direction. The sails above the explosion were tattered and ripped. Some of them were on fire. Human flesh and blood accompanied the burning debris. Three men had been working to clear the misfired cannon and secure its unexploded ordinance. They were all shredded by the blast. Little remained that had the appearance of humanity. All that was left of three souls were splashes of blood and shreds of flesh and bone.

The captain and the other men on the quarterdeck had instinctively ducked below the railing in response to the initial blast. Their ears were still ringing from the concussion. They slowly rose above the level of the railing and gasped in horror at the carnage below. More than a dozen wounded men writhed on the deck, most of them peppered and punctured by shards of disintegrated wood. A handful of sailors darted to their aid. Most of the men were busy fighting several small fires throughout the ship. The misfired cannon that had previously been secured in its position before the explosion was almost completely below the deck, having dropped into the hole created by the explosion of gunpowder. Roughly a foot of the end of the barrel was all that remained visible above the top of the charred hole.

The captain began shouting orders. "Extinguish those fires! Soak the sails! Secure any remaining powder!" He walked quickly to the rear of the quarterdeck and peered over the stern of the boat, resting his hand on the cool barrel of the lone rear-facing cannon. He cursed beneath his breath when he saw the pirate ship's sails fully unfurled and swelling in the wind.

He nodded to the four men standing at the ready beside the nine-pounder chase gun. "Gentlemen, ready the long nine and fire when ready. See if you can drop a little more lead onto those murderous, thieving bastards!"

The men crisply responded, "*Oui, mon Capitaine!*" They jumped to action, grabbing the various implements required to make the weapon ready to fire.

He turned to Pierre and Antoine. "Gentlemen, I find myself short several men for the tasks at hand. I would be most grateful if you would assist my crew."

"Of course, sir," responded Pierre. "What are your orders?"

"Help see to the wounded. My men are a bit occupied trying to hold the ship together and keep it from burning up."

Pierre needed no further instruction. He leapt down the short flight of stairs from the quarterdeck to the gun deck. Antoine followed closely behind. They located an unattended wounded sailor and began to render aid. The man was flat on his back on a large pile of ropes. He was severely bloodied, but conscious.

"Where were you hit?" Antoine asked the man.

The man's face registered shock and confusion as he grabbed at his ears. He almost screamed in response, "What?"

"He has been deafened by the blast," observed Pierre. "His chest and belly are soaked in blood. We need to get his shirt off to examine him."

Antoine whipped an ivory-handled pocket knife from his leather pouch and began cutting the man's shirt. The sailor protested at first, but quickly realized what the two men were attempting to do. He lay back on the pile of ropes and draped his forearm across his eyes. He winced in pain when Pierre lifted him slightly to remove the shirt.

The man's torso was punctured in numerous places by large splinters and shards of wood. Antoine and Pierre began to remove the bigger pieces of wood shrapnel. Most of them came out quite easily. One particularly large piece was lodged deep in the man's left side. It oozed a steady stream of dark blood.

"We need to get that chunk of wood out of him and get pressure on the wound, or he is going to bleed to death," commented Pierre.

"It's pretty deep," responded Antoine. "I can barely see the tip of the wood." He attempted in vain to grasp the foreign object that protruded from the man's flesh. "It's no use. I cannot grab hold of it. There is too much blood."

"We will have to cut it out," Pierre declared.

"I am not cutting it out!" challenged Antoine. "I abhor the sight of blood."

"Well, I am certainly not going to let this man lie here and bleed slowly to death! It has to come out, all of it, or else it will fester and he will die a slow, agonizing death of fever."

Antoine did not budge.

"Give me your knife, you squeamish coward," demanded Pierre.

Antoine silently and angrily slapped the knife into Pierre's open hand.

"Make yourself useful. Go find some rum and some clean cloth."

Antoine grunted and then scurried toward the bow in search of liquor and bandages. Forty feet away from them the rear-facing nine-pounder chase gun fired its first round from its mount on the back of the quarterdeck. The *Auguste* had finally opened fire on the pursuing ship.

Pierre tried to focus on the task before him. He thought it best to try and communicate what he was about to do. He tapped the sailor on the forearm that covered his face.

"What is your name?"

"Huh?" The man merely shook his head and pointed at his ear.

Pierre leaned closer and yelled. "What is your name?"

"Alain Duguay."

Pierre yelled again, "Alain, I must cut this piece of wood from your side!"

The man shook his head in confusion. He clearly did not understand what Pierre was attempting to tell him. So, Pierre took another communicative route. He opened the knife and pointed the blade at the tip of wood that was protruding from the sailor's side. He made a couple of small slashing moves to demonstrate his intent. Alain grimaced and nodded slightly to indicate his understanding. Antoine reappeared by Pierre's side with a large piece of linen and a jug of rum.

"Antoine, tear some long strips for wraps. They will need to reach all the way around his belly. Then fold the rest into a square bandage that we will place directly on the wound. Make sure you have plenty of cloth to plug the hole. We do not know how deep this chunk of wood goes. And give me that rum."

Antoine handed him the jug. Pierre splashed a healthy dose of the fragrant liquid onto the wound. Alain winced from the searing pain of the alcohol that scorched his exposed flesh. Pierre threw back the jug and took a long drink, and then handed the jug to the wounded sailor. The long nine cannon belched concussion and fire as the rearward-facing crew launched another shot at the pursuing pirates. Alain swigged thirstily from the fiery jug.

"Not the best conditions for surgery, eh Antoine?" quipped Pierre.

Antoine shook his head nervously, unimpressed by Pierre's morbid attempt at humor.

Pierre shrugged his shoulders. "All right, then. Here we go."

He leaned forward and made a slow cut from the edge of the chunk of wood toward the man's hip. Alain screamed in pain. Pierre stopped the cut at about one inch, then pushed the jug toward Alain again and encouraged him to drink. As the man tilted his head back to fill his mouth with rum Pierre cut, rather surprisingly and unexpectedly, in the opposite direction above the wound. Alain had little time to respond. He merely gagged on the burning alcohol of the rum and cursed profusely once he was able to regain his breath.

"Help me, Antoine," Pierre commanded.

His companion sighed deeply and dutifully knelt beside him. "What must I do?"

Pierre paid little attention to him at first. He was busy pulling the expanded wound open with his fingers and probing to feel the wood below the man's flesh. In one spot, he had to cut a bit deep, penetrating the muscle beneath.

"Antoine, this splinter is huge and very deep. It feels like the larger part of it is well beneath the flesh. We only have this tiny tip of the wood to work with. I will spread the cuts open with my fingers. I want you to pull on the piece of wood as hard as you can. Do you understand?"

Antoine nodded. "There is not much wood to grasp."

"No, there is not," affirmed Pierre. "And there is much blood making everything very slimy and slick. You may need a small piece of cloth to help you get a better grip and pull more strongly."

Antoine whipped a handkerchief from his haversack. "Will this do?"

"Perfect!"

The long nine cannon boomed again, causing the deck to tremble slightly. Pierre stole a glance at the sails. They were full and tight. A stiff, refreshing breeze swept across the deck of the ship. The *Auguste* was running full with the wind and skimming across the choppy sea.

"Here we go, Antoine. We must give this poor man some relief."

Antoine wrapped his handkerchief round the tip of the wood and then nodded in readiness. Sweat poured from his nervous brow. Pierre carefully but deliberately pulled the skin and flesh apart at the cuts that he had made on the periphery of the invasive piece of wood. The stricken seaman once again howled with pain. Antoine pulled. The wood budged about a half-inch. He reached lower and pulled as hard as he could, but the progress stopped. More dark, semi-clotted blood gurgled from the wound. Antoine's knuckles turned ghostly white as he tried to grip the pointed tip of the wood, but it was to no avail. His fingers soon released and the wood slipped back into the fleshy cave in Alain's side.

Antoine howled in frustration. "I cannot do it, Pierre! I cannot get a good enough grip! If only there were some tool or device that we could use to grasp the splinter."

Pierre, ignoring the loud protests of his friend, bent over and examined the bloody chunk of wood. He noted that just below the exposed tip there was the tiniest of holes in the wood. It wasn't much … just a small remnant of a knot hole in the ancient timber. But it gave him an idea.

"Antoine, fetch a piece of heavy cord. You may have to cut a length of rope and separate a strand. Make sure it is three or four feet in length."

"How will that help?" challenged Antoine. "The tip is pointed. We cannot tie to it."

"No, but there is a slender knothole below the tip. If I can hollow it out just a bit more with your knife we can get a strand of cord through it and then pull the wood out of the wound."

Antoine jumped up and darted toward the bow of the ship as, once again, Pierre picked up Antoine's pocket knife. He patted the man reassuringly on the shoulder. The sailor continued to drink heavy gulps of the rum. He actually smiled at Pierre. Clearly, the rum was doing its job. Pierre carefully inserted the blade of the knife into the open knothole and then gently began to spin the knife in a tight circle. He blew the debris away from the wound as best he could. He could see that the knife was making progress through the blood-soaked wood. He removed the blade from the hole and inspected his work. The hole was definitely bigger.

The cannon boomed again, launching yet another explosive ball toward the pursuing pirates.

Antoine returned just as Pierre began to attack the knothole from the opposite side of the wood. He dropped a piece of hemp cord on the wounded man's leg. He held a ten-inch wooden peg in his hand.

"Any progress?" he asked Pierre.

"Most definitely. We are almost there. What is the peg for?"

"It is for pulling. I'll show you once we have the string through the hole."

Pierre nodded and returned to his work. He gently whittled on the hole for another two minutes. The cannon boomed once again.

"The men on the cannon are getting faster and firing more often," noted Antoine.

Pierre nodded and kept spinning his knife. "Job experience." He smiled.

A minute later he stopped whittling and examined the hole. "I think we can do it. Give me the cord."

Antoine grabbed the strand of thin hemp cordage off of the man's leg and placed it in Pierre's hand. Pierre used the knife to make a clean, unraveled cut on the end of the cord. It took a little coaxing, but he eventually fished the line through the tiny hole in the wood.

He exclaimed, "Yes! This is going to work!"

Antoine straddled his legs across the wounded sailor in preparation for pulling.

"Pierre, I will tie the cord tightly on this peg and use it for a pulling handle. You spread the cut and I will pull straight up. This is going to work!"

"It has to work," muttered Pierre.

Antoine secured the line to the peg and gave it several twists, coiling the hemp into a double-stranded rope all the way down to the piece of wooden shrapnel. He nodded to Pierre.

Pierre gave the numbed sailor a tender pat on his cheek. "Here we go, Alain. This is going to hurt."

He gripped above and below the cut and spread the bloody flesh as Antoine pulled straight up on the rope.

It was over in less than a second. The wood slid out of the fleshy cave with a loud slurping sound just as the rearward cannon boomed again. Alain screamed with pain. Pierre and Antoine screamed with delight. Moments later up on the quarterdeck they heard men screaming in celebration.

Blood poured from the gaping wound.

"Quick! Get the bandage and wraps!" commanded Pierre.

He grabbed the jug of rum from Alain and poured several ounces into the open hole, eliciting yet another scream from the sailor. This time the man passed out from the pain. Pierre pulled the edges of the wound closed and placed the fat bundle of cloth on the bloody crack as Antoine wrapped the strips tightly around the man's torso.

The celebration continued at the rear of the boat.

Pierre examined their work. "This will suffice for now. The wound will have to be stitched as soon as possible, but it looks like the bleeding is under control."

"Let him sleep. I want to know what all of the celebrating is about!" exclaimed Antoine.

The two men checked their patient one last time. He was unconscious and breathing deeply. Satisfied that he was safe, they proceeded up the steps onto the quarterdeck. They saw Captain de Laurent laughing and celebrating, slapping his men on their backs and saluting them.

And then they saw the cause of the celebration. The main mast of the pirate ship was broken and leaning to port. Her sails were on fire. Black smoke billowed into the darkening sky. The vessel had slowed considerably and was moving in a slow starboard arc.

The battle was over. The *Auguste* and her crew were saved.

"Pierre! Antoine!" boomed the voice of the captain. "Look at those sails burn! My boys landed one amazingly lucky shot, eh? Right on the main mast!" He slapped one of the cannoneers on the back. "She'll be lucky if she has any cloth left by morning!"

"Are you certain we are safe?" inquired Antoine.

The captain nodded vigorously. "It will be dark in an hour. We will change course under cover of darkness, just to be prudent. Those scoundrels will limp along for weeks before they find land. Most likely they will be sunk by another ship. Or maybe they'll just dry up and die of hunger and thirst." He grinned wickedly.

"What now?" asked Pierre.

The captain grabbed Pierre around the shoulder and pulled him close. "Now, my young friend, we go to New Orleans!"

# 4

## VOYAGEURS AND VICARS

*July 19, 1769*

"Half price? Whatever do you mean, half price?" screeched Antoine. He stared in disbelief at the two sacks of gold that sat on the floor at Pierre's feet.

"That is all the import house would pay," responded Pierre.

Antoine wadded his hat angrily into a ball and threw it against the wall of their New Orleans hotel room. It landed with a thud on the rough wood floor and rolled dangerously close to the fireplace. He didn't seem to care. His face burned red with frustration and anger. He walked over to the window and stared down onto the busy, dusty street below.

"And what was the total for our cargo?" he asked in a monotone voice.

Pierre took a very deep breath, paused, then replied, "22,000 livres gold for eighty percent of the load."

Antoine gasped and spun around to face Pierre. "You mean, I only get one hundred and ten livres? After all of that travel and all of that work? After risking my life and almost losing it twice?"

Pierre nodded. "One half of one percent. That was your contract. My own payment is a mere two hundred and twenty."

Antoine's mind reeled. How could this be happening? He was counting on at least double that amount of payment to get him established in business in the Illinois Country. His dreams seemed to be dashed.

Antoine collapsed onto the narrow bed near the window. The ropes that suspended the mattress in place squeaked in protest.

He began to pepper Pierre with questions. "Why the change? Why the drop in value? What has happened to business here? Is something wrong upriver?"

"No, not upriver. The problem is right here ... in this city. New Orleans is in a political uproar," explained Pierre. "There has been something of a revolt among a handful of the French leaders. They have swayed the governing council toward their point of view. They are attempting to overthrow the Spanish government altogether and retain French ownership of the city and territory. The Spanish governor was expelled last November. It is a grand mess, for sure. No one quite knows how the Spanish will respond. Some say that they are sending an army from Cuba to quell the rebellion. That is a great fear here in the city."

"What about *Monsieur* de Maxent ... the military officer and company representative in New Orleans? What did he have to say about the decrease in prices?"

Pierre shook his head. "*Monsieur* de Maxent has refused to involve himself. He would not even take a meeting with me. He was arrested by the rebels last fall and accused of collusion with the Spanish. After the Spaniard governor departed for Cuba he was released from the local jail. Just last month he officially terminated his contract with Laclède. He is attempting to remain impartial in the midst of the rebellion. I suspect that he is playing both sides. But whatever his game may be, the company is dissolved, Antoine. We are on our own."

"But *Monsieur* de Maxent was supposed to receive the funds from us and forward them back to France! What will we do now? What will happen to *Monsieur* Daubaret and his business in La Rochelle?"

Pierre responded matter-of-factly. "I suspect that he will be ruined. Let us just be happy that we did not have any investments in the company. We would be ruined, as well. As it stands, I am happy that we did not reach the dock in New Orleans to just get carted straight to jail. That would be somewhat ironic after all that we have survived in order to get here." Pierre smiled in an effort to lift the spirits of his friend. His effort failed.

Antoine leaned back on the bed and sighed. Suddenly his eyes lit up with excitement. "But now you're holding 22,000 livres in gold! That is a lot of coin. What shall we do with it? Is it ours to keep?"

"We will do what is honorable," responded Pierre, shaking his head. "We will finish the job that we started. We must take it up the Mississippi and hand it over to *Monsieur* Laclède, minus our expenses. And do not worry, my friend. I plan to pay for every *denier* of our expense with company money. Our hotel, meals, travel, the rental of boats, and payment of *voyageurs* and crewmen ... all of it. *Monsieur* Laclède will get whatever is left over. We will let him worry about transferring the remaining funds, such as they may be, back to his partner in France. That is beyond our ability and concern."

"Well that is good. I'm out of money. I've spent every coin that I had on this horrid room in this brothel and on the stale bread that we've been eating."

"Not to worry," reassured Pierre, tossing him two gold coins. "This should more than reimburse your monies spent."

"What about the remaining one-fifth of the cargo?" questioned Antoine.

"We do exactly as planned and agreed upon," Pierre stated flatly. "We will take the goods north and establish a trading post in Illinois. If Laclède wishes to remain our partner, we will negotiate a suitable contract. If not, we will retain the goods as payment for our journey upriver."

"That seems a bit extreme, doesn't it? Upwards of 5,000 livres worth of cargo for a river boat ride?"

Pierre chuckled. "It is not a pleasure sail on the Seine with a violinist and *hor d'oeuvres*, you ignorant Austrian. It will be a dangerous journey through native and bandit-infested country. We will have to hire crews and soldiers and row ourselves up the river. Most likely we will have to fight every inch of the way."

"Oh," mumbled Antoine. "On second thought, I may stay in New Orleans." He grinned at Pierre.

Pierre laughed. "I'm hungry. Let us go and find some food and a little rum to feed and drown these sorrows. The dock foreman told me about a tavern where we might be able to hire some men and make arrangements for the trek upriver."

Antoine licked his lips. "That is the most sensible thing you have said to me since you returned from the docks."

♆

Antoine sat alone at a small table along the wall of the tavern. The room was dark and smoke-filled. It reeked of raw meat, fish, grease, alcohol, and body odor. The establishment was filled with men of all types, shapes, and sizes. There were a few who appeared to be wearing military uniforms. Antoine, being from Austria, had no idea what nation or service they represented. There were dozens of sweaty, stinky dock workers. Mixed in among the colorful crowd were men dressed in peculiar mixtures of French apparel, wool blankets, and animal hides. They smoked slender pipes, swilled on great volumes of rum and ale, and laughed boisterously as they enjoyed lively conversation and games with their friends. These men were the *voyageurs* ... the French explorers and guides from the back country in the North.

Antoine was so focused on his observations of the patrons in the colorful establishment that he did not see Pierre approaching from his right side. He jumped in surprise when his friend dropped a large wooden platter of roasted beef flanked with two loaves of steaming bread on the table in front of him. Pierre also hugged three blue, corked bottles against his belly. He handed one of the bottles to Antoine.

"What's in the bottle?" asked Antoine.

"Wine, my friend! A little taste of France to brighten your otherwise dark day. And I have someone I want you to meet." He waved his hand toward a tall, muscular man standing behind him. "Antoine Alexis, this is Charles Rimbault. He is formerly of Quebec, but now a resident of Vincennes, in the Illinois Country. He has agreed to guide us upriver."

Antoine scooted his chair back from the table and rose to his feet, extending his hand and offering a welcoming smile. "*Monsieur* Rimbault, it is a pleasure to meet you. Please sit. Let us eat and make conversation." Antoine looked curiously at Pierre and leaned toward his friend's ear as they sat down. He whispered, "You work quickly, my friend. A little too quickly, perhaps?"

Pierre grinned and patted Antoine reassuringly on the back.

"Charles, tell my young friend from Austria the things that you have told me about Illinois," encouraged Pierre.

Charles Rimbault smiled broadly and drew deeply on his clay pipe. "Well, Antoine, it is a place of unspeakable wildness and beauty. The fields are fertile. Wheat grows thickly like weeds. The rivers are full of fish and turtles. The forests are full of small game, deer, bear, and *beoufs* ... what the English call buffalo. One need never go hungry. It is a place where a strong and ambitious man can make his fortune. I am blessed to live there."

Antoine commented, "Forgive me, *Monsieur* Rimbault, but your French is so ... different ... so raw. I grew up speaking Dutch, but have learned to manage the French tongue. Still, I find it most difficult to understand your words."

The frontier Frenchman threw back his head and laughed enthusiastically. His open mouth revealed stained, decaying, pitted teeth. Antoine grimaced and tried to hide his disgust.

"It is from my many years on the frontier, Antoine. We Canadians speak differently, anyway. But now my Canadian French has become tainted with the languages and accents of the Miamis, Kickapoos, and the Shawnee."

"Who are they?" Antoine asked innocently.

"They are the native savages who roam the forests and fields around Vincennes, of course! They are our partners in trade, and sometimes our enemies in battle. You will get to know them well when you paddle north."

"Oh," responded Antoine, feeling somewhat foolish. "What brought you to New Orleans?"

"Business and commerce, young man! I guided several boat-loads of flour, wheat, furs, and maize downriver to market here in late April. Now I am waiting to return in early August."

"Why so long?" asked Pierre. "That is over a month from now!"

The frontiersman shook his head teasingly. "You fellows have much to learn. We must wait for the water levels on the Mississippi and Ohio Rivers to become lower during the dry summer weather. The current must reduce or we will find ourselves paddling furiously and going nowhere. We float downriver in the early spring, when the water is swift and high, and then paddle back upriver in late summer. It has always been so. There simply is no other way."

"How long does it take to reach Illinois?" inquired Antoine.

"Four months. Perhaps one or two weeks more."

Pierre gasped. He knew that it would be a long journey, but he never anticipated that it would require four months.

"Why so long?" Antoine begged.

Charles leaned over the side of his chair and simulated exaggerated, strenuous paddling. "It is difficult and lengthy labor, young man. Not for the faint of heart. Especially when every savage you see on the banks is shooting at you and making plans to remove your scalp from your skull!"

Antoine's eyes widened in fear, eliciting another raucous round of laughter from the *voyageur*. The strange man slapped Antoine on the leg playfully.

"Do not worry, Antoine! You will be traveling with me, the infamous Charles Rimbault of Vincennes! I will help you secure the proper boats and hire good men for the journey. We will arrive safely at our destination." He paused. "Of course, you gentlemen have other business that you must attend to before we leave New Orleans in August."

"Other business?" asked Pierre.

"Indeed." Charles nodded subtly. "You will need a wife to take to Illinois. You must woo and win a woman's hand within the next month. It will be a challenging task, but not impossible."

Pierre and Antoine sat in silence for a moment, then cast a glance of disbelief toward one another.

"Our partner in France told me the same thing before we left, but I thought that he was merely jesting," Pierre remarked dryly.

"Not at all, Pierre. There are no white women in the North. You need to marry a maiden from good French stock and take her up-river with you. There are only native women and a few slave women in the Illinois Country. They do just fine for wintering, cooking, and washing, but not for wedding, if you know what I mean." He winked mischievously at the two young men.

"Where are we supposed to find wives?" exclaimed Pierre. "The entire notion is absurd! You act as if we can walk out into the street and hire them."

"It is not quite as difficult as you may think," responded Charles. "Did you bring a letter of introduction from your bishop or priest in France?"

Pierre nodded.

"What about you, Antoine? Do you carry papers of introduction?"

"No, I have no letter. I am not religious, and have no dealings with the church."

Rimbault pondered. "Hmmm … then it may be very difficult for you, indeed. You may have to settle for a Kickapoo woman. But don't worry, she will more than entertain your young loins and bear you many healthy little brown babies!"

The strange man laughed, once again, at his own poor effort at humor.

"Thank you, but no," responded Antoine. "I will be fine on my own. A wife is the last thing on my mind."

"You say that now. But we shall see. No doubt you will change your mind when your little cock begins to crow to the north." The *voyageur* slapped the table and laughed uncontrollably for a most uncomfortable amount of time. At long last he calmed down.

"Now you, Pierre, are very much in luck. I will take you tomorrow and seek to make an appointment with a certain Capuchin priest. You must bring your letter from France. The Vicar always knows of one or two damsels in need of a husband. And who knows? You may even receive a nice dowry in exchange for marrying one of the local girls."

"A dowry?"

"Oh, yes, indeed. Some of these New Orleans families pay quite well to relieve themselves of a daughter, especially if their family is suffering legal difficulties or feels desperate to trim the size of their household. You may do quite well. A sack full of gold *and* a tasty young wench!" And once again, the man guffawed at his own crude joke.

Pierre shot another sideways glance at Antoine, who stared thoughtfully at the table in front of him. Clearly, the notion of a dowry payment was causing him to rethink his marriage plans. Perhaps this rough, rowdy frontiersman was right. A bride might not be a bad idea.

Rimbault looked down at the beef, bread, and bottles. "Enough of this talking. Let us eat and quench our thirst."

The frontiersman savagely broke off a large chunk of the fragrant bread and jammed it into the gooey grease that surrounded the slab of beef. He bit the end off of the greasy bread, rolling his eyes with pleasure. After that first bite, he wasted no time in ripping the cork from his wine bottle and taking a long, deep drink.

Pierre and Antoine were a little slower and more refined in their approach to the meal. They were genuinely surprised at the amazing flavor and aroma of the roasted beef, which had obviously been cooked in a stock with an ample supply of onions and garlic. The wine, on the other hand, was not so flavorful. It was very dry and quite bitter. Antoine gagged at the taste of it.

"This wine is disgusting," he whined. "Surely they have something better."

Rimbault glanced around the room and then leaned over the small table toward his new friend. "Be judicious in your complaints, young Antoine. That disgusting wine was imported by your company, and came off of your very own boat." Again, he laughed his deep, booming laugh.

Antoine frowned and shook his head in disbelief.

Pierre sat uncomfortably in his stiff, straight-back chair and evaluated the priest. Friar Dagobert de Languor nodded and grunted as he read Pierre's letter from the bishop in France. He was an enormous, jovial, red-faced man. Pierre liked him the moment that he met him. He seemed to be very kind and genuinely interested in helping address Pierre's needs.

The only problem was that at their dinner the previous evening Charles Rimbault had filled Pierre's mind with volumes of juicy gossip regarding the Friar. According to Rimbault, the local people claimed that the Friar, like most of the other local priests, kept a mulatto mistress and had fathered several mixed-race children who actually ate at his table and quite comfortably referred to him as "Papa." Pierre could not imagine such scandal within the church back in France. And he found it difficult to believe that such goings-on would be tolerated by the church here in the New World.

"Your letter appears in good order, *Monsieur* Grimard," remarked the fat, jolly priest. "I am not acquainted with Bishop de la Chasteigneraye, but his predecessor, Bishop Simon-Pierre de Lacoré, was a good friend. We served together many years ago."

"He was a beloved man in our region. His death was mourned greatly, and he is sorely missed," responded Pierre.

"Indeed. I will remember him in Mass on the Sabbath." He made the sign of the cross, which Pierre mimicked out of respect.

The priest leaned back in his large, cushioned chair and smiled broadly at Pierre. "So, Rimbault tells me that you are planning to make a life on the frontier in Illinois. Is that what led you to depart Germignac and sail to Louisiana?"

"Yes, Father. I find myself in a peculiar position. The company that employed me to come here and deliver their cargo and goods has collapsed, and I find myself holding some significant assets. My goal is to go upriver and surrender the company's assets to the last remaining partner in the venture and then set up my own business in Illinois."

"And you would prefer not to make this journey and life on the frontier a lonely endeavor?" The priest's eyes twinkled and his lips curled in a wry smile.

"That is correct, Father. I have been advised against it. Rimbault strongly encouraged me to wed before heading into the Indian country. It seems that many of the men have taken to making homes with the savage women."

The Friar nodded in understanding. "Indeed, this is true, Pierre. You will find the Illinois Country a colorful blend of white, red, and brown men and women. Yet I understand your desire to marry a woman of French stock. I commend your intention to enter into a marriage that is holy and blessed."

"Thank you, Father. But what must I do? I am ignorant of such things."

The priest waved his hand dismissively. "You simply leave it to me, Pierre. As fortune would have it, I already have a candidate for your consideration. There is a family in my parish that recently suffered a great loss. The father, a well-loved and respected gentleman of New Orleans, passed away last month. His poor widow now holds charge of all of his assets and debts, and she has a young daughter who needs to marry. We have had some difficulty in locating a suitable husband for her. But now here you sit, a young native of France who is also an ambitious merchant and businessman. You are a most excellent candidate to receive her hand."

"What is the girl's name?" asked Pierre.

"I prefer not to disclose any personal details until the child's mother agrees to a meeting. I would not want to betray any confidences. Is that suitable with you?"

"Of course, Father. You said, 'child.' How old is she, if I may ask?"

The priest grinned. "Not to worry, Pierre. She is an exquisitely beautiful damsel of fourteen years. She is the perfect age for marrying and breeding."

The priest rose from his chair. Pierre rose immediately and respectfully and followed the dark-robed Friar as he walked toward the door.

"I will make all of the arrangements for the meeting. You will, of course, have to negotiate the bride price with the girl's mother. But not to worry … the family is quite wealthy. I am certain that you will fetch a fine dowry. It may take me a day or two to make all of the arrangements. Meanwhile, where can you be reached?"

"I am staying at the Hotel Beauchene."

"Ahh. Very well, then. I trust that you are holding your honor intact during your stay at such a less-than-reputable house. Very well. I will send a messenger once the arrangements are made. After the contract is negotiated and the banns are read, I will be most happy to solemnize your union."

"Thank you, Father. I am deeply grateful."

The Friar extended his right hand to Pierre, who respectfully lifted it toward his mouth and kissed the large, gold ring that adorned his priestly finger.

"Go with God, my child."

❧

*July 23, 1769*

It was almost dark on Sunday evening. Pierre had been summoned by the priest's messenger to report to the home of *Madame* Marie-Anne Romagon, the widow of the late Isaac Colon. It was a huge, majestic French home ... a mansion by Pierre Grimard's humble standards.

The messenger had filled Pierre in with most of the details and accompanied him to the front gate of the home, where he promptly gave his leave. Pierre was on his own. He anxiously, almost reluctantly, entered through the front gate and trudged along the torch-lighted walkway to the steps of the front porch.

Pierre performed a last-second check of his appearance. He smoothed his brown wool coat and removed a piece of lint as he adjusted his neck sock. He checked to make sure that his cocked hat was perched properly on top of his head. He looked down at his black buckle-shoes. They were muddy and desperately in need of a shine. Pierre felt a momentary flash of horror brought on by his horrid shoes. He was just on the verge of turning and running back down the path to the gate when the front door of the home swung open. A beautiful, middle-aged woman in a lavender-colored formal gown stood in the portal. Soft yellow candle and lamp light cast a saintly glow from behind her silhouetted form.

"*Monsieur* Grimard, I presume?"

"*Oui, Madame*. I am Pierre Grimard of Germignac. I am pleased that you have invited me to your home this evening."

"Please come inside, *Monsieur* Grimard. I am Marie-Anne Romagon, the mistress of this estate since the passing of my dearest husband, Isaac." She bowed her head and made the sign of the cross on her chest. Pierre did, as well. He removed his hat as he stepped through the front door into the foyer of the lavish home. *Madame* Romagon closed the door behind him.

"Please pardon me for answering the door myself. It is most rude, I know. But I have given the servants the Sabbath evening to enjoy with their families. I hope you are not offended."

"Oh, no, *Madame*. Not at all." He smiled warmly at her. "We always opened our own doors back in France."

The beautiful woman returned his smile. "You do me a great honor by visiting my home this evening."

"I am truly sorry for your loss, *Madame* Romagon."

"My Isaac was a saintly, loving man. This house is empty without him. We miss him tremendously. But come … you are not here to listen to this old woman's troubles. Join me in the parlor and we will discuss the business at hand."

"Are you certain that it is acceptable for us to be here alone?" asked Pierre.

"Oh, dear boy, we are not alone. My son, Elian, is resting in his room, as is my daughter, Genevieve. Our local notary and magistrate, Franche Bois de Bertien, is here and waiting for us in the parlor."

She opened one side on a set of swinging doors and pointed Pierre toward the room where the meeting and negotiations were to be held.

"*Monsieur* de Bertien, this is *Monsieur* Pierre Grimard of the village of Germignac, near La Rochelle, in France. He is freshly arrived in our fair city after a long journey at sea."

The notary, an elderly gentleman, stood stiffly and extended his hand to Pierre. "*Bonjour*, young man. I trust that your voyage was safe and uneventful."

Pierre grinned and elected not to go into any detail about his journey to America. "My voyage was challenging, but interesting."

*Madame* Romagon gracefully seated herself in one of three chairs that surrounded a small table. The notary balanced himself on his cane and plopped somewhat less gracefully into his chair. On the table, there was a small pot and three tiny cups, along with a bottle of brandy and three small glasses. Beside the silver pot there was a saucer with sugar and tongs and a tiny cup of cream. There was a small stack of papers in front of *Monsieur* de Bertien's seat.

*Madame* Romagon nodded toward the extra chair. "Please, Pierre … do you mind … is it all right for me to call you by your given name?"

Pierre spoke as he sat, "Of course, *Madame*."

She smiled warmly. "Pierre, would you like some coffee?"

"I've never tasted coffee before, *Madame*, but I would love to try some."

"Oh, you will love it! I have some sugar and fresh cream to soften the flavor."

She quickly and gracefully poured him a cup of the steaming black beverage and added a dash of cream and a small cube of sugar. She stirred the liquid with a tiny silver spoon and then placed it in front of Pierre.

"*Merci, Madame.*"

Pierre took a sip of the dark, sweet liquid. The burst of bold, bitter flavor was captivating. He was in the midst of taking a second drink when the notary spoke.

"*Monsieur* Grimard, I have conferred with *Madame* Romagon and prepared the appropriate contract of marriage. Since you are new to the city and carry a letter from your bishop we have chosen to dispense with the formality of the reading of banns. We will negotiate the particulars tonight. I have already secured the signatures of Louis Champion and George Antoine Nenninger, legal representatives of *Madame* Romagon. I assume that you can produce two signers of your surety this evening."

The straightforward proclamation by the strange man took Pierre by surprise. He coughed lightly and almost spit his coffee back into his cup. *Madame* Romagon covered her mouth and giggled lightly.

"Now, now, Franche. You're scaring the poor boy half to death. He looks as if he is preparing to run right out of here. Let us get to know one another first before we go signing any contracts."

*Monsieur* de Bertien seemed a bit impatient, but acquiesced to the widow's desire and request. "As you wish, *Madame*."

The widow spoke, "Pierre, Friar Dagobert has informed us of your situation and your plans to establish yourself in Illinois. What did he tell you about my predicament?"

"Very little, *Madame*. Only that your husband passed recently and that you were searching for a husband for your daughter. He would not give me your name or any other details until he had your permission. I only learned of your identity this evening on the way to your home."

She nodded. "Well, Pierre, Friar Dagobert is correct. I do, indeed, seek a husband for my daughter, Genevieve. As you are well aware, New Orleans is in a state of tumult. Only four days ago a Spanish force landed to quell the ongoing rebellion and place a military garrison in charge of the city. Over 2,000 of the beastly Spaniards now roam our streets. New Orleans is rapidly becoming an unwelcome place for those of us who share a French ancestry and heritage."

Pierre nodded his understanding as he took another sip of the fragrant coffee.

The widow continued, "I am currently seeking to divest myself of my husband's holdings and properties in the city. It is my desire to go upriver, as well, and seek refuge in St. Louis or in the Illinois Country. But it may be quite some time before I can do so. Meanwhile, what I want to do is provide my innocent daughter the opportunity to leave this city and escape the growing population of Spaniards. I want her to have a good French husband who will share her heritage. According to Friar Dagobert, you are exactly the young man that we need."

She paused and awaited Pierre's response.

Pierre cleared his throat. "*Madame* Romagon, I am most interested in your offer of marriage to your daughter. As you well know, the options for marriage on the frontier are limited. In the absence of white brides, many men are given to setting up house with the native women."

"As I am all too aware, Pierre," remarked the woman. "My late husband's father arrived in the French New World before the turn of this century. He was a soldier who came through what is now New Orleans. He spent many years in a frontier garrison at Kaskaskia. While there he took a wife from those natives. The red wench mothered a house full of little half-breeds before he was reassigned to Mobile. Thank God, he left that horrid brood behind and sought himself an acceptable wife when he was stationed on the Isle Dauphine. That is where my husband was born."

Pierre listened with great interest to her colorful story and responded, "So your husband's family already has connections to the Illinois Country, then?"

"Indeed. And it so happens that through my husband's inheritance I hold deed on a plot of land that my daughter's grandfather claimed there in 1705. If we reach an agreement, it is my full intention to sign that deed over to you and my daughter. In addition, I will commit to a sum of eight hundred livres in gold coin for my daughter's dowry to use as her own after your marriage."

"That is a very generous and thoughtful offer, *Madame*."

"I extend it out of love and generosity toward my dearest daughter. I wish only the best for her in our rapidly changing and increasingly violent world."

The notary interrupted the pleasantries, "So what do you think, Grimard? Do we have an agreement?"

Pierre clumsily and nervously returned his tiny cup to rest on its dainty saucer.

"Well, *Madame* and *Monsieur*, if I may be so bold … would it be acceptable for me to meet the young woman first?"

"Ahh!" The notary nodded his approval. "You wish to inspect the goods first, I see."

"Not at all, *Monsieur*. In fact, I am offended by your description of my request. Actually, I would like for her to 'inspect' me, as you so callously put it, and determine if she might find me tolerable and suitable as a husband."

"Humph!" responded the thoroughly chastised contract-writer. "Whatever you say, boy."

*Madame* Romagon's approval showed in her smile. "It is a most appropriate suggestion, Pierre. And it confirms in my heart the positive impression that I formed of you the moment that I saw you.

Only a man of honor would be so thoughtful and humble. I will go and fetch Genevieve so that you two may meet."

She rose from her chair and moved quickly toward the door. Pierre rose in respectful response to the lady of the house. *Monsieur* de Bertie rose only part-way before collapsing back into his chair.

As soon as *Madame* Romagon closed the door, the older gentleman hissed, "Well, aren't you just a little smart ass? Such nerve you have … making me look bad in front of Marie-Anne."

"You didn't need any help in that regard, sir. Only an ignorant dolt would refer to a woman's young daughter, in her very presence, as if she were offering up a horse or a slave on the selling block."

"Like I said. Smart ass."

Pierre grinned devilishly. "Careful now, Franche. I'm soon to be a male member of this household. You do not want to endanger your future employment, especially since *Madame* Romagon has so many properties to sell in the coming days."

"Humph!" grunted the offended older gentleman.

The two sparring men sat in silence for several minutes. They listened as tiny footsteps overhead proceeded toward and down the stairs. Then, quite dramatically, the double doors swung open. *Madame* Romagon entered first. She quickly stepped to one side and waved her hand toward the young girl who followed behind her.

"*Monsieur* Pierre Grimard, allow me to introduce to you my daughter, *Mademoiselle* Genevieve Colomb …"

# 5

## THE LAUNCH

Pierre could barely breathe. The young girl who stood before him was nothing short of angelic. She was petite in size, barely an inch over five feet in height. Her hair was a soft reddish-brown. Pierre caught wondrous glimpses of wispy curls that peeked from beneath the sides of her house bonnet. Her skin was soft and pale, and her eyes were the most amazing shade of green. She wore a soft green damask dress that drew out the brightness of her exquisite eyes. She smiled shyly at Pierre. Her teeth were white and perfect. There was the slightest hint of a blush in her cheeks.

Pierre was mesmerized. He was smitten. He fell helplessly and hopelessly in love with the young woman the moment that she stepped into the room. He absolutely knew that he must have this girl as his bride.

*Madame* Romagon observed their reactions for a moment. She could see that both Pierre and Genevieve were pleased. Their instant interest in one another warmed the mother's heart.

She broke the awkward silence, "Genevieve, Pierre is a merchant from France and only arrived in New Orleans last month. He is preparing to travel north to the wilderness of Illinois."

"I am pleased to make your acquaintance, *Monsieur* Grimard." She bowed her head ever-so-slightly and gracefully. Pierre's heart melted at the sound of her perfect voice.

"The pleasure is, indeed, mine *Mademoiselle* Colon."

"You may call me Genevieve."

He smiled broadly. "I am honored, Genevieve." He placed his right hand across his belly and bowed toward her. "And you may call me Pierre."

The notary's voice boomed from the table behind Pierre, "Well, what about it boy? Have we a deal, or not?"

Pierre shot the man a hateful glance, then cast an exasperated look toward the widow Romagon. Her return gaze communicated that she fully understood his frustration and growing impatience with the obnoxious official.

"Pierre, why don't you and Genevieve take a few moments to stroll on the veranda? Perhaps you could sit in the swing and visit for a while ... get to know one another a little."

Franche Bois de Bertien emitted a loud, exasperated sigh from his seat at the table.

The widow had finally reached her limit on patience. She snipped at the impudent man, "*Monsieur* de Bertien, if you have other duties that require your attention, please feel free to leave at any time. I am sure that my son can locate a notary for me when and if I need his professional services later this evening, and on any subsequent evenings when we may be in need of his expertise."

The man sat upright and stammered in response, "Oh, no, *Madame!* I have nowhere else to be. I am quite fine and content to remain here until you call upon me."

"Very well, then. I would appreciate it if you would keep your comments and bodily noises to yourself for the remainder of the evening."

"*Oui*, of course, *Madame.*"

Being sufficiently scolded, the man turned his attention to the brandy bottle and glass that sat on the table in front of his papers. Pierre choked his desire to laugh out loud at the humiliated man.

*Madame* Romagon cleared her throat and nodded encouragingly to Pierre. He took several steps forward and offered Genevieve his right arm.

"Genevieve, would you do me the honor of a stroll outside?"

"That sounds delightful," she replied.

She slipped her tiny hand inside the crook of Pierre's arm. Her touch electrified him. And her scent was amazing. She smelled like sweet summer flowers. The hormones that lay dormant and inactive in Pierre's body for all his years since puberty suddenly surged and flowed freely into his veins. He became excited and almost dizzy with delight.

Pierre somehow managed to guide the beautiful young woman through the parlor doors and into the foyer. Moments later they were on the front porch, strolling slowly around the periphery of the house. They took several steps in awkward silence.

Genevieve spoke first. "So then, Pierre, you are preparing for a journey upriver?"

His knees wobbled slightly when she said his name. Somehow, he managed to keep walking.

His voice shook. "Yes, Genevieve. My partner and I are making all of the necessary arrangements for our voyage to Kaskaskia and St. Louis."

"When is your departure?"

"Very soon, I am afraid. The arrival of the Spanish soldiers has accelerated our plans. Thankfully, because of their presence, there is now a surplus of men who wish to leave and go northward. We are having little trouble hiring oarsmen, riflemen, and boatsmen."

"What are your plans for the end of the journey?"

"After we work out an agreement with a certain gentleman in St. Louis, I plan to become a merchant in Kaskaskia or one of the other villages nearby. I have ample goods and capital to launch such a venture."

They walked for a moment in uncomfortable silence.

"Mother has informed me that you do not wish to make the journey alone. Indeed, she says that the reason you are here this evening is to secure a French wife as quickly as possible."

Pierre stopped abruptly and looked dejectedly at the floorboards of the walkway beneath his feet.

"What is the matter, Pierre? Is what my mother told me not true?"

Pierre took a deep breath, weighing his words carefully. "The information that she conveyed is true. But it is the spirit of those words that is not quite accurate." He turned to face her. Genevieve squared herself before him and met his gaze.

"Genevieve, up until the moment you walked into the parlor, all I had on my mind was securing a wife. It seemed to be a very practical mission. I confess … I was approaching this meeting with your mother as a mere formality … as a matter of business. I have never dealt with this situation before. I have never been wed. I have never sought a mate. I am not familiar with such things."

She lowered her eyes and looked past Pierre, obviously deep in thought. Pierre suddenly noticed that she was trembling slightly. He gently reached out and caressed her soft chin, lifting her face so that their eyes could meet again.

"But then, Genevieve, you walked into that room. I saw your sweet smile. I witnessed your unimaginable beauty and your God-endowed grace. I took one look into your emerald green eyes and fell completely in love with you. And I proclaim to you right now that I do not simply want a wife. My greatest desire is that *you* will be my wife. But it is not up to me, or to your mother, or even to that blowhard *Monsieur* de Bertien. It is entirely up to you."

She stared deeply and longingly into his eyes.

"Genevieve, I do not want to be your husband because your mother wishes it to be so. I want *you* to choose me. If you find me acceptable and suitable as a husband, and if you are willing to have me, then I will be honored to speak once again to your mother and ask for your hand. But if you are somehow repulsed by me, or simply do not wish it, then I will leave immediately and trouble you no further. My heart will be broken in two, and I shall never be satisfied with another. But I will leave you in peace."

Genevieve's chin began to quiver. Her eyes reddened as tears formed. She looked away, ashamed, and raised her hand to cover her mouth.

Pierre touched her gently on the arm. "Genevieve, tell me what you are thinking. No ... please, tell me what you are feeling."

Tears flowed down her cheeks.

"I am afraid, Pierre."

"Afraid of what? Afraid of leaving? Afraid of the river voyage?"

"No. I know that you would protect me and care for me. Of that I have no doubt. But, Pierre ..." She began to cry. "I am afraid of you." The young maiden wept openly.

Pierre was puzzled. He, himself, fought the urge to cry. He felt a sensation of heaviness and dread within his heart. Was the woman of his dreams about to reject him?

"Why should you be afraid of me, Genevieve? Am I that fearsome and repugnant? Am I unpleasant and hideous to you?"

She chuckled lightly and wiped away her tears with her bare hand. "Don't be silly, Pierre! You are a rugged, handsome man."

"What then? Why are you afraid of me?"

"I am afraid of what you will do to me." She looked shyly at him. "My friends have told me about what goes on in the bed-chamber between a husband and wife. They have described to me how vicious and cold a man can be when he takes his woman. I am afraid of the pain and violence and barbarity of it." Once again, she stared deeply into Pierre's eyes. "I am afraid that you will be different in those private moments than you are right now."

Pierre reach out and took her gently by the hand. His face was stolid, sincere, and firm.

"Genevieve, I want you to understand something." He paused. "I have never been intimate with a woman. I have never even kissed a woman before. I am not a worldly man. But if you will be my bride, I will never know any other woman but you. And I will never 'take' you, as your friends have described. I will always be gentle, and kind, and patient. I will wait until you love me, and until you choose to give yourself fully to me. We will explore and discover one another and the marriage bed together, in tenderness and in love. That is my promise to you. You need never fear me."

Silent tears flowed freely down her cheeks. She found it difficult to look Pierre in the eyes. Her body trembled with emotion.

"Genevieve, I only hope that one day you could actually love me."

She reached up and gently placed her finger on his lips to silence him.

"Shh ..." she hissed. "Pierre, you are the most amazing and beautiful man that I have ever met. I already love you. I knew I loved you the moment I saw your wavy, shiny hair and looked into your piercing brown eyes."

Pierre smiled. "Well then, Genevieve Colon." He dropped down on one knee. "I know that you only met me moments ago ... but will you do me the greatest possible honor by becoming my wife?"

She wiped away her tears and smiled broadly down at his beaming face. "*Oui*, Pierre Grimard. It will make me very happy to become your wife."

Pierre kissed her hand. He stood and they embraced fully in the dull lamplight of the porch. Genevieve wrapped her arms around Pierre's neck. He picked her up off of the floor and lifted her face to his, kissing her gently on the lips. It was the first kiss ever for both of them ... innocent, pure, and electric. Pierre's senses reeled at the softness of her lips and the fullness and warmth of her breasts pressed against his chest. He did not want to ever let her go. But slowly and gently, after they released their kiss, Pierre lowered her back to the floor.

Pierre chuckled lightly. "Well, I suppose we can put that boorish notary's mind at ease now. And I suppose I must go and fetch my friends to sign his surety papers."

"There will be plenty of time for that. Come, Pierre, let us go and tell Mama!"

She hugged Pierre again, kissed him lightly, and then grabbed his hand and excitedly dragged him back toward the front door of the Colomb home.

꙯

### August 8, 1769

Pierre ambled down the walkway beside the river pier, munching on a sweet, fresh apple. It was his first day back on the job after a week of honeymooning with his young bride. There was a song in his heart and a skip in his step. He was convinced that he must be the happiest man in the world. He saw Charles and Antoine standing near a shack at the end of the pier. Antoine was inspecting a writing board that was stacked high with papers. He could see Rimbault "talking with his hands" and heard the man's raucous laughter as he bellowed at one of his own jokes. Pierre smiled as he watched Antoine shaking his head in disgust.

Pierre called out, "*Bonjour,* river travelers! How is our little fleet shaping up?"

Rimbault threw up his hands in celebration, clapping them together loudly and cheering the approaching groom. He added loud catcall whistles to his obnoxious din.

"How wonderful of you to join us, *Monsieur* Grimard! So, you decided to come out from under the covers for a little air! How is our lover boy? Have you tamed that little temptress? Is it true? Can a Frenchman survive only on love?"

The rowdy frontiersman howled with laughter at his own eternally crude and always inappropriate humor. Antoine fought the urge to laugh, as well. Pierre was less than amused.

The cretin continued, "Only God knows how you tore yourself away from that tasty little beast. My, oh, my ... I'll bet you she's as sweet and juicy as a summer melon!"

Rimbault laughed so hard that it seemed that he might choke on his own spittle. Pierre almost wished that he would.

Pierre snapped, "I will tolerate no more of your disrespectful, vulgar talk, Rimbault. That is my wife that you are speaking about! Civilized men do not discuss women in such terms. You would do well to remember who is paying your salary for the next five months. I will not hesitate to have your ass thrown out on the riverbank somewhere between here and Kaskaskia."

Rimbault bit his lip and feigned humble regret. "A thousand apologies, Pierre. I was merely jesting … having a little fun at your expense."

"Fun at my expense is fine, Rimbault, just as long as it does not involve my wife. Do I make myself clear?"

"Very clear, *Monsieur* Grimard."

"Good. Now, to the business at hand. How are the preparations coming? We need to launch soon. There are rumors that the Spaniards are about to clamp down on river travel, perhaps even close the river altogether. They're beginning to pry around the import house and docks."

"Two more days, Pierre," responded Rimbault. "That is all we need. I must secure one more bateau and finish out her crew."

"How many bateaux do we have committed already?"

"Seven," responded Rimbault. "Each with full crews of twenty-four men. We need about a dozen men for the last boat."

"That is a lot of men, Rimbault. Eight crews of twenty-four! How will we ever pay them all?"

Antoine joined in the conversation. "Not to worry, Pierre. There are so many Frenchmen wanting to escape New Orleans that we do not even have to pay some of them a salary. With Charles' help I have hired experienced captains for each bateau, along with proven soldiers for our defense. But the vast majority of our oarsmen have signed up for a free ride north, along with food, lead, and gunpowder for the journey. I have promised each man who survives the trek a twenty-livre bonus when we reach Kaskaskia. We even have a couple of wealthy businessmen who are paying a hefty fare for passage north. Of course, they will not swing an oar. But at least they can shoot!"

Pierre nodded his approval. "Excellent planning and work, both of you. You are to be commended. Will it be difficult to staff the final bateau?"

Charles responded, "Oh, no, Pierre. That is the least of our worries. I will have the necessary men enlisted by noon today. I should also have possession of the final bateau before sundown. Tomorrow we will gather the crews, load the cargo and provisions, and make final preparations. We can depart at dawn the next day."

"Excellent. I will make sure that Genevieve and I are prepared for the departure."

Charles paused, taking a short, thoughtful breath. For the first time that Pierre had ever witnessed, the man seemed to be choosing his words carefully and deliberately.

"Pierre, I need you to truly understand the peril of this voyage upriver."

"Charles, I am well aware of the possible danger."

"There is nothing 'possible' about it, Pierre. There *will* be danger. Grave danger. We will encounter marauders, thieves, and savages. You can bet on it. There will be horrible, foul weather. The first month will be unbearably hot. In November, there will be bone-chilling cold. There are insects, leeches, snakes, and disease. Many good men have perished on this muddy river. It is torturous to the women. Some members of the fairer sex lose their minds on this journey, never to be the same again."

"I am so glad that I did not take a wife!" exclaimed Antoine. "I already have enough trouble, as it is."

Pierre grinned at his friend, then turned to Charles. "Genevieve is a strong young woman. No need to worry. I will watch over her and protect her."

"Sometimes that is not enough," responded Rimbault.

"Companions may be of some help. Are there any other women going on the journey?"

"I believe that there are five other married men who are bringing their wives with them. There are none with children, though. I would not allow families in our little flotilla."

Pierre nodded enthusiastically. "I agree. That is for the best. But it is good that there are some more women. Genevieve will have the fellowship of other ladies. Perhaps they can all be an encouragement to one another."

"We shall see, Pierre. We shall see," responded Charles, somewhat unconvinced.

Pierre sighed. "Well, gentlemen, keep up the good work. I will be here bright and early tomorrow for the loading of goods."

Pierre shook hands with both men and then sauntered back up the boardwalk toward town. He purchased a bouquet of lovely flowers, two bottles of fine wine, and a basket of fruit on the way back to his small apartment. He intended to make the most of his final day of honeymooning.

᪐

*August 16, 1769*

The morning was hazy and humid. The sun had been up for almost an hour. Alongside the wide dock eight French boats, *bateaux de roi*, were tied snugly to posts. Though certainly not seaworthy, the large boats were perfect for transporting men and cargo throughout a river system. These larger versions of a traditional bateau had been designed and used for several decades for cargo travel on the Mississippi River.

Twelve men sat on rowing benches on each side of a bateau, each commanding a long oar for propelling the vessel upstream against currents. A modest mast and sail stood amidships, ready for deployment on the days when a wind out of the south might lessen the burden on the oarsmen. The center hull of each bateau was deep and held ample room for cargo, food, supplies, and passengers.

Most trips upriver from New Orleans consisted of two to four of these vessels. Pierre and Antoine's little armada was double the usual size. They were moving an impressive amount of cargo and men up the Mississippi River. Because of the unusual size of their party many spectators had gathered along the bank of the river to observe the launch. The area was a veritable sea of humanity and there was something of a carnival-like atmosphere. The observers seemed excited and jolly.

The travelers, on the other hand, were much more subdued and grim. The boat captains diligently checked their cargo and inspected their vessels. The men of the boats busied themselves with their personal property and weapons. It was clear that most of them were growing tired of waiting and were anxious to get underway.

Pierre sensed the tension and called out to the throng of crewmen that crowded the dock, "Gentlemen! Gather around, please!"

The crowd silenced quickly and gathered as close to Pierre as they could. He struck an impressive, commanding stance and cradled a shiny Charleville musket in the crook of his arm.

He spoke with as much authority as he could muster. "Men, the time of departure is upon us. I am grateful to each and every one of you who have chosen to make this journey with our company. My name is Pierre Grimard. I am the man who is financially responsible for this venture. Like you, I am anxious to reach the Illinois Country. As most of you have undoubtedly heard, I know absolutely nothing about bateau travel or life on the Mississippi River."

Most of the men chuckled lightheartedly.

"However, as we prepare to launch our convoy, I want everyone to be absolutely clear about who is in charge. Charles Rimbault, *voyageur* of Vincennes, is the commander and master of our little fleet. He has made this perilous journey many times. He knows the river and is well acquainted with the hazards and travails that await us. Once we are on the water, we all answer to him. You will obey his commands. I will obey his commands. Have I made myself clear?"

The throng of travelers grunted and nodded in affirmation.

"Excellent. Now, I yield to *Monsieur* Rimbault. He will issue final orders and instructions." He turned to Rimbault. "Charles, the men are yours."

Rimbault nodded respectfully. "*Merci*, Pierre." He cleared his throat to address the crowd. "Boys, my instructions are simple. Do what I tell you to do when I tell you to do it. We will stay in the center of the river channel unless I command otherwise. You will keep your weapons loaded and primed at all times. Always make sure your powder is dry and protected. If you are not on an oar, you will remain on constant watch and maintain a careful eye on the riverbank. We have plenty of stores and supplies, but we will attempt to supplement our diet with wild game, fish, and turtles as much as possible.

"We will establish nightly security in our camps on a rotating system by boats and crews. The boats are numbered according to their order along this dock. Learn your boat number and get to know your fellow crewmen quickly. We will not be swapping boats unless absolutely necessary ... and by necessary, I mean that someone has been killed and must be replaced for the boat to function."

The group of two hundred and thirty men and women listened intently and in thoughtful silence. Many stared at the boards beneath their feet. If, before this moment, they had been unaware of the danger of their endeavor, they were now being thoroughly and bluntly educated by their swarthy commander.

Charles continued, "I will command the first boat and lead the fleet. *Messieurs* Grimard and Alexis will be in my boat. If there are questions or concerns during travel on the water you may pass word along the line of boats and we will communicate by simple relaying of messages.

"Gentlemen, I suggest that you become accustomed to the water quickly. We will not be making unnecessary stops during daylight hours. Those hours are for traveling. Understand me well! We are not stopping a fleet of eight bateaux for you to empty your bowels. You will have to relieve yourselves over the side of the boat."

There was a murmur of surprise and disgust among some of the men. The eyes of the six women dispersed throughout the crowd were open wide with shock.

Genevieve tugged Pierre's arm and pulled his ear to her mouth. "Is that man serious? I will not relieve myself over the side of any boat."

"Do not worry, my dear. I have made provisions for you."

She nodded, but maintained her expression of shock and concern.

Rimbault picked up on the consternation among some of the passengers and crew. "Do not worry, gentlemen. After four months on the water you will become accustomed to dangling your jewels over the rails. Just be careful of splinters, swinging oars, and snapping turtles."

The crowd erupted into enthusiastic laughter. Finally! Someone else besides Rimbault had laughed at one of his crude jokes.

"We will stop to make camp and send out hunting parties approximately two hours before sunset each day, unless there are potential threats to our security that require us to stay on the water and proceed at night. We will eat a cold breakfast and a hot supper. Those will be our meals each day."

He paused and took a deep breath. "There is not much left to say. Some of you are about to experience the most backbreaking work that you have ever attempted. We will use the sails whenever possible, but for the most part, your arms and oars will propel us to our destination. But when we do reach Kaskaskia, you will be stronger and better men ... and you will have ownership of a story that you will someday tell your children and your children's children.

"Above all else remember that your job ... what you have signed on for ... is to transport Grimard and Alexis and all of their cargo and goods to Kaskaskia. All other purposes are of no consequence to your employers. Your passage north and your personal plans for the future are secondary to our mission." He looked at Pierre. "Is there anything else, *Monsieur* Grimard?"

"Just one thing," responded Pierre. "For each boat that arrives in Kaskaskia with all of their cargo intact and undamaged, I will pay each crewman on that boat an additional bonus of ten livres gold. This is in addition to the bonus promised by *Monsieur* Alexis."

His announcement elicited an enthusiastic cheer from the men.

"All right, then!" shouted Rimbault. "Crewmen, to your boats! Make ready for the launch!"

There was a mad scramble on the dock as the men filed toward their assigned bateaux. Pierre escorted Genevieve to her place in the first boat. In the very center, right next to the mast, he had prepared a small, comfortable nest for her. There were blankets, several pillows, a basket full of fruit, and a piece of canvas for shade. In one corner of her cubby lay a weathered, well-used chamber pot.

Genevieve placed both hands on her hips and nodded toward the pot. "*Excuse-moi.* Is *that* the provision that you made for my personal needs? A chamber pot in the center of this boat?" She stomped one foot. "*Quel désastre!*"

"It is a perfect solution, my darling. You will be under the canvas and out of view. We can even use the cloth from the sail for more privacy if needs be. Anyhow, you will have the hem of your dress spread over your personal areas and the pot when in use. No one will see anything."

"Humph!" she retorted. "And have all of these strange men listening to my business striking the bottom of that thunder pot? Not in this lifetime! And not in this boat! This simply will not do. Pierre Grimard, you must find a better solution."

"Sweet wife, it is either that or hanging your tender backside and lovely dress over the gunwale of the boat. Or I suppose you could hold your bladder and bowels for upwards of twelve hours a day until we stop to make camp for the evening. The choice is yours. But this is simply the best that I have to offer." He looked as sympathetic as he possibly could. "Remember … the other ladies on the other boats are in the same predicament as you. We have made the same provision for each of them."

Tears welled in her eyes. Pierre thought that she was on the verge of erupting into some type of tantrum. He glanced around and saw that the other men on the boat were all fully engrossed in the ongoing marital drama being played out in front of them. No one moved or even blinked. Genevieve took note of the two dozen enthralled observers, as well. She took a deep breath and attempted to compose herself.

"Very well, then, husband. I realize that this is a burden shared by every female on this voyage. I will bear it with as much dignity and resolve as I possibly can." She paused and faked a smile. "Thank you for arranging this special provision of privacy for me."

"You are most welcome, my bride. Now gather your things and make your place as comfortable and restful as possible."

She smiled again. This time it was genuine. Pierre reached out and lightly stroked her cheek with his finger and then gave her a playful tap on the nose.

He whispered, "Everything will be fine, I promise."

Genevieve knelt down in the bottom of the boat and began to prepare what was to become her home for the next four months.

His wife somewhat appeased, Pierre joined Charles on the dock to help organize and secure the remainder of the boats and men. It took almost another half-hour to get everyone loaded and positioned properly. Rimbault pranced like a peacock up and down the length of the dock, shouting orders, cursing in French and various Indian tongues, and giving enthusiastic direction to the men. Occasionally he jumped into one of the boats to lash down a piece of equipment or check the swivel on an oar. He griped and fussed and acted as if he were thoroughly disgusted with their slow progress.

Pierre pulled him aside. "You seem incensed and impatient. Are you having second thoughts about this endeavor?"

Rimbault chuckled. "No, Pierre. I am having the time of my life! This is the most fun that I have had in months. It always takes an unreasonable amount of time to prepare for launch. I just enjoy giving the men a hard time. Allow me to have my fun." He winked at Pierre, who shook his head in disbelief, smiled, and patted him warmly on the back.

At long last it appeared that everyone was in place and prepared to depart. Rimbault made one more inspection walk up and down the line of bateaux. When he reached the first boat he climbed on board and made his way to the center, right next to Genevieve, where he planted his boot on a small peg that stuck out of the base of the mast. Grasping the mast, he lifted himself up so that he could see all the way down the line of boats. He took off his red *voyageur* hat and waved it high over his head.

He shouted, "Cast off all lines! Push away from the dock!"

The men on the starboard side of each boat used their oars to push away from the dock. All eight boats eased into the slow current and began to drift slowly southward.

"We're headed the wrong way, gentlemen! Let's get those oars in the water! Boat captains, find your rhythm! Not too fast, and not too slow! Stay in formation, and follow me to Illinois!"

The oars of the French bateaux began to slap the water. The strokes of the men were haphazard at first, but within minutes each boat and crew found its rhythm.

Pierre observed the line of boats as they made their way into the center of the river channel. Less than a half-hour later his bateau rounded a bend and the buildings of New Orleans slowly disappeared from view. The landscape soon changed from that of estates, fields, homes, and civilization into a wilderness of virgin timber, muddy banks, and bubbling streams.

Pierre looked down at his young wife and smiled as he watched her adjusting her wide-brimmed straw hat to shield her eyes from the sun.

"We're actually doing it, darling!" he exclaimed. He glanced at Antoine. "Antoine, old friend, we're actually going to Illinois!"

"Yes, Pierre. Yes, we are," responded Antoine, grinning from ear to ear.

Pierre peered northward with a great sense of accomplishment and satisfaction. His face beamed with optimism and joy. He felt like the master of the world.

"The time will pass quickly. I am convinced of it. We will be there before we know it!"

Charles Rimbault, sitting in the rear of the boat, smiled grimly and shook his head.

# PART II

*The Journey North*
*1769*

# 6

## DELUGE

Pierre was mortified by their astounding lack of progress. He looked back down the ragged line of eight bateaux, four of them trailing wide, cargo-laden pirogues tied to their sterns by short ropes. He winced at the almost two hundred souls struggling and fighting against the invisible yet supremely powerful current of the river.

Day after day these men leaned into their oars and labored against the onslaught of the mighty Mississippi River, and yet on each of those days they only managed a meager six or seven miles of travel. Each evening they stopped, made a quick camp, and ate a boring meal. Each morning they ate a cold breakfast, loaded their personal items, and began rowing again. The boredom of it all was beginning to drive Pierre insane. After four days of laborious travel the convoy of cargo-laden boats was still following an overall westerly path and had not yet even reached the point where the river made its northward turn.

He had envisioned a great wilderness journey, but thus far all that Pierre had witnessed were the familiar sights of typical Louisiana bayou civilization. Small French villages and plantations dotted the edges of the busy river and its tributaries. As they progressed westward they entered a unique area settled entirely by Germans.

"At least that was something different," Pierre thought sarcastically.

Local residents and their colored slaves paddled up and down the channel in their pirogues as they tended to their daily lives and commerce along the river. Sometimes the pesky locals guided their smaller craft in and among the larger bateaux, asking their nosy questions and making conversation with the crewmen. Many of the slave children attempted to sell their wares, especially garden produce and fresh homemade bread and pastries. The more aggressive sellers relieved quite a few of the oarsmen of their copper coins.

Pierre was relaxing after spending a couple of hours on an oar. He and Antoine had taken it upon themselves to give relief and rest to the occasional oarsman who might be exhausted, sick, or otherwise indisposed by nature's frequent call. Pierre swatted a mosquito that had begun to feast on his left arm. Thus far, the blood-sucking bugs were the most dangerous things that the river travelers had encountered. The frustrated Frenchman shot a look of bored disgust at Rimbault.

"Charles, you made it sound like this journey was going to be a trek of great danger and adventure. To me, it feels like an evening cruise along a New Orleans bayou. The wildest things that I've seen have been these pesky mosquitoes and the slave boys who constantly attempt to sell us their melons and baguettes."

"What did you expect, Pierre?" challenged the grungy voyageur. "Did you think that wild Indians would be lying in wait around the bend from the wharf in New Orleans? Are you *that* anxious for trouble?"

"No, not anxious for trouble … but anxious for something beyond this dreadful boredom and monotony."

"Be thankful for the monotony, Pierre. It will disappear soon enough. I pray that every single day of our journey will be just like the last four. I can most definitely live with this dull, comfortable warmth and dry days and nights. I would venture to guess that your bride would be in wholehearted agreement with me."

Pierre stole a quick glance at Genevieve. She was napping peacefully under her canvas shade.

"I suppose you're right, Charles. There is no amount of adventure that is worth endangering my wife." He sighed. "I do apologize for sounding so childish and headstrong. I just had some different expectations, I suppose."

Charles chuckled and spat over the top of an oarsman's head into the muddy water beyond. "Do not fret it in the least, Pierre. Young men like you are filled with visions of adventure and glory. But the simple truth is that most of life is made up of routines ... dull, boring, glorious routines. The older you get, the more you will come to appreciate them. You may crave adventure, but all that I crave is peace."

Pierre smiled warmly. "I suppose you're right."

"Oh, I assure you young friend, I am quite right. There will come a day when all that you will desire will be a warm fire, a warm meal, a warm bed to sleep in, and a warm woman beside you to keep your feet and your manhood toasty." Charles cast an exaggerated wink toward Pierre. "After that, Pierre, everything else is just gravy."

Pierre laughed out loud at his crude, river-running friend.

Charles nodded admirably at Pierre. "I commend you and Antoine for taking a turn on the oars. Most masters of the boats would not think of lowering themselves to such a level of labor and servitude."

"We're just trying to do our part," responded Pierre.

"I know. And it has made quite the impression on the men. They respect you. They will fight for you when the time comes."

Pierre sighed. "Well, let's hope that time never comes."

"And here I thought that you were a voyageur adventurer!" teased Charles.

Pierre looked back over his left shoulder and saw Antoine pulling smoothly on one of the oars. He was shirtless and soaked with sweat. Like all of the other men on the boat, he was suffering with the pink, puffy, blistered skin of sunburn. Pierre reached up and touched the tender skin on his own shoulders. He winced at the pain.

Charles saw that he was testing the skin under his shirt. "Does is still hurt? The sunburn?"

"It is better, I believe. It's difficult to tell what irritates me the most ... the mosquito bites or the cooked skin. Genevieve has been rubbing a generous amount of bear grease on my shoulders and back at night. It seems to help a bit."

Charles grinned and teased, "That sounds like fun ... Maybe I need to try to get a sunburn when I get back home. Perhaps my Julie will want to rub some of that bear grease on me. It might liven things up just a bit!" He laughed out loud, as usual, at his own bawdy joke. After several seconds, he finally stopped.

"Pierre, the only thing that will truly help your cooked skin is time. You need to keep your shirt on during the heat of the day. But do not worry. The blisters and tenderness will soon go away. By the time we reach the Chickasaw Bluffs, you will be as tanned and bronzed as a Shawnee warrior. We will not be able to tell the difference between you and the savages along the riverbank."

"I'll believe that when I see it," teased Antoine from the back of the boat. "Pierre is so white that the men behind him are blinded when he takes off his shirt. They have to pull their hats down low over their eyes!"

The oarsmen chuckled enthusiastically at the Austrian's joke. Charles Rimbault joined in the teasing. "It is true, Pierre. I was not going to say anything. But yesterday when you took your shirt off the reflection was so bright toward the stern of the boat that I thought one of the men had deployed the sail."

Truly raucous laughter ensued. Pierre could not help but laugh, as well, even though he was the object of the joke. The rambunctious noise awakened Genevieve. She rolled over onto her side and peeked at Pierre from underneath the canvas cover. She smiled. It brought her great joy to see happiness on her husband's face. She stretched and slowly began to crawl out into the sunshine.

Her tiny voice emanated from beneath the canvas shade, "Pierre, may I join you all?"

"Of course, my love. Come out and enjoy this beautiful Louisiana afternoon."

The beautiful woman's appearance brought a sudden end to the laughter of the men. None of them wanted to be found guilty of even a hint of shameful behavior in front of their master's young wife. They instantly focused all of their attention on their oars and the waters of the river. Rimbault called out a modest pace for the rowers, directing them into a steady rhythm.

The crewmen tried not to look at the young girl, but most of the men could not resist stealing a glance. She was, indeed, a stunningly beautiful female. Her green eyes were captivating and piercing. Her generous curves demonstrated themselves quite nicely despite the conservative petticoat and short gown that she wore. Genevieve gracefully seated herself on the narrow seat beside Pierre and leaned against the wooden mast.

She sat quietly for a moment and surveyed their picturesque surroundings. She giggled and pointed at a group of slave children playing nearby in the water of the river. Moments later she took off her mob cap and allowed her soft reddish-brown curls to fall loosely to her shoulders. Her hair was somewhat displaced and unruly from sleeping while wearing the bonnet. Sensing her disheveled appearance, she leaned forward and fluffed her hair vigorously with her fingers and then tossed her head backwards to shake the curls from her eyes. Her shiny hair arced high in the air and then settled softly over her shoulders.

The sudden fluffing and flinging of her hair was innocent enough, but it was intensely and undeniably sensual and completely torturous to the crew of woman-starved men. It elicited an almost audible gasp from within their ranks. Genevieve innocently glanced around to see what all of the commotion was about.

The men quickly diverted their collective gaze toward their oars. Charles Rimbault watched the entire episode from his seat midway toward the stern of the boat. He just smiled and shook his head.

Genevieve shielded her eyes and looked toward the sun. She commented to no one in particular, "We are still heading west I see. When will we make a turn to the north?"

"Soon, young lady," Rimbault answered from behind her. "We are approaching Little Colapisas. We should make the bend at the Plateau Breton some time before noon tomorrow. We will be past the Piakamenes and Iberville Rivers the following day."

"And then the British territory will be to our east," she commented.

"Yes, madam. Indeed." Charles seemed surprised. "You sound as if you are familiar with this country."

"*Oui.* I've been here before ... two summers ago."

Pierre was shocked. "Really? Pray tell, why were you on this river?"

"Papa had business in the village at Baton Rouge. My brother was uninterested in travel, so Papa invited me to accompany him. It was a glorious experience that I shall never forget. The trip upriver took ten days. We were in the area for almost two weeks. I met many new people and explored the wilderness around the village with Papa. It was a very special time for me, and a precious memory of him that I hope to never forget."

"You loved him very much, then?" asked Pierre.

"*Oui, mon mari.* He was a wonderful, loving man. He and Mama made quite a pair. I miss him very, very much." She paused and stared at Pierre. "You remind me of him in some ways."

"Really? How so?"

"Well, not in a physical sense. Papa was a short, plump, red-faced fellow. But your warm sense of humor and thoughtfulness remind me of him very much. You are a conscientious, hard worker like he was. And you are concerned very much for the welfare of those who are under your charge. Very much like my Papa."

Pierre leaned close to her and whispered, "Perhaps I might make a good Papa one day to some little Grimard children?"

She smiled and reached out to take him by the hand. She whispered, "I expect that you shall one of these days. But I would like to keep you all to myself for a little while, at least."

"I quite agree, *ma femme précieuse*."

In the rear of the bateau Rimbault rather obnoxiously cleared his throat. "Pierre, we need to be on the lookout for an adequate place to camp for the night. We will need to make our stop within the hour."

"*Oui*, Charles. On the north bank or the south bank?"

"It matters not. I want a spot that is well above the water line. Just find us a place with good elevation. I smell rain coming."

Pierre looked incredulously toward the blue, crystal-clear sky. "Charles, there is not a cloud to be seen. How can you 'smell' rain?"

"Trust me, Pierre. It will rain this very night."

꒚

Pierre cuddled against his wife's back as close as space would allow. He attempted to stretch their wool blanket to its maximum size to help chase away the damp chill of the night air. Outside their tiny tent the thunder roared and the rain fell in a great torrent.

Pierre whispered in his wife's ear, "Are you all right, my darling?"

"*Oui*. I am safe and warm with you."

She wiggled her hips and invited him closer. He wrapped his left arm around her waist and pulled her shoulder blades tightly against his chest. Then he prayed that all of the preparations that he had completed just before nightfall would keep them dry throughout the night.

The travelers were perched on the side of a small hill on the north bank of the river, with tents pitched against the edge of the tree line. The forest was thick and almost jungle-like behind them.

It was the best site that they could manage to locate as darkness fell on the river bottom.

Once they had pitched camp, while the other men ate and drank their rum, Pierre busied himself with the task of digging a shallow drainage trench around his tent. He hoped that it would be sufficient to divert water. He also constructed a small dam of smooth stones and earth on the uphill side of their shelter. While he held little hope that his precautions would be of much help in a real downpour, his goal was to at least steer the majority of the rain water around their tent.

But, tragically, he failed to achieve that goal. Pierre winced as he felt a stinging sensation of wetness and cold in the small of his back. His timid hope for a dry night disappeared. A rivulet of water had found its way through his makeshift berm. The cool water began to soak his back. Beyond the walls of their shelter Pierre and Genevieve could hear men cursing and screaming as the water flowed into their shelters and soaked their blankets and bedrolls.

Genevieve sighed. "It is going to be a long and miserable night."

Pierre grunted. "And an even longer day tomorrow, I am afraid."

※

Pierre awakened with a start. He did not know how he had managed to fall asleep, but somehow, he did. His back was thoroughly soaked and ached immensely. He was stiff in his spine and hips from lying on his right side for the entire night. And he felt like his bladder was about to explode. Genevieve purred quietly, still asleep and completely dry. Pierre was the only water dam that she needed, blocking all of the cold moisture with his own back. Soon he realized what had awakened him. It was the harsh voice of Charles Rimbault shouting orders down by the riverbank.

"Make sure all of that canvas is dry before it is folded!" barked Rimbault. "I don't want black mold and rot growing in my boats! We'll stay here as long as it takes. Damn you, boy, stop your excuses and get that fire going! And build it big. I want lines strung in the sun. Hang out all your laundry, boys!"

Pierre extricated his numb right arm from beneath Genevieve's neck and head, replacing it with a small cloth sack full of wool that she used for spinning yarn. He slowly and quietly crawled out of the tiny two-man tent, fighting against the stiffness in his knees, neck, and back. He tossed open the flap of the tent and discovered a camp full of activity. Everyone was attempting to wash away the mud and silt from storm water runoff and dry their clothing and equipment. Everything had been thoroughly soaked during the night.

Pierre glanced upward to discern a forecast for the day. The sky directly overhead was still filled with broken clouds, but an expanding shade of blue revealed itself to their west. After such a miserable, rainy night, it appeared that the men were going to be blessed with a clear, warm, and sunny day to recover.

He thought, "God, I hope the cargo is not damaged."

His bladder cramped sharply and reminded him of its distended state. The cargo would have to wait. Pierre slogged gingerly through the spongy, muddy grass and found a quiet spot at the edge of the tree line to relieve his bladder ... which took a while. Mosquitoes tortured him the entire time that he was urinating. They were out in swarms and looking to feed. After attending to his needs and killing at least a dozen of the blood-sucking pests, he made his way toward the boats.

The boisterous Rimbault saw Pierre approaching and shouted a greeting, "Good morning, Pierre! I was beginning to wonder if we had lost you in the flood!" He smiled mischievously. "I trust that you and the little lady remained warm and dry throughout the night." He slapped a mosquito on his own cheek.

Pierre turned and revealed his half-soaked back and right leg.

"Genevieve is dry and still sleeping like a newborn. I slept on the uphill side and managed to catch all of the water that leaked into our tent. It was a miserable night. I do not think that I slept except for the last hour or two before dawn."

"You need to get those clothes off and get them dry, Pierre. You could contract all manner of skin maladies in this wet environment. It's not yet cold enough to worry about croup or *le grippe* or the pleurisy, but those days are certainly coming in the months ahead."

Pierre smiled and nodded. "I understand. I just wanted to check on the cargo and boats before taking care of my laundry."

Rimbault waved a dismissive hand in the air. "The cargo is fine, Pierre. I checked all eight bateaux and all of the cargo pirogues first thing this morning. The stretched oilcloths did the job nicely. Every yard of that greasy canvas was a good investment. The interiors of all twelve of our boats are absolutely dry."

Pierre exhaled a sigh of relief. His investment and future business were still intact.

"How long will it take for the men and the camp to dry out?"

Rimabult sighed. "I'm quite certain that it will take the entire day. Full sunshine is still a few hours away. The fires are slow in starting. Most of the men did not make adequate preparations around their tents … not that it would have helped much in a downpour like the one we experienced last night. Our shelters, clothing, and leather are all soaked. We need to make sure everything is dry before proceeding northward. It will be an all-day endeavor."

"So, we'll be here another night?" asked Pierre.

"Yes. I think we should simply plan on it. After all, there is no reason to rush. Illinois is not going anywhere. It will still be there whenever we arrive." He saw the mild look of disappointment on the young man's face. "Do not be discouraged, Pierre. This is at most a minor setback. Our four months of planned travel includes almost three weeks of extended camp due to weather and hardship."

Pierre humbled his strong will before the wisdom of the weathered *voyageur.* "Very well then, Charles. What do I need to do?"

"First, attend to your wife and get on some dry clothes. If you have any decent tinder, try to get a fire started. We need the ladies to pitch in together and prepare us a hot breakfast. We have ample rice, nuts, and raisins for a fine porridge. Then we could use some fresh meat for the evening. We're going through our stores pretty quickly with this crowd. I will appoint a team for hunting and place you in charge, if that is agreeable with you."

"As you wish, Charles. I've been aching to try out my shiny new Charleville musket. We'll not be hunting parrots, will we?"

Rimbault looked thoroughly bewildered. "*Quelle?* Parrots? What the hell are you talking about, you crazy Frenchman? There are no parrots in Louisiana!"

Pierre chuckled and waved his hands at his friend. "Never mind. It's a long story. Perhaps one that we can share over a cup of rum tonight."

Charles laughed lightly. "I think that I would like to hear it! But what we need is deer, Pierre. At least four of them to feed this mob. Or a nice heifer cow would be nice … though I doubt you will discover one of those in the Louisiana backcountry. And speaking of rum … it would probably serve us well to break out a keg and give the men a snort. It might do wonders for the chill and the foul mood that hovers over this camp."

"Good idea, Charles. But only one small keg, and only one ration of rum per man. We don't want a drunken rabble on our hands."

"Agreed. I will see to it."

"And I will see to my wife and my wardrobe. Choose your hunting party and have them meet me by the riverbank nearest the lead boat after breakfast. And be sure to pick some good shooters."

"I will, Pierre. I already have several men in mind."

Pierre turned and trudged back up the small hill toward his tent.

❦

Genevieve was awake and gone when Pierre returned. One of the men from the crew of the second boat had built her a small fire and was working diligently to keep it lit. She had already raised both sides of their shelter and lashed the corners with leather thongs to nearby trees and bushes to expose them fully to the sun and dry them out.

"*Bonjour*," Pierre spoke kindly to the fellow. "Have you seen my wife?"

"*Oui, Monsieur.* She has stepped into the forest just beyond the tent to attend to her needs. I am keeping a lookout to make sure no one disturbs her while I get you folks a good fire started."

A tiny voice called from the darkness of the trees, "I am here, husband! I will join you in a moment."

Pierre chuckled and turned to the fellow kneeling beside the smoking pile of kindling. "*Merci, mon ami* ... for the fire and for your gentlemanly kindness toward my wife. What is your name? I have seen you several times, but do not believe that we have been introduced."

"I am Francois Turpin, formerly of Acadia."

The man stood as Pierre stepped forward to shake his hand. "Francois, I am pleased to make your acquaintance. Have you always been a boatsman and *voyageur*?"

Francois smiled and laughed lightly as he shook his head. "Not hardly, *Monsieur.* I was a cattle farmer in Canada before the English came and took my home. It was my father's home and land, and my father's father's before him. Yet someone somewhere signed a treaty and then it suddenly was not ours anymore." He paused, and his face became grim. "My wife and daughter died on the ship to New Orleans. I have no family or connections to Louisiana, so I jumped at the opportunity to join your party and leave. I hope to begin a new life in Illinois." He knelt down again and gently stirred the smoking twigs and coals.

"As do we all, Francois, as do we all. I am grieved by your loss. I pray that you will find happiness and prosperity in the North."

"Amen to that, *Monsieur.*" He made the sign of the cross on his chest as he stared into the smoldering fire. Pierre followed his lead and made the sign, as well.

Genevieve emerged from the woods as their conversation dwindled.

"I see that you two have become acquainted. Francois was quite the gentleman, Pierre. He has been most generous with his fire-making skills."

"Do not sing my praises just yet, *Madame*. I am struggling to get this fire lit."

"Oh, I have faith in you, Francois." She turned to her husband. "What is the news, Pierre?"

"We are staying in this camp all day and for another night. Charles wants all of the equipment dried thoroughly before we resume our journey."

"I would say that is wise," she affirmed. "And what is expected of me today?"

"Charles would like for the women to work together to cook a hot meal for the camp. He suggests using our stores of rice, raisins, and nuts to cook a cauldron of sweet porridge. Coffee and tea would be nice, as well."

She nodded, pleased with having an assignment and some responsibility. "I will gather the women and tackle the task. It should not us very take long."

"I will assign some men to bring up the supplies from the pirogue," offered Pierre.

"That is not necessary, husband. I am quite sure that I will have no shortage of volunteers if a hot meal is on the other side of the labor." She examined him a bit more closely, noting his awkward stance. "What is wrong with your back?"

"I am just stiff from the night. I got a little wet."

She grabbed him by the arm and spun him around. Her eyes widened in shock.

"A little wet!" she exclaimed. "Your back is soaked! How did that happen? I was dry all night!"

"I think I took most of your water." He grinned sheepishly.

She pushed him toward the tent. "Get out of those wet clothes this instant! You have another outfit in your portmanteau. I want you in all fresh garments ... even your socks. While we have the entire day at our disposal, I will launder your breeches, shirt, and weskit so that all of your clothing will be clean."

"*Oui, Madame,*" he responded jokingly, as he crawled under the spread-open canvas and began to change. She stared at him with both of her hands on her hips.

She continued, "I will bring you some fresh water and a cloth for washing. You might as well wash your filthy body before your put on those fresh clothes. Your smell is pungent."

"You didn't seem to mind my smell when you snuggled against me in the rainstorm last night," he teased.

"Humph!" she responded wordlessly and then spun to go in search of a basin.

A half-hour later Pierre was clean-shaven, washed, and outfitted with fresh clothing. He looked quite the gentleman in his black linen breeches, indigo shirt, and buff weskit. The campfire was roaring and Francois was busy placing a kettle of water for tea on a rock beside the fire.

"Is breakfast almost ready?" Pierre teased.

Francois laughed and pointed with his head toward the center of camp. "Your bride is quite the little general. She has all of her cooking staff and subordinate laborers toiling over the fires right now. Charles has been griping at her about taking so many men away from their other tasks ... but I know that he is just teasing her."

Pierre laughed. "That sounds like Charles, all right."

"I expect that we will have a hot, satisfying meal within the hour, *Monsieur.*"

"Francois, please just call me Pierre. That is my name. I'm tired of all of this '*Monsieur*' business."

"Very well, Pierre." He paused. "Word about the camp is that you are leading a hunting party into the wilderness after our meal."

Pierre nodded. "Rimbault has assigned me the task of bringing a supply of venison back to camp. He wants us to get at least four deer for an evening feast."

"I am an experienced hunter and a decent shot. It was a requirement for survival in Acadia."

"Then you shall join us!" declared Pierre, heartily slapping the fellow on his shoulder. "It will be an honor to have you along."

"*Merci*, Pierre. I was hoping that you would invite me."

Five hunters were spread out in a line roughly thirty yards apart in the dense, humid virgin woods. The trees were still soaked and holding water from the previous night's heavy rain. Noisy squirrels dislodged a soaking spray of the moisture every time they jumped from one limb to another. The sound of the forest showers was almost deafening beneath the otherwise silent canopy. The air was thick, dank, and earthy. Moss grew on the tree trunks and most of the forest floor. Fresh tracks and the telltale fecal pellets of deer littered the ground. Surely there were more of the elusive animals nearby.

Three other hunters had left the campsite as part of Pierre's eight-man hunting party, but they were a few hundred yards back toward camp, busy gutting the three deer that they had already killed. There were two medium sized does and a single large buck with the velvet still on his antlers. It was a good amount of meat, but with over two hundred travelers, they still needed more. They were in search of at least one last kill.

Pierre was on the far-left end of the line. His heart was thumping loudly in his chest. He was almost certain that he had seen the flash of a white tail through a break in the trees about a hundred yards ahead. He desperately wanted to shoot his first deer. He did not want to mention it to Charles Rimbault, but this was the first time that he had ever actually been hunting. His former friends back in the vineyards of France would have made much fun of him for taking part in such a barbaric activity.

But France was in his previous life. He was now in the untouched forest of the New World and stalking an animal that would later feed him, his wife, and his comrades. The raw, primal thought of it exhilarated him. It awakened a side of his manhood that he did not know existed. He wanted to pull that trigger and hear the metal clash with the meat.

Suddenly a cluster of brush and briars about twenty yards ahead of him exploded with movement. Three does burst forth out of the thicket and scampered toward Pierre's right. He instantly realized, "They are running right across in front of the other hunters!"

Pierre quickly pulled his hammer back to full cock and aimed the barrel at the nearest animal. It was almost forty yards away and moving fast. He led the animal just a bit and aimed a little high to account for the distance. The crack of his own musket surprised him when the charge exploded in his pan and breech. A haze of white smoke filled the area around Pierre. He stepped forward a few steps to get away from the smoke of his discharge. Two other shots exploded to his right.

He looked anxiously toward the spot where he had aimed to see if he had registered a hit. Seeing nothing at first, he was thoroughly disappointed. But then he saw the deer. It had been down on the ground, but was attempting to get back up on its feet. The animal took two timid steps forward and then collapsed face-first onto the ground. Pierre saw no more movement. He kissed the stock of his Charleville and then raised the weapon high in the air. He surprised himself again when he emitted a barbaric war whoop that echoed beneath the high canopy of trees. Further down the line two more happy voices answered his celebratory call.

"I got one!" he yelled toward the others. "What about the other two?"

An anonymous voice responded, "I got one, as well!"

"I did, too!" responded a second voice.

Pierre's legs were shaky, and then they began to cramp and ache. The adrenaline of the kill was beginning to burn off. He felt like sitting down, but he resolved himself to get on with the nasty business that followed the shot. He began to make his way to the area where his doe had gone down. As he walked he braced himself for the nauseating job of bleeding and gutting the animal. He just hoped that the deer would be dead when he got to it. Off to his right he could hear the excited chatter of the other hunters. Oh, my! How proud Rimbault would be! Six deer would provide a veritable feast for their little fleet of Frenchmen.

Pierre quickly reached the doe. She was a large and beautiful animal. Pierre's heart leapt into his throat when he saw that she was not yet dead. Her sides billowed up and down, struggling for life in the thick forest air. Her breathing was shallow. Then the deer emitted a hollow cry. Clearly the animal was in much pain. Pierre felt a tear well in his eye as he knelt beside the animal's head. She instinctively tried to kick her legs in defense and lift her head off of the ground, but she was too weak.

"I must end this quickly," Pierre proclaimed out loud.

He grudgingly pulled his hunting knife from its sheath with his right hand. He placed his left knee on the animal's shoulder and his right knee on her neck just below the jaw. Grabbing the handle of the knife with both hands, he plunged it into her neck just beneath the spine. He stoutly pulled the blade down and toward him, severing the arteries and veins in her neck. She seized involuntarily and thrashed for just a moment as thick, dark blood poured out of the cut and onto the ground. It was quite the mess. Pierre jumped up onto his feet quickly to prevent the tide of blood from getting onto his clean breeches.

Pierre sobbed. Then he felt ashamed. He glanced around to make sure that no one could see his moment of weakness. He wiped his face with his left sleeve and then bent over to wipe the blood off of his blade onto the doe's furry, soft belly. As he cleaned the blade he realized how stupid it was to do so, since he would soon have to slit open her abdomen and remove all of her innards.

"Idiot!" Pierre scolded himself.

He hoped that at least one of the other men would wander over and help him with dressing the carcass. Truth be told, he had no idea what to do next. As he steadied himself for the gruesome task at hand an ear-splitting, other-worldly, piercing scream shattered the silence of the woods.

# 7

## A RED-COATED CHALLENGE

Pierre crashed and stumbled through the woods as he made his way toward the horrid screaming. At last he saw some of his men. Three of them were standing in a small clearing. All were leaning on their muskets and looking toward the ground. They appeared to be somber and grim. He climbed over two large logs and then ran to their location. The screaming continued, though it sounded weaker.

"What has happened?" he demanded as he approached the men.

One of the men pointed. Pierre gasped when he saw Francois, the widower from Acadia, writhing on the damp, leaf-covered forest floor. The poor fellow clutched at his left leg.

When he saw Pierre, Francois exclaimed, "Help me, Pierre! These scoundrels simply stand and stare at me!"

"What happened to you, Francois?"

"Something has bitten my foot! It burns like fire all the way to my knee! Oh, God! What is happening to me?"

"It is the *serpent congo*," commented one of the other men, rather matter-of-factly.

"*Oui*," added the second man. "They are the treacherous water snakes of Louisiana. It looks like he stepped into a nest of them. I count at least three bites."

Pierre's eyes widened. He reached down and ripped off the moccasins and socks from the man's feet. On his left foot, he discovered four pairs of puncture wounds roughly an inch apart. His foot was already swollen and distended. A strange redness streaked his skin and appeared to be climbing his leg.

"There are four sets of holes," confirmed Pierre.

"They are very close together," commented the third man. "Most likely juvenile serpents, all hidden together in a ground nest. And the poor fool had to be wearing moccasins. It is tragic, but this man will be dead before sundown."

Francois wailed hysterically at the man's words.

Pierre shot an angry look at the man. "Not if I can help it!"

"There is nothing that you can do," responded the aloof hunter.

Pierre's ire was stoked. He shifted swiftly into command mode and began barking orders. He pointed to one of the men. "You ... get to work dressing the animals that we have on the ground. We need to get the meat back to the river as quickly as possible."

He shifted his gaze toward to other two men. "I want both of you to get back to camp quickly and bring back a dozen men and a piece of canvas for a litter. We'll need help with all of this meat and with the task of carrying Francois back to camp."

"But it is a foolish endeavor, *Monsieur*, I told you ..."

"Do as I say!" screamed Pierre. "And stop wasting this man's valuable time. Now go!"

Pierre took his knife and cut the rope from his leather-wrapped bottle canteen. He wrapped the rope double around the wounded man's thigh, inserted a large stick beneath the rope, and began to twist.

"What are you doing, *Monsieur*?" asked one of the idle hunters.

"I am preparing to reload my musket and put a ball in your brain if you do not do as I say!" Pierre growled angrily. He stood to his feet, clenching his fists as he glared at the three men who still leaned lazily on the barrels of their spent muskets. "I swear before a holy God that I will see you all hung for mutiny if you do not do as I say!"

The men frowned as, at long last, they each turned and walked deliberately toward their assigned tasks.

"And bring back some rum!" Pierre shouted at their backs. The men grumbled their acknowledgement.

Pierre knelt down and resumed his work. He twisted the rope until it dug deeply into Francois' flesh. The stricken man winced at the new source of pain.

"What *are* you doing, Pierre?" asked Francois through clenched teeth.

"The poison of the serpents will get into your bloodstream and travel all over your body. I want to slow it down. Hopefully we can get the worst of it out of your foot."

"How?"

"I will draw it out. Now be still, and try to calm down."

Quickly, methodically, Pierre took his hunting knife and slashed deeply across the four sets of bites in Francois' ankle and foot. Dark blood began to pour from the cuts.

"Stop, Pierre! I will bleed to death!"

Pierre placed a hand on the man's shoulder and spoke reassuringly, "I will not let you bleed to death, my friend. But we must bleed you a little in order to remove this poison. Just trust me, Francois. I have seen this done before. When I was a boy one of my father's workers in his vineyard was bitten by a *vipère péliade*. I watched the doctor treat him. The man survived. I will do all that I can to save you, but right now the best thing that you can do is to calm yourself. Now ... do you have any rum?"

Francois shook his head in the negative.

"No matter. The men will bring some when they return. It will help you relax. But for now, just remain still, do as I say, and allow me to do my work. Understood?"

Francois nodded and smiled grimly.

"Now, take hold of this stick, and when I tell you to, release the pressure on the rope just a very little bit."

Pierre knelt down and cupped his hands around the small of the man's calf, just below the knee.

"Now, Francois. Release the rope, just a little."

More blood flowed from the wounds. Pierre squeezed tightly around the man's shin and his calf muscle and pulled downward toward Francois' foot, effectively 'milking' the blood from his leg. A very large volume of blood poured out onto the ground. Pierre repeated the process three more times. When he was finished, there was a huge pool of blood beneath Francois' foot.

Pierre looked at the man's face. He was becoming a little pale, but his breathing had steadied and he seemed calmer.

"That is good, Francois. Now let me have the stick."

Francois released his grip. Pierre spun the stick a couple of times until the rope became loose. He tossed the stick into the bushes and removed the rope.

"Is that it?" asked Francois.

"Yes. That is all we can do for now. We will get some rum in you and get you back to camp. You will likely have a fever, for there is certainly some poison still in your blood. But perhaps we removed enough to save your life, Francois."

"*Merci*, Pierre."

Pierre heard shouts and the sounds of men thrashing through the vegetation to the south.

"You are most welcome, my friend. You must rest now. I hear the men coming. We will have you back at the river very soon. My Genevieve will have you healthy and back swinging your oar in no time."

Rimbault grunted and spat into the brown water, "We should be there by mid-afternoon, Pierre."

It had been two weeks since the overnight deluge and the snake-bite incident. The flotilla had enjoyed relatively pleasant weather and no injuries since. Pierre glanced at Francois as he lay sleeping in the bottom of the boat. Amazingly, the man had survived. His leg turned a strange purple-blue from the knee down on the second day after the bite. He endured a raging fever for four days. But slowly, steadily, he had begun to recover. After the fever broke, his leg turned a dull yellow color and then slowly began to return to normal.

Francois was much improved, but he was still severely weakened by his body's response to the venom. Genevieve deserved much of the credit for his improving state of health. She had insisted that Francois be placed in the lead boat so that she could care for him. She treated his fever, bathed his wounded foot, and kept him fed and hydrated for days. She was quite the impressive frontier physician.

Pierre stole a glance at his beautiful wife as she lay napping beneath her cloth shade. He was so very proud of her courage and resilience. The other men on the journey were impressed by her, as well. In less than three weeks on the river she had already earned a reputation for her feisty demeanor and seemingly tireless work ethic. Pierre smiled lovingly at his bride.

Pierre turned to Rimbault, "Tell me again, what is the name of this place?"

"It was known as Fort Rosalie when it was a French outpost. Our countrymen established the fort very early in this century. But forty years ago there was a horrible massacre there. Over two hundred settlers were slain by the Natchez Indians. It is a frightful story."

Charles continued, "The fort was turned over to the British, of course, after the war. They renamed it Fort Panmure ... whatever the hell that means. They stationed about fifty Scotsmen there in 1766. Now that was a wild crew! Always drinking and shooting off their muskets and causing trouble with the native women. They were a jolly bunch, indeed. I always enjoyed my visits with them.

But those fellows were gone when I came downriver in March. The operator of the trading post said that London had ordered them back to St. Augustine in British East Florida. I was disappointed that they were gone."

"So, there is still a British presence there?"

"Just one man when I was there six months ago … a crazy plantation owner named John Bradley. Surely, he must be crazy! Only a mad man would remain at this outpost all alone, totally defenseless, and with a family."

"How do you think he will react to such a large contingent of Frenchmen?"

"Oh, he will be quite thrilled to see us, Pierre. He is a businessman, and not very interested in international politics. You may be able to sell some of your goods or make a decent trade or two."

"Really?" asked Pierre, his interest piqued.

"Of course. He inhabits the only civilized outpost for hundreds of miles. He is forever eager to do some dealing."

"That is good. I would not mind lightening our load. Perhaps we can relieve ourselves of a couple of these pirogues, eh?"

"Could be, Pierre … could be. But whether you do any bartering or not, it will be a good place for us to stop for a couple of days of rest."

❧

The flotilla passed the narrow mouth of the northward flowing Little River and then turned due west. Minutes later the river made another hard turn to the right. The boatsmen skirted a long, narrow island on their left. Suddenly the brilliant red and white colors of the British Jack came into view just above the treetops on top of a large bluff on the eastern bank of the river. It was roughly one half-mile upriver from their location.

Charles Rimbault exclaimed, "There it is, boys! Fort Panmure!" He whipped his flintlock pistol from his belt and fired a shot of celebration into the air.

A cheer erupted in the lead boat that spread quickly through the remainder of the other vessels in the tiny fleet of bateaux. Several other men joined in the celebration by firing their weapons, as well. The sight of the flag and the knowledge that they would camp comfortably and safely in a civilized setting that night caused the men to increase the pace of their paddling. Their oars attacked the water and fought valiantly against the river's quiet, powerful current.

It took an entire agonizing hour to reach their destination. As they neared the base of the tall bluff upon which the fort was positioned, they noticed several small buildings and shacks near the river on the flat ground beneath the cliff. Amazingly, just on the other side of the row of shacks, there was a formation of roughly two dozen British soldiers. The red-uniformed men stood smartly at attention. At the far-left end of their formation the British Jack and a colorful red, yellow, and white regimental flag dangled loosely in the light breeze. Two other men, one an officer and the other dressed in rather fancy civilian clothing, stood near the water's edge.

Pierre turned and stared incredulously at Charles. "I thought you said that the British had evacuated this fort."

Rimbault shrugged. "That is what John Bradley told me back in the spring. I assure you, Pierre, there were no soldiers here six months ago."

Antoine butted in on their conversation. "Well, they're here now! Is that John Bradley standing next to the officer?"

Rimbault peered past Pierre and examined the man. He shook his head.

"No. That is not John. I've never seen that gentleman before. But he looks important." Rimbault turned and shouted to the boat behind them, "Pass the word! Keep all weapons loaded but within reach and out of sight. Everyone smile and look extra friendly. We do not want to provoke an incident with the British, but we will not allow ourselves to be bullied, either."

The individual boat commanders repeated the instructions down the line of boats.

Rimbault moved from his place in the rear of the boat and climbed up onto the step beside the mast. He grasped the pole with his left hand and waved in as friendly and enthusiastic a manner as possible. The British officer returned the gesture with a rather cool wave.

"Pierre, you need to be prepared to join me on the bank. You are, after all, the financier and commander of our fleet. You and I will speak for our interests."

"Of course, Charles. Antoine will accompany us, as well." Pierre glanced at his wife. She peered anxiously from her nest in the bottom of the boat. She nervously tugged at the locket that dangled from her smooth, creamy neck.

"There is nothing to fear, my dear," Pierre reassured her. "We will observe the formalities and then enjoy a couple of quiet days inside the fort."

"Are you certain that they will allow us to land?" she inquired timidly.

"I hope so. They have no reason to deny us."

The boats were well within speaking distance from the riverbank when the British officer stepped to the very edge of the water and called out to the lead boat in perfect French. "I am Major Henry Hamilton of His Majesty King George's army, and commander of this troop. Who is in charge of this contingent of boats?"

Pierre answered, "I am, sir. Pierre Grimard, recently of New Orleans. I am an entrepreneur and responsible for these men and boats. This is my adjutant, Charles Rimbault of Vincennes. He is a professional *voyageur* and captain of the boats and crew."

"You have a very large group of men, *Monsieur* Grimard. What are your intentions and destination?"

"We are bound for Kaskaskia in the Illinois Country and have boats laden with cargo for sale and trade."

"Your mission is not military in any manner whatsoever?"

"No, Major. We are all civilians in search of new homes and businesses."

"Very well, then. You may land your boats. But only one man will disembark from each vessel and tie off while we consult with you and *Monsieur* Rimbault."

"Of course." He turned to Charles. "Rimbault, please give the orders."

Charles shouted to the line of boats, "Ground all bateaux! One man to tie off and secure each boat! Everyone else remain on board until the parley is complete!"

The men of Pierre's boat guided the bow toward the rocky bank. The man in front jumped out, grabbed the line, and pulled until the boat was sufficiently lodged in place. The other seven boats followed suit.

Antoine, Pierre, and Charles climbed over the right side of the bow, jumped off into the shallow water, and then approached the major.

The officer spoke first. "Gentlemen, please allow me to introduce the honorable Sir Montfort Browne, Lieutenant Governor of East Florida. I am commander of his personal guard."

"Governor Browne, I am pleased to make your acquaintance," offered Pierre. "I am Pierre Grimard, formerly of Germignac, France, and more recently of New Orleans. This is my business partner, Antoine Alexis of Austria and our *voyageur* guide, Charles Rimbault."

Charles and Antoine nodded toward the British official. The noble governor offered his handshake to all three men in a most common and friendly manner.

"What brings you to this fort, Governor?" Rimbault inquired boldly. "I thought that the British government ordered all troops back to Florida."

"Oh, we are merely here for a visit, *Monsieur*. I find this region of the Natchez to be most charming. It is an amazingly fertile and abundant place. If we can only tame the local natives, I believe that this will be a prime location to divide lands and establish a permanent settlement. I plan to lobby Parliament to pursue such efforts."

"Well, good luck with that," Rimbault teased, chuckling. "Time and rum may be the only things that will tame the Natchez Indians."

The governor smiled. "You are probably right, *Monsieur.*"

The governor turned to Pierre. "So, your expedition is traveling to Illinois, *Monsieur* Grimard?" inquired Sir Browne.

"*Oui.* Antoine and I have brought goods from Europe to trade with the settlers and natives in the North. Our crewmen have signed on with our mission in order to earn safe passage to the Illinois Country."

"There aren't many Frenchmen left in Illinois, *Monsieur.* Most have fled British governance and moved across the river into the Spanish territories," interjected the British major. "It seems most curious that you would be moving such a large contingent of Frenchmen to the very place that so many other Frenchmen seem to be abandoning in great numbers."

Pierre did not like the man's tone. In fact, he did not like the man, himself. This Englishman was obviously quite pompous and arrogant.

"I was not aware of any relocation of my countrymen from Illinois. Your news surprises me. It has been my understanding that there are many of our people still living and thriving there," responded Pierre. "But whatever the case, I am willing to trade with anyone who wishes to do honest business. Major, I am only attempting to begin a new life on the frontier. I left my father's home in France to make a future for myself in this New World. I assure you that I am not interested in anyone's politics. I merely want to establish a company and raise a family."

Rimbault added, "And I assure you, Major, not all Frenchmen are abandoning their homes in Illinois. Many of us remain and are not troubled in the least by British governance, as long as it is peaceful and equitable."

"You are an established resident of the territory?" inquired the major of Rimbault.

"*Oui.* I emigrated from Montreal and have lived peacefully in Vincennes for six years. I make regular trips to New Orleans and back to transport goods for the farmers and merchants in my area."

Major Hamilton mulled over their words. "Then I have your testimony as gentlemen that yours is not a military flotilla on a hostile mission?"

"How could we be French military?" retorted Rimbault sarcastically. "The Spaniards now control New Orleans. They just landed two thousand troops and are actively quelling an attempted rebellion by the French citizenry. There is no more French military in America. No, Major, we just want to go north and be left alone."

"Do you have duty papers for your cargo?" inquired Major Hamilton.

"Of course," responded Pierre. "We provided all the necessary manifests to the Spanish customs officials in New Orleans. I paid all required duties and I have all of the necessary legal documents."

"That was in accordance with the laws of Spain, *Monsieur* Grimard. Kaskaskia is in British territory. We will be required to inspect and inventory your cargo and impose the appropriate British duty here at this station."

"And then have the British officials in Kaskaskia assess another duty when we arrive there?" exclaimed Rimbault incredulously. He shook his head vigorously. "I do not think so, Major. I have stopped at this station at least ten times in the past several years and have never once been assessed any duties, even when there was a permanent station of soldiers present! Our desire was to stop here for a brief respite and, perhaps, do some business with *Monsieur* Bradley. But if it is your plan to impose upon us an illegal and unprecedented tax, then we will gladly loose our boats and be on our way."

The major's temper flared. "How dare you, sir, accuse me of imposing an illegal tax! My commission as Major in His Majesty's army is all of the license that I need to tax citizens, travelers, and cargo. And you will not untie or remove a single one of these boats until I am satisfied that the King's requirements have been met!"

The major glanced over his shoulder at the formation of soldiers. A young lieutenant jumped to action.

"Squad! Spread ranks! Secure the beach! Take the boats and men into custody!"

Twenty-four soldiers fanned out across the riverbank and encircled the small landing area where all eight of Pierre's bateaux were beached. One of the women in the boats uttered a muffled scream of horror.

Rimbault yelled over his shoulder, "Frenchmen, to arms!"

In an instant almost two hundred muskets and pistols appeared from the bottoms of the bateaux. The men held them at the ready. Their guns bristled like thorns above the weathered wood of the gunwales of each boat. The men sighted their weapons directly at the dispersed British soldiers.

Pierre shot a quick glance at the armed armada behind him. "I don't think we'll let you take our cargo or boats into custody today, Major. Clearly, we have you outmanned and outgunned. Is your pride and arrogance worth triggering an international incident?" Pierre sighed, frustrated. "All we wanted was some rest and fresh food and, perhaps, even a hot bath. We were not planning on any backwoods British tyranny. And, by the way, most of these men lost their homes to your countrymen in Acadia. I daresay that there is quite a bit of French anger and frustration represented in these boats. The outcome of this standoff is up to you, Major."

It was an incredibly tense moment. The Frenchmen held an almost ten-to-one advantage. The British soldiers glanced nervously at their commander, unsure as to how they should respond. They had not expected such resistance. The Frenchmen in the boats hunkered low. They did not want to open fire on the British, but they would perform as ordered.

Lieutenant Governor Browne broke the tension of the encounter. "Now, now, Major Hamilton ... none of this is necessary. Good Lord, you're a headstrong man, aren't you?" He glanced at Pierre and Charles, then turned to the officer. "William, call off your men. We didn't come here to start a war. *Monsieur* Rimbault is quite right. It is neither our place nor our interest to levy taxes on their cargo. How did you even come up with such a notion? We are here on an unofficial visit. I have every confidence that our people in Kaskaskia will judiciously perform their duties and tax these materials accordingly."

"But, Governor Browne ..."

"No 'buts,' Major!" the man snapped. "My decision is final. There will be no blood shed on this river today! These men intend us no harm. They are our friends. We would be doing Mr. Bradley a great disservice if we rob him of the opportunity to relieve them of some of their coin and cargo. Now ... dismiss your men and allow these weary travelers to disembark. I am quite sure that they stand in need of food, fire, and shelter."

Charles Rimbault grinned teasingly at the major, who obviously did not like the humiliation of the moment. He was even so bold as to cast a subtle wink at the officer. If looks could kill, Charles Rimbault would have been vaporized by the man's hateful gaze.

"As you wish," growled the major, thoroughly disgusted and humiliated. He snapped his fingers and the two dozen red-coated soldiers withdrew back into formation in front of their lieutenant. The major then looked inquisitively at the politician. "Your orders, sir?"

"No orders are necessary. There is no threat here. You are dismissed, Major. You may join your men and return to the fort. I will be along shortly. I have many questions for our new acquaintances."

The governor turned and focused his attention on Pierre. The slighted, dismissed officer trudged away, barked a few orders at his men, and then marched them smartly up the trail toward the fort.

The governor implored Pierre, "Sir, can you urge your men to put away their weapons? I assure you that they are no longer necessary. This is a friendly outpost."

"Of course, Governor," Pierre responded. "Charles ..."

Rimbault nodded his understanding. He turned to face the boats. "Men! Secure your muskets, cargo, and equipment! Tie off the boats! We sleep in the fort tonight!"

The men emitted a gigantic cheer as they began to stow their long guns and oars.

"Our men will, of course, retain their pistols, Governor," stated Rimbault. It was not a request. He very deliberately tucked two pistols into his own belt and handed one each to Pierre and Antoine. They followed his lead and inserted the pistols into their belts just in front of their left hips.

Governor Browne smiled broadly. "Of course. All men are entitled to their self-defense." He turned to Pierre. "Come, now, *Monsieur* Grimard. You must tell me all about your journey thus far and your adventures on this great river!"

"Please sir, call me, 'Pierre.'"

The governor chuckled. "Wonderful! Very well, then, Pierre. Let us stroll and talk."

Pierre suddenly heard the dull whack of a tiny shoe striking wood and the high-pitched sound of a throat clearing behind him.

"Oh! Good heavens, Governor! I almost forgot my wife!"

He spun around and ran back to the boat. "My love, I am so very sorry. I was caught up in the excitement of the moment."

She grunted. "I'm sure that you were, husband."

She allowed Pierre to lift her over the gunwale of the boat and then, once on dry land, she broke from his grip rather quickly and marched deliberately toward the governor.

"*Monsieur* Browne, I am Genevieve Colomb, the daughter of Isaac Colomb and Marie-Anne Romagon of New Orleans. Pierre is my husband."

"Gracious me, Pierre, how could you ever forget such an exquisite young woman?" The governor bowed deeply. "*Madame,* I am honored to meet you. You are an oasis of beauty and refined grace in this wild and untamed place. But, pray tell, what are you doing here? I am shocked that you are making such a perilous voyage up this river!"

"New Orleans with its scores of loathsome Spaniards is no longer a safe place for a French lady, Governor. And besides, I am compelled to accompany my husband. My place is by his side."

"Indeed, it is." He extended the crook of his right elbow to Genevieve. "Well, then, *Madame* Colomb ... *Monsieur* Grimard ... let us find our way to the fort and enjoy some hearty food and friendly company."

Pierre responded, "First, Governor Browne, I have a man who needs medical attention. He was bitten by venomous snakes several days ago. He had recovered somewhat, but he remains in a very weakened state. Is there a physician available?"

"My surgeon has accompanied me on this journey, Pierre." The governor chuckled. "He was still sleeping off last night's liquid celebrations when I came to greet you at the river. He will be more than happy to evaluate and treat your man. Come, we will go to the fort and send back my horse and carriage to retrieve the poor fellow."

Genevieve smiled. "Thank you, kind sir. I have been dreadfully worried about young Francois."

"You are most welcome, young lady. Now come! Let us go to the fort and seek some shade and refreshment."

The governor and Genevieve led the way up the trail that wound its way around the northern edge of the bluff toward the summit and Fort Panmure. Pierre and Antoine followed closely behind.

☙

True to his word, Governor Browne immediately dispatched his driver to take a small carriage down the narrow trail and fetch Francois back to the surgeon. Afterwards he gave Pierre and the other leaders of the tiny French fleet the tour of the fort grounds and buildings.

The fort was an impressive structure, encompassing almost an entire acre of land. The outer wall was comprised of a combination of blockhouses connected by a sturdy wall constructed of logs and stone. Several other small houses and buildings were dispersed throughout the interior of the fort. John Bradley's store and tavern were located in a whitewashed wood building in the very center. It was a picturesque, peaceful scene. Try as he might, Pierre had difficulty imagining it as the former site of a bloody massacre. He shuddered at the thought of the amount of French blood that had been shed at this distant outpost.

John Bradley, the British operator of the trading post was, indeed, thrilled upon the sight of his unexpected guests. He always enjoyed hosting French travelers, and considered the present day's arrival to be a perfect opportunity to do some volume business. He knew all too well the profit that was to be found in an eager throng of hungry, thirsty travelers.

After negotiating a price with Pierre for two days of food and lodging, the businessman flew into action. He called in every member of his family and a few faithful native servants to begin the process of cooking a grand feast for the newly arrived Frenchmen. They stoked several large fires and slaughtered a variety of livestock for the coming meal. Bottles and jugs were opened and glasses and dishes cleaned and wiped. Within minutes the rum and ale began to flow ... in liberal quantities.

As Mr. Bradley's wife, daughters, and Indian servants attacked the task of meal preparation, his sons began to heat water and fill tubs in the designated bathing area, located in a secluded alcove between two windowless sheds. A large hemp curtain strung between the buildings insured the privacy of bathers. The ladies of the boats were invited to enjoy the first baths. They jumped at the opportunity of such luxury. After inspecting the area and placing two armed guards outside the curtain, Pierre gave permission for the women to bathe.

Four hours later, just as the sun was beginning to set, the meal was served. There were two huge pots of stewed meat mixed with potatoes, beans, and onions. Copious loaves of fragrant bread accompanied the stew. There was also a table stacked high with fresh garden vegetables and several different types of sliced melons.

Governor Browne invited Pierre, Genevieve, Antoine, and Charles to join him at his table. It was a gesture or honor and respect, and greatly appreciated by the Frenchmen. Major Hamilton and his lieutenant joined them, as well. As darkness fell upon the fort the travelers ate, drank, conversed, and greatly enjoyed the mealtime company, despite the broody major's sullen and most intemperate disposition. Pierre and the others decided to simply ignore the prideful man.

The travelers ate until they could hold no more. The other British soldiers dined and drank, as well, but remained aloof and at a distance from the Frenchmen on the far side of the compound. It appeared that they were under orders to remain separate from the French travelers.

After the meal, the revelry continued as the boatsmen drank rum, smoked pipes, danced, and sang bawdy songs. Rimbault laughed at the drunken spectacle that was beginning to unfold. Pierre shook his head and frowned.

"My dear wife, I think that it might be the right time for you and the other ladies to retire for the evening," Pierre announced with authority.

"As do I," affirmed Governor Browne. "It appears that this evening's celebrations are on the verge of becoming a little less than ladylike. We would not want to tarnish your fragile, innocent eyes and ears." He smiled warmly at Genevieve.

"Of course," she replied. "I have no interest in watching these men dishonor themselves. Besides, I am quite tired, and have been looking forward very much to sleeping in a real bed this evening." She smiled at Pierre. "Husband, will you escort me to our chamber and deliver me safely? I do not know my way around this fort, especially in the darkness."

"Of course, my dear. Gentlemen, if you will excuse us ..."

Pierre and Genevieve rose to their feet. The other men at the table stood out of respect for the young woman and bowed gently in her direction. Pierre picked up a candle from the table, offered his arm to Genevieve, and then escorted his beautiful wife toward their quarters. The eyes of the other gentlemen at the table followed them until they disappeared around the corner of the tavern.

The couple walked briskly toward a small guardhouse on the southwest corner of the fort. Mr. Bradly had ordered the tiny room cleaned and specially prepared for the couple.

"We have a room all to ourselves, Genevieve. *Monsieur* Bradley has seen to everything."

"That was very kind of him." She smiled in the darkness.

"Oh, he has been reimbursed quite nicely, I assure you," declared Pierre. "Now, come. Inspect what will be your new home for the next couple of days."

Pierre escorted his wife through the rough wooden door. Pierre used his beeswax candle to light three others inside the room, bathing the space in a soft yellow glow. Inside the tiny chamber, they discovered a tattered but serviceable rug on the dirt floor, clean sheets and blankets on the small bed, and fresh cut flowers in a cracked vase on the end table. A chamber pot and wash cloths were tucked beneath the bed near the footboard. There was even a tiny four-inch-square looking glass hanging by a yellow ribbon on the wall above the wash basin table. Pierre nodded. "This will do quite nicely. It appears that Bradley has taken care of everything."

Genevieve walked over to examine herself in the looking glass. She glanced down at the basin and pot. "Well, not quite everything, husband," she responded, holding up an empty water pot. "We have no water for washing."

Pierre smiled. "Never fear, my love. I will fetch you some water for your personal needs. Go ahead and prepare for bed. I will return in just a moment."

Pierre grabbed the jug and strolled out of the door, carefully closing it behind him. He sauntered off toward the well on the far side of the compound.

Genevieve busied herself in her bedtime preparations. She quickly shed her freshly-cleaned dress and hung it on a nail beside the door. She used the chamber pot and cleaned herself with one of the small, clean cloths that had been left for just such a purpose. Afterwards she grabbed her hair brush from her *portmanteau* and returned to the looking glass, dressed only in her shift, to brush her hair. Moments later the door opened quietly.

Genevieve teased, "That did not take long, husband. Did you make one of those horrid soldiers draw you some water from the well? Or perhaps you could not wait to get back and satisfy your lonely wife?" She reached down and untied the top ribbon on her shift, gently parting the soft cloth and exposing the milky white skin along the center of her chest. She subtly dropped the top of the undergarment to her left, exposing her bare shoulder. She teased, "Maybe this is why you returned so quickly to my chamber instead of going back to rum and pipes with your friends?"

A dull grunt-like chuckle and the scuff of leather shoes on the hard-packed dirt floor was the only response. Genevieve fluffed her hair and smiled, turning ever-so-slowly, and teasingly running her fingers along the exposed skin between her breasts. But her smile melted away in an instant when she saw the man who was standing a mere four feet away from her.

It was not her beloved Pierre. Instead it was a tall, muscular hulk of a man wearing the red coat and black hat of the British army. The man reeked of rum. His face was flushed red from the alcohol. Beads of sweat dotted his brow and upper lip. The man licked his lips as he removed his hat and tossed it to the floor. He began to unbutton the front flap of his white linen breeches.

The man growled lustily, "I knew that you were a tasty, clean wench the moment I first laid eyes on you. And that was with all of that fluffy cloth covering you up. Now I can truly see how right I was. I will make sure that you are satisfied this night, little lady. I will introduce you to some delicious, real manhood ... something that little Frenchy could never dream of doing."

Genevieve opened her mouth to scream, but in an instant the powerful man was upon her. He cupped his hand over her mouth, ripped her shift in two from top to bottom, and pinned her violently against the stone wall. Genevieve tried to cry out through the hard muscles of his hand, but she could not manage a sound. She could not even breathe. The helpless girl wept as the man used his hands to explore the most private places of her naked body.

# 8

## A BITTER ENEMY

Pierre whistled gaily as he walked back toward his quarters with a pitcher of fresh water in hand. He was extremely excited about sharing an unusually quiet and private evening with his new wife. He figured that they still had a bit of honeymooning to do. He pulled the string on the latch and stepped with eager anticipation through the door of the blockhouse.

"My love, here it is! A jug full of clean, cold wa ..."

Pierre stopped mid-sentence. His eyes registered complete terror at the horror that greeted him inside the dark room. An enormous British soldier hovered over his naked wife and had her firmly pinned against the outer wall. The man's filthy right hand covered his tiny wife's entire face from her nose down. His left hand was planted firmly between her legs. Her terrified, begging eyes reached toward Pierre, pleading with him for rescue and deliverance. The attacker stared at Pierre also, peering over his left shoulder through sinister, red eyes. Clearly, the man had not expected Pierre to return to the room quite so quickly.

Pierre felt a deep rage welling up within his breast. The heat of his hatred washed upward through his body. It formed within his lungs a deep, guttural, barbaric yawp. He screamed out of hurt, anger, offense, and passion. Then, without even thinking about physics or tactics, he bull-rushed the huge man.

The soldier spun to his left and released Genevieve as he prepared to meet Pierre's attack. She collapsed onto the floor, dazed and weakened from shock and abuse. She recovered quickly, however, and emitted a partial scream just as Pierre collided with the drunken, violating soldier. She watched in frozen horror as Pierre slammed the ceramic pitcher that he was carrying against the left side of the man's skull. The vessel shattered into dozens of ceramic shards and the water it had contained exploded all over the upper portion of the soldier's body.

Charles and Antoine sat and relaxed at the table with Governor Browne. He was turning out to be a very jovial, friendly, easygoing character. The men were drinking and smoking, sharing stories about their adventures, and enjoying the spectacle of the ongoing celebration in the courtyard of the fort. John Bradley, the post proprietor, and two of his oldest sons had joined the group at the governor's table. Major Hamilton remained at the table with his superior, but he clearly had no desire to engage in conversation with the French visitors.

A muted female scream from the distant reaches of the compound carried across the fort grounds. The governor looked curiously at the other men at his table. "What in the blazes was that?"

"It sounded to me like a young woman in the throes of pleasure," quipped Rimbault. "One of those Indian women, perhaps. What say you, Major? Have you authorized one of your privates to do himself a little native wenching tonight?" The men around the table chuckled at Rimbault's offensive joke.

"I will not dignify your lewd and undignified statement with a response, *Monsieur.* I suggest that you change your tone and change the subject."

Charles placed both hands in the air in a feigned symbol of surrender. "I'm sorry! I'm so sorry! Sincerely! I was merely joking,

Major. No need to get your fancy breeches stuck in your tightly-puckered British arse."

Antoine resisted his own urge to laugh at Rimbalt's crude dig at the British officer, but the governor could not seem to resist. Partially inebriated, his rum-enhanced sense of humor unleashed a side-splitting crescendo of uncontrolled laughter ... all at the major's expense. The officer exhaled in response and stood angrily.

"If it pleases the governor, I will retire for the evening."

"Of course, Major." He bit his lip as he tried to control his laughter. "You are free to go. I am in good hands."

"Indeed," the major responded snobbishly, raising his nose high into the air. "Then I bid you goodnight, sir." He turned to his second in command. "Lieutenant ..."

The young officer jumped to his feet and scurried along after his superior.

The other men at the table held their composure until the major was about ten steps away when Rimbault muttered, "Make that two tightly-puckered British arses."

Another wave of contagious laughter exploded around the table.

♌

The heavy blow of the water jug slowed the man momentarily, but not long enough to give Pierre any advantage in the one-sided fight. The soldier easily outweighed Pierre by fifty pounds. He shook his head twice and then growled as he grasped Pierre around the neck with both of his enormous hands. The powerful man pushed Pierre with all of his might and slammed his head against the log wall on the far side of the room. Pierre was dazed. The man picked Pierre up off of the floor by his neck, pressing him against the wall, and growling louder and louder as he choked the flow of air to his victim's lungs. The soldier squeezed even harder as he attempted to snap the bones in Pierre's upper spine.

Pierre slapped weakly and ineffectively at the man's arms with both of his hands. The soldier's grip was overwhelming. Pierre reached down with his right hand and tried to retrieve his pistol from his belt, but the man's hold on him was far too strong and his body pressed against Pierre with a tremendous force. Pierre was simply unable to fit his hand between their compacted bellies. He soon resolved himself to his fate. He knew that he was about to die, and that this man was going to have his violent way with his beloved wife. A single tear of brokenness and frustration trickled down his cheek.

The attacking Englishman muttered, "Why don't you just hurry up and die, you worrisome little French bastard, so that me and your tasty bitch can have ourselves some fun?" He gave Pierre's neck one final, powerful squeeze.

Suddenly a blood-curdling, piercing, lingering scream filled the room. The rabid scream was accompanied by the sound of cracking wood. Something exploded against the back of the man's head. Splinters and shards of wood flew into Pierre's open mouth and eyes. He tasted blood. He didn't know if it was his own or the Englishman's. He blinked as he tried to clear his vision, then caught a brief glimpse of his naked wife standing behind the man. She held one leg of the wash basin table in both of her hands. Blood trickled from her nose and the corner of her mouth.

໔

The wailing scream echoed across the courtyard. The men outside knew that there was something different about this scream. It carried a tone of distress. The singing and dancing of the Frenchmen stopped. Their drinking, jokes, storytelling, and games ceased. Over two hundred men stared silently and curiously in the direction of the far corner of the fort.

"That did not sound right at all, gentlemen. I heard pain in that voice. Something is definitely wrong," proclaimed the governor.

Charles exclaimed, "That sounded like the voice of Genevieve!" He slapped Antoine on the arm. "Come, Antoine! Let us go! Quickly!"

Charles and Antoine jumped up from the table and took off running toward Pierre's room. They drew their pistols from their belts as they ran. Two dozen pistol-wielding Frenchmen followed them. As they ran they heard more screaming. Then they heard the dull report of a pistol.

Genevieve's attacker, partially dazed by the sudden blow of lumber to his head, instantly released the lethal tightness of his grip around Pierre's neck and stumbled backward a single step. That brief stumble provided the opportunity that Pierre needed. He reached down with his right hand and drew his French flintlock pistol, pulling it back to full cock as he brought it upward toward the man's head. He did not stop until the barrel made contact with the bottom of the attacker's chin. Pierre angled the barrel slightly toward the center of his brain and without hesitation pulled the trigger.

A deafening explosion rocked the room. The man's head exploded with a dull pop. The top of his skull erupted in a geyser of blood, bone fragments, and brain matter as the soft lead ball flattened out and forged an uninterrupted path through his tongue, sinuses, skull bone, and cerebrum. The bloody spray that moments ago was his brain splashed wet and sticky against the rough boards of the ceiling. The man seized and trembled for a mere second or two and then collapsed to the floor in a lifeless heap.

All of Pierre's senses were overwhelmed by the explosion of the pistol within the confines of the small room. The scorching fire from the powder blast and the acrid smoke burned his nose and eyes. The pistol was so close to his face that he was blinded temporarily by the flash of the exploding powder. The report of the weapon was so close to his right ear that it caused an overwhelming ringing. He was partially deafened by the explosion. The one thing that he could hear was the high-pitched wail of Genevieve as she screamed and sobbed on the far side of the room.

Pierre dropped his pistol to the floor, pushed himself away from the wall, and stumbled numbly toward his wife. When he got to her he took the table leg from her hand and then tossed it against the wall. He opened his arms reassuringly.

"Genevieve, my love. It is over. You are safe. That man is dead. You have nothing else to fear."

The terrified, naked girl leaned into him and buried her face in his chest. She continued to sob uncontrollably. Her entire body heaved and convulsed, and then quite unexpectedly she pushed violently away from Pierre and quickly spun to her left. She vomited into the center of the floor, emptying her stomach of the meal that she had enjoyed earlier in the evening.

Pierre grabbed a towel and dabbed it in a small puddle of water on the floor. He used it to wipe her mouth and face clean of the putrid emesis. He tossed the rag into the corner and embraced her again. He comforted her for a moment, then lifted her chin so that he could look into her eyes.

"Did the beast violate you, Genevieve?"

She shook her head. She mumbled, "Only with his hand. He just kept touching me all over. And he groped me down ... down there. Oh, Pierre, you returned just in time! He was about to ... about to ..." Again, she buried her head in his chest and wept.

"Do not talk about it anymore. Try not to think about it." He became aware of the issue of her stark nakedness. "We must cover you, my dear. Men will be coming in response to the gunshot."

Pierre was just grabbing the blanket from the bed to cover his wife when several men burst through the partially open door. Charles and Antoine arrived first, followed quickly by some of their fellow Frenchmen. The men all respectfully turned their heads until Pierre had sufficiently covered his wife.

Charles and Antoine looked at the dead soldier in the middle of the floor. Blood and other fluids dripped slowly from the ceiling, landing upon and staining the man's pristine, white linen breeches. They quickly surmised what had happened.

"Are you all right, Pierre? Is Genevieve unharmed?" inquired a very concerned Charles.

Pierre nodded subtly as he held and consoled his wife. A moment later the red-faced, winded governor burst into the room. His mouth flew open at the scene that greeted him. The room was thoroughly wrecked with pieces of wood, ceramic debris, and puddles of water and blood scattered all over the floor. Blood and tissue coated the ceiling. A dead British soldier lay crumpled in a heap. There was a huge pool of vomit just a few feet from the dead body. It was a spectacle, indeed.

Genevieve swayed slightly as she leaned against Pierre. She was remarkably close to fainting. Pierre leaned over and placed his right arm beneath the backs of her knees and effortlessly scooped her up off of the floor. He walked over to the bed and gently placed her on it, facing her away from the center of the room and toward the interior wall. He pulled the top sheet over her to further preserve her modesty. The poor girl lifted up her arm to cover her head. She went numb as she closed off her mind and spirit to the crime that had befallen her.

The dazed governor stared at Pierre in confusion. "Pierre, what has occurred here?"

Pierre felt a bit shaky, himself. He began to fight his own desire to collapse. His neck, back, and legs ached. He started to tremble.

"Fetch this man a chair!" ordered the governor.

Antoine grabbed a straight-back chair from the corner and placed it beside the bed. He and Charles urged Pierre to sit. He collapsed onto the seat.

The governor placed his hand on Pierre's shoulder and spoke gently. "Now tell me, son, what happened?"

Pierre's voice was shaky and scratchy because of his bruised, inflamed throat muscles. He croaked, "I went to get us some water from the well. When I returned, I found this man assaulting my wife. He had torn her chemise from her body and pinned her against that stone wall. He was just about to violate her." Pierre choked briefly, emotionally. "I hit him with the water jug, but it did not seem to stun him at all. He came after me. He managed to get his hands around my neck and pinned me against the opposite wall."

The men stared at the room, attempting to visualize the attack as Pierre described it.

"I was dead, for certain. I could not break his hold on my neck." He pulled down his collar to reveal the red and blue flesh of his swollen neck. The outlines of the man's fingers were evident.

Pierre continued, "Just as I had given up Genevieve somehow managed to smash the wash table across his back. He released his grip for a moment … just long enough for me to draw my pistol. Then I shot him dead." He choked up slightly. "It is only the second time I have ever fired a gun."

Then Pierre began to weep, himself. The flood of emotions poured forth out of him.

Charles Rimbault knelt beside him and placed a hand on his knee. "It is all right, my friend. You did what you had to do. You defended your wife and yourself against this wicked man's assault." He glanced at the body sprawled awkwardly in the floor. The flap of the man's breeches was open and his manhood was partially exposed. Charles added, "May the loathsome bastard rot in hell."

Major Hamilton stepped into the room just as Charles declared his curse upon the dead soldier's soul. His lieutenant followed two steps behind him. Hamilton looked down at the floor at his dead private. He glanced upward at the blood and brains splashed on the low ceiling. He asked a single question. "Who shot this man?"

"I did, Major," confessed Pierre, wiping the tears from his face. "I caught him attempting to rape my …"

The Major coldly interrupted Pierre's explanation, "Lieutenant, take this man into custody. He has murdered one of the King's soldiers."

Pierre exclaimed, "Excuse me, Major?"

"Shut your mouth! There is no excuse for you, insolent French dog. A British soldier under my command is dead. You just confessed to having killed him. And you will pay the price." He nodded at the lieutenant. "Take this man to the guardhouse to await tribunal and execution in the morning."

A pistol clicked near the major. Two others clicked in rapid succession. Then a chorus of clicks echoed from outside the door. The major turned to find Charles Rimbault aiming a pistol directly at his forehead. He aimed his other at the lieutenant. Antoine had a pistol pointed at the major's gut. The men outside all held their firearms menacingly.

"Just one damned minute, Major," growled Rimbault. "I don't believe I'll let you take Pierre or anyone else from our party into custody on this night." He glanced at Pierre. "My friend, I think, perhaps, that you should reload your pistol." He looked toward the door where two of the other boat captains stood peering into the room. "Henri, Marcel, go and fetch every armed man that we have in this fort. See to it that the remainder of the soldiers are relieved of their arms. It shouldn't be that difficult. Most of them are thoroughly drunk or passed out by now."

"*Oui*, Charles," both men responded. They turned and trotted off into the night. Pierre got up from the chair, retrieved his pistol from the floor, and with shaking hands began the process of reloading.

Charles reasoned, "Now, Major, you have not made even the slightest effort to take a logical look at what has occurred in this room. Your dead soldier attempted to violate this man's wife. Pierre caught him in the act, fought him, and killed him. It was a fair fight and clearly self-defense, pure and simple."

"That is your story, or rather Grimard's version of it. Unfortunately, Private Bevins is entirely too dead to speak for himself. But what I do see before me is a slain British soldier. I see his brains dripping from the ceiling. And I see a couple of filthy Frenchmen aiming pistols at me and others who seem ready to take this fort by force! I have all of the evidence that I need to hang this criminal."

"I am Austrian, not a Frenchman, you pompous arse," retorted Antoine in heavily accented English, spitting at the man's feet.

"I don't give a damn about your nationality. This man has killed one of *my* soldiers! He must suffer justice for his actions. He will stand tribunal at first light and he will hang for his crime."

At long last the governor intervened. "Henry, are you really so daft or are you simply blinded by your exceedingly abundant arrogance and pride? It is quite clear to me and to everyone else here that your boorish private, with his head and hormones polluted with copious amounts of rum, entered this couple's quarters and assaulted that young girl."

"So, you're taking the side of your French friends, I see. I submit that yours is the position of a traitor to the Crown. I wonder what London would have to say about that?" The major's demeanor was terse and threatening.

"No, Major, I'm not taking the side of Frenchmen. I'm taking the side of common sense. And don't you dare threaten me you spoiled, insolent, pompous arse! I'll have you reassigned to India or to some other armpit of the British realm if you attempt to cross me! Look around you, man! You see the signs of the struggle. You see a bleeding, traumatized, sobbing, catatonic girl lying on yon bed. You see your soldier lying there with his breeches unhinged and his manhood exposed. You know full well what happened in this chamber."

The Major retorted sarcastically, "Oh, I'm quite sure of what happened, Governor. That little French trollop probably invited this handsome soldier into her bed and then screamed 'rape' when her husband happened upon their frolicking. I've seen it before with these French whores."

Another pistol lock clicked to full cock. Pierre placed the muzzle of his weapon directly against the major's temple. His hand trembled with rage as tears of emotion flooded his cheeks. He growled, "Major, if you speak one more word of insult against my wife ... if you call her one more unwholesome name ... I am going to give Governor Browne cause to hang me at sunup. I've killed for my wife once tonight, and I wouldn't mind sending you to the hereafter, as well."

The governor pleaded with Pierre, "Son, none of this is necessary. Please, put your weapon down. I will handle the major. Please don't sully your honorable actions of this night by shedding this fool's blood."

"Honorable actions?" challenged the major.

"Yes, Henry, honorable actions. And if you had just one drop of true honor in you, I should think that you would be able to recognize it! You dined with the lady this very evening. You know full well that she is a refined young woman and a doting, loving wife. That you, personally, have experience with trollops and ill-reputed women I certainly have no doubt. But this dear child is not one of them."

The governor pointed at the dead soldier. "That horrid man was a drunken rapist. In the end he received what he deserved. You claim that *Monsieur* Grimard must suffer justice for his actions? I declare that he has already, in the process of defending himself and his wife, meted out the only justice required this night! Your man died for his crime of assault and attempted rape ... at least I hope that is all that he committed." He offered a consoling glance at Pierre, who nodded in response.

Pierre confirmed, "It was an attempt, only, Governor. He did not succeed in violating my bride sexually. I returned from my errand of retrieving water just in time."

"And I praise God that you did, Pierre. We are all greatly relieved. Indeed, she suffered enough dishonor from the touch of his filthy hands." He paused. "*Monsieur* Grimard, it is with a deep sense of sorrow and regret that I offer to you my most sincere apologies, as well as the apologies of King George III and the British Empire."

"But, Governor!" the major protested.

The governor exploded with rage. "Henry, you will remain silent! Not another damned word! Every time you open your mouth you heap further insult and shame upon the Crown!"

He turned his back on the officer. "As I was saying, *Monsieur* Grimard, I sincerely do offer my deepest apologies. I know of no other form of restitution or satisfaction that I can offer you. You have already disposed of the shameful criminal who assaulted your beautiful wife, and for that I am most grateful. You have saved me the trouble of prosecution. It is quite clear that you acted in defense of self. Absolutely no charges will be filed. As far as the Crown is concerned, this matter is closed."

"But Governor, this soldier was in *my* charge! *I* am in command of this detachment!" boomed Major Hamilton.

"Indeed you are, Major. But that is a matter that I can rectify immediately. As the commander of this criminal I am holding you personally responsible for his abhorrent actions. Therefore, Major Hamilton, I hereby relieve you of your duties as commander of my personal guard. You will return to your quarters where you will remain until our guests have departed this post."

The major stood silently, his mouth agape. He could not believe what was happening to him. He had never been treated thusly. He had never experienced the challenge or rebuff of his authority as a British officer.

"But sir ..." he began.

"I do not want to hear it, Major. Not another word! I am tired of your unreasonable attitude. I want you out of my sight!" He turned to the young lieutenant. "Lieutenant ... what is your name, son?"

"Thomas Dowling, sir."

"Lieutenant Dowling, you will receive Major Hamilton's sidearm and blade and have him escorted to his quarters. You will assume command of the troop until I inform you otherwise."

"Yes, sir. As you wish, Governor."

Lieutenant Dowling was quite literally shaking in his boots. He turned to the major and spoke in a somewhat timid voice, "Sir, your weapons, please."

"Are you really going to do this, Dowling?" challenged Hamilton.

His voice trembled. "I have no choice, sir. You heard the governor's order. Both of us serve at his pleasure. Your pistol and sword, please."

The major never removed his gaze from the eyes of the lieutenant as he handed over his pistol and then unhinged his sword.

The lieutenant motioned toward the door. "Please lead me to your quarters, Major."

As he turned to depart the room the officer hissed at Rimbault and Pierre, "I'll not forget this, French scum. You have not seen the last of me!"

Charles retorted, "The feeling is mutual, Hamilton. We'll not forget you, either. And unless you plan to relocate to Illinois in the foreseeable future, I daresay that we have seen the last of you, miserable prick!"

The major stiffened at the insult. He lifted his shoulders and head and pridefully thrust his chest forward. Just as he turned to exit the room Charles once again, as he had done at the water's edge earlier that day, cast a subtle wink toward the man. The officer's face flushed with rage and he stormed angrily out of the room.

The governor muttered, "Good riddance! Good God! You think you know people, and then they manage to put their true colors on full display." He addressed Pierre again, "I am truly sorry, son. I do not feel that I can say it enough. No expressions of apology can make right the wrong that you and your wife have suffered this night. Please have your men gather your things and then you and your wife are welcome to have my quarters for the night … or for as long as you would like to stay."

Pierre nodded gratefully. "Thank you, sir. We will accept your offer for tonight. But I think that this is the one and only night that we will be staying at this particular fort."

"That much is certain," affirmed Rimbault. "No offense, Governor. You have been a gracious ally and a good friend, but I have suffered from all of the British hospitality that I can stand. We will depart at first light. Pierre, I will go and inform the men." He tucked his pistols into his belt as he headed for the door.

"I am truly sorry, Charles," the governor called after him. He faced Pierre again. "I am heartbroken. Truly heartbroken. You will suffer no further harm or harassment from the troops under my command. I will confine all of them to their quarters for the remainder of your stay."

Pierre turned and scooped his wife up off of the bed, shielding her from viewing the body that lay sprawled in the floor. "I humbly accept your apology, Governor. Like Charles said, you are a good man and a gentleman. I will forever remember your kindness. I only wish that all Englishmen exhibited the same measure of wisdom and grace."

"Most of us do, Pierre. I assure you. Most of us do."

"I pray so, sir," Pierre responded tersely. "Please lead the way, Governor. I want to get my wife out of this cursed room."

𝔔

The Frenchmen packed their belongings in the pre-dawn darkness. Few of them had slept during the night. They were too angry and agitated to rest. For most of them sunrise could not arrive soon enough. They all wanted to put distance between themselves and the British soldiers.

At long last the dull glow of dawn began to emerge in the eastern sky. Pierre fetched his wife well before sunrise in order to take her to the boat. The governor's surgeon had visited shortly after the attack and administered an opioid sedative to help her sleep. The strong drug did its job most effectively. Genevieve barely stirred when Pierre picked her up out of the governor's comfortable bed. He gently and thoughtfully carried his exhausted, semi-conscious wife to their bateau and placed her in her familiar covered nest located just behind the mast and sail. She snuggled in and continued to sleep.

Francois, weakened as he was by his body's reaction to the snake venom, had carried the Grimards' baggage to the boat. He spoke to Pierre once Genevieve was resting comfortably. "Do not worry in the least, Pierre. I will help take care of your wife, just as she took care of me when I was so very sick. You know that I am no good for rowing or physical labor in my present weakened state, but I am well enough to see to Genevieve's medical and practical needs. You have my word that I will not allow any harm or discomfort to come to her."

Pierre smiled at his friend. "Thank you, Francois. I gladly and gratefully accept your offer. My responsibilities are many, and your friendship and care are a tremendous comfort."

"It is my honor, Pierre. And it is the least that I can do in return for Genevieve's kindness to me."

A half-hour later the little fleet of Frenchmen departed quietly and without fanfare just as the sun peeked through the treetops. No residents of the fort arose to see them off, not even the kindly Governor Browne. But that suited Pierre just fine. He had his fill of the British. He just wanted to get to Illinois.

Soon the men fell into a rhythmic pace of rowing. The sound of it satisfied and soothed Pierre. He smiled as he considered his newfound love of the routine of the boat. It was just as Charles Rimbault had declared all those many weeks ago. Dullness, boredom, and routine were, indeed, good things.

Pierre had his fill of adventure. He prayed that the remainder of the journey would be insanely tedious and boring.

But he had absolutely no notion of the trials and tribulations that still awaited him and his countrymen among the forthcoming islands and curves of the ancient, deadly, muddy Mississippi River.

# 9

## TEMPEST AND TOSSED

*October 10, 1769*

I t had been almost a month since the incident at Fort Panmure. Genevieve was fully recovered from the shock of her experience. It had taken about a week for her to find her way out of the dark and sorrowful emotional state induced by the wicked attack. Slowly and steadily she emerged from the fog of trauma and returned to her former self. She had once again reestablished her position as the "queen of camp" when the flotilla landed each evening, barking out orders to the men and attending to the preparation of the evening meal. She doctored wounds, treated blisters, and mended garments. She chopped meat, stirred soup pots, and rationed food. It was within these mundane tasks that she found meaning and rediscovered her peace.

Francois had finally recovered from his near-fatal snake bites. His hovering care over Genevieve during the week that followed her attack had been good medicine for him. He soon regained much of the strength that had been sapped from his members. He had been back at his duty on an oar for a little over one week. He could still only manage about a half day of rowing, but he was happy to be doing his part once again. Pierre insured that Francois remained a member of his personal boat crew. The men of the other crews were somewhat jealous because of Pierre and Antoine's willingness to take their turns at rowing. Counting Francois, the lead boat had a total of three rowers in relief ... a luxury not enjoyed by any of the other crews.

In just under two months bateau number one had become something of a home for the men of its crew. Counting Charles Rimbault, there were twenty-nine souls on board, and there were many colorful characters included in the mix. There was no shortage of complaining, joking, teasing, and horseplay. It bothered Pierre at first, but Charles reassured him that it was all normal behavior and part of the healthy everyday life of a boat crew. Pierre yielded to the *voyageur's* wisdom and experience. Before long he, too, included himself in the banter and barrage of remarks and insults that were often tossed about among crew members. The men appreciated and respected his levity. He was warmly received into the crew.

The routine and labor of river travel continued. The boats slowly and methodically inched northward, though one could not tell it at any particular moment during the journey. Most of the time the boats moved almost due east or due west as they wound their way around the convoluted curves and bends of the river. Amazingly, there were several places where they actually rowed due south, sometimes spying to their left or right the channel where they had been traveling northward less than an hour before. It was maddeningly frustrating to Pierre to spend so much time and effort doubling back over geography that they had already traversed. But such was the nature of travel on the snake-like Mississippi River.

Those who had never before traveled the river were enamored by its unspoiled landscapes, rugged wildness, and unparalleled beauty. And they saw many strange things throughout the journey. A few days after departing Fort Panmure they passed the mouth of the Tioux River, which marked the northern border of the land of the Natchez Indians. At that location, there was a most amazing whirlpool, known as the "Great Gulf," where the swift-running waters of the smaller river collided with the Mississippi. Charles Rimbault expertly guided the boats well away from the dangerous eddy.

Even when facing certain danger and deadly river currents Rimbault never ceased sharing interesting stories of ancient Indian settlements, abandoned French villages, ancient wars, and bloody massacres. He pointed to the east and described strange tribes known as the Chackhumas, Tapuchas, and the ancient Ibitupas. The boatsmen were mesmerized by the lore of the region. They attempted to visualize the ancient Indians and their villages which, according to Rimbault, had been adorned with an obscene amount of silver, gold, and jewels. The numerous ancient ruins that dotted the riverbanks seemed to lend credence to the *voyageur's* tales and claims.

The men rowed their bateaux past the mouth of the wide, powerful Yazous River, which emptied its pale green waters into the muddy, brown Mississippi. The two different shades of water ran parallel to one another until they disappeared around the bend and intermingled along their common journey toward the Gulf of Mexico.

One evening the travelers camped at a fascinating bow-shaped turn in the river called Little Point. Even though it was not an actual island, their campsite was almost completely surrounded by the water on all sides. The environment was lush, green, and jungle-like. It reminded Pierre of the thickets and forests that he had visited on Cayman Brac.

They paddled past various islands with curious names ... Alligator Island, Corn Island, and a tiny cluster of knobs in the water known as the Mulberry Islands. They saw amazing birds, which seemed to fascinate and entertain Genevieve more than anything they observed during the journey. Some were large, gray-blue cranes with long necks and huge beaks that looked like spears. There were also enormous eagles with heads that were shaded a brilliant white. They encountered huge turtles and fish, gigantic frogs, and strange-looking tailed amphibians. On one occasion, they watched in silence as the body of an Indian woman drifted swiftly downstream on a tiny makeshift raft. A cluster of colorful flowers adorned her chest. The Mississippi River never failed to provide them all with a strange, bewildering, unforgettable experience.

The weather was quite agreeable. October brought slightly cooler air on most days. There had been a few rain showers, but for weeks the weather had been remarkably clear. They experienced a storm one night in late September, but it was nothing like the Louisiana deluge they experienced on the first week of the trip. The fact that they were much more prepared for the weather greatly lessened the impact of the most recent storm on their travel time. Charles Rimbault was more than pleased with the conditions thus far on the journey, but he knew that their fortunes could and would change sooner or later.

It was Friday of the second week in October. That day, compared to the days previous, was extremely warm and humid. When the group made camp on the previous night there had been cool winds blowing from the north. They awakened to much warmer air and almost no breeze at all. The air was heavy, thick, and still. As they slowly paddled upstream an enormous dark gray formation of clouds developed to their west and southwest. Charles kept a careful eye on the clouds, fearful that extreme weather was drawing near. He saw that the men of his boat were also wary and fearful of the ominous skies, so he decided to make conversation and attempt to divert their attention.

"Look to your left, gentlemen. Do you see those ruins?"

The men craned their necks toward their immediate west.

"Do you mean that unremarkable pile of rocks on that small bluff?" asked one of the men.

"That is it, indeed! It is all that is left of one of the formerly majestic villages of the ancient Arkansas Indians. They do not exist as a people anymore. Their descendants now number among all of the other smaller tribes in this region."

"So, they are all dead?" asked another man.

"No, you imbecile, they are not dead. They are scattered among the other nations, much like *les Juifs*, eh? The children of Israel ..."

The confused man nodded his understanding.

Rimbault continued, "There are many similar ruins of the great civilization that once defined this region. They are here along the Mississippi and along the many other rivers and creeks that flow toward this valley from the west."

He paused and scanned the water ahead. "Just ahead of us there is a sharp bend to the east. It is the place where that old gold-hunting Spaniard, Ferdinand de Soto, discovered the Mississippi River way back in 1541 ... over two hundred years ago!"

"How could a Spaniard discover something that has always been here since the beginning of time?" asked a crewman from the rear of the bateau. The other men chuckled at his query.

"That is a most excellent question, young David. Maybe you can ask him about it in the hereafter someday ... if you both land in the same place beyond the grave."

The men chuckled again. The young crewman named David responded, "I think I shall ask him, instead, why he could not have discovered an easier way to travel up this muddy beast!"

His retort elicited a round of rowdy laughter and a chorus of affirmation. The men had certainly grown weary of rowing the bateau.

Once the laughter had died down Rimbault spoke again. "This spot is of the utmost importance to us and our great venture north-ward."

"Why is it important to us?" inquired Genevieve, joining in the conversation.

"It is important to us, *Madame*, because it marks the 34th parallel ... our half-way point to Kaskaskia."

"Really, Charles?" Genevieve inquired excitedly. She slapped Pierre excitedly on his arm. "Are we truly half-way to our destination?"

"Of course, we are, my dear."

"Then that is a very important milestone, indeed," she stated as she stared forward in silence at the waters of the river. "I am so very ready to reach our new home!"

Her simple, wishful statement brought a chorus of, "Amens!" and whistles of celebration from the men of the boat. Pierre hugged his wife tenderly. Excitement washed through the crew. The men broke out into a well-known song as they enthusiastically and rhythmically attacked the water with their oars.

Less than an hour later the weather began to change. The eight bateaux were traveling directly to the east in a huge bend of the river when the first winds struck the surface of the water and pierced the stillness of the dead air. Those winds rapidly became gusty, tossing the treetops to and fro and blowing the bateaux along at a much quicker pace. The temperature dropped significantly and the wind became almost ice cold. Thunder groaned far to the west.

"Deploy the sails!" shouted Charles. "Let us take advantage of this stout wind!"

Genevieve gripped her husband's arm in fear. Pierre turned to speak to Rimbault and noted that the same fear was evident in the eyes of all of the crewmen.

"Charles, I have never seen weather like this. There has been such a dramatic change in the air and the temperature. And these winds are becoming so violent!"

The men began to mutter and mumble their agreement to Pierre's concerns.

"A storm approaches, Pierre. I have seen such storms before. They move very quickly and often times carry devastating winds. We need to move upriver as fast as we can and secure shelter. Do you see that bend to the north just ahead?"

Pierre craned his neck to see ahead of them. Thunder boomed. Its powerful echo rumbled for several seconds. It was much closer than before. Yellow lightning illuminated the skies to the west. The fierce storm was approaching rapidly.

"Yes, I see it," Pierre responded. "It looks like every other bend that we have encountered in this cursed river. What is so special about that one?"

"That is known as Ozier's Point. There is a huge sand bar on the western edge of that bend. During the low water of summer and autumn there is a small, exposed bluff and a broad, sandy beach. We must reach that beach, land and secure these bateaux, and take shelter beneath the bluff. In addition to powerful winds, such a storm may have deadly *grêlons* that could harm us or even kill us."

"*Grêlons?*" asked a bewildered Genevieve. "I have never heard of this word. What are they?"

"Madame, they are stones made of ice that sometimes fall from the clouds during these violent storms. Sometimes they are small, like cherries or grapes. But I have seen them as large as apples, sometimes even larger." He paused, his face growing dim. "I have witnessed those huge balls of ice kill entire herds of cattle."

Genevieve's eyes grew wide with shock. She nervously eyed the sky. The deep blue-gray clouds churned and rolled like a steaming cauldron. The lightning was almost directly overhead. The atmosphere began to assume a queer yellow-green hue. The black cloud that approached them was low, bow-shaped, and almost looked like a huge wall.

The wind gusted more powerfully than it had before. The tiny sail on their bateau strained against the overpowering wind. The men heard a dull crack at the base of the mast.

"Our masts are not equipped for such high winds!" exclaimed Charles. "Lower the sail immediately!" He turned and screamed at the boat behind them. "Lower your sail! The wind is too powerful! Pass the word!"

But relaying the new orders to the other bateaux would be an impossible task. The stormy winds had served to disperse their little fleet. Earlier they had maintained intervals of approximately twenty yards between each boat, but the use of sails and the variations in the gusty winds had scattered the boats across the width of the river. The eighth boat in the formation was well over a quarter mile back from the lead craft. It appeared that their mast and sail were broken and the crew was in a state of disarray.

The thunder and lightning roared directly over their heads. The wind screamed and howled an eerie tune. The tops of the trees along the river's edge were bent low and leaning with the wind, which had shifted. It was now blowing directly out of the south. Small branches were ripped loose and flying through the air. Leaves and twigs slammed into the sides and backs of the hapless members of the boat crew. The lead bateau was a mere one hundred yards from the bend. Pierre soon spotted the dark brown sand of the exposed sandbar on the left side.

"I see it!" he screamed over the screeching wind. "We are almost there!"

Rimbault urged the men, "Dig, boys! Attack that water! We must get to that beach!"

Suddenly Genevieve screamed, "What is that?" She pointed downriver behind them, directly toward the west. The men on the oars began to turn and look toward the direction that she was pointing.

Rimbault scolded them, "Face forward and keep paddling, men! Paddle or die!" He turned to look back down the river.

About a mile to their west, just where the river made its eastward curve, the leaves were being stripped from the trees and the dark waters of the river splashed and churned as humongous hailstones plummeted from the sky like mighty missiles. It was a surreal vision. Each stone sent a gray-white spray of water high into the air upon impact.

Rimbault screamed, "*Grêlons!* Large ones! We will be crushed! Quickly men! We must ground the boat and seek whatever shelter we can find!"

The men paddled feverishly. They grunted and yelled as they tore at their paddles. Sweat dripped from their brows and soaked their shirts despite the numbing cold of the storm-cooled air. The men attempted to steal glances toward the west, but could not see over the high stern of the craft. They could not see the wall of hail that was pounding the waters of the river a half-mile behind them. The wave of wind-driven ice bombs quickly made their way toward the northeast, where they began to devour the forest on the northern bank of the river. The sound of it all was deafening. The thunder, crashing ice, howling winds, and the snapping of limbs and trees all combined into a cacophony of terror and destruction.

At long last they reached the sand bar. The men in the front of the boat leapt out onto the sand and pulled on the forward guide lines. The others jumped out and heaved as they attempted to push the heavy, cargo-laden bateau onto the dry sand. The other boats began to land all around them. Dozens of men fell in together and struggled to secure their boats. Meanwhile the deadly thunderstorm churned its way toward the northeast.

"There are only seven!" screamed Pierre, having counted the boats. "Where is the last bateau?"

Rimbault pointed downriver. The final bateau was about three hundred yards to the west. The men were paddling it toward the southern bank of the river. The mast and sail hung haphazardly over the center of the boat. The captain was pointing and screaming. The men appeared frantic.

"They are trying to reach the shelter of the trees!" shouted Rimbault.

"My God!" yelled Pierre. "The ice is upon them!"

They watched in horror as the huge hailstones assaulted the hapless boat. They could hear the cries of the men and the hollow crack of the hail against the hard wood of the bateau. The boat captain, an old friend of Rimbault's named Claude Duvalier, was standing near the stern with his hands held defensively over his head. The men standing on the distant beach watched in horror as he tumbled clumsily into the water, no doubt struck by one of the deadly hailstones. A few of the oars fell loosely into the ice-churned river. The other men were barely visible as they cowered and sought cover in the bottom of the bateau. Some held fast to their oars and tried to shield their heads with the narrow pieces of wood.

Then the sound of the wind changed. A strange whistling roar filled the skies. The air above them literally screamed. The sandy ground beneath their feet trembled and vibrated with the power of an earthquake. The clouds overhead tumbled, spun, and churned.

The source of the screaming air emerged over the trees to their southwest. A gigantic tornado stretched from the low, black cloud. It curved majestically from the dark sky and slammed into the forest about a half-mile to their southwest with a tremendous crash. The cloud groaned its destruction with a sound that could only be the voice of Satan, himself.

The roughly one hundred and eighty men and women from the first seven boats stood mesmerized on the distant sandy bank. They could not force their feet to move. Most of them made the sign of the cross on their chests. The spectacle was captivating. The tornado consumed the forest, sucking entire trees into its funnel and pulling them high into the air. Even from the distance of a half-mile the refugees on the beach could hear the trees snapping like twigs. The massive virgin timber did not have the strength to stand to the onslaught of the cloud's destructive winds. The tornado churned its thunderous path toward the northeast.

"God in heaven!" shrieked Genevieve. "What is this devilish cloud that descends and consumes the land?"

"It is a cyclone, Genevieve," responded Rimbault, attempting to shout over the din of the storm. "It is more powerful than any other force of nature on the earth. You cannot flee from it. You cannot hide from it. All that you can do is pray."

Debris began to rain down around them. It was the remains of the devastated forests along the river's edge. Leaves, splinters, and chunks of wood slammed into the water and sand. The tornado chewed its way through the trees on a straight path toward the river.

"We must take shelter in the trees!" exclaimed Pierre.

Charles shook his head sadly. "It will not do any good, Pierre. Our fate is in the hands of God. There is nowhere for us to hide. The only place safe from a cyclone is below the ground in a cellar or cave. We can only pray that it will somehow miss us." He yelled to the congregation of boatsmen, "You had best make your peace with God, men!"

Dozens of the oarsmen dropped to their knees in prayer. Many wept. Some spat angrily on the ground and shook their fists toward the heavens. The different faiths, attitudes, and life experiences of the travelers all combined together to form a variety of remarkable responses to the deadly cloud that appeared poised to claim all of their lives.

Pierre slipped his arm around the fragile shoulder of his wife and hugged her close. He whispered, "I will love you forever, Genevieve. Either here or in the hereafter."

She lifted her incredible green eyes to meet his gaze. "And I you, Pierre. Forever. No matter where this devilish wind may take us."

They kissed, gently ... sweetly. She slowly turned her head and rested it against Pierre's chest.

One of the men exclaimed, "Look! The bateau!"

All of their eyes and emotions were fixed upon the helpless, stranded bateau. The tornado emerged from the trees and descended upon the river. It sucked the muddy water up into its funnel, forming a strange, tan-brown streak in the massive cone. The front edge of the huge cyclone snatched the bateau and its men from the surface of the water and tugged them upward toward the heavens. The people on the beach heard the deathly shrieks and screams of the men above the roar of the cyclone. The grounded crews watched in disbelief as the dark speck of the boat circulated around the periphery of the funnel and then disappeared into the massive shelf cloud above.

"Quick!" encouraged Charles. "Let us press against the bluff! I think that the cyclone is going to miss us, but the wind and debris are still very dangerous!"

The men and women did as Charles urged. The darted toward the tiny bluff, a drop-off of the bank behind them that was barely four feet high and about sixty feet in length. They knelt down and crowded two-deep against the bare earth and tree roots as they sought the meager protection from the stinging leaves, branches, sand, and rocks that pelted the ground around them.

The curtain of hail, followed closely by the tornado, continued on its northeasterly path, skipping off of the river and crashing into the forest a mere two hundred yards to the west of the grounded bateaux. The muddy water of the Mississippi River, having been sucked upward into the cloud, soon completed its skyward journey and began to rain down on them from the above. Amazingly, though large amounts of wood and debris fell in waves from the sky, not a single hailstone reached their beach. They huddled fearfully and listened as the winds churned behind them. Trees crashed to the ground in the woods that were to their west, beyond the bluff and out of their view. The beleaguered travelers held their breaths and prayed. It was all they could do.

Amazingly, almost as quickly as the storm had developed and descended upon them, it started to dissipate. The giant whirlwind chewed its course through the forests and lands on the eastern side of the river. The howling roar of the cloud moved far into the distance to the northeast. The winds died down rapidly. There was a brief shower of light rain, just enough to give the freshly-devastated environment a thorough rinsing. Then the sun revealed itself immediately and bathed the landscape in its brilliant orange light.

Pierre and Genevieve walked to the edge of the water and peered to the northeast. Where there had once been dense, high forest there was now a chewed avenue of destruction that was almost a quarter mile wide. Huge trees were snapped off at the ground and lay in haphazard piles. Through the huge crevasse in the trees they gazed upon a brilliant rainbow to the east.

Charles Rimbault and several of the other men climbed up on the bank above the bluff and looked behind them to examine the pathway of the tornado. One of the men emitted a low whistle of disbelief. The outer edge of the destruction was a mere fifty yards away. That was how close they had all come to certain death and destruction.

Charles took off his hat and wiped the sweat from his brow with his shirt sleeve. He gazed down at the dazed throng of boatsmen who huddled together on the sandbar near their undamaged boats.

He proclaimed, "By the grace of God we live to paddle another day!" He paused thoughtfully. "But now we must go and look for our friends."

An hour had passed since the disaster of the devastating storm. It took that long to organize the boats, make camp, and develop a plan. Rimbault assigned a small group to stay with the women and build fires on the beach and then dispatched the remainder to search for bodies. By nightfall they had only located two on the western side of the river. Both were in the line of destruction left by the devastating tornado. There was no way to tell how many bodies may have been concealed beneath the logs and treetops that covered the ground. Early on they held some hope that there may have been survivors, but it was clear from the ravaged condition of the two bodies they located that there was absolutely no hope of anyone living through the powerful cyclone.

The search party hastily buried the men they had found in shallow graves near the river and returned to camp just before the sun set in the unimaginably dazzling, clear western sky. It was an unthinkable contrast of peace and beauty to the darkness and violence of the early afternoon. The group numbly ate a modest supper and then gathered around several soul-warming campfires. Charles, Pierre, Genevieve, Antoine, Francois, and several of the individual boat captains reclined around a particularly large fire. They sipped rum and, for a long while, stared in silence at the flames. They were still in shock from the sights, sounds, and death of the day.

Pierre broke the vigil of silence. "Charles, what is our plan for tomorrow? How do we proceed?"

"We continue the search, Pierre. We owe it to our comrades to find their remains, if possible. We will locate and bury as many of our friends as we can."

Pierre nodded. "Yes, we do owe it to them. There were twenty-six souls on that bateau, including one of our women."

"Her name was Josephine Levron, and her husband was Gaspard Dubois," added Genevieve wistfully.

Pierre reached over and touched his wife's hand. "Did you know her well, then?"

"Well enough. We worked and cooked together many times. She was a quiet girl, and very young. She and Gaspard were married less than a year." Genevieve paused as tears welled in her eyes. "She was with child." She looked at Pierre with hollow eyes of sadness and despair.

"Really?" asked Pierre, shocked. "I did not know."

"She had only found out days before our departure. They wanted to keep it secret. Gaspard was afraid that you might not allow them to come on the trip with a wife in her condition. She was confident that since it was so early in the pregnancy she could keep her secret until we reached Illinois."

"She was right. I would not have let them come. How I wish I had known ..." Pierre's voice trailed off woefully.

"They died searching for their dream, Pierre," Charles interjected. "They died looking for a better life ... looking for freedom and their rightful place in this world."

"And now they are dead," Pierre responded bitterly.

"Yes they are, Pierre, as we all will be some day." He shrugged. "It was their time."

"I have heard you say that twice now, Charles ... *'It was their time.'* I did not know that you were such a man of faith and one who holds such deep beliefs in the providence of God," Pierre remarked.

"One need not spend time kneeling in cathedrals, counting beads on a necklace, or hiding in dark closets talking to fat, virgin, pale-skinned priests to be a man of faith, Pierre. I have faith. One would have to be an idiot to see the sights that we have seen this very day and still deny the sovereignty of an all-powerful, almighty God." He paused thoughtfully and tossed a stick into the campfire. "I fear God, and I am His friend. Whether or not He considers me a friend of His is entirely a matter of speculation."

There were a few understanding, light hearted chuckles around the fire.

Pierre rose from his seat. "All right, then. Tomorrow we will search for the missing boat and crew. As we lie down and sleep tonight let us pray for their eternal souls."

Several of the men made the sign of the cross in the dull glow of the dancing flames.

"Come, Genevieve, let us retire for the evening. Gentlemen, we will see you at sunrise."

A chorus of quiet 'good nights' followed them as they retreated to their nearby spot on the beach and crawled between their blankets for the night. There were no tents in the camp that evening. The travelers all pitched their bedrolls on the pleasantly soft, sun-warmed sand under cloudless, dazzling, star-filled skies.

Out of respect for the dead there was no profuse drinking, storytelling, laughing, or singing of songs on this sorrowful night. The entire camp was overwhelmed by a morose quietude. Within a half-hour, the entire entourage was bedded down and sleeping quietly, if not soundly.

On more than one occasion that night the silent darkness was pierced by the hollow cries and whimpers of nightmares. Many of the weary men, even though they escaped the cyclone in life, could not escape the fearsome cloud in their dreams.

꙰

The women awakened well before the dawn and prepared a hot breakfast of gruel, accompanied by steaming pots of tea. The men were well-fed and prepared physically, if not emotionally, for the gruesome task of the recovery of bodies.

Having already covered all of the ground on the western bank of the river inside Ozier's Point, the search parties needed to move to the eastern side of the river in order to continue searching the debris path. The immediate issue that had to be resolved was the matter of transportation. Charles Rimbault elected to use the first bateau as a shuttle. Since they were just crossing the narrow river, it would only require a minimum rowing crew. Eight men could easily move the heavy craft back and forth across the river. It took four separate trips to move all of the personnel to the eastern side, but the now-expert boatsmen completed the task in magnificently short order. Pierre assigned twenty armed men to remain behind and maintain security at the camp. Francois was placed in charge of that group.

So, the men quickly fanned out and began their search. By mid-morning they had located only six bodies. Since the corpses were severely maimed and beginning to bloat in the unseasonable heat, they buried the men where they found them. Some men on the far northern flank of the search zone found one other man, but his body was lodged high in a tree, almost eighty feet off of the ground. There was absolutely no way that they could retrieve him, so they joined together around the tree to pray for the unknown victim and then moved on to continue their search.

The teams moved steadily toward the northeast, following the two-hundred-yard wide swath of destruction through the almost unrecognizable forest. The men spread out and searched in a line roughly two hundred yards to the north and south of the debris field, as well. By noon they had found and buried only four more bodies. They had hiked almost a half mile. The shattered trees so cluttered the terrain that men often had to climb over huge, twisted mountains of tree trunks and branches. It was back-breaking, thirst-inducing, frustrating work.

While taking a water break Pierre looked questioningly at Charles. "What do you think? We've only found thirteen out of twenty-six. I'm beginning to think that it's a miracle that we found most of those. And we haven't seen the first sign of the bateau. Not even a single paddle or piece of cargo!"

Charles nodded his agreement. "Pierre, there's no telling how many bodies we have stepped and climbed over in the debris field. We've most likely passed them by. And there is no way to tell how far that cyclone carried the bateau. Hell, it could be in Illinois already, for all we know! I think that we should just call an end to the search and consider that our lost friends are already entombed under this devastated forest. Their bodies will return to the ground, as they were intended to. Ashes to ashes ..."

"And dust to dust," Pierre finished the sentiment. He nodded at Charles. "Let's tell the men."

Charles cupped his hands to his mouth and was just preparing to shout the recall to the searchers when an excited scream erupted about a hundred yards to their right. It came from the untouched woods to their south. A deep voice carried through the forest on the light breeze. "We have found it! We have found the bateau!"

Pierre and Charles popped the corks into their tin canteens and trotted toward the sound of the voice. They could hear the footfalls of dozens of other men running through woods around them. They quickly reached the growing gathering of men in a small clearing. Antoine was one of the men standing nearest the boat. They all stared sullenly at the wind-battered bateau. It was upside-down and solidly wedged between two large trees.

"The boat appears to be remarkably intact, Pierre," remarked Antoine. "We may be able to salvage a few things from it. I believe there were muskets, flints, and lead bullion strapped in the bottom of this boat. No items of glass or other breakables, as I recall."

Pierre concurred, "I think you are right, Antoine. It is amazing that the boat was not demolished altogether. We may, indeed, be able to salvage most of our goods. Has anyone attempted to move the boat?"

"We tried to move it when we first found it, but it is wedged in tightly between the trees. The four of us could not budge it."

"We can try with more men," stated Pierre. "If all else fails, we will take an axe to the hull where it contacts the trees."

"Did anyone from the search party bring an axe?" inquired Antoine.

"Of course," remarked Rimbault. "Four men carried axes in case we had to cut debris in order to move bodies. I believe that they had to exercise their skills on two of the recoveries this morning."

"You should probably go ahead and pass the word that we need them over here," suggested Antoine.

"I will take care of it," stated Charles. He turned to one of the men standing nearby. "Jacques, go and fetch the axe men."

"*Oui*, Charles. I will return as quickly as possible."

"Meanwhile, let us attempt to move it by force. We have over twenty strong men here now," observed Pierre.

Charles organized the group and placed the men at strategic areas along the hull of the boat. The bow was the portion that was so firmly embedded between the two trees. It was slightly elevated off of the ground, providing an ideal point to insert a lever. The men fashioned a crude lever from a large branch. The men then pushed and heaved, screamed, and grunted as they attempted to dislodge the boat, but it refused to move. They made absolutely no progress at all. After two more tries they gave up and waited for the axes.

The cutting crew arrived in relatively short order. They quickly went to work on the hull at its two contact points. Minutes later the men were able to rock the hull in place. They tilted it slightly toward one side ... just enough to allow the bow to slip out from between the trees. Rimbault gathered the men together and they gave one final, mighty push. The bateau popped free. Two dozen men then lined up along one side and easily flipped the boat upright. The broken mast was wedged in place inside the hull, trapping the tattered sail on the floor of the bateau and covering the central cargo area.

"Cut that line and get that mast and sail out of there!" ordered Rimbault. "We have to get this cargo unloaded and back to the river. We have a lot of stuff to move and only three hours of daylight to get it done."

Two of the men leaned over the edge of the hull and sliced the lines that tied the sail to the mast and riggings. One of the men reached down to grab the sail, but he instantly screamed and tumbled backwards, falling soundly on his arse. The others laughed at his seemingly foolish behavior.

"Bertrand, what is wrong with you?" scolded Rimbault.

"There is a body in the boat!"

The other men eased forward to look, none of them eager to see another dead, distended human corpse. Antoine jumped over the side of the boat and gingerly eased his way toward the center. He slowly pulled the torn sail away from the body below, revealing a small, soft face.

He looked at Pierre and Charles, who stood peering over the far side of the boat. "It is the woman."

He looked at her tender features. She was a pleasant-looking, if not pretty, young girl. Her lips were full. Blonde hair peeked from beneath her bonnet. Her cheeks were pink and plump.

Then suddenly Antoine realized the implication of her skin color. Her cheeks were pink! He leaned forward and placed his hand over her mouth. The air inside the bateau was already hot and he could not feel any breathing, so he leaned forward and placed his head on her chest. Several of the men groaned in shock and disgust.

Charles scolded him, "Antoine, you fool, what are you doing? That is sacrilege! Leave that poor dead girl in peace!"

But Antoine heard deep in her chest the faint but steady thump of her heart. He heard her shallow, almost indiscernible breathing.

He stood and shouted with glee, "Charles, this girl is not dead! She is alive!"

# 10

## ON TO ILLINOIS

Amazingly, a little over a month had passed since the horrible cyclone and storm. During that time, the miles crept slowly by. The remaining seven bateaux continued the agonizingly slow journey northward toward their destination in the Illinois Country. As the days passed the landscape along the river morphed from the bright green hues of summer to the browns, oranges, and reds of autumn. The air became much more cool and crisp and less humid. They had not yet experienced the first frost of the season, but the nights were significantly colder. The travelers slept close to large fires each night and pitched their tents and shelters whenever they had the opportunity.

During that month of travel, they passed several important landmarks and locations. They paddled past the mouth of the *Riviere a Mayot*, the Wolf River, and the corresponding cliffs of *Mayot*. This high bluff was the site of the short-lived French Fort of the Assumption. Charles explained how the French outpost was abandoned after repeated attacks by the Chickasaws. It was also the site of an ancient abandoned city known as Chucalissa, and a perpetual hotbed of Chickasaw activity. The fleet slowly made its way past the other Chickasaw bluffs and past the mouth of the snake-like River of the Chickasaws. As they paddled along this particular stretch of river the men remained vigilant at all times, scanning the eastern bank and nearby hills for any sign of the notoriously violent Indians.

By the time they passed the final Chickasaw bluff, only one pirogue remained in tow. The other three were abandoned once their supplies and stores were consumed during the journey. The men supplemented their diet with fresh fish and game. Pierre was somewhat concerned that their food stores were going to run out. Charles Rimbault assured him that their rate of consumption was right on schedule for a group their size.

Two weeks after the storm the travelers added an amazing and surprising treat to their menu. They had camped on a sandbar on the western bank of the river and promptly dispatched hunting teams in search of venison. One of those teams stumbled across a small herd of *boeufs*, the cattle-like animals that were known among the English settlers as buffalo. They shot three of the gigantic beasts and had to send a runner back to the camp to fetch extra help to haul the enormous quantity of meat back to their fires. The group spent an extra day and night on that sandbar cooking, eating, drying, and smoking the lean, delicious flesh. They did not have enough time to properly clean and dry the hides. That was most unfortunate, for those pelts would have fetched a handsome price in trade goods at Kaskaskia.

The miraculous Josephine Levron, the lone survivor of the cyclone, had become something of a celebrity among the men of the boats. She was in an amazingly good state of physical health, having only received a few bruises, mostly from hailstones, and some minor cuts as a result of her stormy ordeal. Everyone was thoroughly confounded as to how she could have survived being swept up into the deadly cloud, tossed about in the heavens, and then deposited, alive and relatively uninjured, over a half-mile away. Truly, it was a miracle. It was the main topic of speculation and conversation most days.

Unfortunately, Josephine did not contribute much to those conversations. She regained consciousness soon after the search party located her. It only took a bit of cool water to awaken her from her slumber. She was talkative in those first moments, peppering the men with questions and demanding to know the whereabouts of her husband. When she learned that she was the lone survivor from her boat she simply stopped talking altogether. The poor girl shut herself off from the group and stared into the sky in apoplectic silence. She remained that way for well over a week. It took several days of constant attention and care from Genevieve to slowly draw her out from her emotional cocoon and back into the flow of daily life. Francois was a big contributor to her care, as well. As Genevieve and Francois kept her busy and drew her back into the work of camp life she did, eventually, return to some semblance of normalcy.

Genevieve agonized over the girl's future. She was a widowed young woman and carrying the child of a dead man. Genevieve worried what would become of the girl once they reached Illinois. But Rimbault assured her that she would not remain a widow for long. French women, or white women of any sort, were a precious commodity on the frontier. There would be no shortage of men willing to take her as a bride, baby or no.

Rimbault joked, "But I sincerely doubt she will make it to Illinois without attachment. Someone in this crowd will woo and win her before our bateaux touch the banks of Kaskaskia."

*November 23, 1769*

"That is our destination for the night," declared Charles Rimbault. "It is *Île de Loups*, the Island of Wolves."

They peered ahead at a huge island between two channels of the Mississippi. It was thickly forested with an impenetrable barrier of trees and brush. The island looked dark, unspoiled, and menacing.

"It does not sound very inviting," observed Antoine. "Why must we camp in such a frightening, desolate place?"

"Trust me, *Monsieur* Alexis, you do not want to camp on either the eastern or western banks of the river at this location. There are dangerous tribes of natives in both directions. I do not know what the western Indians are called, but the area to our south and east is the wilderness known as Kentah-Ke. It is Chickasaw country, and they do not care the least little bit for Frenchmen. Wolf Island is a common stopping point and camp site. The river splits into two channels around this enormous island. The deeper, slower channel is to the left. We will pursue that course. On the northern side of the island are very large, sandy beaches that are perfect for temporary lodging. I believe that you will be most pleased with the site of our accommodations."

It took them over two more hours of rowing to reach the site where Charles wished to camp. It was a very broad, sandy beach on the northeast corner of the island. The beach was littered with large logs and smaller pieces of driftwood. Beyond the beach there extended a broad, fertile grassland. They saw a large herd of deer foraging among the tall, dry grasses that covered the small plain. Dense forests began about a quarter-mile inland beyond the rolling plain. It was, indeed, a perfect place to camp.

The men grounded the bateaux safely on the sand and set about the daily business of making camp. Everyone had a role to fulfill and an assignment to perform. After three months of traveling together it seemed that the group worked in almost perfect harmony. With all of the driftwood on the beach the firewood gatherers had an easy job. Hunting parties were dispatched into the forests. Some men went in search of clean drinking water. Others constructed fire pits, shelters, and tents. The women began preparation of the evening meal, which was always their primary meal of the day. They made their preparations quickly as nightfall would arrive in less than two hours. Charles predicted that they would have their first frost of the season that evening. He encouraged the men to use tents or construct lean-to shelters utilizing the ample driftwood and logs from the beach and brush from the nearby thickets and fields.

When darkness fell, everyone was sheltered and well-situated. The camp was almost festive that evening. The men were well aware that they were nearing their destination. After a satisfying dinner of hearty stew made from smoked buffalo meat, ground maize, and beans, the travelers rested by their fires and sipped mugs of hot tea flavored with pungent rum. The temperature dropped noticeably after dark. The conversation, as it did most nights, centered upon their progress in travel.

"What remains, Charles?" asked Pierre. "We have journeyed over three months now. Surely we are nearing the end."

"Indeed, we are. We are three days south of the confluence of the Ohio and Mississippi Rivers. That marks the beginning of the Illinois Country."

"We are truly that close, Charles?" asked Antoine.

"*Oui, Monsieur.* At our present rate and barring any other set-backs, we have less than ten days of travel north of the Ohio. In two weeks, we should reach Kaskaskia."

A small cheer erupted around their fire, and those magic words, "two weeks," spread quickly to the other fires. More cheering ensued, followed by festive songs. It was late into the night before the rum-tainted travelers crawled into their cozy shelters.

The attack came at dawn. There was no advanced warning, because there were no lookouts. Rimbault believed that the party was so safe on the mid-channel island that he never even considered posting sentries. He knew that no one had ever been attacked on Wolf Island before. But, tragically, Charles Rimbault had miscalculated.

The Chickasaws emerged from the forests to the south, crouched low, obviously intending to slay the Frenchmen in their sleep. They would have succeeded had not a lone crewman been awake to answer nature's call. He saw dozens of bald heads with scalplocks and feathers bobbing toward him in the grassy area just beyond the beach. He took off running back toward the shelters even as the urine continued to empty from his bladder, soaking his breeches and socks.

The man screamed, *"Attaque! Attaque! Sauvages!"*

The men in the camp struggled to escape their rum-enhanced slumber. Once the man's cries of terror pierced the waning moments of night, the Indians had lost their advantage of total surprise. There was a single gunshot and the hysterical Frenchman's cries fell silent. Within seconds, dozens of the warriors' wicked, wailing screams of battle pierced the atmosphere and bathed the camp in terror.

Pierre kicked open the flap of his tent and pulled on his black leather shoes. He grabbed his musket and searched frantically in the darkness of the tent for his shooting bag. Genevieve stirred beside him, groggily. She heard the terrifying wailing of the Indians. She grabbed his arm.

"Pierre, what is that ungodly sound?"

"Indians, my dear. We are under attack. Stay here and lie low to the ground. Do not move unless I or Charles or Antoine instruct you differently. Do you understand?"

"Yes, husband. But what are you going to do?"

"Fight, Genevieve. We must fight for our lives. Remember always that I love you."

He kissed her quickly on the forehead and then darted out of the tent. He shoved his pistol into his waist belt as he ran. More gunshots erupted from the south. All around him Pierre heard the dull thumps of lead against lumber, canvas, and logs. Tiny eruptions of sand indicated other nearby shots. A few arrows dropped silently and impaled into the sand. He surveyed the situation. Men were slowly crawling from their shelters. Some were beginning to return fire in the general direction of the attackers. The entire engagement appeared loose and unorganized. He spotted Rimbault and Francois about twenty yards to his left, in the direction of the boats.

He shouted to them, "Charles! Francois!"

Both men dropped to their knees as a ball slashed through the tent that was to Charles' immediate left. They motioned for Pierre to come to them. He bent over low and scurried to their position.

Pierre was almost breathless with fear when he reached them. "Charles! What is going on? Who are they?"

"They sound like Chickasaws to me. The bastards! I have never known them to venture onto this island. As if they do not already have enough territory to roam!" He spat on the ground.

"How many do you think there are?" Francois inquired excitedly.

"Enough," Rimbault grunted. "Probably forty or fifty warriors. They saw our boats today, no doubt, and cooked up a plan to relieve us of our cargo. They likely planned to cut our throats while we slept. It is only good fortune that someone was awake. This is all my fault, Pierre. We should have posted sentries for the night."

"It is too late for that, now. What must we do?" asked Pierre sternly.

"We must evacuate as quickly as possible. We must salvage as much of our equipment and camp supplies as we can and get these boats into the water. But we need a perimeter of armed men for cover. If the Chickasaws get onto this beach there will be a bloodbath. They will unleash their knives and war clubs on every one of us."

The shooting from the tents and shelters began to increase even as the light of dawn began to glow just a tad brighter.

"All right, then ... so tell us what to do!" Francois countered anxiously.

"Pierre, you and Francois organize the resistance. We need thirty or forty men on a skirmish line from there to there," he declared, pointing at spots on their left and right flanks. "I will find Antoine and organize the evacuation. You men must hold them off. It may take several minutes to organize this mob. Good enough?"

Both men nodded their understanding.

Charles encouraged them, "All right, then. Now get going. Cover us well and we just might make it out of this alive."

Pierre responded, "Before you do anything else, make sure someone sees to my wife, Rimbault. Get her into our boat immediately."

"And Josephine, as well!" chirped Francois. "She has no one to care for her!"

Rimbault chuckled suspiciously. "It looks like she does now, eh?" He winked at Francois. "Don't worry, boys. I'll take care of your women-folk. Now get going!"

Pierre checked the powder in his pan and felt in his shooting bag for cartridges, confirming that he had about a dozen pre-rolled charges for his .69 caliber Charleville. He barked at Francois, "Let's go, brother!"

They rose to their feet and ran toward the rear of the camp, recruiting men as they went. They only drafted the ones who already had their muskets or rifles in hand. Pierre especially wanted the men who already had the wherewithal and common sense to open fire and fight back against the screaming invaders. They ordered all of the weaponless crewmen they encountered to find their weapons and their personal belongings and report back to Charles at the boats. They had fifty shooters on the line in a matter of minutes. They were strung out along a bow-shaped protective perimeter approximately sixty yards in length.

The attacking savages suddenly grew quiet. There was no sign of them in the grass or the trees. The sky had become significantly brighter in the pink glow of the sunrise. Though the bright orb was not yet above the horizon, there was enough illumination to see all the way to the distant tree line.

"What is happening?" shouted one of the men. "Have they fled?"

"I did not see anyone running to the trees," answered Francois. "They must be down in the grass, planning their next move. Remain at the ready!"

Pierre screamed as loudly as he could, "Men, we need to flush them out. I don't want them to crawl undetected to this beach." He walked toward a spot directly behind the center of the line. "Men, when I give the signal, I want all of you on my right to lie down flat and fire into the grass. Aim low, no more than a foot off of the ground. Men to my left, remain at the ready but do not fire until you have a clear target. We must give the others time to reload. Is that clear enough?"

The men answered, "Yes, sir!" in relative unison.

"Very well, then. Gentlemen, I hope you are primed and loaded. Full cock!"

The men to his right all clicked the hammers on their flintlocks. "Take aim! Remember ... shoot through the grass!" He paused for just a moment as he scanned the terrain to their front. "Fire!"

Over twenty rifles and muskets roared on the right side of the line. The flash of the explosions lit up the dim field. Smoke billowed into the air and rose quickly to form a dull haze. There were a few distant cries of pain downrange. Somewhere in the grass metal had found meat. Pierre smiled with satisfaction.

"Reload!"

One of his men shouted, "*Monsieur,* there is a fire!"

Pierre shot a quick look to the right. Apparently, the muzzle blasts had ignited a grass fire in an area where the men were deployed particularly close to the vegetation.

Pierre had a sudden revelation. He pointed to the three men lying closest to him. "You men! I want the three of you to leave your weapons and run back to the fires. There are a couple of them still burning. Make torches from bear grease and cloth. Bring back fire so that we can ignite this grass. We'll make a wall of fire for these bastards to run through. If we're lucky, maybe we can burn them out!"

The men obeyed immediately, realizing the wisdom of the plan. Pierre scanned the line to his right. Most of those who fired in the first volley were already reloaded. The Indians still lay concealed in the grass.

"We need to keep their heads down, boys. Men to my left, lie down and prepare to fire a volley."

The men obeyed his commands quickly.

"I want the same execution as the first shot. Low and straight through the grass. Full cock!" The weapons clicked in obedience. "Take aim! Fire!"

A second thunderous volley sent another shower of lead through the fragile grass.

"Reload! Men to my right, are you prepared to fire?"

"Yes, sir!" they howled.

"Full cock! Take aim! Fire!"

For the next five minutes Pierre ordered alternating volleys from the two groups of shooters. He was successfully buying precious minutes for the other men on the beach to load and launch the boats, as well as time for the fire crew to return with their torches. When at long last Pierre saw five bouncing balls of fire approaching him from the camp he ordered a cease fire.

"Everybody check your weapons. Clean your pans and touch holes. And don't shoot us!"

Two of the men carried two torches each. The third man held only a single flame.

"I'm sorry, *Monsieur* Grimard, I could not get my second torch to light properly. So I finally gave up."

"Not to worry," Pierre reassured him. "Excellent work, men. Now give Francois and me one of those extra torches."

He and Francois each took one of the flaming sticks. The five men crouched low and fanned out along the front of the defensive line. They stuck the flames into every cluster of thick vegetation they could find. In a matter of minutes there was a four-foot-high wall of flames across the entire front. The flames slowly inched their way southward as they sought fresh fuel in the dry field.

"That should flush them out," remarked Pierre.

Rimbault pranced around the boats as he shouted orders and directed men. He noticed that the random shots of lead and arrows had stopped after the first hail of gunfire from Pierre's perimeter line. The lull in the attack gave him the opening he needed to get the camp moving. Men were throwing everything they possibly could into the bateaux. Cooking equipment, canvas shelters, weapons, food … all of it was stacked haphazardly and deep in the center of the boats. The women attempted to help at first, but Charles insisted that they take cover behind a cluster of driftwood logs that lay near the westernmost boats. Antoine fetched Genevieve from her tent and stashed her under cover with the other women. He and two other riflemen remained on watch to guard their safety.

The work of evacuation was progressing quickly. They would be ready to launch the bateaux in a matter of minutes. The men were already pushing some of the vessels back into the shallow water. Charles glanced back toward the action to the north. The firing had stopped. He noticed a small fire burning to the right and several men dispersed along the line, all of them setting fire to the dry autumn grass.

"Smart boy! What a smart boy you are, Pierre!" cheered Rimbault. "Let those savages burn!"

A sudden explosion of shots rang out to his left, from near the direction of the easternmost river channel. Those shots were followed quickly by the screams of dozens of Chickasaw warriors.

Charles shouted, "*Mon Dieu!* The Indians have flanked our fighters! To arms! To arms!"

The native raiders were upon them in seconds.

≥

Pierre watched the burning grass with great satisfaction. There was no way that the Indians would attempt to attack through such a hellish conflagration. Then the hail of gunfire erupted to their rear. Pierre spun around, confused. He saw men on the beach firing sporadically toward the southeast in the direction of the water. Then he heard the screams of the Indians. He also saw the muzzle flashes from the east.

"They've gone around us, men!" screamed Pierre. "They are almost upon the bateaux! To the beach!"

The men scrambled to their feet and sprinted toward the attacking savages. Many of them paused and fired as they ran.

Pierre yelled at Francois, "Get the women to one of the boats and get it launched! I will attempt to hold them off." He paused. "Francois, my friend, please see to my wife."

"I will, Pierre. I promise. Now stay low and aim true! Hold them off as long as you can!"

Francois spun and ran toward the boat that was furthest to the west.

෫

The Chickasaws overran the first boat in the line before the men even knew the Indians were upon them. The combat was bloody, hand-to-hand, and very one-sided. The savages screeched as they cracked open the heads of their victims with their gruesome war clubs. They unleashed an indiscriminate barrage of arrows at the huge assembly of Frenchmen. Many of the natives, sensing blood and victory, dropped their muskets to the ground in favor of their more familiar bows, knives, and clubs. Their dark, painted faces and bodies were like fearsome apparitions in the ghostly early morning light. They struck fear in the hearts of the hapless Frenchmen, most of whom had never tasted of combat before.

The fight seemed all but lost and the travelers doomed until the sudden return of the forward skirmishers interrupted the Chickasaws' charge. The fifty riflemen and musketeers unleashed a concentrated hail of lead into the screaming Indians just as they were about to attack the next boat and crew. Several of them fell screeching and writing upon the dark sand. The deadly wall of bullets brought the advance of the Indian horde to an immediate, if only temporary, halt.

"Reload! Reload quickly, men!" shouted Pierre. "Here they come!"

Half of the Chickasaw warriors had broken off from their attack on the boats and were charging headlong toward Pierre's formation of shooters.

Francois was almost completely out of breath. He was overwhelmed by the confusion and din of battle that raged all around him. He struggled to see through the thick haze of gunpowder smoke that blanketed the boats and beach. It took several minutes for him to locate Charles Rimbault.

"Charles! Pierre sent me to check on Genevieve. Do you know where she is? What are we doing?"

Rimbault pointed at the cluster of logs thirty yards behind him. "She and the other women are in safety behind those logs."

Francois craned his neck to see over the logs.

"Do not worry, Francois. Your Josephine is there and safe. Antoine is guarding them, along with two other men. And we are fully prepared to leave. Some of the bateaux are already launching." He pointed at two boats already hovering in the edge of the water. "We need the women loaded and men dispersed in the boats. We are going to be short several oarsmen."

Francois nodded grimly.

Rimbault continued, "It looks like Pierre and his men have stalled the attack from the east. We need to recall his men and get them in the boats, as well. You go and help Antoine with the women. I will send a man to Pierre. We need to be in the water in five minutes."

"How can we attempt to paddle into the current with these heathens shooting at us, Charles? They will use us for target practice!"

"We're not going upstream. We're going to paddle with the current and cover as much distance as we possibly can. We will stop on the western bank a mile or two downstream to repack our boats and see to our wounded. We will proceed north in the full light of afternoon. Now off you go! I want those women in the two westernmost boats."

"Yes, Charles!" Francois sprinted past his friend in the direction of the women.

Approximately fifteen warriors ran screaming into the face of Pierre's formation. Most of the men had reloaded, but not all were prepared to resist. Dozens of shots rang out, dropping half of the warriors at close range. Still, the others ran on ... screaming hysterically and swinging their war clubs. Soon the men were locked in a fierce, life-or-death, hand-to-hand struggle. They used their muskets as shields against the blows of the blades and clubs. Some of them used their firearms as clubs, as well. The men fought with their knives. Some even resorted to using rocks from the sandy ground to smash the skulls of their attackers.

Pierre got off a quick shot with his musket and then dropped it to the ground just as one of the fast-running warriors slammed into him. The wild-eyed, howling attacker was holding his war club high over his head, just preparing to swing it in a mighty arc against Pierre's head. Pierre clumsily yanked his pistol from his belt, pulled back on the cock, and fired from his hip. The ball impacted the warrior's sternum with a loud, hollow pop. The man's eyes expanded wide in horror. He careened to his left as he clutched at the enormous hole in his chest. The stricken Chickasaw fell to the ground, trembled, and then kicked his left leg twice as the blood and life ebbed out of his body.

Antoine threw up his musket and took aim at the dark form approaching from the east. He was just about to fire when he heard a familiar voice.

"Antoine!" shouted Francois. "We must get the women in the boats! We have to launch!"

"I almost shot you, Francois!"

"That would have been most unfortunate," quipped Francois as he jumped over the log and knelt beside Antoine and the women. "And here I thought that we were becoming good friends." He reached out his hand and touched Josephine tenderly on the arm. "Are you all right?"

She covered his hand with hers, smiled, and nodded.

"I'm serious, Francois! I almost shot you! You should have shouted a warning."

"It is all right, Antoine. You did not shoot me. Calm down. We have to focus on our job."

"What is that, exactly?"

"Getting the women into these first two boats. Rimbault is ready to launch. There is no time to waste."

"Where is Pierre?" demanded Genevieve.

"I do not know, *Madame.* The last time I saw him he was fighting on the front line against the Indians, but then they snuck around the side and attacked along the beach. You must not worry. I am sure that he is fine."

Francois grabbed Josephine by the arm and nodded to the other women. "Ladies, please follow us. These men and I will escort you to your bateaux. Do not ask questions or make comments. Go to the boat that we assign you. Once you are over the side, get in the very bottom and lie still. Understand?"

The women nodded fearfully. Before anyone else had the opportunity to speak, Francois lifted Josephine over the log and began leading her to the boat. The other men assisted the remaining women. Antoine escorted Genevieve. They ran in parallel lines with the men placing their bodies as shields between the women and the fighting.

They reached the bateaux quickly. The men hurriedly lifted the women off of the soft sand and unceremoniously dropped them over the sides into the bottoms of the two boats. Francois released Josephine and turned to cover the others with his musket. Antoine had just released Genevieve into the same boat and was attempting to turn around when something prevented him. He glanced quickly and discovered that his weskit was hung on the oar lock. He tried to pull away from the tangle but the strong linen would not budge.

Genevieve saw his predicament and rose up on her knees inside the boat to assist him. She pried at the cloth with her fingers, attempting to dislodge it from the metal brace.

"*Madame!*" Antoine exclaimed. "You must get down in the boat. It is not safe."

"It is almost clear!" she responded.

Antoine turned and pawed frustratingly at the tangled garment. At last the cloth gave way with a mighty rip. He spun around to face the battle to their east and see if the remaining men were getting loaded into the boats. Suddenly his head recoiled backward from a mighty blow. The back side of his skull exploded into a wet mist directly into Genevieve's face. The horrified woman tasted his coppery, warm blood in her open mouth. She screamed hysterically as Antoine's heavy, lifeless body tumbled backward into the bateau and landed directly on top of her. She pushed against the weight of his body and continued to scream incessantly as the men pushed the bateau into the water and then jumped into the seats and secured their oars.

Pierre stared, dazed, at the dead Indian at his feet. The sounds of gunfire and combat diminished dramatically. The Chickasaws had fought angrily and valiantly, but they were greatly outnumbered by the Frenchmen. There remained only a dozen or so alive on the battlefield. It seemed that the survivors all experienced a simultaneous realization of their defeat. The Indians broke off from the engagement and ran toward the southeast.

He heard Rimbault's voice calling from the edge of the water. "Pierre! We are ready! All men to the boats! We must launch now!"

"Let's go, men!" shouted Pierre. "Gather any weapons you see! Launch all the bateaux!"

He picked up his musket and two other abandoned weapons from the ground and sprinted to the nearest bateau. He tossed the muskets into the boat and joined a dozen other men as they pushed the heavy craft into the water. They quickly clamored over the sides and grabbed the oars. All of the bateaux were in deep water and moving in less than a minute.

"Downstream, men! Paddle downstream!" barked Rimbault. "We want distance from these savages! We will make up the lost miles later when it is safe!"

The seven bateaux lumbered into the current, allowing it to carry them swiftly to the west and then south. They paddled feverishly to add to the speed. Many of the men wept as the adrenaline and emotion of battle escaped from their bodies. Most of them prayed. Some vomited over the sides of their boats. At least ten men were bleeding from the wounds of the Chickasaw's blades and clubs. Some of those wounds were mortal.

And behind them on the bloody, sandy beach of Wolf Island lay thirteen of their dead or soon-to-be dead comrades. Antoine Alexis, the young adventurer from Austria and best friend of Pierre Grimard, lay dead in the bottom of one of the boats.

*December 12, 1769*

The weather was bitterly cold. Three inches of snow coated the banks of the Kaskaskia River. Two hundred yards ahead they could see the tiny makeshift docks near the small fort. There were a few men milling about near the water. Some pointed curiously at the approaching bateaux. None seemed overly concerned or impressed.

Pierre turned to look at the men in his boat and in the other boats that followed. There were significantly fewer of them. Three more souls succumbed to their wounds in the weeks following the Indian attack. Including those who died in the tornado, forty-three men had perished on the deadly Mississippi. Those who remained alive were frozen, haggard, hungry, exhausted, and hollow-eyed. They were all wrapped in multiple layers of wool blankets, canvas, and hemp cloth in an effort to stave off the bitter, wet cold. Pierre looked down sadly at his traumatized wife as she lay sleeping fitfully in her mid-boat cocoon.

He turned to Charles. "I thought it would be different, my friend. I expected to celebrate when we arrived. But our arrival seems so pathetically empty ... so anti-climactic."

"What did you expect, Pierre? A welcoming party? Perhaps a band or a parade? How silly of you! The journey is done. You have reached your new home, and you are alive. It is a good day!"

"But so many have died," responded Pierre. "Surely it could not have all been worth it."

"Stop punishing yourself, Pierre. Ours is a harsh and unforgiving world. People die. Indeed, all of us have an appointment with death. Just be glad that you survived, and that you still have your wife at your side. Stop looking backward. Look forward, and make the very most of your new life here in the wilderness. Launch your business. Make your fortune. Start a family. The future is all yours, Pierre."

"And what about you, Charles? What will you do now?"

"My dreams are simple ones, Pierre. I will find a hot meal, a warm bed, and a fire for tonight. Then tomorrow I depart for Vincennes. I must go to my sweet Julie. We have much reacquainting to do over the long, cold winter." He smiled broadly, exposing his stained teeth, and offered Pierre a very long and animated wink.

# PART III

*Shattered Peace*
*1778*

# 11

## WHISPERS OF WAR

*July 20, 1778*

**"P**ierre! Son! Bring my belt and hat! I am in a grave hurry!"

It was Monday, the day of the weekly militia muster at the fort. On Mondays past the French militia reported mid-morning for a head count with Edward Abbott, the British lieutenant governor of Vincennes, and then received their dismissal. Lately, however, the three companies of Frenchmen had been forced to spend a significantly greater amount of time performing drills and discussing tactics. They had even been deployed on occasional patrols in the fields and forests that surrounded the village. Though they were a world away from the rebellion against King George that was ongoing along the eastern coast of the continent, the conflict had caused all British forces to seek a greater state of readiness, even on the faraway frontier.

Thankfully, Governor Abbott had recently departed Vincennes for Detroit, leaving a Frenchman, Captain Francois Bousseron, in command of the local troops. The captain's military style and expectations were not quite as stringent as their British overlord's. And much to the delight of the men, he paid little attention to formalities and time schedules.

That was very good for Pierre Grimard, Sr., who sat perched on the edge of his porch chair and proudly worked the oil cloth over the length of his prized flintlock weapon. It was an exquisite .54 caliber long rifle made in a faraway place called Lancaster, Pennsylvania, by an American gunsmith named Jacob Dickert. Its striped curly maple stock almost glowed with its amazing soft-toned, orange-brown luminescence. Its lock and hardware were of the highest quality. Pierre had absolutely no idea who Jacob Dickert was, but was more than convinced that the Pennsylvania gunsmith knew his craft very well.

The exceedingly long and heavy rifle had cost Pierre dearly. He obtained it from a Ohio River trader who had wandered up the Wabash with a load of English goods to sell to the French and the Indians who lived in the vicinity of Vincennes. In exchange for his prized rifle the trader relieved Pierre of four hundred pounds of flour, thirty beaver pelts, forty otter pelts, ten jugs of rum, and ten livres in gold. Genevieve had almost passed out from disbelief when she heard the almost obscene cost of the gun. But to Pierre it was worth every bit of the steep payment. The weapon was perfectly balanced and shockingly accurate. He was the envy of all of the other Frenchmen in the militia who manned the British outpost at Fort Sackville.

Pierre should have been on duty already, but he was running well behind the scheduled time for muster. He was not very concerned, though. Like most of the Frenchmen in Vincennes, he was not about to let the clock become his master. Life was too precious and short. Indeed, the relaxed atmosphere and lazy mornings in Vincennes were exactly what had drawn him to the locale in the first place.

Pierre, though he was a successful businessman, was an active member of the local militia. He had served in the citizen-military since his arrival in the Illinois Country. Word had spread quickly in Kaskaskia about his leadership during the attack by the Chickasaw

Indians on Wolf Island. The local militia captain at Fort de Chartres and Prairie du Rocher, Jean-Baptiste Barbeau, recruited Pierre two days after his arrival in Illinois. From that moment forward Pierre's life had been a mixture of business and military. He somehow managed to strike a healthy balance between the two tasks, and over the years he had experienced success in both.

After amassing a modest profit doing business with the local Indians and Spaniards along the Mississippi River, Pierre packed up his family in the autumn of 1772 and moved overland to Vincennes, a small French village on the eastern bank of the Wabash River. Frenchmen had lived and thrived in this remote village for many decades, living peacefully among and having commerce with the many Indian tribes in the area. Pierre moved to the village to establish a new grain mill to grind locally-grown wheat into flour. It was a service that had been long-needed in the community. Pierre's business thrived and soon expanded to three horse-drawn mills. His export business, which served to transport tons of flour and grain downriver to the bread-hungry Frenchmen in New Orleans, grew as well. Of course, all of his river and transport ventures were carried out under the expert guidance of the rugged *voyageur* and Pierre's good friend and partner, Charles Rimbault.

Pierre was, indeed, a patient man. But his patience for waiting on this particular morning finally reached its limit. He tossed his oilcloth onto the table, exhaled loudly, and gazed impatiently toward the front door of the house. He quickly shifted his gaze to his lovely bride. Genevieve reclined in a small rocking chair in the shade of their front porch. She was attempting to absorb every possible whisper of morning coolness from the thick, humid July air. She had been sewing a new baby smock, but now the cloth lay loosely in her lap as she sat peacefully with her eyes closed. Her cheeks were slightly flushed from the heat.

"I swear, woman, your son moves as slowly as the backwaters of the Wabash."

Genevieve never opened her eyes. She quipped, "He moves with as much enthusiasm as his father, I'm afraid, when there is actual labor to be done."

"Are you inferring that I am lazy, *Madame* Grimard?" challenged Pierre, feigning indignation and offense as only a real Frenchman could do.

"I am not inferring anything, dear husband. I am only stating that as the father is, so must be the son. You are the only model of industriousness in his life. I quite imagine that young Pierre is grooming himself to be an entrepreneur and supervisor like his father, not a common laborer like most of the other men of the village." She smiled, eyes still closed.

Pierre climbed quietly and nimbly from his stool and crept toward his wife. He thought that he had managed to successfully sneak up on her but her right eye opened suddenly and aimed directly at him.

"Do you think that you can actually sneak up on me, Pierre Grimard? You sounded like a bull trotting down a cobblestone street."

"I'll show you a bull!"

He descended rapidly upon her. Dropping to his knees beside the chair, he grabbed her sides and tickled her ribs with teasing, wandering fingers. She laughed and squealed with a mixture of anger and delight as she thrashed and kicked against his powerful grip. She placed her hands in his face and tried in vain to push him away.

"Pierre! Stop it this instant!" She giggled as his fingers dug deeper. "You should not treat a woman in my condition in such a way!"

Pierre stopped tickling her and laid his head on her soft, warm belly. He wrapped his powerful arms around her waist and hugged her close, breathing deeply of her pleasant, flowery scent.

"I am sorry, my dear. I was not thinking. I forgot about that."

She tousled his hair and caressed his head in her hands. "Oh, Pierre, it is quite all right. You could never harm me. I pray that you will never want to stop tickling me and touching me."

He lifted his head and met her gaze. He grinned. "I believe this one is a girl. And we will call her Genevieve, because she will be tiny and sweet and beautiful like her mother."

"I certainly hope it is a girl!" she responded. "Lord knows we have enough noisy, messy, stinky, troublesome boys running around here."

Genevieve had given birth five times since their arrival in Illinois. Only three babies survived birth, and all were boys. The first was Pierre, who was baptized by the Vicar General of their diocese, Father Pierre Gibault, on September 1, 1770, in Prairie du Rocher. Pierre and Genevieve had calculated the math and reached the conclusion that little Pierre must have been conceived on Wolf Island on the night before the Indian attack. Genevieve considered the little boy a precious token of God-sent irony and grace … a gift of life in the midst of a place of violence and death.

Jean-Baptiste was baptized on October 22, 1773, shortly after the family's move to Vincennes. He was the namesake of Pierre's close friend and militia commander at Prairie du Rocher. And then there was little Charles. He was baptized on October 17, 1776, by Father Gibault. He was, of course, named after the infamous Charles Rimbault. The ruddy *voyageur* was humbled and at the same time enlarged with pride at the fact that Pierre had named a son after him. Baby Charles was already following in Rimbault's foot-steps. The precocious toddler was bold, fearless, inquisitive, and headstrong. Twice already the little tyke had escaped the Grimard house and disappeared into the dense woods that surrounded Vincennes. The second time he was missing for almost four hours before he was returned by a grinning, painted Piankeshaw Indian warrior who had found the child almost a half-mile away, playing in a large puddle of water. The Indian declared the boy to be, "great in courage and spirit."

The eldest of the boys, his own father's namesake and a rather rambunctious eight-year-old, darted quickly out of the open front door. He was winded and red-faced, holding a black cocked hat in his left hand and a wide leather belt in his right.

"Here I am, Papa! I had a most difficult time finding your belt."

"It was in my trunk, where I always keep it," responded his father.

"No it wasn't, Papa. I looked there first. I finally found it hanging on the nail beneath your capote."

"Oh!" responded Pierre. "I don't remember hanging it there. Most strange …"

"You did not put it there, husband. You left it dangling on the back of one of my dining chairs. I accidentally knocked it off and that gruesome hunting knife popped out of its sheath and almost sliced off my toes. So, I hung it under the safety of your winter capote so that Jean-Baptiste and Charles could not reach it."

"Thank you, my dear."

"You are quite welcome. Try to put things in their place from now on."

"Yes, Mama," Pierre replied, rolling his eyes at his son. Little Pierre covered his mouth and choked back a giggle.

"I saw that!" snapped Genevieve. "I think you had better get to the fort before they hang you for mutiny, or before I string you up for messing up my house and keeping me pregnant all of the time."

Pierre winked at her as he strapped his belt around his waist. He tucked his hunting knife inside the belt on his left side and his tomahawk on the right. He grabbed his rifle off of the table and popped his cocked hat sportily onto his head. As he bounded down the steps from his porch he called over his shoulder, "Woman, I'll be home at noontime for dinner."

"See that you are," she called back. "And do not be late!"

Pierre marched steadily up the street from his house to Fort Sackville. It was a rather puny, pitiful excuse for a fort. Governor Abbott had seen to its construction but then paid little attention to its upkeep or improvements. Captain Bousseron was even less interested in investing French labor and funds to fortify the British outpost.

Truth be told, the Frenchmen served the British cause simply because they had no other choice. They answered to the British governor who was sovereign over them only because of geography and politics. They actually detested many of the tactics of war used by the British. Pierre was heartbroken by the all-too-frequent parade of so-called "prisoners" from Kentucky that the Indians marched regularly through Vincennes on the way to British prison in Detroit. These groups of white settlers, tied in ragged lines by their Shawnee captors, often contained as many women and children as they did men. The British leadership in Detroit was, apparently, paying hefty bounties for the American settlers. Rumors abounded that the British were now also paying a bounty for scalps. That news set the French settlers of the region on edge. Payment for scalps endangered everyone, since the top of one's head did little to identify one's nationality or political allegiances.

Precious few of the Frenchmen in Vincennes held any real allegiance to England. Their true allegiances were to business, profits, prosperity, and liberty. And it was becoming harder and harder to find such things under the sovereignty of King George III.

Pierre heard the crunching of footsteps behind him. Then came a familiar voice.

"Pierre! Wait for me!"

It was his friend and next-door neighbor, Francois Turpin, who was also reporting for the muster. Francois and Josephine had migrated to Vincennes with Pierre and Genevieve. The couple had been wed three days after their arrival at Kaskaskia. The local priest, Father Gibault, had seen the wisdom of a quick marriage for the very pregnant widow. She gave birth to the child of her dead husband in early April. They named the boy Gaspard, in honor of his father. Francois loved the boy very much and raised him as his own. The couple had long believed that they could not have children together until they at long last welcomed another son the previous October. Little Francois was a healthy, active nine-month-old.

"*Bonjour*, Francois. And how are you on this lovely Monday morning?"

"*Bonjour* to you, Pierre. I would be better if I did not have to waste part of my day at this stupid fort. Lord knows I have plenty of other places to be and have much work that needs to be done."

"Josephine is keeping you plenty busy, then?" teased Pierre.

"Always, Pierre!" He was not joking. "God knows I love the woman, but she is a tireless taskmaster, indeed."

"But such a lovely taskmaster, and with good benefits." Pierre winked at his friend.

"True. That is true, *mon amie*. She is, indeed, worth it. She is still my little miracle, dropped out of that deadly cyclone just for me."

"You are quite the miracle, yourself, Francois. You should have never survived those snake bites. I daresay that you two were saved for the purpose of completing one another."

"Indeed," responded Francois. He paused thoughtfully. There was an extended period of awkward silence. "Still, she can be a very harsh and demanding woman."

Pierre laughed. "Then perhaps you should treat our weekly trips to the fort as little holidays of temporary distraction rather than burdens upon your time. It is all about your perspective, Francois."

"I suppose you're right," Francois muttered.

"I know that I am right, old friend. Now, come. Let us report in with the captain and see if we have any unusual or exciting assignments for today."

Francois chuckled. "That would be a first!"

The two men joined about a half-dozen others who were striding through the front gate of the fort. They noticed many others trotting along rather quickly behind them. Inside the fort there was an unusual flurry of activity.

Francois and Pierre looked at one another quizzically.

"Something is not right," declared Pierre. "I've never seen the fort like this. It's so busy."

"What do you think is going on, Pierre?"

"We shall know soon enough. Look." He pointed in the direction of the blockhouse. Captain Bousseron was just emerging from his headquarters. The captain appeared to be on a mission, pointing in different directions and issuing orders to his adjutants.

Suddenly a loud whistle carried across the compound.

One of the officers sounded the call. "Form up, men! Formation in the courtyard! All soldiers of the militia!"

Men scurried from all directions within the fort to gather in the center of the walled compound. A few climbed down from their stations along the tops of the palisade walls. No one seemed to be in a particular hurry, but there was definitely an air of excitement and intrigue inside the fort. It took a few minutes for the seventy-five men to form up in loose lines according to their companies.

Captain Francois Riday Bousseron marched deliberately toward the head of the formation. The captain was a well-known, highly respected, and successful businessman of Vincennes. Born in French Canada, he relocated to Vincennes at a young age. He loved the quaint, quiet village so much that he remained even after the British took control. He operated the largest general store in the town and traded enormous quantities of furs and goods with the local Indians. He was respected by both red and white men, and he was the unanimous choice to be captain of the French militia. He carried the respect and authority of a commander, yet at the same time never forgot that the men under his military command were also his neighbors and friends. He somehow managed to maintain a delicate, perfect balance of those two very different responsibilities in his life.

One of the men shouted from the formation, "Francois! What the hell is going on? You don't actually expect us to play soldier today, do you?"

The other men giggled and howled with laughter. Captain Bousseron smiled sheepishly in response and shook his head in disbelief.

"No playing today, gentlemen. We actually have to do some soldiering. We have received some alarming information."

A quiet hush befell the previously rowdy formation.

"A messenger arrived in the pre-dawn hours this morning bearing news from Kaskaskia and villages to the east. It seems that a force of Americans, Virginians to be precise, have invaded the Illinois Country. The local Indians have taken to calling them the 'Long Knives.' The size of this invading force is unknown, but word has it that they are operating from a central base at the Falls of the Ohio. So we should assume that they are significant in number."

There was an audible gasp from among the men. They had heard the dreaded word, "Virginians." The sound of it struck fear in the hearts of Frenchmen. According to the British all Virginians were bloodthirsty barbarians who killed indiscriminately. The local Frenchmen were afraid of all of the American rebels, but they reserved their greatest fear for the apparently heartless and vile Virginians.

"We have confirmed that the following locales have surrendered to this force: Kaskaskia, Prairie du Rocher, Fort de Chartres, and Cahokia."

There was yet another audible gasp, this time louder, from among the men. Those were all French villages, protected by French militias! Why would the Americans attack there? Why were the Virginians making war upon Frenchmen?

A question emerged from the formation. "How many are dead, *mon Capitaine?*"

Bousseron shook his head. "We do not have any such details, I am afraid. I believe that we must assume the very worst. Therefore, I must declare that the Vincennes militia is now officially called up. You will remain on duty and in a state of vigilant awareness until such time as this threat has been addressed and defeated. In the event that an attack seems imminent, we will, of course, bring our families inside the walls for our common protection. Meanwhile, for the remainder of the day we will see to the needs of our poorly prepared fort. We will shore up defenses, organize and add to our provisions, stockpile lead and powder, and see if there is some way we can figure out how to use these damned cannons." He grinned warmly at his men.

His weak attempt at levity drew a nervous chuckle from only a handful of the men.

Bousseron shrugged. "That is it, men. That is all the news I have for you. Sergeants, see to your companies. Lieutenant Lacroix has your assignments. Please do not wander off and pursue your own interests, men. This is serious. We must respond accordingly. Understood?"

The men mumbled a rather ragged, "*Oui, Monsieur.*"

"Very well, then. Make sure you all come back to the fort after your mid-day meal. For now, you are all dismissed to your duties."

The captain turned and strolled back toward the headquarters building. Pierre shot a look of disbelief at Francois.

"What do you think about all of that?" Francois mused.

"I am not quite sure what to think. I hold no place in my heart for the British. But neither do I wish to have any part of their civil war. This rebellion of their colonies should have no bearing upon us here in Illinois. I do not understand why the American soldiers have come here."

"I daresay it is because of what the British are doing here, Pierre. Do you think, perhaps, that the Virginians have grown weary of these Indian agents of the British kidnapping their citizens off to prison in Detroit? Or perhaps it is Detroit's payment for scalps that has finally brought their armies here. I, for one, cannot blame them," declared Francois.

"Are you saying that you might join in their cause?" challenged Pierre.

Francois mused, "I think that, perhaps, we may all soon be joining in their cause."

"Not likely!" retorted Pierre.

⌇

The men labored all morning on the fortifications. Pierre and Francois' company was assigned the task of repairing the main gate and adding some log barriers just inside the entrance. The other companies repaired portions of the wall where the palisade logs were leaning or otherwise out of place. The heavy labor continued until after noon, when the captain dismissed all of the men for their mid-day meal.

Pierre and Francois trudged down the dusty street toward their homes. As they approached the houses they noticed their wives were together, hovering over a dining table in the Grimard front garden. Little Pierre and Gaspard both ran to meet them.

"Papa! Papa!" exclaimed Gaspard. "Mama has been working with *Madame* Genevieve to prepare a huge meal for us all. They said that you men would be ravenous with hunger from your physical labors."

"Indeed, they are right, my boy! Bring on the food!" teased Francois.

Each boy took his father by the hand and escorted him to the bountiful table prepared in front of the Grimard house. There was a large pot of stewed beef and gravy, a platter stacked high with steaming loaves of fluffy bread, and several bowls of fresh garden vegetables. Tepid ale and hot tea were available to wash down the hearty food.

"Gaspard and I have already eaten, Papa. Will it be all right if we go and play?" begged little Pierre.

Pierre glanced at Francois, who nodded his assent. "Of course, boys. Have fun, and stay out of trouble."

"*Oui*, Papa!" The two boys took off running toward a nearby field.

"Ladies, you have outdone yourselves," proclaimed Pierre. "But what is Francois supposed to eat?"

Genevieve threw a hand towel in his face. "Sit down, Pierre, and stop with your games. Josephine and I have children and other tasks to attend to while you gentleman play soldier this afternoon."

Pierre and Francois plopped down beside one another on the wide bench beside the table.

"Unfortunately, Genevieve, we are not playing soldier this time," responded Francois.

Josephine looked at her husband fearfully. "Then it is true?"

"What have you heard, my darling?"

She responded, "We heard that the Americans are here in Illinois and that they have taken over all of the French towns to the west along the Mississippi River. The word has spread like wildfire throughout Vincennes. Is it, indeed, true?"

Francois and Pierre nodded.

"And are they killing civilians?" demanded Genevieve. "*Madame* Descoteaux said that she heard the Virginians are killing all of the men, taking the woman as slaves for pleasure, and eating the children." Her lip quivered with despair and fear.

Pierre exploded, "Oh, Genevieve! That is nothing but the absurd rambling of a gossipy old woman! No one is eating children! We do not have any word that anyone has been killed, at all. As far as we know, the French militias all surrendered to the Virginians without firing a single shot. We must not jump to conclusions, and we must not be a party to spreading wild stories and rumors. Do you hear me?"

She nodded silently.

"You should know that I would never let anything happen to you or the children. Francois and I, and every Frenchman in this village, would fight to the death to protect you. You know this, don't you?"

Genevieve nodded and smiled.

"Good. Now come, ladies, and let us dine on this fine meal that you have prepared. We have less than an hour before we must report back for duty at the fort."

The two families surrounded the table and attacked the bountiful table. They ate, drank, talked, and laughed. The pleasant meal did much to lift the spirits of the women. Afterwards the children ran off to play while the adults sipped hot tea and continued their conversation. Francois and Pierre pulled out their clay pipes and enjoyed some of the tobacco that Pierre had obtained in a trade the previous autumn with a very odd Kentuckian and frontiersman named Simon Kenton. It was the perfect ending to a delightful dinner.

"Well, I hate to be the one to break up a good party, but we must get back," announced Pierre. "We are probably already late. Let us hope that *Capitaine* Bousseron does not throw us into the stockade!"

The women chuckled at such an absurd notion. They both kissed their husbands and shooed them toward the street. The men grabbed their hats and weapons from beneath a nearby tree and were just opening the front gate to leave when little Pierre and Gaspard suddenly came sprinting toward home along the south road, both of them red-faced and out of breath.

"Papa! Papa!" both boys shouted. "Someone is coming! I think it is Father Gibault. And there is a strange man with him."

"What is the Reverend Father doing here today?" wondered Francois aloud. "He is not due to visit and administer the Sacraments for two more weeks."

Pierre shrugged. "I do not know. Let us go and find out."

Both men trotted down Main Street toward the south, in the direction opposite the fort. Minutes later they saw a small contingent of men on horseback approaching the outskirts of town.

"The boys are correct," affirmed Francois. "That's Father Gibault, all right. And some of the elders from Kaskaskia. I recognize Dr. LaFont. But who is that tall fellow in the middle?"

Pierre strained to see the strange man. Even in the saddle they could see that he was a full foot taller than the men of Kaskaskia who accompanied him. He wore a plain brown weskit over a white shirt and a black hat cocked on the left side and decorated with a white cockade. The man wore buckskin from the waist down and carried a long rifle cradled across his lap.

"Whoever he is, he looks to be armed well," observed Pierre. "Let's go and greet them."

Pierre and Francois walked toward the visitors. When they were about fifty yards away, the Father threw up his hand in an enthusiastic wave of recognition. They witnessed the Father saying something to his companions. Soon the group of men on horseback picked up the pace to a light trot, throwing up a dim haze of dust in their wake. They quickly reached Pierre and Francois on the road.

Pierre greeted the priest, "*Bonjour*, Father Gibault. What brings you to Vincennes at such a curious time?"

"*Bonjour*, Pierre. And *bonjour* to you, Francois. How are your families?"

"They are well, Father. But tell us please, why are you here? Vincennes is in an uproar. We have heard horrible stories of atrocities to the west."

"We are here to deliver the news about recent events along the Mississippi. I and the elders of Kaskaskia come bearing news of the situation in our town."

"We heard that you were invaded by the dastardly Virginians. Is everyone all right in the river villages?"

Father Gibault laughed joyfully. His plump belly jiggled and his face turned bright red. "Oh, Pierre, we are just fine! Everyone is well and uninjured."

"So, the rumors are not true, then?" asked Francois.

"Rumors?" inquired Dr. LaFont, a local physician from Kaskaskia.

"There are all sorts of horrid rumors circulating about the village. Some say that the Americans have killed all of the men, taken the women for their sexual perversions, and even roasted and eaten the children!" replied Francois excitedly.

Francois' enthusiastic outburst elicited a rather uproarious laugh from the strange fellow in the brown weskit and buckskin breeches and leggings. The men from Kaskaskia joined him in the good-natured laughter.

"Those are nothing but childish rumors, Francois," declared the priest. "They are unfounded, I assure you. Now, if you fellows will allow me to make a proper introduction … Pierre Grimard and Francois Turpin, please extend a hand of fellowship to Lieutenant William Asher of the army of Virginia, and a representative of his American commander, Colonel George Rogers Clark."

Francois and Pierre stared with open mouths and wide eyes at the strange, tall foreigner.

⚬

"And you are certain of this information, Father Gibault?" challenged Captain Bousseron. "You have verified the sources?"

The captain stood behind his chair in his small office and faced his guests. The contingent of men from Kaskaskia and their American friend stood in the center of the room and faced the militia commander. Various officers and sergeants lined the chinked log walls. Pierre and Francois, because of their personal discovery of the American soldier, were invited to remain and witness the conference from an obscure corner of the room.

"Yes, Francois," the priest assured Bousseron. "As I have already told you, Colonel Clark presented documents and newspapers from the east to verify his claims. The Kingdom of France declared war against Great Britain on March 17 of this year. Our mother country is, most definitely, at war with England."

"And the Americans have treated you all well?" asked Captain Bousseron as he turned and stared out the minuscule window of his fort headquarters at the curious, anxious faces of dozens of French militiamen standing in the courtyard beyond.

"Oh, quite well, Francois. They restricted our movements at first and naturally, because of the misinformation that had been imposed upon us by the British, we feared the worst. We assumed that we would have our lands and property confiscated and that the men would all be taken to a prison of war. But Colonel Clark has been most kind and generous. He released us from confinement in our homes and then allowed us to choose our own side in their revolutionary conflict. He freely offered an oath of allegiance to Virginia and the United States that most of our citizens readily and wholeheartedly swore. That is why we have come today. Rather than appearing with a fearsome army, Colonel Clark thought it best to send one of his officers and a contingent of local leaders from Kaskaskia to address the leaders and citizens of Vincennes."

"Was there any resistance to their army or to the oath?"

"No military resistance, Francois. Nary a shot was fired in any of our villages or outposts. The handful of Frenchman who bore loyal allegiance to the British Crown fled in the darkness of night. There was one fellow who was caught attempting to get word to the British through a group of hunters. The Americans dealt with him most severely."

The captain pondered his words. "And if we take this oath to Virginia, what then? What will become of our village? What will happen to the fort and our own militia companies?"

The American officer spoke up, "Your companies will remain intact and you will continue as their commander, Captain. Colonel Clark may assign an officer of the rank of captain or higher to assume command of the fort, itself. But you will remain as the liaison for the local militia. Indeed, we will rely upon your militia for the proper defense of this fort and village."

"Are you saying that if we swear your oath we will become soldiers for the American cause?" Captain Bousseron asked bluntly.

"Yes, sir. That is exactly what I am saying. If your men swear their allegiance to Virginia and the Congress of the United States, your people will become citizens of the United States of America and I will, this very day, record your enlistments and place your names on our army payrolls. You will be reimbursed at some point in the future for your service to the government of the United States. I will deliver those documents in person to Colonel Clark at the first possible opportunity."

Father Gibault reasserted his role in the negotiation. He stepped forward and placed his hand on the captain's arm. "Surely you see the wisdom in pursuing this path, Francois. These Long Knives from Virginia are powerful. The rebellion against England is gaining strength. France has chosen the side of the United States and is openly at war with England. These mighty armies are about to clash right here on our very own soil, among our fields and homes. These Virginians have been good to our people and made clear their desire for our freedom and prosperity. They treat us as equals, not as subjects. I urge you to follow the lead of the other villages and take their oath."

The captain turned once again toward the tiny, hazy window and peered at his men outside. Beyond those men, he could see the open gate of the fort, and in the distance, women strolling and children playing in the street. His heart ached over the certain and unavoidable change that lay in store for their picturesque, peaceful Vincennes.

"Francois ... *Capitaine* Bousseron. What are you thinking? What do you intend to do?" asked the Father.

The captain reached for his hat that rested on a nail beside the window. He turned and faced the group.

"Gentlemen, this is not a decision that I can make for an entire village. I know where my sentiments lie. But each man and each family must make their own decision. I will not force a single citizen of Vincennes to conform to my politics ... or to yours, Father." He paused thoughtfully. "We must allow the people to decide for themselves."

The captain nodded toward his officers. "Men, sound the alarm and notify the citizens that there will be a town meeting in one hour. All men age sixteen and older are expected to be present. This meeting will take place at the church ... if that is agreeable with you, Father Gibault."

"Most agreeable, Francois, and an excellent idea," responded the priest.

"Very well then. Off you go, men. Inform the people. In one hour's time, we will convene and choose sides in this war of rebellion against England."

# 12

## AN OATH AND A FLAG

The air inside the tiny church was stifling, and it seemed that the tempers of some of the parishioners were beginning to flare in collusion with the oppressive July heat. The discussion was animated and boisterous. Such was the nature of enormous, life-altering decisions. The men of Vincennes seemed to have reached a diplomatic impasse.

Father Gibault, anxious to avoid potential bloodshed and trauma for his parishioners, tried to bring the meeting to a close and achieve the outcome that he desired. For well over an hour he and Captain Bousseron had entertained multiple questions, comments, and insights. Still, it seemed that the men were a bit on edge and not quite convinced of what they should do. The questions and comments were becoming repetitive and frustrating to the elders and leaders.

The Reverend Father rose and spoke frankly. "Friends, we have been at this for an hour or more, and we are beginning to endure questions already asked and answered. Enough of this incessant, empty talk! The time has come for your decision! Men of Vincennes, I submit to you that there is no need to resist this army from Virginia. I urge you, as souls under my charge, to follow both my counsel and my example and swear by this oath, thus uniting yourselves with the United States of America and the causes of freedom and liberty for which the people of this new nation now fight. If you are willing, I am prepared to administer the oath given me by Colonel Clark. Right here. Right now."

The men in the crowd looked left and right. Many of them cast glances behind them. All were trying to gauge the reactions and intentions of their peers. Everyone was waiting for someone else to "jump" and declare their intent. The men wanted a leader from among their ranks, but no one seemed prepared to take this monumental leap of faith into such radical change of government and allegiance on such short notice and in such a public venue.

Pierre was struggling. He hated the British. That much was certain. His heart still burned with rage from that horrible night nine years previous when he had been forced to kill a British soldier who was attempting to defile his wife. Likewise, he hated the incorrigible officer who tried to cover up the disgrace of the soldier under his command and then sought to have Pierre executed for a supposed crime.

Yet Pierre also feared change. Political change, in particular, frightened him. He was just as confused and worried as all of the other men in the room. But then, quite suddenly, he experienced a clarity of thought and a rush of courage.

He cleared his throat and stood to his feet. "Father, if I may … I have only one final question before I am prepared to render my own decision."

"Yes, Pierre. What is your question?" The portly priest sounded frustrated.

"I need to know the intent of *Capitaine* Bousseron."

He stared at his commander who rested in a chair beside the pulpit. The captain met his gaze.

"That is an excellent query, Pierre," affirmed Father Gibault. He looked at the militia commander. "Francois, one of your men has an important question for you."

Pierre spoke again, this time directly to his captain. "Francois, what would you have us do? What are you planning to do?"

Captain Bousseron breathed a deep, cleansing sigh. He glanced from side to side, capturing the gaze of all of the men. He pursed his lips and at long last rose to his feet.

"Pierre, the decision is surprisingly simple for me. The allegiance of my heart is to Vincennes. The allegiance of my blood is to France. I have absolutely no love for the British ... the pompous, arrogant bastards."

The men erupted into laughter.

The captain flushed from embarrassment. "I'm truly sorry, Father."

"You are forgiven, my son. But see me for confession when we are done with our business."

The men erupted into laughter again.

"Of course, Father. But to continue ... I have no allegiance to King George or Great Britain. I serve them now only because of a treaty signed many years ago and thousands of miles away from here by men I do not know. But here ... today ... I get to make my own choice. I believe, based upon their actions here in Illinois, that the intent of the Americans is liberty and freedom from tyranny. Therefore, I plan to join with their cause. I will swear their oath and join their army."

A rumble of excitement erupted throughout the room. Most of them could not believe the bold proclamation of their captain. Father Gibault's face expanded to accommodate a huge smile.

Pierre looked to his left. His eyes met the gaze of Francois Turpin. His friend smiled and nodded at him with a look of resolve. Francois tilted his head toward Bousseron and the priest. It was a nod of encouragement, affirming Pierre's inclination to be bold and to speak his mind.

Pierre, the lone man standing in the midst of the congregation, called out over the din of the boisterous crowd, "Then, *mon Capitaine*, and men of Vincennes, if you will swear the oath and join the Americans today, then so will I!"

Francois jumped to his feet, "As will I!"

Then, one after another and in rapid succession, every man of Vincennes rose and proclaimed his intent. The moment was electrifying. The room was filled with passion, excitement, and boldness.

Father Gibault called to the American officer, "Lieutenant Asher, you hear the declarations of the men of Vincennes. Do I have your permission to administer the oath?"

"You do indeed, Reverend Father!" The lieutenant held up a piece of parchment. "And once sworn, I ask that each man come forward and add his name to this list of signatories. This will be the document in evidence that I will forward to Colonel Clark."

"Very well, then," replied the priest as he received the paper from the Virginia officer. "Men of Vincennes, please raise your right hands."

The men complied.

"Do you make an oath to the Holy Evangel of Almighty God to renounce all fidelity to George III, King of Britain, and to his successors, and to be faithful and true subjects of the Republic of Virginia as a free and independent state?" The Father paused. "Men, you must say, 'I do.'"

The Frenchmen responded awkwardly, "I do."

"And do you swear that you will not do or cause any thing or matter to be done which may be prejudicial to the liberty or independence of the said people, as prescribed by Congress, and that you will inform someone of the judges of this county of the said state of all treasons and conspiracies which shall come to your knowledge against the said state or some other of the United States of America?"

Again, the men responded, "I do."

The priest beamed with pride. "Very well, then. Citizens of Virginia and the United States of America, come and add your name to this roll."

A great cheer erupted in the room. Benches and chairs scraped against the rough floor as the men clamored toward the front of the room to sign the oath. After they signed the document, the men quickly made their way to the door. They were eager to return to their homes and inform their wives and families about the monumental change that had just come to Vincennes.

Father Gibault and Lieutenant Asher caught Pierre just as he was about to leave the church. The lieutenant offered his handshake to Pierre. "*Monsieur* Grimard, I just wanted to thank you for your words today. Your question came at just the perfect time and was critical in encouraging your commander to stand up and lead."

"I only spoke from my heart, *Monsieur* Asher. I am compelled by honor to follow my commander, therefore I had to know his thoughts and intent."

The lieutenant nodded. "Most wise, *Monsieur*. Most wise indeed." He paused. "Well, one thing is for sure, today's events will certainly be a thorn in the side of Governor Hamilton."

"Governor who?" responded Pierre.

"Governor Henry Hamilton. He is the British official in charge in Detroit. He commands this entire region in the eyes of the British. He is one ruthless bastard ... pays a bounty to the heathens for scalps. We call him the 'Hair Buyer.'"

"Are you talking about Major Henry Hamilton of the British army?"

The lieutenant looked intrigued. "Perhaps. I believe that Hamilton was an officer in the British army for a number of years, but I do not know the rank he attained. I believe he fought against our countrymen on this continent in the Seven Years' War. But a few years ago he resigned his commission and went into politics. He's been governing this entire region for over two years now. Why? Do you know him?"

Pierre was stunned. His face grew pale. He looked at Francois, who stared back at him in wide-eyed disbelief. Pierre nodded numbly at the lieutenant. He began to speak in a dazed, rambling voice. "How did we not know that Henry Hamilton was governor in Detroit? Did you know this, Francois?"

His friend frowned grimly and shook his head.

"I ... I had absolutely no idea," Pierre stammered. "The only Englishman we dealt with here was Governor Abbott. He was a nice enough and likable fellow."

The lieutenant responded, "Well, Henry Hamilton is no likable fellow. He is a vindictive, evil, bloodthirsty arse."

Pierre met the man's gaze. "As well I know, Lieutenant. If you will excuse me ..."

He turned without further comment and walked away, leaving a confused priest and an even more confused American officer in his wake. Francois followed closely behind. They exited the building and walked slowly toward their homes. As they proceeded they mulled the events of the day in their minds. Neither of them, when they rolled out of their beds that morning, anticipated being citizens of another nation before supper time. Neither of them had any idea that they would become involved in a faraway war of rebellion against Great Britain. And neither of them ever guessed that they would once again be dealing with the likes of Major ... now Governor ... Henry Hamilton. The weight of the decision and the events of the day grew heavier upon Pierre's heart with each step toward home.

He spoke blandly as he stared straight ahead, "Francois, I hope we did the right thing."

"It was the right thing to do, Pierre. You will see."

꙰

*August 6, 1778*
*Fort Detroit*

"Who has invaded the Illinois Country?" screamed Governor Hamilton.

"Rebels under the command of one Colonel George Rogers Clark," responded his adjutant, Major Jehu Hay.

"Who, in God's name, is George Rogers Clark?" screeched the exasperated governor.

"He is a young rebel officer out of Virginia, sir. Apparently, his entire army is comprised of Virginians, all of them operating from a clandestine base near the Falls of the Ohio. It seems that the entire lot of them are unkempt, ungentlemanly, bloodthirsty savages."

The governor's mind reeled. He had never anticipated an attack on his far western flank. All of his attention had been on the east and the taking of Fort Pitt in the wilderness of Pennsylvania. He had long assumed that his payments to the Indians and their constant, harassing raids on the settlements in Kentucky would keep the American forces in check along the Kentucky and Illinois frontiers.

The governor plopped down into his chair and took a quick drink of the dark, fragrant brandy that still lingered in his crystal glass. His face reddened with anger and embarrassment. This impudent Colonel Clark had caught him napping. Henry Hamilton could not allow such an insult to stand unanswered!

"How much damage has been done? What are our losses?" he asked Major Hay.

"I am afraid that the losses are quite extensive sir. All of the French villages along the Mississippi and Wabash Rivers have surrendered to the rebels."

"Including Vincennes?"

"Yes, sir. It was the last to succumb."

"Did the French fight well?"

The major did not respond. He stared sullenly at the rough, gray floorboards beneath his feet.

"Major, I asked you a question. Did the French fight well? How many casualties?"

The major cleared his throat. "Well, Governor ... there were no casualties. All of the towns were surrendered without actual combat. Apparently, the towns along the Mississippi were taken by surprise at night. Vincennes surrendered after a brief negotiation."

Henry Hamilton seethed. He cursed and then spat on the floor.

"I might have known as much!" he thundered. "Damned simple-minded, selfish, cowardly French!" He pounded his fist on his desk. "I warned London! I told them repeatedly of the dangers to our west, and they have either scoffed at me or ignored me! Now look at our predicament. The entire frontier is exposed. Our Indian allies will be driven from the country. Sooner or later Spain will enter this war, no doubt on the side of the rebels, and will sail convoys of troops right up the Mississippi."

He took another swig of his fiery brandy.

"Major, we cannot allow this to stand. We will liberate those villages from the rebel horde, starting with Vincennes."

"Of course, sir. What are your orders?"

"All provisions earmarked for the invasion of Fort Pitt are to be re-routed to action in the west. We must field an army as rapidly as possible. Since my authority does not extend to the regular army here in Detroit, we will be required to assemble a force from volunteers."

"Our pool of volunteers among the British subjects is limited, Governor. Will we supplement our army from the ranks of the red men?"

Hamilton sighed. "Yes, Major. Of course. We have no choice. Just make sure that they are Indians that we can control."

"Indeed, sir. I will begin posthaste, but it may take some time. I daresay it will take until spring to assemble such an army and arrange the necessary logistics."

"Two months, Major."

"I beg your pardon, sir?"

"Two months. That is the maximum that I will allow. Assemble the army, bateaux, canoes, and supplies. Do not dawdle. We launch the first week in October."

"'We,' sir?"

Henry Hamilton fixed his blank, steely gaze upon the major. "I will lead this expedition myself, Major Hay."

❧

*August 7, 1778*
*Fort Sackville - Vincennes*

The American officer rode through the gates of the fort at mid-morning without announcement or fanfare. He was accompanied by two other Virginians, one of whom was the familiar Lieutenant William Asher. The three men trotted their horses in the direction of the headquarters shack.

Captain Bousseron was reclining at his desk and reading the report from the morning patrol. As usual, there was absolutely nothing of alarm or interest. The door popped open and one of the militiamen stuck his head into the office.

"Francois, three riders have entered the fort. One is Lieutenant Asher. One of the others appears to be his superior."

"*Merci*, Rene. I will be out shortly."

The militiaman nodded and closed the door.

Captain Bousseron resolved himself to go out and meet the new commander of the fort. He dreaded the awkward nature of the entire situation, and hoped that the American officer would be an agreeable fellow. Francois did not know if his French comrades could withstand an uptight, regulation-obsessed, career military commander. He fetched his hat from the nail on the wall, walked to the door, took a deep breath, and lifted the latch.

A boisterous voice thundered the moment he stepped out of the door. "Captain Bousseron! I am thrilled to finally meet you!"

The American officer approached Bousseron with a friendly air of confidence. His hand was outstretched as he walked, eager to shake the hand of his French counterpart.

Francois stammered, "I ... I am afraid that you have me at a disadvantage, sir."

Lieutenant Asher intervened. "*Capitaine* Francois Bousseron, allow me to introduce you to Captain Leonard Helm of the Illinois Regiment of Virginia. Colonel Clark has dispatched him to take command of this fort."

The two officers shook hands as they examined and sized up one another.

"This other gentleman," added the lieutenant, "is Private George Williams. He has volunteered to assist the captain and myself in our duties at this post, primarily in the role of messenger and runner."

"Indeed," responded Francois, nodding to the private. "Captain Helm, gentlemen, welcome to Fort Sackville."

"Ahh … that is incorrect, sir," responded Helm.

"Pardon me?"

"Colonel Clark has discarded that name. He considered it inappropriate that it should continue to sport a title of British choosing. He has officially re-designated this post with the name Fort Patrick Henry, in honor of the great governor of Virginia."

Bousseron nodded. A name change made sense. He had no idea who Patrick Henry was, but he certainly had no objection to renaming the fort.

"Very well, then, Captain Helm. Fort Patrick Henry it is. Won't you come inside? I will, of course, vacate my office and surrender it to you as the commandant of this post."

"Oh, no, Captain Bousseron," objected Helm. "I would not dream of displacing you from your headquarters. I am quite sure that I can find other accommodations within the fort. I would like to have a space that could be utilized both for my command office as well as my own personal quarters. Is there such a space available?"

"Certainly, sir." He pointed across the compound. "The ground floor blockhouse on the northeast corner is spacious and well-suited for your purposes. We have a few items stored in there, but I can have my men remove them to another location forthwith."

"That would be most excellent, Captain. Meanwhile, would you care to show me the fort and brief me on its defense?"

"Of course, Captain Helm."

"Then, perhaps, we can find us a hot dinner and a jug of rum?" inquired Captain Helm. "We have friendships to forge and stories to tell." Captain Helm's rugged face beamed with levity and friendliness.

Bousseron's face broke out into a broad smile. He liked this American. He could already tell that they were going to get along in grand fashion.

*August 21, 1778*
*The Outskirts of Vincennes*

Pierre watched with satisfaction as the team of four horses trudged slowly and methodically in their perpetual counter-clockwise circle, rotating the main shaft that delivered power to the crude mill's grinding wheel. He never ceased to be amazed at how this group of slow-walking animals could deliver so much torque to the system of shafts and gears that delivered power to the heavy millstone. He could hear the stone crunching and pulverizing the wheat on the other side of the stone wall.

Francois Turpin popped his head around the corner. "We're getting a good cut on the grain, Pierre, but the pieces are still a little large. We'll have to run it through again."

"As usual," remarked Pierre. "Such is the nature of a horse-driven mill."

"I suppose. If only we could figure out how to build a mill on the river and harness the power of the Wabash," dreamed Francois.

"Someone would first have to figure out how to keep the Wabash within its banks," countered Pierre with a chuckle.

"It's just good to be back at work, isn't it?" declared Francois.

"It certainly is, my friend. And we have plenty of work to accomplish. Just look at the wheat piled up in our shed!"

The men listened contentedly to the familiar sounds of the mill. They were thrilled that life had returned to a somewhat more familiar pattern. The men of the militia were spending less and less time at the fort. Captain Helm established a rotating schedule of duty so that the men could return to their normal lives, jobs, and routines as much as possible. Since Pierre's mills were considered critical to the provision of food for the region, he was allowed to spend significantly less time on guard duty and devote more hours to grain processing.

It helped that Captain Helm was extremely relaxed in his military bearing and expectations. He had pretty much stopped work on the fort improvements that Captain Bousseron had initiated. The affable American officer seemed more interested in hot meals, copious amounts of rum, and the pursuit of romantic interests among the local women than he was in the defense of Fort Patrick Henry. The lack of preparations caused some minor concerns for Captain Bousseron, but it delighted the other Frenchmen in the village. They simply wanted to return to their farming, hunting, and trapping. The had sworn their oaths, and were happy to do so. But it seemed that the war was now hundreds of miles away. There had been no sign of the British in their region since the Long Knives came. For the Frenchmen of Vincennes, it was a case of "out of sight, out of mind."

"How is Genevieve? Is her health good? Is the pregnancy difficult for her?" inquired Francois.

"She is in excellent health. The sickness in the morning ended last month. She gets a little tired in the afternoons and has to nap, but she was the same with all of the other babies."

"When is she due to deliver?"

"We suspect early January, if she has calculated correctly."

"Right in the middle of winter. That's a tough time."

"Indeed," agreed Pierre. "But our house is tight and warm. She and the baby will be fine. Besides, we may not even have much of a winter to speak of this year. You know how mild the seasons have been for three or four years now."

"Let us hope so," responded Francois. "And let us hope that Hamilton stays in Detroit and leaves us Frenchmen on the frontier alone."

"I'll drink to that, brother. Now let's focus on turning this grain into some delicious, white flour. There will be big profits in our surplus come springtime. We want to make sure that Rimbault has plenty of barrels and sacks to fill his flatboats."

*October 4, 1778*
*Fort Patrick Henry - Vincennes*

"A flag?" inquired Captain Bousseron.

"Yes, Captain! A flag!" responded Captain Helm. "That's what this post needs ... a unique flag that demonstrates the area's allegiance to Virginia and the United States."

"But we do not have an American flag," countered the French officer. "And we do not even know what one looks like."

"It has thirteen stripes to denote the thirteen states," answered Helm.

"That does not help much," retorted Bousseron. "Besides, serge cloth is very rare here, indeed. And that is what you would need for a flag. We may not be able to find cloth in the colors that you require."

Captain Helm responded, "We would need red, white, and blue serge. Those are the colors of our nation's flag."

Bousseron shook his head. "Impossible. There is no blue to be found. I can tell you that right now. I have never seen it used in Vincennes. Likely there is no white, either."

"Well then, what colors do you think may be available?"

"*Madame* St. Marie recently completed a project for me using red serge. That is most likely the color of cloth that will be readily available. After that, your guess is as good as mine. We may be able to find some green."

"Green? There is no green in the American flag!"

"So you say, but those are the two colors that you are likely to find around here. They actually represent our area very well. Local Indian tribes trade in wampum that is red and green. It has long signified the colors of the Wabash River."

"Is that so?" pondered Helm. "Then that just may be the perfect answer. A simple flag of thirteen stripes of alternating red and green. It will be the Fort Patrick Henry flag!"

"Are you willing to spend significant money for such a flag? The cloth will be expensive, as well as the seamstress costs."

"Of course, of course," remarked Captain Helm. "Whatever it takes. I will issue a certificate of reimbursement, payable by the state of Virginia."

Francois Bousseron raised an eyebrow. He was beginning to grow weary of these certificates from Colonel Clark's army. They already owed his general store well over three thousand livres gold, and Bousseron had never seen a single coin of gold, silver, or copper. In every instance, all he received was a piece of paper written by Captain Leonard Helm acknowledging the debt. Interestingly, a noticeable portion of that debt was for liquor and food consumed by Helm and his other two men. It was quite remarkable how the three Virginians were putting such a significant dent in the local stores and supplies. Francois was beginning to wonder if he would ever be adequately reimbursed for what he already had invested in this American army.

"That will be all, Captain Bousseron. Please see to it. I want to see that flag flying by the end of the next week."

"Yes, Captain Helm. I will contact the ladies immediately."

The following day Francois Bousseron hired *Madame* Marie Goderre as seamstress for the Fort Patrick Henry flag at a rather handsome sum of twenty-five livres gold. She managed to locate five *elles* of red serge and almost four *elles* of green serge at the hefty price of eighty-two livres in gold. Madame Goderre recruited three other women to help in the project and they completed their work in a remarkably short period of time.

Less than a week later the large, beautiful flag of seven red and six green stripes flew high atop the pole of Fort Patrick Henry. The massive banner measured almost seven feet across. There was even enough cloth left over for a smaller flag, which the captain placed on a pole beside the small dock on the bank of the Wabash.

⚜

*November 14, 1778*
*Between the Maumee and Wabash Rivers*

"Governor, the men are desperate for rest," pleaded Major Hay. "This portage is over nine miles, and we have goods that are measured in tons. The men, especially the Indians, are at the very edge of mutiny."

Governor Hamilton glanced behind him at the haggard men. "I will not tolerate their rebellion, Major. Mutineers will be shot on site."

"It is not their spirits or their loyalties that are in question, Governor. It is their bodies. Many of the men are injured. Several are ill. Moving these boats and goods over land is excruciating work. The men are physically exhausted. I beseech you, sir, to call a temporary stop. Just one day of rest would do wonders to lift the spirits of these men."

"That would give our enemy the advantage of one more day of preparation, Major."

"But, sir, our spies in Vincennes have revealed that there are only a handful of the rebels in the fort. The majority of the men on duty are the Frenchmen, who will most certainly flee at the sight of our army." He paused and allowed his logic to sink in.

"Sir, Vincennes will be just as ripe for the picking one day later in December. Fort Sackville is not going anywhere, Governor. Please, sir ... allow these men some rest. Let us build fires and cook a hot meal."

Governor Hamilton looked again down the long column that stretched for almost a half-mile to the east. He saw the fatigue and desperation on the faces of his men. He breathed a long, deep, cleansing breath.

"Very well, Major Hay. Halt the column and make camp. We will rest for the remainder of the day today and all of tomorrow. We will proceed the following morning. Good enough?"

Major Hay smiled and saluted his commander. "Most excellent, sir. I will inform the men."

✑

*December 10, 1778*
*Fort Patrick Henry - Vincennes*

Captain Helm huddled by the tiny fireplace in his quarters. The night was bitterly cold. There could be no doubt that winter had arrived in full force. He pulled the wool blanket a little tighter around his shoulders as he waited for Captain Bousseron to arrive. It was not long before he heard the hollow knock at his door.

"Come!"

The door opened and Bousseron entered, removing his cocked hat and peeling off his gloves as he strode toward the fire.

"Good evening, Leonard. My, it is a cold one!"

"Indeed, it is, Francois. Have a seat. Grab a cup and help me dispose of some of this rum."

"I believe I will."

Bousseron detoured to his left to retrieve a cup from Helm's desk. He poured himself a generous dose of rum from the bottle that sat beside it. He soon joined the other officer beside the crackling fire. Leonard Helm wasted no time in addressing the reason that he asked for this late evening meeting.

"Francois, I just received dispatches this evening from Colonel Clark. Our spies in the North have passed along some disturbing news about a British force out of Detroit headed in this direction. The word comes through one of the more remote Indian tribes along the Maumee River. That would mean that they are headed for the Wabash, and moving on Vincennes."

Francois grunted and stared into the fire. "I cannot imagine that the British would launch an expedition of such great distance at the onset of winter." He stared at Captain Helm. "Do you believe that these reports are reliable?"

"I doubt it. I daresay it is probably just one of these savage tribes attempting to sow a little fear and mayhem among out forces. But Colonel Clark has ordered that we investigate."

"He wants patrols?" asked Francois.

Captain Helm nodded. "Daily patrols to the north along the Wabash and lookouts posted several miles upriver."

"That remote outpost duty will be frigid and perilous," remarked Captain Bousseron.

"I know. But it is necessary. I need you to see to it, Francois. Four-man patrols starting tomorrow and a single long-range patrol deployed five miles upriver with well-horsed runners to notify us in case a British fleet were to come floating down the Wabash ... as unlikely as that may seem."

"Very well, Captain Helm." Francois stood and drained his cup. "I will take care of it. The first patrols will depart in the morning."

"Thank you, Francois." Leonard Helm shook hands with his French counterpart. "If we don't see anything over the next week or so we will put a stop to this nonsense."

*December 15, 1778*

*Outpost on the Wabash River - Four Miles North of Vincennes*

"Pierre, how, exactly, did you aspire to this horrible assignment?" asked Francois Turpin.

"I took Bousseron's promotion to sergeant," Pierre Grimard responded with a hollow, dispassionate voice. "I thought it was a good thing, until the next words out of his mouth were, 'Good. Now you will lead the northernmost patrol.'"

"That is what you get for agreeing to be in charge of anything," Francois chided him.

"Well, if I am so stupid, then why are you here, Francois?"

"Because I always go wherever you go, you moron."

The other two men who huddled with them beside the tiny fire burst into laughter.

"Oh, so you think that is funny, Rene? And you, as well, Desmond? We will see how funny it is when I send all three of you a mile further north in the morning, all the way to the mouth of Maria Creek."

The laughter ceased abruptly. The other three men stared at one another and barely breathed.

Desmond hissed, "He is not serious, is he Francois?"

This time Pierre burst into boisterous laughter.

"Actually, gentlemen, all of us are moving to that location in the morning. There is a large western bend in the river there and a much better vantage point," Pierre clarified.

"I thought that perhaps we might be heading back to Vincennes in the morning," mused Rene.

"Three more days, gentlemen. Just three more days, and then we will head back home to our warm houses," Pierre responded.

"And our even warmer women," quipped Desmond.

"Speak for yourself," griped Pierre. "My Genevieve is about to burst with child. She has swollen legs and feet and is absolutely miserable. She has gotten to where she runs me out of the house if

I cast an even remotely romantic look at her. I've been sleeping on the floor in front of the fireplace for two months now. Once this baby comes out she may never allow me to lay a hand on her again."

The men around the fire chuckled at Pierre's musings. They were all very familiar with the tribulations of pregnant wives.

Pierre sighed. "But it will still be good to get home. I miss my boys."

The men grumbled their agreement.

"Let us get some sleep, gentlemen. Rene, you have first watch."

Rene threw a flimsy salute toward Pierre. *"Oui, Sergent!"*

The clicks of a dozen or more flintlocks shattered the stillness of the winter night.

A shrill English voice called from the darkness of the trees, "All right, you Frenchies! Hands in the air. We have you surrounded, so do not attempt anything heroic."

Francois whispered to Pierre, "What do we do?"

Pierre raised his hands into the air. "We do as they say."

All four Frenchmen of the patrol raised their hands high into the air. Moments later ten white men and almost as many Indians materialized from out of the darkness. Six of the white men appeared to be French. The other four wore the distinctive red coats of the British army.

# 13

## OLD ENEMIES

*December 16, 1778*
*British Camp on the Wabash River - Eleven Miles North of Vincennes*

Pierre winced as the guard knocked him down onto the frozen, hard ground. His right hip and shoulder throbbed from the impact. With his hands tied behind his back it was completely impossible to do anything to break the blow of the fall. Moments later his compatriots landed in a haphazard pile on top of him as the enemy soldiers tossed them to the ground, as well. The men kicked and wiggled to separate themselves.

"What will they do with us, Pierre?" whispered Rene nervously.

"No talking among the prisoners!" barked one of the red-coated guards.

Pierre smiled reassuringly at his friends and nodded with confidence. He tried to calm them with his countenance, but it was difficult to give a convincing performance. Pierre was, himself, terrified beyond measure.

The captive Frenchmen shivered from the bone-chilling cold. They were soaking wet from being dragged into the water of the river and then tossed into Indian canoes. The British soldiers, assisted by their Indian and French Canadian allies, had paddled upriver all night to reach their base camp. During that time, the prisoners received no cover or protection from the winter cold. The exposure to the elements was torturing. A deep chill had set into their limbs and bones. Pierre could not feel his own hands or feet. As they sat alone in the waning darkness he could hear Francois' teeth chattering violently from several feet away. Poor Desmond was unconscious, having passed out from exposure at some point during the frigid trip upriver.

The dull glow of dawn was just beginning to break over the British camp. Pierre studied his surroundings in a attempt to assess their situation. He counted two dozen fires and roughly seventy white men, a combination of British and northern French, in the area immediately around him. Approximately one hundred yards away there was a separate Indian camp occupied by hundreds of natives. He could see dozens of bateaux, canoes, and pirogues tied to small trees along the riverbank. Pierre shuddered at the sheer immensity of the enemy force.

Pierre heard some boisterous laughter and voices with a distinctively French Canadian accent coming from the opposite side of the clearing. A group of French-speaking men surrounded one of their comrades, slapping him on the back and congratulating him on his good fortune. Then Pierre realized the object of their congratulatory celebration. The Canadian held Pierre's prized Jacob Dickert Pennsylvania long rifle in his grimy, muddy hands. He had claimed and taken it as a war prize. Pierre felt the sinking sensation of heartbreak deep inside his chest. His precious long rifle appeared lost.

A deep voice interrupted his mourning and captured his attention. The voice spoke in very proper, educated French. "Who is in command of this patrol?"

Pierre snapped his head toward the sound of the voice. It was a distinguished-looking uniformed British officer.

The man sighed somewhat impatiently. "I ask you again, who is in command of this patrol?"

"I am, sir. My name is Sergeant Pierre Grimard."

"Where are you and your men from, Sergeant?"

Pierre stared at the man with a rebellious resolve. "I do not believe that we have been properly introduced, sir."

The British officer smiled warmly. "Of course. Please pardon my ill manners, *Monsieur* Grimard. I have been in this wilderness with these savages for far too long. I am Major Jehu Hay, adjutant and deputy commander serving our noble Lieutenant Governor Henry Hamilton."

Pierre's innards wrenched at the mention of Hamilton's name. He tasted bile in the back of his mouth.

The officer continued, "Now ... remind me ... what is your given name? Pierre?"

Pierre nodded subtly in response.

"Please, Pierre, tell me the name of your village and the militia that you represent."

"I am not going to tell you anything, Major, until my men are cared for. Your soldiers herded us into the frigid water of the river before they dumped us into their canoes. We traveled all night without any blankets or other protection from the weather." His teeth chattered mildly. "I have one man who is already unconscious. Indeed, he may be dead. Surely this is not how the Crown treats prisoners taken without resistance."

Major Hay stepped forward and examined the men. He bent over and felt of Desmond's face and neck.

"You are quite right, Pierre. This man is alive, but barely." He pivoted and called over his shoulder to a cluster of men gathered around a large campfire. "Lieutenant Moore, remove the bindings from these men and relocate them to your fireside! And find some blankets and rum. One of these Frenchmen is almost dead." He turned back toward Pierre. "Please pardon the barbarity, *Monsieur*. We will have you in a comfortable, warmer environment in just a moment. I will also have my men prepare hot broth and tea. We will get you warmed up, and then we will speak in just a little while. But rest assured ... we will not be leaving this camp until you and your men have been properly interrogated."

Pierre nodded. "I am grateful for your kindness and attention to our needs, *Monsieur.*"

The officer nodded and smiled as he rose and walked away.

Minutes later the uniformed soldiers cut the ropes from their wrists and escorted the prisoners to the location commanded by the major. Two of them dragged the unconscious Desmond and deposited him near the fire. The Frenchmen felt the immediate relief from the roaring flames as they warmed their flesh and bones. Pierre's feet and hands began to burn with the fire of a thousand pin pricks as the flesh began to thaw. Then the pain began. It worked its way into their members as their circulation returned to normal. The men fought through the discomfort of their thawing skin and flesh as they soaked up the life-renewing heat.

A few minutes later soldiers brought blankets and hot tea spiked with a healthy dose of spicy rum. Desmond awakened after a short while, but he said nothing. He merely stared blankly into the fire. Rene and Francois finally coaxed him to take some sips of the rum and tea. The color slowly began to return to his pallid cheeks. The warmth of the fire, combined with the alcohol in the rum, relaxed their limbs and their minds. One by one the men stretched out beside the fire. Within minutes all of them were asleep.

🐚

"Wake up, gentlemen!"

Pierre rose slowly and struggled to shake away the fog of slumber that clouded his mind.

Major Hay spoke, "You fellows have been sleeping for almost an hour. I trust that you all feel better after your brief rest?"

Pierre nodded. "*Oui, Monsieur.* We are most grateful for the reprieve."

"You will find, Pierre, that soldiers of the British Crown are, above all else, gentlemen. We hold very high opinions of the protocols and rules of war."

"Does that include paying bounties for prisoners and the scalps of settlers from Kentucky?" chirped Francois.

Major Hay glared at Francois, obviously perturbed by his insolence. After a long, uncomfortable period of staring, he shifted his eyes to Pierre.

"*Monsieur* Grimard, you will come with me, please. The governor wishes to be included in your interrogation."

"The governor?" asked Pierre nervously.

"Yes. Governor Hamilton is in his headquarters awaiting our arrival. Now, come, please. Time is of the essence."

Pierre used his arms to help push himself up into a squatted position. His legs were still somewhat numb and his right knee was very stiff. He took a moment to balance himself and then rose to his feet. Once he knew that he had mastered his balance and regained command of his legs, he turned to face the major.

"I hope that we can all behave as gentlemen, Pierre. You strike me as a man of honor. Therefore, I have chosen not to bind your hands again or secure extra guards. I pray that I am correct in my assessment of your character."

"You are, indeed, Major. I pose no threat to you. I promise not to attempt any violence or escape. I just want to go home."

Major Hay smiled warmly. "That is what I thought. Come with me, Pierre."

The two men walked slowly toward a medium-sized marquee tent near the western edge of the encampment. Pierre's heart and mind raced as they neared the open flap on the tent. Would Hamilton recognize him? Would he even recognize Hamilton, for that matter?

The major held the linen of the tent to one side. "After you, Sergeant."

Pierre dipped his head slightly as he entered the tent. The inside of the shelter was bright from the light of almost a dozen candles. It was warm, as well, no doubt from the small wood stove that glowed near the rear wall. Henry Hamilton sat in a folding chair in front of a beautiful chestnut camp desk. He was scribbling a note with his quill on a small piece of paper. Pierre recognized the man immediately. There could be no doubt. It was the evil officer from Fort Panmure in 1769.

The governor peeked over the top of his reading glasses. "Ahh! Major Hay … you have one of our guests. Most excellent!" He folded the paper in his hand and placed it in a small basket on his desk. "Welcome, gentlemen. Sit." He motioned to a small, crude bench that sat along the wall of the tent near his desk.

"I do apologize for the lack of comfortable seating. It seems that a simple bench is the best that I can provide in this rugged environment."

The governor stood and moved his chair to face his guests and then sat down again. He fetched a teacup from the table beside him and then crossed his legs comfortably. He also retrieved a document from the same table.

"Let us begin. *Monsieur* Pierre Grimard, I understand that you are the sergeant in command of your patrol and a member of your local militia. Where is your home?"

Pierre stared at the table beside Hamilton, trying as best he could to avoid looking into the man's eyes. He remained silent.

"Come now, Sergeant Grimard. I am not asking you to divulge any military secrets. I am merely inquiring as to the vicinity of your home and headquarters. You are from Vincennes, no?"

Pierre's eyes darted at the governor. For the first time they made significant eye contact. The governor read Pierre's response and emotion. He slapped a hand in victory on his knee.

"Yes! Of course, you are from Vincennes. No doubt on a long-range patrol tasked with detecting the advance of our forces and notifying the Virginians in command at Fort Sackville."

Pierre's eyes widened. How much did the British know about Vincennes?

Hamilton seemed to discern the question in Pierre's mind. "Oh yes, *Monsieur*, we know all about the events that have transpired in your village. We know that the men of Vincennes have all sworn oaths to the rebel cause. And we know that a mere handful of the rebel Virginia soldiers are lodged at the fort. The remainder of the forces there are your local militiamen."

Hamilton uncrossed his legs and leaned forward toward Pierre. "So, you are, indeed, from Vincennes. Correct?"

Pierre nodded glumly.

"And what do you do in Vincennes? What is your vocation?"

"I am a miller. I own several small, horse-drawn mills that process the grains grown in our region."

"Really? That is very interesting. Then you provide the flour for your fellow Frenchmen to cook their delicious bread and pastries?"

"*Oui*, Governor. And for trade in areas to the south, primarily in Louisiana."

"And you ship by boat to New Orleans?"

"*Oui, Monsieur.* And to other places along the river."

"Excellent! Good for you, *Monsieur* Grimard. You have done quite well for yourself on this frontier, then? You prospered under British rule?"

"My family is healthy and happy. We enjoy our life here."

"And are you a native of Louisiana or Canada? Your accent is difficult to discern."

"I am a native of France, *Monsieur.* I immigrated here a long time ago."

"Well, you certainly have an interesting story, *Monsieur.* Now tell me ... how far from Vincennes are we now?"

"I do not know," Pierre answered honestly. "We were approximately five or six miles north of our village when your men surprised us in our camp. But we traveled many hours during the night in the bottom of a canoe with our hands bound behind our backs. I had no way to maintain my bearings."

Hamilton nodded. "The location of your capture tells me all that I need to know." He looked at Major Hay. "We are only ten, perhaps eleven, miles from Vincennes, Major. We will be upon them tomorrow!"

Major Hay nodded. "Indeed. At long last the journey is almost complete. But what shall we do with these prisoners, sir?"

Pierre looked fearfully at the Major, and then glanced subtly at Governor Hamilton.

Hamilton chuckled and reassured him, "Do not worry, *Monsieur*. We intend you no harm. We want to see you back home in Vincennes and living your life as a loyal British subject. I look forward to enjoying some of the delicious products of your mill this very winter." He addressed the major. "The prisoners will accompany you and our British and French troops to Vincennes. You may release them after the fort is pacified. We will administer a new oath to the men of the village once your detachment has contained the rebellion there."

"Are we dividing our forces, sir?"

"Indeed, we are, Major. You will lead the British and French troops to Fort Sackville and demand its surrender. I will remain here with most of our Indian allies. I will send two scouting parties of Indians toward the southwest in order to cut off any possible messengers the Americans in Vincennes may attempt to send to Kaskaskia. We do not want any of the Indians near Vincennes. We both know how they would behave and what they might do if they were unleashed on the village. These savages would pillage, murder, steal, and rape. But hear me clearly, and understand … if the rebels or the Frenchmen there offer any resistance, at all, then I will bring these Indians downriver and we will utterly destroy Vincennes. I will allow them to have their way with its people."

"You will put your demands and your ultimatum in writing, Governor?" asked the major.

"Indeed, I will, Major Hay." He looked coyly at Pierre. "But, then, I am quite sure that *Monsieur* Grimard and his comrades will be very handy in communicating our intentions. Won't you, Sergeant?"

Pierre nodded in defeat and shame. "*Oui, Monsieur.* I will tell my countrymen of your plans. Our people will not desire for your savages to be unleashed on our town and families. We will obey your commands and do as you require."

"Just as I suspected," commented the governor in a haughty, condescending tone. "Like I told you, Major, these Frenchmen will roll over and play fetch for whoever provides them with wood, wheat, and wine. They are not men who are apt to fight or stand upon any foundation of principle or honor. They never have been."

The governor stood. Major Hay rose in response to his commander's lead. He grabbed Pierre's arm and helped lift him to his feet.

"Yes, sir," responded the major. "If it pleases the governor, I will see that the prisoners and our troops are fed and prepared for the journey. We will depart within the hour and make camp a few miles upriver from Vincennes tonight. We will take the fort in the morning."

"Excellent," affirmed the governor. "I will follow downriver tomorrow and hold off two miles to the north. I will proceed to Vincennes once I receive word from your scouts that the fort has fallen. At that point in time I will redirect our Indian friends to other locations."

Pierre, in a moment of courage, allowed his judgment to lapse. He had thus far played a good game of submission before his British captors. But the governor's comments about his countrymen and the flood of memories from nine years previous at Fort Panmure seized his heart and soul. Pierre looked directly into the governor's eyes and his gaze converted, for a brief moment, from fear and trepidation into utter hate, vitriol, and rebellion. Just as his angry gaze fixed on Hamilton, the major tugged at his arm and began to direct him toward the exit.

"Hold on, Major!" barked the governor. He stared at Pierre with a puzzled look. "Frenchman, what is your name again?"

Pierre kept his eyes fixed on the British commander. "Pierre Grimard, *Monsieur.*"

"Have we met before, Grimard? You suddenly seem very familiar to me."

Pierre did not respond. He just kept staring blankly past the governor.

"Did you serve your nation in the last war, perhaps? Is that what brought you to America? We faced one another in battle, did we not?"

"I have never served in the military, Governor. I am a businessman, nothing more."

"And yet I cannot escape the notion that I know you from somewhere. Just as you rose to leave you cast a most rebellious look in my direction. I saw in you a glimpse of anger and disdain ... a measure of courage and rebellion. And it looked strangely familiar to me."

He stepped closer to Pierre. Their noses almost touched.

"I recognize you from somewhere, boy. Tell me immediately, Pierre Grimard, how do we know one another?"

Pierre remained silent. The governor spun around and paced to and fro in front of his desk. He mumbled short words and phrases as he searched the distant memories that lay dormant in the depths of his mind. He was trying to take the tiny pieces of fact that he had gleaned from Pierre and assemble them into the puzzle of familiarity that baffled him so.

"May we go sir?" asked Major Hay.

"Not yet!" snapped the governor. "I know this Frenchman and, by God, I'm going to figure out where I have encountered him before. Clearly he is hiding something from me!"

"I don't quite see how you could know a man from Vincennes, Governor. You have never visited there before. This man appears, to me, to be a humble merchant."

"Shut up, Major! I'm trying to think!"

The Major sighed and stared, bored and impatient, at the trampled brown grass that comprised the floor of the governor's tent.

The governor mumbled, "France ... New Orleans ... business-man ... river ..."

Then, quite abruptly, his head and body snapped around as he turned to face Pierre. He was smiling in victory, encouraged by a memory that he had dredged from deep in his mind.

"Fort Panmure! That is it! Fort Panmure ... in 1769! I was there with that idiot Montfort Browne. There was an entire fleet of French bateaux. You were with that group!"

But then his smile of victory morphed into a glare of seething anger.

"You!" hissed Governor Hamilton. "It *is* you, isn't it?" His voice boomed, "You're the one who was bedded with that tasty little French tramp! You're the one who murdered one of my men!"

Major Hay's eyes grew wide in fear and confusion. He stared at the humble Frenchman with a perplexed look.

The governor collapsed into his chair in disbelief. He stared at Pierre with a glaring hate, but soon his face burst into a huge, red-dened grin. He laughed out loud and slapped his hand in victory upon his desk. Then his laughing stopped almost as suddenly as it began. He glared at Pierre with a full measure of hate.

"Major, this Frenchman is an enemy of Great Britain! He mur-dered one of the King's soldiers at Fort Panmure on the Mississippi in 1769, and made his escape the following day."

"That is not true!" exclaimed Pierre. "Your man tried to rape my wife and I killed him in self-defense! Governor Browne gave me his pardon and dismissed your notion of pressing charges!"

"Well, Governor Browne is not here, is he, you greasy little French bastard?" He addressed the major, "Jehu, I want this man separated from the others. You may release the other three once you reach Vincennes. This one will remain in custody at Fort Sackville. He will hang for his crime of murder." Hamilton emit-ted an evil chuckle. "We'll hang him on Christmas Day! That will make a festive holiday gift for the folk of Vincennes. Now get him out of my sight!"

Major Hay tugged at Pierre's capote and brusquely removed him from the tent.

҂

*Fort Patrick Henry - Vincennes*
*December 16, 1778*

"What are your concerns, Genevieve?" inquired Captain Bousseron. He smiled at the extremely pregnant woman sitting in the chair opposite his desk.

"My concerns, Francois? Well, my one and only concern is the fact that I have not heard a single word from my husband in over a week! Should not he have returned by now?"

"Genevieve, you well know that Pierre and his men are on a long-range patrol. It should come as no surprise that they have not yet returned."

"But shouldn't we have received some word by now? A note from a messenger? Something?" She was almost hysterical.

"It is a bit odd that we have received no reports from him in the past three days. But there are any number of explanations for that. He may have moved his team upriver for a better vantage point. There were rains a few days ago. They may be dealing with swollen streams and backwaters. It is best not to jump to any unfounded conclusions."

He stood and walked around the desk, extending his hand to Genevieve in a most gentlemanly manner. She took his hand and rose awkwardly to her feet. It was no small task, as she had to contort her body and almost slide out of the chair, such was the volume of her extremely large belly. Captain Bousseron smiled and choked back a laugh at the sight of this tiny, waif-like woman sporting such an engorged bubble on the front of her body. She waddled beside him as he escorted her toward the door.

"*Madame* Grimard, I urge you to return to your home and care for your family. You must assume the best, not the worst. The moment that I receive word from Pierre, I will send a runner to fetch you. All right?" He smiled warmly.

"*Oui*, Francois. I am grateful for your time."

"You are most welcome, Genevieve. My door is always open to you and to any of the other wives of my men."

Captain Bousseron was just about to reach for the latch on the door when it suddenly exploded open in his face. He had to block the door with his foot to keep it from slamming into Genevieve.

He scolded the young private who had burst into his office. "Philippe, what gives you call to come barging into my office in such an ungentlemanly manner?"

"A runner just returned from upriver, sir! The British are upon us! They are camped two miles to our north!"

"Good God!" exclaimed the captain.

"That's not all, sir." The soldier reached into his shooting pouch and pulled out a crumpled, folded correspondence marked with a red wax seal. "The runner brought this letter, given to him under parley, by a British officer of their advanced guard. He was instructed to deliver it to you, Captain, and not to the Virginians."

Captain Bousseron reached for the note with a trembling hand. He carefully broke the wax seal and unfolded the letter. He scanned its words quickly. His face became gray and pale.

"What does it say, Francois?" demanded Genevieve.

The captain cleared his throat and read the note aloud.

> *To the Commander of the French Militia in Vincennes,*
>
> *The combined forces of Great Britain and her Indian allies are within striking distance of your village. We will enter your town and lay siege upon Fort Sackville before the noon hour tomorrow. The French militia in the fort are hereby instructed to lay down their weapons and return to their homes in peace. If you do not resist, you will be treated fairly and allowed to pursue your daily lifestyles and vocations. There will be no repercussions or retribution for your*

*recent mutinous alliance with the Virginia rebels. You will be administered new oaths and welcomed gladly back into the fold of the British Empire. However, if you offer any resistance, whatsoever, I will regard the entire village as being hostile to the Crown. I will unleash the several hundred natives under my command to enter and pillage your community in accordance with their bloodthirsty customs.*

*I am,*

*Henry Hamilton, Lieutenant Governor - Fort Detroit*

Genevieve made brief eye contact with Francois, then her eyes rolled back in her head as she collapsed and fainted into his arms.

Captain Leonard Helm raged at his French counterpart. "A fine lot you Frenchmen turned out to be, Bousseron! Your militiamen tucked their tails and ran the moment they heard the word, 'British!'"

"You must understand, Leonard. They had no other choice!"

"That's a damned lie!" bellowed Helm. "They could stand with us and fight!"

"Stand with who? The three of you? And with a single cannon? Don't you understand the implication of Hamilton's threat? This is not some foreign battlefield at a distant, forgotten location. This fort stands only a few hundred yards from our homes. Our wives and children and grandchildren are just a short distance down the street. The British have threatened to unleash their Indians upon us. You know what that means! They would slay and scalp every Frenchman in this town. The would rape our wives and sell our children into slavery among the western tribes. The would burn and utterly destroy our homes and our livestock. There is no way that these local men could be expected to resist such a powerful force arrayed against them!"

"Yes, they could, Captain. Courage is a choice. Cowering down and running from a fight is a choice. And it seems that your men have already made their choice. There aren't a dozen Frenchmen left inside the walls of this fort. The rest of them have melted into the darkness and are now hiding under the skirts of their women!"

"What would you do if this were your home, Leonard?"

"Come again?" responded Helm.

"I said … what would you do if Vincennes were your home? What would you do if your wife and children were sleeping in a house down the street?"

"That has nothing to do with the matter at hand," retorted Helm.

"It has everything to do with it!" shrieked Bousseron. "That is the true issue here! My men are loyal. They want your liberty and freedom. They are willing to pay a mighty price. But not at the expense of their families and homes. There is a limit to every man's resolve."

"Your people owe me, Francois!"

"Owe you?" shrieked Bousseron in disbelief. "You think we owe you? I daresay that shoe is on the other foot, Leonard. You owe us! You certainly owe me! Since you and your men arrived here all that you have done is eat our stores, drink our liquor, chase our women, and play cards. The businesses in Vincennes have cash drawers full of worthless notes of promise from you and from Virginia. I, myself, have personally extended you over 8,000 livres in credit. If I am not paid by your government someday, I will be financially ruined! That is how dedicated we are to the cause. But, again I say, we will not sacrifice our women and children to the war clubs and knives of Hamilton's savages."

Helm grunted his disdain. "I still say that you're all a bunch of squirrelly, cowardly, half-hearted traitors."

"Well, I'm still standing here, aren't I, Leonard? Am I not demonstrating my dedication to the cause?"

Helm paused and stared at Bousseron. "I suppose so."

"If you would only allow me some input into your decision-making, I believe that we can minimize some of our losses in this predicament."

"What do you mean? Do you have an idea?"

Francois nodded. "Leonard, we need to get all of the powder and lead out of the fort and hide it in the village."

"Hide it? Where?"

"We can bury it. I know of a couple of good places. And we can take all of the food and equipment stores and distribute them in the households so that the people can hide those, as well. The less that we leave inside this fort for the British, the less comfortable and more harsh their winter will be. We can repatriate the gunpowder and stores when Colonel Clark returns to retake the fort in the spring."

"Where will you hide everything?"

Bousseron paused. "Leonard, I think it's best that you do not know. We would not want the British to extract such information from you, would we?"

Captain Helm's eyes widened as he imagined and visualized his interrogation at the hands of the British. He stared past Bousseron, focusing his gaze upon the dancing flames of the fireplace. He pondered the words of his French counterpart.

"You're right, Francois. It is best that I do not know. The secret will be yours. You must proceed immediately. Meanwhile, I will write a dispatch for Colonel Clark and send Private Williams to Kaskaskia this very night."

"Very well, Captain Helm. I will have this fort cleaned out and all provisions concealed before dawn."

The men shook hands.

"Thank you, Francois. I am truly sorry for the things I said to you."

Captain Bousseron bowed slightly and then made his way toward the exit from Captain Helm's quarters. The moment that the door closed behind him, Helm grabbed a piece of paper and began to scribble his report to Colonel George Rogers Clark.

> *Dear Sir,*
>
> *At this time, there is an army within three miles of this place. I heard of their approach several days ago and dispatched spies to verify. My spies were taken prisoner and I never received intelligence until they were within three miles of the town. The French militia have abandoned me. Captain Bousseron has behaved much to his honor and credit, but I doubt the certainty of the others. Please excuse my haste, as the enemy is within sight. My determination is to defend this garrison, though I only have 12 men left for its defense. I refer you to Mr. Williams, the bearer of this dispatch, for more information. I am determined to remain brave. Please remember my condition. I know it is out of my power to defend the town, as not one of the militia will take up arms. Their flag is at a short distance. I must conclude.*
>
> *Your Humble Servant,*
> *Leonard Helm*

Captain Helm yelled toward his door, "Private Williams!"

The door popped open immediately. The private walked deliberately and confidently toward his commander. "Yes, Captain."

Captain Helm handed him the piece of paper.

"George, I want you to secure this dispatch in a marked satchel and select a fast horse. You must ride for Kaskaskia immediately and get word to Colonel Clark regarding our situation here and the nearness of the British. Make sure he understands how dire our situation truly is."

"Yes, sir!" He his hand to the captain. "And good luck to you sir."

"Good luck to you, as well, George. Ride swiftly and be careful, son. Our hope lies in the note that you carry."

*December 17, 1778 - 3:15 AM*
*Eleven Miles Southwest of Vincennes*

Private George Williams rode as swiftly as he possibly could through the dense, dark forest. There was only a sliver of a moon, and very little light filtered down through the canopy of bare but tangled winter limbs.

"At least it's not frigid cold," George thought.

Indeed, it was a mild and almost pleasant night. It would have been a perfect night to stop and build a small fire and camp beside one of the many small streams or lakes that adorned the beautiful, rugged Illinois Country. But there would be no stopping on this night. Instead George leaned low over the pommel of his saddle to maintain his balance and avoid as many face-slapping, skin-slashing limbs as possible. He rode like a man possessed. He knew full well that the fate of Vincennes and Fort Patrick Henry lay in the dispatch to Colonel Clark that he carried in his messenger bag.

Private Williams had just jumped his horse over a narrow ditch-like stream when he saw a blinding flash of smoky light about twenty yards in front of him, slightly to his left. Less than a second later he heard the dull boom of a musket.

The ball impacted his belly just to the left side of the midline and below his ribcage. The huge chunk of lead tore through the fatty flesh of his torso and passed intact through his upper intestines. The soft lead stopped, however, when it impacted directly into his spine. The force of the lead against bone ripped George from his saddle. He somersaulted over the back of his horse and landed face down on the dank forest floor.

George lay still for a moment. He heard his horse as it continued to gallop away from him. Then he heard something that caused his skin to crawl and his heart to miss a beat. It was the wicked, piercing, high-pitch war cry of at least a dozen Indians. They were noisily making their way toward him through the dense underbrush.

George struggled to breathe. He felt as if the wind had been knocked out of him. He was dazed from the fall and his head had hit something hard on the ground. He felt warm blood trickling into his right ear. George thought it curious that he did not feel any pain other than the throbbing in his head. He attempted to roll over onto his back to assess his wounds, but he could not complete the maneuver. No matter how hard he tried to lift his weight with his arms, the lower portion of his body simply would not move. Then he realized what was wrong ... he couldn't feel his legs. Indeed, he couldn't feel anything below his chest.

George clenched the cold, wet leaves of the forest floor with frustrated hands. He pounded his fists on the ground and screamed in anger. Then the tears came. George wept. He was ashamed at first, but then decided that it didn't matter. There was no one to see him other than the savages who were about to snuff out his life. His breathing came faster. He could feel his heart racing. He knew that the end was coming soon. He could hear their footsteps only a few feet away.

Suddenly George felt a vicious kick in the ribs on his right side. The kick was followed by several angry commands in a strange Indian language that he had never heard before. After several seconds two of the Indians bent over and tossed George mercilessly onto his back.

They laughed mockingly at his wound. George looked down at his belly and saw that his wool coat was thoroughly soaked with blood from his crotch to his neck. He tried to reach down and feel the hole made by the musket ball, but he had no strength in his arms. His face tingled and his lips were growing numb.

One of the Indians bent over with his hunting knife and sliced the leather strap of George's messenger satchel. He opened it and rifled through the contents, quickly locating the sealed letter to Colonel Clark.

George could not understand anything the Indians said except for one word. He heard the Indian say most distinctly, "Hammeltahn." He had spoked the name of Henry Hamilton, the British governor. These were, no doubt, some of his Indians from the north.

One of the scouts, seemingly the commander of the raiding party, spoke a quick phrase to another Indian standing nearby. The second Indian quickly and skillfully whipped his tomahawk from his belt and knelt beside George. The Virginian's eyes widened in fear and disbelief as the native lifted the tomahawk high over his head and then savagely drove the razor-sharp blade into George's skull, splitting his right eye and socket in two.

George experienced an immediate flood of senses. He felt the warmth of sunshine on his face. He tasted the sweet flavor of watermelon, his favorite food in the entire world. And he smelled the tangy sweetness of the French perfume that his wife wore. Then he saw her ... his beautiful bride. Violet leaned forward over his face and kissed him gently on the lips. He tasted her sweetness and felt the amazing sensation of her soft flesh against his.

He cried out her name into the darkness ... "Violet!"

There was a brilliant flash of yellow light, and then there was nothing. Just darkness.

The Indian who murdered him laughed and repeated the strange word, "Violet," as he yanked the tomahawk from the bone of George's ruptured skull. He then whipped out his hunting knife and in a single, fluid motion sliced George's scalp from his head. The savage held it high in the air as his companions screeched in celebration and victory.

# 14

---

## BLOODLESS SURRENDER

---

*The Morning of December 17, 1778 - Vincennes*

**M**ajor Hay and his contingent of British soldiers and French militiamen arrived about an hour after daybreak. There were approximately sixty men in the invasion force. They quickly grounded their canoes and then fanned out along the riverbank before moving toward the village and fort. Major Hay left a squad behind to guard the boats and to keep watch over the four prisoners. Pierre and his team of spies were forced to sit on a large log beside one of the beached canoes. Their hands were bound tightly. Three of the Canadian Frenchmen guarded them with their muskets at the ready.

Pierre craned his neck in an effort to see over the riverbank and discern what was happening in the village, but no signs of life or activity greeted his homesick eyes. Vincennes was curiously silent. There was not a soul to be seen in the streets, shops, or businesses. The only movement within the town was the occasional chicken, dog, or goat that wandered across the otherwise deserted streets. He could see the gate of his home about three hundred yards to the southeast. It was closed. The Catholic church was only a hundred yards away. Its windows and doors were shuttered and silent. There was no sign of life. Pierre awkwardly moved his bound hands to make the sign of the cross on his chest as he uttered a desperate prayer for his wife and children.

Major Hay approached the town. He surveyed the area, maintaining watch for any sign of ambush or resistance. To his right, he could see that the gates of Fort Sackville were closed. There were a few heads revealed over the tops of the fort palisades, but the major knew that he and his men were being watched from both the fort and the town. The hair on his neck stood upright. He could feel the hundreds of eyes that followed his every footstep. He caught glimpses of fluttering curtains in the windows of nearby homes. Clearly, the town had not been abandoned. The people were merely concealing themselves within what little protection their houses could afford.

Major Hay halted his men at the mid-point between the fort and the town. The soldiers were tense. They held their muskets high and scanned the area for any sign of enemy movement or resistance.

A sergeant standing beside the major muttered, "I do not like this, sir. This place is unsettling. It feels like a thousand people are watching me. I think we are in the midst of a trap."

Major Hay continued to scan the houses and lots adjacent to the fort. He shook his head.

"No, Sergeant, I disagree. I believe that these people are simply afraid. They need some reassurance. Have the men take cover and remain in place. I am going to approach the nearest of the buildings." He pointed toward Busseron's place. "It appears to be a store."

"That is not a good idea, sir," responded the sergeant. "You will be an easy target."

The major smiled at his soldier. "I think that I will be quite all right, son. Just keep a sharp eye on the fort and all of the other buildings."

Major Hay stepped forward into the street and walked twenty paces to his left, placing himself in plain view of the fort and most of the nearby homes.

"Citizens of Vincennes! I am Major Jehu Hay of the army of Great Britain. I come from Detroit in the name of King George III and his worthy representative, the honorable Lieutenant Governor Henry Hamilton. We have come today to liberate this village and its people from their occupation by the rebels of Virginia. Is there a representative of the citizenry willing to step forward for conference and parley?"

Just a few yards away a door opened at the village store and a tall, distinguished young man stepped out and ambled deliberately into the street. He was dressed in an off-white blanket capote trimmed with a dull red stripe. Fresh, clean buckskin leggings showed beneath the coat. He wore thick, fur-lined moccasins on his feet. On his head, he wore a bright red wool *voyageur's* cap with the word, "*Liberté*," embroidered in white across the brow. It was Francois Bousseron. He waved at Major Hay in a friendly manner and smiled broadly to demonstrate his lack of hostile intent. He could see that at least a dozen muskets were trained upon him.

Bousseron walked to within ten feet of the British officer, stopped, and bowed slightly. "Major Hay, I am Francois Riday Bousseron, *capitaine* of the militia and mayor of this village."

"Then you are authorized to speak for the people?"

"*Absolument*, Major. I am the elected spokesman for all citizens of Vincennes, and I come to allay any fears that you may have regarding our intentions."

"Believe me, *Monsieur* Bousseron, when I say that we have no fears, at all, with regard to your intentions. We are prepared to deal with whatever response that you or your militia may bring to bear upon our forces." The major glared at the Frenchman with a look of confidence and pride. "I am not sure whether to be encouraged or offended by the message emblazoned on your cap, sir."

Bousseron smiled wryly. "Indeed, Major. Well, you may interpret my garment however you wish. But believe me when I say that we have no intentions of resisting your army. We received the dispatch from Governor Hamilton yesterday and have responded accordingly. The vast majority of the men of Vincennes have laid down their arms and returned to their homes and families."

"Majority?" questioned the Major.

"*Oui, Monsieur.* A few remain inside the fort with the Americans."

"How many?" demanded the major.

"Perhaps a dozen or so. The remainder are concealed within their homes."

"And the disposition of their arms?"

"They have retained their arms, *Monsieur.* They will need them for hunting and feeding their families."

Major Hay nodded. "I understand the need, but that may not be an acceptable circumstance for the governor. I will leave that as a matter for him to decide."

"Of course," responded Bousseron. He bowed respectfully before the major. "Then, Major Hay, I hereby offer you our surrender and declare that the town is yours. I implore you not to unleash your Indians upon our people. We have complied with your governor's demands."

"He is your governor now, as well," Major Hay corrected him.

Bousseron nodded in submission, but offered no verbal response.

"Now," continued the major. "Will you please order the citizens to show themselves so that my men might cease their surveillance of the village and focus their attention upon the fort?"

"Certainly, Major." Francois turned and cupped his hands to his mouth. "People of Vincennes! All is well! The British commander has asked that everyone exit their homes and reveal themselves!"

Slowly and with some measure of trepidation the doors of the homes and cabins along the main thoroughfare began to open. The people exited their safe havens very slowly. It took several minutes before the majority of the people were outside their homes and standing in the open. Soon over five hundred souls stood upon the dead grass and mud of the thoroughfares and lawns of Vincennes. They stared forlornly at the red-coated Englishmen and blanket-coated French militiamen deployed near the fort.

"Most excellent, Captain. You appear to be a man of your word."

"Yes, I am, sir," responded Francois.

"You may release your people. Order them to remain in their homes until the fort is pacified. Anyone seen out of doors will be regarded as the enemy and shot on sight."

"*Oui, Monsieur.*" Bousseron turned and called to several of the men, "Adam, Alain, Thibault, Hugo ... come here, please!"

The four men trotted toward their captain. He issued the order of sheltering within the homes until informed otherwise. The men trotted down the street and repeated the instructions and warning to the citizens of the village. The streets cleared quickly as the men shooed their families back into their warm homes. Major Hay was clearly pleased with their obedient response.

Francois appealed to the British officer, "Might I make an inquiry, Major?"

"Of course, Captain."

"Four of my men are missing. They were dispatched on a patrol to the north last week and we have not heard from them in several days. Did your party encounter these men?"

Major Hay nodded. "Yes. Our forward scouts captured your patrol two days ago. They are in custody and in reasonably good health. We brought them with us this morning, and they are under guard near our boats."

Francois looked past the governor in an attempt to spot his men. He could not see them, but he could see a cluster of soldiers standing guard near the river.

"That is good news, Major. We were very concerned that they had fallen upon some grave misfortune."

"As I said, your men are well. It is our intention to release them to you once we are established in the fort ... all except one."

"*Excusez-moi?*" asked a confused Francois.

"One of the prisoners is under sentence of death. It is the leader of the group, Sergeant Pierre Grimard."

"Why, on earth, is Pierre under such a sentence? What has he done?"

"Governor Hamilton has sentenced him to hang on the charge of murder. I cannot comment further."

"Murder?" exploded Francois. "Who did he murder?"

"I am not at liberty to discuss the situation with you, Captain!" snapped Major Hay. "It is a matter for the Crown. Now, if you would please return to your home, as well. I will fetch you if I need you. I must send for the governor and prepare to take the fort."

"But, Major …"

"That is all, Captain. You are dismissed. Please go away."

Major Hay turned his back to Bousseron and focused his attention on Fort Sackville. Francois turned and trotted quickly down the street toward the Grimard home.

꧁

"Murder? They've charged him with murder?" screeched Genevieve in disbelief.

The expectant woman huddled near the fireplace as she sought its meager heat in an effort to combat the frigid December air. She had only recently returned to the refuge of her home after parading her children into the street in response to the demands of the British commander. The combination of cold air and disturbing news caused her to be a bit light-headed. She placed her hand on the mantle to steady herself.

Little Pierre stood near the door. He was still wearing his blanket coat and wool cap. Without asking for permission from his mother he threw open the door and ran outside.

"Pierre!" his mother yelled. "Come back this instant!"

But it was too late. The lad had already jumped the fence and was running in the direction of the fort.

"Let him go, Genevieve. He is upset and needs to find some friends to console him."

"But the British!" she protested.

"Do not worry. Not even the British are dastardly enough to make war against little boys. Young Pierre will be just fine."

Genevieve nodded and turned her attention back toward the fireplace. She took hold of the iron poker and stirred the logs and coals in an effort to revive the flames.

"Who, in God's name, is my husband supposed to have murdered?" she mumbled as she stared at the glowing coals. "The entire notion is preposterous. Something must have gone horribly wrong on that patrol." She snapped a look of despair at Bousseron. "Francois, you know Pierre better than most of the men in this village. Surely you know that he is not capable of murder."

"Certainly, I know that, Genevieve. But I do not know any of the details. Major Hay stated only that the other men were to be released, and that Pierre was being held under sentence of death."

A heavy tear trickled down her cheek. "What am I to do, Francois?"

"I do not yet know, my dear. But rest assure that we will do something. This will not stand. There is no way that I am going to stand idly by and allow the British to hang your husband."

Genevieve turned and darted toward her bed. She collapsed on top of the wool blankets, buried her face in her plush feather pillow, and wept from despair.

⁊

*Mid-Afternoon - December 17, 1778*
*At the Gate of Fort Patrick Henry - Vincennes*

Captain Leonard Helm watched from his place of concealment along the top of the fort wall as the second contingent of boats landed along the banks of the Wabash River. There were twice as many boats in this group as there had been in the first arrival in the early morning. The men traveling in these boats were frighteningly different. There were well over one hundred Indians manning the canoes. Helm's stomach churned with a mixture of anxiety and excitement.

As the Indians disembarked their canoes and gathered on the shore another boat came into view from the northeast. It was a larger flat boat, and the cargo that that was displayed on the deck of that vessel made Helm's heart skip a beat. It was a cannon ... a very large cannon.

It took almost a half-hour for the enemy troops to wrestle the enormous artillery piece onto the riverbank. The daunting task required several ropes and dozens of tugging, grunting, heaving Indians and militiamen. Once the cannon had cleared the steep riverbank and was securely on shore, the task of maneuvering it appeared to be quite easy. The artillerymen expertly rolled the gun into place directly in front of the main gate of the fort and prepared their load. Then they waited. The Indians began to disperse and make their way around the periphery of the fort. They quickly surrounded the structure.

Several minutes later a very well-dressed, confident Governor Henry Hamilton strode forth into the open street beside his exceedingly large cannon. Major Hay joined him. The governor nodded to the major.

Major Hay called out with authority and confidence, "Attention, defenders of the fort! You must, by now, know that you are completely surrounded and outnumbered. Resistance is both foolish and futile. I hereby order you to surrender this post at once. There is no need for bloodshed."

Captain Helm called down from his position on the wall, "Who makes such a demand?"

"Henry Hamilton, the King's Lieutenant Governor from Detroit," responded Hay.

There was no further response from inside the fort. Several minutes of uncomfortable silence ensued. Major Hay cast a curious glance at the governor. They thought that the negotiations were over and were just about to turn and leave the street when the fort gate opened slightly and a lone man emerged. Captain Leonard Helm stepped boldly out into the open street in front of the fort. He surveyed his surroundings quickly and then proceeded to approach the men standing near the cannon. He walked to a spot within three paces of the two British officials.

Helm bowed slightly. "Governor Hamilton, I presume."

Hamilton returned the gesture. "At your service, sir. And you are?"

"Captain Leonard Helm of Virginia, in command of the United States garrison at Fort Patrick Henry."

Hamilton raised an eyebrow in a mixture of amusement and disdain. He thought, "These impudent rebels have actually changed the name of my fort!" Hamilton choked back a chuckle and dismissed the insult from his mind in order to focus on the matter at hand.

"Captain Helm, this is my adjutant, Major Jehu Hay."

Helm nodded to the soldier. "Major."

Governor Hamilton began, "Captain Helm, I encourage you to order your men to lay down their arms and surrender to our forces under the command of Major Hay."

"What are your terms, sir?" responded Helm.

"I offer no terms, Captain. I promise only humane treatment of you and your men."

"There are only two of us who serve in the American army from Virginia, Governor. I assume that we would be held as prisoners?"

"That is correct, Captain. You will be held here at the fort until such time as we can make other arrangements. But I quite think that you will winter here with us. Soon the rain and snow will begin in earnest and no one will be traveling throughout this country."

Helm glanced over his shoulder toward the fort. "May I assume that I and my other officer will retain our property and baggage?"

"Certainly, sir. I would never deprive a fellow officer of his personal effects."

"And the handful of Frenchmen inside will be allowed to return to their homes without repercussion?"

"Absolutely, sir. We have no desire to make war upon these provincials. We want them back at work and providing the goods needed by the Crown and the King's forces."

Helm pondered the governor's words as he surveyed the dozens of Indians that stood in the shadows of the nearby trees and houses.

"What about your natives, Governor Hamilton?" asked Helm. "Do I have your assurances that they will not pillage our property?"

"I assure you that I have made every effort to control our Indian allies. They will behave in a civilized manner."

"Humph!" grunted Captain Helm. "I'll believe that when I see it. To be honest, sir, I do not believe that you will hold this fort for very long. I dispatched a messenger to Kaskaskia to alert Colonel Clark regarding our predicament. No doubt he will be here within days with a relief force. Your army will be driven from this fort."

Governor Hamilton was growing tired of the rebel captain's impudent posturing. "Are you referring to this correspondence, sir?"

The governor reached into the pocket of his coat and produced the bloody dispatch, written in Helm's own hand and entrusted to his servant, Private George Williams. No doubt it was George's blood that stained the document.

The governor tossed the letter to the ground in a dramatic gesture. "Sir, as you can see, there is no relief coming to deliver you. Your cause is lost. So ... do we have an agreement? I require your answer immediately. If you are unwilling to surrender, then I urge you to return to the fort and prepare for an attack." He paused and stared at Captain Helm with a look of haughty confidence. "Because we *will* take it by force before sundown this day."

Helm stared dejectedly at the ground at the governor's feet. He realized all too well that his cause was, indeed, lost. There was no honor in getting his tiny remnant of a command killed. The defeated officer drew in a deep, resolute breath.

"Lieutenant Governor Hamilton, I accept your terms. The fort is yours."

Helm turned and yelled toward the men behind the walls. "Gentlemen, we have surrendered! Throw open the doors! Exit the fort and lay down your arms!"

Seconds later the timber door swung open and the men began to march out in single file. As they approached Captain Helm they lifted the frizzens on their muskets and rifles and dumped the powder from their pans onto the ground. The men piled their weapons in front of the cannon. Captain Helm's deputy, Lieutenant Asher, stood near his commander. The twelve Frenchmen from Vincennes lined up in front of the fort in a loose formation.

"Is that everyone?" inquired Major Hay.

"Yes, Major. That is everyone," responded Captain Helm tersely.

"Very well, then. Citizens of Vincennes, you may retrieve your weapons and return to your families. You will be notified of a community meeting to be held at some point over the next few days. At that time, you will renew your oaths to Great Britain and King George. Captain Helm, you and your man will, of course, be residing with us for a while."

"As you wish, Major." Captain Helm bowed to his captor.

Suddenly a rather unexpected and infuriating sound emanated from inside the fort. It was the din of breaking glass and screeching, yelping Indians. Captain Helm spun around and saw dozens of the savages running to and fro within the fort walls.

He spun back around and faced the British official. "Governor! You said that you would control your Indians!"

"Oh, calm down, Captain! They must have made their way in through the gun ports or some other poorly constructed location in your defenses. They are just like little children. Let them play for a while and satisfy their curiosity. I assure you that any personal property of yours will be returned."

"But your word, sir!"

"I will keep my word, Captain!" snapped Hamilton. "But surely you understand that I cannot tie a leash on every single one of these Indians. Grow up, man! Besides ... you are a prisoner. I am growing weary of your whining." He turned to his adjutant. "Major Hay, take these men inside and confine them to their quarters. When you are done, take care of the other prisoners on the waterfront. Release the three underlings, but bring the murderer inside the walls and see that he is properly incarcerated."

"Murderer?" inquired Captain Helm.

"It is none of your concern, Captain. Am I to assume that you have a guardhouse or some other quarters suitable for housing a prisoner under capital sentence?"

"Capital sentence?" mumbled Helm. "You mean you aim to execute somebody?"

"Again, I say, it is none of your concern. Now ... is there a suitable guardhouse or other jail inside the fort?"

"Yes, Governor. There are plenty of places for you to house a prisoner. Indeed, as I am one of your prisoners, I pray that you will exercise some mercy in your choice. But I will have no part in your plans to execute anyone, nor will I assist you in any way in this matter. The fort is yours. I am quite sure that you are intelligent enough to figure out what to do with your own damned prisoners."

"Very well, then. Major Hay, please see to the captives. Captain Helm, after you, sir."

The governor motioned toward the gate of the fort with his open hand, obviously intending for Leonard Helm to lead the way inside. Captain Helm ambled at a rebelliously slow pace through the gate. He choked back a tear as he watched a gang of rampaging Indians cut the line to the glorious red and green flag of Fort Patrick Henry, irreverently releasing it to fall onto the muddy ground.

❧

Young Pierre burst through the door of the Grimard house just as the evening sun descended below the horizon. He was breathless and red-faced.

"I saw him, Mama! I saw him!"

His mother was hovering over a pot beside the mantle and tasting a stew that she had prepared for supper. She turned and placed both hands on her hips and began to scold the boy, "Pierre Grimard, where have you been all the long day? I have been worried sick about you! There are British and Indians all over this town! I thought for sure that one of them had apprehended you!"

"You are not listening to me, Mama. I saw him! I saw Papa!"

She scurried toward him and placed her hands on his shoulders. There was a glint of joy and hope in her eyes.

"Where, boy? Where did you see him?"

"They brought him up from the river about an hour ago. I saw *Monsieur* Turpin and the others, as well. The British released them, but they took Papa into the fort."

"So then ... the fort has surrendered?" she asked.

"Yes, Mama. No one fired a shot. I saw the tall American go out and talk to two British men. I heard him call one of them, 'Governor Hamilton.' A few minutes later they threw open the gates and the Indians and British rushed in."

Genevieve bit her lip nervously. "Well, at least they have not unleashed the Indians upon our village and houses."

"I don't think they plan to, Mama. After the savages plundered the fort, I saw most of them get into canoes and paddle back upriver. All that remains in the fort now are British and what looks like some Frenchmen they brought with them. There might be a handful of Indians, but not many."

She nodded her understanding, then her face registered a measure of shock. "Wait! Did you say 'Governor Hamilton?'"

"Yes, Mama."

"Governor Henry Hamilton? He is here? In Vincennes?"

"I did not hear a first name. Only Hamilton."

Genevieve was trembling. "Did you see where they took your father?"

He shook his head. "No, Mama. But he was most definitely being held prisoner. His hands were tied together in front of him."

A single tear crept down her cheek. "Was he injured?"

"I do not think so, Mama. I saw no blood. He appeared to be in good spirits. He walked with strength and pride." Young Pierre smiled proudly, himself.

"Why have you waited so long to come home and tell me?" she chided the boy. "I have been sick to death for news!"

"Because I was hiding, Mama. I was concealed on top of *Monsieur* Pineau's shed. I had to wait until their patrols went in for the night. The fort is locked up tight now. I do not think anyone will be going in or out until morning."

His mother smiled slightly at him and then tousled his light brown hair. "You are a brave boy, Pierre. Just like your father. Our very own little spy of Vincennes. Now, come and get some stew and bread in your belly. I know that you must be hungry. After you eat you need to go and report what you have seen to Captain Bousseron."

Pierre smiled sheepishly. "Mama, I already went to see him first. He said that he would be here in about an hour. He had to meet someone else first before coming here to make a plan."

"Make a plan?" she asked, confused.

"Yes, Mama. A plan to get Papa out of that fort."

🐚

Captain Bousseron took a generous swig from his cup of wine and then wiped his lips on his shirt sleeve. He was numb and somewhat in a state of disbelief from the story that Genevieve had just recounted for him. It was the tale of that nightmarish evening at Fort Panmure in 1769 ... the night when Pierre shot and killed the British soldier in order to protect his wife from the man's violent, perverse attack.

"I cannot believe that Pierre has never told me about this," Francois declared.

"We do not talk about such things, Francois. We believed it all to be in the distant past. It was a horrible event. I have tried to forget it as best I could. Pierre has done the same."

"Do you think that is why Pierre is being held now?"

"There can be no other reason!" Genevieve exclaimed. "Why else would he be singled out from the other men on the patrol? Henry Hamilton is here in Vincennes. Surely, he must have recognized Pierre! He wanted to hang Pierre on that horrible night at Fort Panmure, but the British governor who accompanied him overruled his orders and declared the shooting to be justified."

"Which it was!" exclaimed Francois.

She nodded. "Of course, it was. Any fool could see that. But Henry Hamilton is a sinister, bloodthirsty, prideful man. He called me horrible names ... accused me of being some type of trollop or whore." She stopped speaking suddenly and cast a quick glance at her son. The boy did not appear to understand what she had said.

"I suspect that you are right, Genevieve. And that is all the more reason to go ahead with our plot to free your husband."

She shook her head vigorously. "I cannot allow you to use my son in your plans. I may have already lost my husband. I will not sacrifice his namesake on the altar of British violence."

"But I know that it will work, Genevieve! It is a simple, foolproof plan. We will get Pierre out of his British chains, but first we need to know where he is. We need intelligence from inside the walls of the fort."

Genevieve, ever the overprotective mother, shook her head in protest. "I cannot send my boy into a fort occupied by the British and their allies on a mission of subterfuge! What if he is found out? What if he is arrested? No! No! I simply cannot allow it."

Little Pierre's small voice emanated from a dark corner of the cabin near the fireplace. "I can do it, Mama. It sounds easy. I will just deliver dinner for Papa on Sunday, let him know that we are all just fine, and find out exactly where they are holding him. I will also try to see what changes the British are making to the inside of the fort. Afterwards I will come right back home and make my report to the captain."

Bousseron added, "Father Gibault has already agreed to the plan, Genevieve. He will accompany the boy. He will enter the fort on Sunday in order to administer the Holy Communion to soldiers and prisoners. The priest will serve as escort for little Pierre and secure permission for him to deliver a hot meal to your husband. The entire visit should take no more than a half-hour at most."

"Why do you not enter the fort and check on Pierre, yourself? He is, after all, a soldier under your command," challenged Genevieve somewhat spitefully.

"My dear, they will not allow me into their fort! They consider me to be something of a traitor to their cause. Which I am, by the way!" He winked toward little Pierre. The boy smiled broadly. "It will be some time before I will earn enough of Hamilton's trust to be given access to Fort Sackville."

"Then I, myself, will take him his meal! I will find out what you need to know!"

Bousseron shook his head vigorously. "No, Genevieve. That fort is no place for a young woman, pregnant or not. Besides, like you just told me, you have some bad history with Hamilton. He may remember you. And he, apparently, already has a very low regard for you. What if he did recognize you? What if he somehow decided to hold you equally responsible for the events at Fort Panmure? No, Genevieve. I will not place you in that precarious situation."

"But you place my boy in danger," she responded in disbelief.

"Your boy has already proven his worth to our cause. He was able to move throughout this town undetected today. As a child, he enjoys a degree of anonymity and invisibility. Besides, the lad wants to serve his father! He is a very capable and worthy spy. No one would suspect a young boy," Bousseron pleaded passionately.

Genevieve buried her face in her hands as she agonized over the entire situation. Her nerves were shattered. She was a very frightened woman. She was physically exhausted. She was barely a month away from giving birth. The emotions of pregnancy were already enough for any woman to endure. But now her husband was in British bondage and headed for the gallows! And her eight-year-old son was eager to sign on as a spy and perform a secret mission on behalf of the militia! She thought, "How much more must I bear?"

Francois Bousseron spoke quietly and respectfully. "Genevieve ... we need your permission. We have precious little time to make all of the arrangements."

Pierre rose from his chair and walked over to her. He placed his arm reassuringly around her shoulder and rested his temple on the top of her head.

"Mama, it will be all right. I promise you it will. I am not afraid. I will be brave." He cupped her chin with his small hand and turned her face toward him. "I have to do this, Mama. I do not want you to go anywhere near those men. Please let me go. Please let me fight for Papa."

Genevieve wiped the tears from her face and embraced her son. She released him and then rose from her bench and walked over to the curtain at the far end of the cabin. She glanced between the two partitions of cloth and stared at Charles and Jean Baptiste. Both of her younger sons slept peacefully on their shared feather mattress. She closed her eyes and uttered a silent prayer. She made the sign of the cross on her chest.

She turned and faced the militia commander. "All right, Francois. Pierre will be your little spy. Now ... what must I do?"

Francois grinned broadly. "You simply need to cook your husband a delicious dinner. What do you think he would like? Venison or beef?"

# 15

## ESCAPE!

*Sunday, December 20, 1778*

The gates of Fort Sackville stood open, but four French-Canadian militiamen stood vigilant guard nearby. Father Gibault shuffled toward the entrance to the fort. The hem of his brown robe hovered just above the muddy ground. His portly belly jiggled with each of his enthusiastic steps. He carried with him a basket containing a small bottle of wine, a round loaf of communion bread, and a gold chalice. Pierre Grimard, Jr., walked one step behind him. The little boy carried a rather large basket of food covered with a pale brown linen cloth.

They were a mere ten steps from the fort when one of the Frenchmen confronted them. "Stop! I am sorry, but you may proceed no further, Father."

"Surely, my child, you will not inhibit the work of the church within the walls of this fort," pleaded Father Gibault. "What is your name, boy?"

The young soldier seemed somewhat ashamed. "Alain Dupuis, Father. I apologize, sincerely, but citizens of the village are not allowed inside the fort under any circumstances. Major Hay's orders."

"My son, I have come to administer the Sacrament of Holy Communion to the men of this fort. Today is the Sabbath day, after all. It is my responsibility to minister to the men here, no matter their nationality or current political allegiances."

The soldier's eyes lit up. "We have not received Communion for over three months, Father."

Father Gibault shook his head in an exaggerated gesture of shock and shame. "Just as I suspected. Your commanders departed Detroit without the provision of adequate spiritual leadership. I did not even see a humble Brother or Friar among your troops."

The soldier nodded. "It is true, Father. And a shame it is, too. There are many Frenchmen here who would be most grateful for the Sacrament."

"And I assume that there are some who might enjoy the confessional, as well." The priest's eyes twinkled.

The soldier grinned and nodded. "Of that I am certain, Father."

"So, we have ourselves something of a dilemma, do we not? I come to provide ministry, but your commander will not allow me inside the fort. Do you think, perhaps, that we could make a small exception and ask for special permission for me to enter?"

"What is the boy's purpose in being here?" inquired the soldier.

"He is merely here to assist me. I have received word that there is a man of Vincennes being held inside the fort under sentence of death. I have brought the condemned man a hot, satisfying meal."

"Yes, there is a man sentenced to hang on Christmas Day, but I am not sure that the major will allow any benevolence on his behalf."

"Might you summon an officer, perhaps even Major Hay, himself, so that I can appeal my case directly to his authority?" pleaded Father Gibault.

"Of course, Father. I will fetch someone straightaway."

The militiaman turned and gave brief instructions to his men and then walked quickly into the fort. He followed a path toward the office of the commandant. Several minutes later he returned with a somewhat aloof British officer.

"I am Major Jehu Hay, commander of the military forces of Vincennes and Fort Sackville. The sergeant has explained to me that you have come to administer Holy Communion to the men."

"That is, indeed, the truth, Major. I would count it an honor to hold Mass and administer the Sacrament to my brethren within your ranks."

"Are you the priest who regularly serves this village?"

"I am, sir. I am well-known by all the residents here, having baptized most of their children. Any one of them can offer testimony to my office and ministry in the Holy Catholic Church."

The major exhaled slightly and considered the request. He looked judiciously into the priest's eyes.

"I suppose that your administration of Communion would be acceptable to me, Father. And what of this boy? What is his purpose in being here?"

"You are holding one of my parishioners under sentence of death, Major. One of the women of our town has prepared him a hot meal. I invited this child to carry the basket and deliver it to the man."

The major raised an eyebrow. "One of your parishioners, you say?"

"*Oui*, Major. Everyone knows that you are holding Pierre Grimard and that he is to be hanged. No one questions your authority of governance. We would merely like to minister to our brother until such time as the sentence is carried out."

"I suppose there is no harm in that," responded the major. "Sergeant Grimard seems to be a decent fellow. I, personally, loathe the current circumstances surrounding him and his subsequent treatment. I know for certain that he would enjoy the gesture and the meal. We will, of course, have to inspect the contents of the basket."

"*Absolument*, Major. You will discover that it is merely a bowl of venison stew, some slices of fresh bread, a small pie, and some wine."

"My man will examine the basket and then escort the boy to the blockhouse where the prisoner is being held. You may set up your altar near the main office. I will notify the garrison of your availability."

"Thank you. You are most gracious, Major." Father Gibault nodded respectfully.

"And you are most welcome, Father," responded the Major. "Sergeant, please inspect the boy's basket and then escort him to the prisoner's quarters."

"*Oui*, Major!"

The sergeant of the French militia flipped back the linen cover on little Pierre's basket and examined the contents quickly. He seemed satisfied that they were safe enough.

The sergeant mumbled, "Come with me, son."

Pierre walked obediently beside the strange, bearded Canadian. As he walked he scanned in every direction within the fort. Men were working feverishly throughout the post, repairing the palisades and building lookout positions high on the walls. Some were even building new buildings that looked like houses along the southern edge of the compound. Pierre made a mental note of it all so that he could make a thorough report to Captain Bousseron.

The sergeant inquired quietly, "Do you know this man to whom you are delivering the food?"

Pierre answered honestly, "He is my papa."

The Frenchman grinned. "I suspected as much. I thought that I noticed a resemblance." Pierre looked up at the man, who winked at him in return. "I will allow you to visit with your father for a nice, long while. It will be our secret ... one Frenchman doing another a favor, *oui?*"

Pierre nodded and smiled.

It took a couple of minutes for them to cross the compound. The man guided Pierre toward the westernmost corner block-house. It was the structure nearest the Wabash River. When they reached the entrance, the guard pulled back the heavy iron latch and cracked the door to look inside at Pierre. His face betrayed his pity for the prisoner.

"I will give you as much time as I possibly can with your father. It may be the last time you ever see him, so make the most of it. I am very sorry."

He pushed the door open all the way and encouraged Pierre to step across the log threshold. The door closed quietly behind him. It took a moment for the boy's eyes to adjust to the darkness inside. Then he saw the dark outline of a body lying against the wall to his right.

"Papa!"

His father raised up slowly onto one elbow. He stared in disbelief at his son. Little Pierre placed the basket on the ground and ran toward his father just as the heavy timber door slammed shut behind him.

"Pierre! My boy! What in God's name are you doing here?"

*Grimard Home - Later That Evening*

"And you are certain this is where he is being held?" inquired Captain Bousseron, pointing at his crude, hand-drawn map.

The captain and all of the other people in the room stared intently at young Pierre. In addition to Bousseron, there was Father Gibault, Genevieve Grimard, and two of Bousseron's loyal militia lieutenants.

Little Pierre nodded vigorously. "I am certain, *Monsieur*. It is the blockhouse that is to the left rear of the compound when you enter through the main gate. It is right along the river. You can even hear the sounds of the river from inside his room."

Lieutenant Oscar Hamelin added, "Father Gibault said that the British are improving the defenses of the fort. Did you notice that, as well?"

"*Oui, Monsieur.* There were dozens of men hard at work on the buildings and fort walls. They were sealing several wide places between the logs. One group of men was even building a series of small buildings along the wall on the western side."

The lieutenant looked grimly at Bousseron and said one word, "Barracks."

"Indeed," responded Bousseron. "Our British friends are preparing themselves for a long, cold winter. They do not have the luxury of homes and hearths that we enjoyed as the local militia."

A frustrated Genevieve interrupted their military assessment, "That is all quite interesting, gentlemen, but what are you planning to do to free my husband? I care nothing about your talk of walls and barracks. They plan to hang my Pierre in five days!"

"That corner blockhouse is thirty yards from the rear gate. It is a long way to move in the open, even under cover of darkness," remarked Lieutenant Hamelin.

"The new barracks are in direct line of sight of the structure, so I doubt that it would even be a possibility to infiltrate the inner compound and reach the door of the blockhouse," stated Bousseron. "We must think differently."

"What are you saying?" inquired Father Gibault. "How else could we possibly get him out?"

"I do not know!" exclaimed Bousseron, slamming his fist on the table. "I have absolutely no ideas! But we must do something! I cannot abide by the notion of these pompous, red-coated bastards hanging my friend!" He glanced at the priest. "I'm sorry, Father."

"It's quite all right, my son. I share equally in your frustration."

Little Pierre's high-pitched voice penetrated the room. "What about that old shed down by the river?"

"What old shed?" demanded Bousseron.

"There is a very old, broken down shed between the fort and the river. Part of it has fallen down completely … the section closest to the water. It has been washed out by the floodwaters, I suppose.

But most of it is still standing. I have never seen the building used for anything. I think it was there even before they built the fort."

"I have neither seen nor heard of such a structure," retorted the captain.

"You cannot see it from the fort, *Monsieur.* It is in that thick cluster of big cedar and pine trees right beside the corner blockhouse. But I have played in it for years. We children like to pretend that it is our very own fort."

Bousseron responded, "I know of the stand of trees that you describe, but I was unaware of any building. Still, I do not see what use that information is to us, Pierre. Your father is imprisoned inside the fort walls. A shack beside the river is useless in our situation."

"But, can we not dig him out?" Pierre asked innocently.

His words lingered dramatically in the dark, cold room. The adults tried to envision the execution of Pierre's outlandish idea.

"That is impossible," responded Lieutenant David Aubin, another of Bousseron's officers. "The distance is too great, and we would be discovered."

The little boy pointed at the map. "But it is not even twenty feet to the wall." He grinned. "Besides, we have already started the digging for you."

"Whatever do you mean, Pierre?" demanded his mother.

"We started digging just for fun way back in the summer. We were going to try to get into the fort and cause a little mischief. We got about half-way to the wall but the sides kept crumbling."

"Good Lord!" his mother shouted.

The boy pleaded innocently, "It is all right, Mama. We stopped as soon as the dirt started giving way. No one was hurt."

"Only by the grace of God!" she barked at him.

Bousseron interrupted the mother-son argument, "I think the boy is onto something." He looked to his lieutenants. "David, we could use the scrap lumber from the building to shore up the sides and roof of a tunnel. If what Pierre tells us is true, we only need to dig another ten to fifteen feet to reach inside the wall. The building is already well out of view. After all, none of us have ever even seen it! We could infiltrate the shed under cover of darkness and have our men dig night and day. Daytime digging would actually be better because there is more noise and activity to mask any possible sound."

Lieutenant Hamelin's eyes widened. "We could even reach that spot by canoe if we need to. And we could toss the loose dirt into the river and simply let it wash away!" He looked with renewed confidence at his commander. "It might work!"

Bousseron grinned and slapped a happy hand on the table top. "Yes, it *will* work! We begin tonight! We only have four days to dig a sufficient, safe tunnel to free our fellow compatriot." He playfully tapped his fist against Pierre's chin. "Let us see if we can get inside those walls and cause a little mayhem. Eh, Pierre?"

The boy beamed with pride and pleasure.

∿

*December 24, 1777*
*Early Afternoon - Near the Mouth of the Tunnel*

Captain Bousseron had joined the daytime shift of tunnel diggers in the pre-dawn darkness. It was Christmas Eve. Pierre Grimard was scheduled to be hanged at noon on Christmas Day. A rough set of gallows had been completed just outside the main gate of the fort. Governor Hamilton had already issued a summons to all citizens of Vincennes. He expected every man, woman, and child of the village to attend the execution of this enemy of the Crown. Bousseron knew that his men were working against the clock. He wanted to personally check on their progress.

The men had worked diligently for three days and nights. Eighteen men volunteered to take part in digging the tunnel. They worked in threes in shifts of five or six hours each. During the daytime they approached the riverbank from canoes on the Wabash. At night they reached the shack by sneaking along the tree line near the river. In either case reaching the old shack was relatively easy. There were only occasional sentries along the top of the palisade wall on that side of the fort. The British paid little attention to the river. Instead, they directed most of their surveillance toward the town.

While on "digging duty," one man whittled at the rock-hard face of the tunnel while the other two removed the loosened earth and passed along boards and heavy stones for shoring the overhead and sides. The wood patches were haphazard and irregular. The silence of the operation did not allow the use of saws for cutting exact length boards. In a couple of instances the men had to dig deeply into the sides of the tunnel in order to add stone columns and longer overhead boards.

Still, the men progressed steadily over the three-day time period. They believed that they had dug enough to be exactly under Pierre's cell. Bousseron wanted to examine the tunnel and verify its length for himself. Candle in hand, he crawled along the shaft until he reached the terminus. He had a string attached to a button on his weskit that dangled loosely behind him toward the mouth of the tunnel. One of his men inside the shack held the remainder of the bundle of string. When Francois reached the face of the shaft he untied the string, held it against the wall, and gave a deliberate, swift tug. That was the signal for the man at the mouth to tie a knot in the string to mark the opening of the tunnel. After a couple of minutes Francois began to crawl backwards toward the entrance. He quickly emerged into the dim daylight inside the old shack.

"Did you do as I instructed?" he hissed.

The man whispered his response, "*Oui*, Francois. I made the knot at the entrance."

Bousseron grabbed the string and reached for his haversack that hung on a rusty nail on a nearby wall. He pulled a short stick from his bag.

"What is that, Francois?" whispered one of the other men on the digging crew.

The captain muttered quietly, "It is for making measurement. This piece of oak is exactly one foot in length."

With the help of the other men Francois carefully worked the ruler along the length of the string and counted in one foot increments. The string measured just over twenty-seven feet.

Captain Bousseron grinned and then whispered, "That is it, gentlemen. We are beneath his room!"

"What do we do now, *Monsieur?*"

"We dig no further. But we need to widen the spot at the end of the tunnel. It needs to be a slightly larger box so that a man can drop down from above and turn his body in order to exit the tunnel. That is your job for today. But do not dig upward! Pierre does not know that we are coming, yet. We must inform him today. Tonight, we will dig up through the floor and get him out of there. Excellent, work, men!" Bousseron was very excited. It was difficult for him to remain quiet.

The captain shook the hands of the three tunnelers and then donned his hat, coat, and bags and scurried out of the old shack. He made his way quietly through the thick trees toward the south and then circled around the outskirts of the village and entered Vincennes from the northeast. He headed straight for the Grimard home.

🐚

"I do not make this request lightly, Francois," replied Genevieve, her voice firm and her chin held high. "I should take the final meal to Pierre. His captors will think it odd that his wife has not been to see him during his captivity. They will be doubly suspicious if I do not go to him this afternoon."

"But Genevieve, what about your history with Governor Hamilton? I still do not like the notion of you going inside that fort."

"You worry too much, Francois. Father Gibault will accompany me, as well as my boys. We need to make the British believe that we are resolved to accept this execution. They will expect that his family would visit before he goes to the gallows."

"She is right, Francois," chimed in Father Gibault. "We need to keep the British off of their guard and not even entertaining the notion of an escape. They will, for certain, expect his family to visit him today. I can make all of the necessary arrangements."

Bousseron inhaled deeply, shifting his gaze between the priest and Genevieve. "Do you think you can convince them of your despair? How good of an actor are you?"

Genevieve sported a devilish grin. "Oh, they will believe me, Francois. I will become a blathering, hysterical wife. They will enjoy the show."

Captain Bousseron chuckled. Father Gibault smiled thinly.

🍥

Major Hay and Governor Hamilton watched the proceedings from the covered porch of the command office. They sat beside a small table nestled against the rough log wall. It was a cold day, but the governor insisted upon observing the family of Pierre Grimard. He insisted upon being seen by the family, as well. The two men sat proudly, dressed in their finest uniforms with their black cocked hats perched proudly on their heads. The governor sipped nonchalantly from a cup of hot tea.

"Is that the woman?" asked Major Hay.

The governor grunted. "That is her, all right. She is a few years older, but that is definitely her. And just look at her! Her belly all swelled and that little gaggle of French roosters plodding along beside her. That French whore cannot keep her legs closed, can she?"

A pang of guilt struck the major. "They appear to be a respectable, handsome family to me, sir." He paused. "She is a very stunning woman, isn't she?"

Hamilton shot an angry glance at his officer. "Do not let appearances fool you, Major. That trollop lured a British soldier to his death many years ago. She is as much an enemy of the Crown as that greasy Frenchman to whom she is wedded. I wish that I could stretch her whorish neck, as well."

Major Jehu Hay did not respond. He merely felt a sinking pang of despair for the woman who was about to lose her husband and for the fatherless children trudging behind her through the sticky mud of Fort Sackville.

The small entourage made their way slowly across the compound. The chubby priest supported the very pregnant Genevieve as best he could. The woman wailed and cried every step that she took across the fort grounds. He soon found himself unable to support her weight.

"Sergeant, can you please assist me?" he implored the French militiaman walking beside them.

"*Absolument*, Father." The soldier reached and took hold of Genevieve's other arm.

The woman wailed even more ferociously at the strange man's touch. The younger boys, Charles and Jean-Baptiste, both cried, as well. They did not cry because of the circumstance, because they did not understand what was happening. They merely reacted to the extreme emotion of Genevieve. The fact that their mother was so upset was enough to elicit their tears of confusion and fear.

Pierre marched proudly beside his mother and the priest. He carried his father's final meal in a beautifully decorated basket. The French guards had inspected it diligently, but were careful not to disturb the contents. The two younger boys each carried a wool blanket. The guards gave them a cursory inspection, as well. They were most respectful of the emotional, mourning family. Father Gibault noticed a tear in more than one eye. Clearly, the imported Frenchmen were not in favor of the execution of one of their distant countrymen. The Father smiled within his heart, for he knew that their ruse was working.

As they neared the blockhouse the French guard released Genevieve to Father Gibault's grip and reached into his leather bag to retrieve a large key. He then reached for the enormous lock that hung on a newly forged iron latch. Little Pierre noticed that the lock assembly was brand new and had replaced the older wooden latch. Clearly, the British were taking no chances on allowing the condemned man to escape.

As the French guard opened the door he mumbled to Genevieve, "*Madame*, I will secure the gate in one hour. You may have that much time to spend with your husband. I will come and fetch you before we close the fort for the night."

Genevieve and Father Gibault nodded. Just as they were about to enter the cell another Frenchman approached them with a lighted candle lantern. The tall candle glowed brightly inside its glass casing. In his other hand, he carried a small three-legged stool.

The man bowed as he handed the lantern to Genevieve. "*Madame*, you will need this lantern. It is very dark inside. And you will need this stool to sit, as well. I assume that your boys can all sit on the floor." He smiled glumly at the forlorn woman and handed the stool to Father Gibault.

Genevieve wiped her ample tears and snotty nose with a linen handkerchief as she muttered, "*Merci, Monsieur.* Your kindness will not be forgotten."

Father Gibault escorted Genevieve into the blockhouse. The boys followed. After the heavy timber door slammed shut behind them, an emotional family reunion began to take place inside the dark, low-ceilinged room.

A deep, congested cough gurgled in the darkness. Pierre's weak voice mumbled from the far corner, "Genevieve? My love! Is that you? Or is it an angel that has come to visit me and take me on to heaven?" He coughed another deep, thunderous cough.

"It is I, husband. And I have brought your boys."

The two youngest boys screamed, "Papa!" as they swarmed their father. The youngsters embraced him and showered him with kisses.

"Oh, my boys! My boys! My boys! I am so glad to see you! I have missed you so!"

"Papa, you have big whiskers," teased Charles, giggling.

"I grew them to tickle your neck, Master Charles." He grabbed the boy and buried his chin beneath the lad's soft neck, causing him to emit a delighted squeal.

Tears filled the man's eyes. He struggled to stand.

"Do not try to get up, Pierre. Stay where you are. Conserve your strength. We will join you, instead," encouraged Father Gibault.

The priest placed the stool next to the wall beside Pierre and helped Genevieve get seated comfortably beside her husband. Pierre draped his arm across her lap and buried his face into her swollen side. He wept openly and without shame.

"My darling, I have missed you so much that it hurts." His tears flowed. He coughed.

Genevieve stroked her husband's stringy hair and wept with him. She felt of his forehead. "Oh, my Lord! You have a high fever! I need to get you home and take care of you properly. This cold has moved into your bones and afflicted your throat and chest."

Pierre removed his face from his wife's soft, fragrant dress and wiped his cheeks with his sleeves. He took hold of his wife's tiny hand. He coughed again, deeply.

"How I wish that were possible, my love. But you and I both know the injustice that confronts us in the morning. I have heard the gallows being built outside the gate. I have endured the teasing and derision of my British captors. They plan to hang me tomorrow at noon. There is no escape for me. See ... my son has brought me my last meal. Come here, Pierre."

The solemn eight-year-old walked over to his father, leaned down, and gently hugged him. He kissed his papa's cheek. Pierre grabbed his son and pulled him close and tight.

"How is my big boy? Have you been taking care of your mother?"

"Yes, Papa. Mama says that I have been an excellent 'man of the house.'"

Pierre chuckled and hugged his son again.

"You must have faith, my son, that you will be delivered," declared the priest, interrupting the father-son embrace.

"My faith has escaped me, Father. I see no other possible outcome for me. I am afraid that you will bury me in your churchyard before sundown tomorrow."

Father Gibault leaned closer and whispered, "I do not think so, Pierre. In fact, I quite expect that you will be far away from Vincennes before dusk on our Lord's birthday." The priest's eyes gleamed with mischief and joy. His face erupted into a wide, plump grin.

Pierre glanced at Genevieve. He could see her equally huge smile in the warm glow of the lone candle.

"What is he talking about, Genevieve?"

She leaned toward him and took his chin in her hand. She hissed quietly, "We are breaking you out of this prison tonight, my love."

"What? How?" Pierre exclaimed a bit too loudly.

Father Gibault threw his finger up to his lips. "Shhhh! There are curious ears beyond these walls."

Now Pierre was excited. He felt new energy creeping into his limbs. He scrambled onto his knees.

"Tell me ... what is going on?" He coughed again.

Father Gibault nodded at Genevieve.

Genevieve whispered into his ear, "Captain Bousseron and his men are getting you out tonight. They have tunneled underneath the wall and have reached a point directly beneath this room. Tonight, after dark, they will dig upward to reach you and set you free."

Pierre's eyes grew wide with disbelief. "They are under this room?"

"Yes, Pierre," responded the priest. "At this very moment. They started from beneath a shack just beyond the wall and by the river." He paused. "It was all little Pierre's idea."

Pierre glanced proudly at his son. "Is that so?"

The boy glowed with pride. He nodded silently at his father.

Pierre whispered to his wife, "What happens once I am free?"

"The men will have a canoe hidden at the river's edge beyond the shed. The entire area is concealed very well by thick brush, pine trees, and cedar trees. Your canoe will be stocked with extra clothing, blankets, provisions, and weapons. You must go south on the river and then make your way west to Kaskaskia and the protection of the Virginians."

Again, tears began to flow down Pierre's tired, filthy cheeks. He simply could not believe the news that his family had brought to him. His joy was quickly overshadowed by a series of violent coughing spasms.

He managed to get out a single question through the coughing. "When will they come?"

"Late tonight, after the garrison is bedded down. That will give you several hours head start on the river before sunrise. You will be well beyond their reach by dawn and will leave no trail," answered Father Gibault.

"But, husband, you must insure that the escape hole is covered with these blankets and the food basket. Simply scatter your refuse on the blanket and try to stretch it over the hole as best you can. The diggers will attempt to make a minimal opening in order to disguise the tunnel. The longer we keep the British guessing and in a state of confusion, the further you can travel in safety."

"Yes, my love. That is an excellent idea. Now I am so excited, I do not think I will be able to eat this fine meal!"

His wife tenderly pushed back the hair from his eyes. "You must eat, Pierre. You need strength. I have a small jar of rum, and I have some fragrant salve in my bag. I will coat your neck and chest with the ointment. The aroma should help loosen up that horrid cough."

Father Gibault assumed his priestly authority. "Before you eat, my son, we will pray for your meal, and for your health, and for our little conspiracy. And then you can eat while your family catches you up on all of their latest news. Afterwards, when we leave, Genevieve and the children will have to wail and cry with convincing despair and emotion. We need the British to hear how broken-hearted you all are about Pierre's appointment with the gallows tomorrow. Do you all think you can do that?"

Every member of the family grinned and nodded vigorously.

"Good!" responded the priest. "Now let us pray …"

Pierre was finally warm. The moist cold of the blockhouse had been insufferable for the past week. Though the room had a small fireplace, the British would not allow him to have a fire out of fear that he might attempt to ignite the building and fort. Neither would they allow him a blanket or even a pallet to provide a barrier between his body and the heat-sapping ground. The two blankets that his family had brought him were luxurious, indeed. He folded one length-wise and used it for a pallet, and then he wrapped his frigid body with the other one. Together they provided him with a cocoon of warmth.

At first Pierre found it difficult to sleep. He was too excited. Even as he slumbered fitfully he continued to awaken and glance around the room, searching for any sign of his rescuers. After almost an hour of tossing and turning he finally faced the wall and succumbed to a deep, rum-enhanced sleep.

Then he felt his leg shaking.

A voice hissed in the darkness, "Pierre!"

He thought he was dreaming until he received a harsh slap on the shoulder.

"Pierre! Wake up! It is time to go!"

He rolled over onto his back.

He stared into a very familiar and unexpected face in the darkness. It was his good friend, neighbor, and compatriot Francois Turpin.

"Francois! I cannot believe it is you!"

Pierre tossed his blankets aside and embraced his friend.

"Come, Pierre. We have no time to waste. The tunnel is over near the fireplace. We barely made it into the room, but we made it. Close enough, eh?" He smiled. "Leave your blankets and other things beside the hole. I brought a couple of small boards. I will do my best to conceal the opening."

Pierre barked a deep, guttural cough. "I've been sick, Francois. I really want to take one of these blankets with me."

"We have plenty for you in the canoe, my friend. Genevieve has thought of everything. She has gathered blankets, medicine, and more food and provisions than a man should need." He shoved a dark bottle into Pierre's face. "Here ... take a good drink of this liquor. And keep the bottle. We cannot have you coughing once we get you out from under the ground."

Pierre took two long gulps of the fiery fluid. He then picked up his food basket and blankets and deposited them beside the small hole in front of the tiny fireplace. The opening was barely big enough for a man to fit through. He looked curiously at his friend. "What must I do?"

"It is simple, Pierre. Just go down feet first. It is only a three-foot shaft down to the tunnel. We dug out a larger room below." He grinned. "It is not really a room, but it is big enough for you be able to bend over and get down onto your belly. Then all you must do is crawl toward the moonlight. It is about thirty feet. Take your time and do not worry. I will be right behind you."

"There are men waiting at the other end?"

"Yes, Pierre. You have friends there waiting for you. Now ... enough of the talk. Let us go!"

Francois helped Pierre lower himself into the tiny hole. He held on to Pierre's hands for a moment and then released him into the tunnel below. Pierre scraped against the coarse, rocky sides of the vertical shaft and landed in the bottom of the tunnel with a jarring thud. He knelt down for a moment to compose himself and get his bearings. He quickly located the horizontal shaft. He bent forward and contorted his body and kicked his legs. Somehow, he managed to get onto his belly. Once he was pointed toward the exit he did not waste any time. Pierre crawled with reckless abandon toward the dull blue glow at the far end of the tunnel.

It was a long, painful, energy-sapping endeavor. When at long last he reached the end, a set of strong hands pulled him out of the shaft. The invisible assistant steadied Pierre and helped him stand upright. His legs were weak and trembling from the sudden exercise involved in crawling such a long distance. Pierre looked into the man's face and recognized Lieutenant Oscar Hamelin of the militia.

"Oscar!" He hugged his friend.

"It is damned good to see you, Pierre."

"You cannot imagine how good it is to see you, Oscar."

"What about me?" inquired another voice from the darkness. It was Captain Bousseron.

"Francois! You are here as well!" hissed Pierre.

"There was no way that I was going to miss seeing you off this night," retorted the captain. "We have worked much too hard for this. Our men needed a victory after the humiliation of our shameful surrender."

Francois Turpin's head soon poked out of the end of the shaft. "Give a fellow a hand!" he whispered.

The captain and lieutenant grabbed his arms and pulled him out of the shaft.

"Did you cover the hole?" inquired the captain.

"Somewhat. It was very difficult to accomplish from below, especially since I had to brace myself inside the downward shaft while disguising the opening above my head. I do not think they will suspect anything at first. But it will not take them long to discover what has occurred."

"Good work, Francois," affirmed the captain. "Still, we have no time to waste." He moved closer to Pierre. "You need to get moving right now. We have the canoe ready. You will launch immediately. Drift south until you reach the mouth of the Embarrass River, then turn and head upstream. Go to Indian Creek and paddle two miles west. There is an old cabin on a small hill near the creek. You can hide out at that location until you feel a little better. But you need to move on to Kaskaskia as soon as possible."

"I understand the urgency of your plan, Francois, but I am very weak. I do not know if I have the muscle or strength to paddle against a current, even the minor current of the Embarrass. Will someone go with me? Francois Turpin, perhaps?"

A deep voice muttered from the darkness in the far corner of the shack, "What good will that city boy do you in the backwoods? He is likely to be bitten by a snake and die ..."

Pierre recognized that gruff voice, even though it was one that he had not heard in many months. His lips broke into a broad smile when the face of the brash, obscene *voyageur* Charles Rimbault appeared in the moonlight.

"Charles, you old skunk! Where have you been? You should have returned from New Orleans a month ago!" He shook hands with his long-absent friend. The rugged river man grabbed Pierre and hugged him with a warm embrace. Emotional tears flowed down Pierre's cheeks. Though he would never admit it, Charles had tears of joy, as well.

Charles broke the embrace and gave Pierre an enthusiastic slap on the arm. "I got tangled up in Kaskaskia, old friend. The town is full of those strange, interesting men from Virginia. I have been there for three weeks enjoying their company and their rum and relieving them of what little money they carried. It seems that none of them have any skill at cards or dice." He grinned slyly. "I only returned this very evening. Captain Bousseron informed me of the circumstance and the mission ... so here I am. Fresh as a daisy. Are you ready?"

"You are going with me?" Pierre asked in disbelief.

"Neither the fires of hell nor the gallows of these British pigs could keep me from it."

Pierre smiled. "Then I am ready."

Pierre's friends helped him walk to the edge of the water and then climb clumsily into the canoe. Charles insisted that he lie down in the bottom in the front of the boat and cover up with the blankets that awaited him there. The *voyageur* took up a paddle and seated himself in the rear steering position.

"Good luck, and Godspeed," whispered Bousseron.

The captain and Francois Turpin both waded thigh-deep into the water and gave the heavy, cargo-laden canoe a vigorous shove out into the current of the Wabash River. They watched with pride as the canoe that carried their liberated compatriot disappeared silently into the winter darkness.

# PART IV

*The Return of the Long Knives*
*1779*

# 16

## WINTER

*December 25, 1778*
*An Hour Before Dawn*

Pierre felt the waves slamming against the great ship. He heard the wind screaming and tearing at the timbers of the hull. Somewhere nearby he heard a voice calling for him ... pleading for his help. It was Antoine, his old friend from Austria! And the boy was drowning, dying, and crying out to Pierre for salvation.

"How did you get here, Antoine?" asked Pierre. "I saw you die beside that muddy river."

Antoine's head appeared mysteriously out of the water that surrounded Pierre. He reached and grabbed Pierre's leg. Blood poured from a hole in his forehead. The wounded fellow shouted, "Run, Pierre! Run, my friend! They are coming for you!" Then he released Pierre's leg and disappeared once again below the waves.

Pierre screamed, "Antoine! Antoine! Come back! Please do not leave me again! Come back!"

Pierre felt a sharp, painful whack against his backside. There was a sudden, frigid breeze against his face. He felt his body rocking gently from side to side. There was no storm. There was only silence. Pierre rolled quickly onto his back, causing the canoe that he was lying in to teeter precariously.

"Whoa! Careful now! Wake up and shut up, you fool. You are going to arouse every Indian within fifty miles. And try to be still. You almost tipped us over."

That voice did not belong to Antoine. It was the gruff, gravelly voice of Charles Rimbault. Though slightly disoriented, Pierre managed to recall his current circumstance. He was freshly escaped from the British jail and spared from Henry Hamilton's gallows in Vincennes.

Pierre surveyed his surroundings. It was still the dark of night, with no hint of the dawn. Pierre could see intermittent stars peeking between the thick, bare branches of the winter canopy overhead. He could hear Charles vigorously yet silently paddling the heavy canoe.

"I apologize, Charles. I must have been dreaming."

"Indeed, you were, complete with all manner of moaning and wailing. Your ceaseless hacking and coughing have been bad enough. But when you started shouting hysterically to our departed friend, Antoine Alexis, I had to put a stop to it. You were howling enough to wake the dead. I hope you do not have a bruise on your arse. Tugging your shoe did not seem to be enough to awaken you. I had to use my paddle."

Pierre chuckled in the darkness. "I have not received a spanking in quite some time, Charles."

"I suppose you were long overdue for one, then," his friend teased.

Pierre glanced over the side of the canoe. "Where are we now?"

"We have been on Indian Creek for a while. We will reach the cabin soon. It is on a small, cedar-covered hill on the western bank, inside a tight horseshoe bend in the creek. With the water almost completely surrounding us, we only have to keep watch to the southwest. It is an excellent hideout, and far from any roads or trails. We will be very safe there."

"How long have I been asleep?"

"Several hours now, ever since we pushed off at Vincennes. How are you feeling? Genevieve said that you have been extremely ill. You cough sounds very bad."

"I do not feel well, at all, Charles. I think I have a fever."

"Well, my friend, just cover up with those blankets and hold on a little longer. We will be warm and snug inside that old hunting cabin within the hour. Then the renowned physician Charles Rimbault will get you cured of that cough and fever."

Pierre grinned in the darkness and pulled the wool blanket tighter beneath his chin.

☙

*December 25, 1778*
*Mid-Morning - Fort Sackville - Vincennes*

Governor Hamilton leapt from his desk chair, knocking over his glass of Christmas brandy and spilling the contents on a stack of freshly-written dispatches.

"Whatever do you mean? How can he be gone?" he thundered. "How in God's name can a prisoner simply disappear from our guardhouse? Your men must have been derelict in their duties, Sergeant. Asleep at their posts, no doubt. You will pay for their mistake, sir! If that man is, indeed, gone then your career is finished!"

The British sergeant stood proudly, cocked hat held high in his left hand in front of his red-coated chest. He stood at attention in front of the governor's desk. Major Hay stood silently beside the door, his eyes open wide in disbelief. The prisoner from Virginia, Captain Leonard Helm, sat quietly in his chair beside the fireplace. His eyes gleamed with delight.

The sergeant sighed. "Sir, if I may … no one was derelict in their duties. The men remained on vigilant watch throughout the night. I checked on them myself each hour. The iron bolt and lock on the door were secure and undisturbed. No one broke the lock or otherwise inflicted damage upon the door or walls. We have inspected them inside and out. The man is simply gone, sir."

"So he's just up and disappeared like a fart on a summer breeze?" screeched the governor. "Is that what you claim? That he has simply vanished? Not likely, I say! There is a conspiracy afoot, Sergeant, and I aim to get to the bottom of it." He darted from behind his desk. "Major!"

"Sir!" answered Major Hay.

"Dispatch patrols in every direction. Three-man teams are to scout to a perimeter of five miles. Our French 'fart on the breeze' cannot have traveled very far on foot."

"Yes, sir. I will see to it immediately."

"Send only the Frenchmen and whatever Indians we have available. I want the Englishmen to remain here for our defense. I do not trust these locals. They are a vile, lazy, treacherous lot who will shift their allegiances on a whim."

"Yes, sir," responded the major.

Hamilton cast a livid glance at the sergeant. "What about the Spaniard ... Mr. Vigo? Is he still in his room, or has he vanished, as well?"

"Mr. Vigo is secure and comfortable in the other blockhouse, sir. I checked on him the moment that I discovered that Grimard was gone."

"Well, at least you had enough common sense to do that!" the governor snapped.

"Shall I join the patrols, sir?" asked the chastised soldier, attempting to change the subject.

Hamilton grabbed his coat and hat from a nail behind his desk. "No, Sergeant. You will accompany me and show me the quarters of our French phantom. I intend to get to the bottom of this mystery."

"Of course, sir."

The sergeant turned and opened the door for the governor, who stormed angrily through the portal into the muddy courtyard of the fort. Hamilton marched angrily across the compound toward the blockhouse where six French militiamen lounged against the log wall. The sergeant followed him in humble submission.

"What are those men doing milling about?" asked the governor.

"I instructed them to remain outside but near the cell, sir. They are the six men who were on guard at various times throughout the night. I assumed that you would want to speak with them personally."

"You assumed correctly, sergeant. I also want lanterns and torches."

"There are six lanterns inside the room already, sir. We left them in place after our initial inspection. The chamber is well-lighted."

The governor strode angrily to the door and kicked it with his right foot. He hissed at the nearest Frenchman, "Well, don't just stand there like an idiot! Unlock and open this door!"

The Frenchman moved aside as the sergeant stepped forward with his key to open and remove the lock. Once the door was open the governor stormed inside.

"Nothing has been disturbed?" he confirmed.

"No, sir. I left everything exactly as I discovered it. I secured and relocked the door before making my report to you."

The governor paced around the periphery of the room and examined the walls. "Who was the last person to visit this room?"

"Private Jamison, sir. It was just before dark and the closing of the fort. He confirmed the prisoner's status after the man's family departed."

The governor nodded. "I saw Grimard's blabbering brood when they entered, along with that fat, mutinous priest. Were their belongings sufficiently inspected?"

"Yes, sir. There was nothing but a basket full of food and two blankets. The priest also carried a Communion set to administer the Sacrament to the prisoner. We examined everything very thoroughly. You can see that the items carried by his family remain. The basket, refuse, wine bottles, and both blankets."

"Where was the prisoner when the private checked on him last night?"

The sergeant was confused. "Here in this room, sir."

"I mean … where in this room?" screeched Hamilton in frustration. "Where, exactly, was he sitting? Or was he lying down? What was his disposition?"

The sergeant pointed toward the spot. "The private said that he was lying over there near the interior corner and wrapped snugly with both blankets. Grimard appeared to have a chill or fever and was attempting to get warm."

The governor looked curiously at the pile of crumpled blankets and the food basket perched on top. The items sat near the unused fireplace on the opposite side of the room.

"Don't you think it odd that a freezing, ill man would leave his blankets behind? And why would they be located on the opposite side of the room, far from the place where he slept?"

Hamilton walked toward the pile of blankets and refuse. He kicked angrily at the food basket, knocking it and the two wine bottles into the wall nearby. As he kicked his foot made a hollow, scraping thump against the ground below the blankets. It did not sound or feel right to him. He dropped to one knee and threw back the pile of crumpled blankets. Below them were two small boards. He tossed both boards to one side and peered, aghast, into the deep, dark hole below.

The sergeant standing behind him exclaimed, "Oh, my God!"

Governor Hamilton seethed with rage. "It appears that we do, indeed, have a conspiracy on our hands, Sergeant. Fetch me that fat priest and the French whore."

⅂

*Later that Day - Governor Hamilton's Office*
Hamilton stared angrily out the window as cold, heavy rains soaked the bleak landscape around Vincennes. His prisoner, Captain Leonard Helm of Virginia, sat silently beside the fireplace and sipped wine from a crystal glass. Although a prisoner, Helm had

become quite chummy with Hamilton and his officers over the past two weeks. Hamilton enjoyed the Virginian's jovial company and treated him more like a guest than a prisoner.

Genevieve Grimard responded angrily to Hamilton's repeated and intrusive interrogation. "I will not tell you again, Governor Hamilton. I do not know the whereabouts of my husband! Yesterday, when I saw him last, he was freezing to death and feverish in your horrid excuse for a jail cell. And how evil it was of you to allow neither fire nor blanket for a man to keep warm in the dead of winter!"

The governor faced her and angrily stomped his right foot three times. "It did not seem to slow him down, *Madame* Grimard! He ably made his escape, and you assisted him!"

Genevieve choked back a giggle. The vision of this grown man stomping his foot reminded her of one of her young sons throwing a tantrum. She elected to smile within her heart.

"What an interesting picture that would make!" she retorted. "Do you suppose that I crawled in here under cover of darkness, swollen to eight months of pregnancy, with ankles the size of melons, chewed my way through an oak door and iron lock, and then set my husband free? Do you not hear how utterly ridiculous you sound?"

"Of course, I do not believe *that* is what occurred. But you know something!" he hissed as he drew his face closer to hers. "You know what has happened. You know who is responsible."

"I know nothing."

"You lie! Now tell me where your husband is!"

She stated flatly, "I do not know where he is."

"You are lying to me, you insolent French hussy!"

"I am not! And I have nothing else to say, you pompous, arrogant little slush bucket!"

The governor responded without thinking. He slapped Genevieve viciously with the back of his right hand. He struck her with such force that the horn comb she wore in her hair flew against the log wall and shattered into pieces. She raised her hand to cover her sore, red cheek. The wounded woman choked back her tears through sheer power of pride.

Captain Helm, ever the gallant American, jumped to his feet. "Governor! I must protest this crude violence! Do not forget that this is a fragile lady and that you are supposed to be a British gentleman!"

"Remain where you are and shut up, Captain Helm! Or would you like me to find a blockhouse cell for you?"

Helm returned quietly to his chair and continued nursing his glass of wine.

The governor took a deep breath and regained his composure. He leaned over Genevieve's chair. "Let us pretend for a moment that you are telling the truth." He paused. "Would you actually tell me if you did know of his location?"

"Of course not," she replied tersely. "I simply rejoice that he is gone and beyond your wicked, bloodthirsty reach."

The governor stood upright and walked around the side of his desk.

"And what about the priest … that insufferable Father Gibault? Where has he gone?"

Genevieve could not conceal her surprise. "What?"

"Oh! So, you did not know that he has disappeared, as well? That is very interesting, indeed."

"No, Governor. I had no idea. He escorted us home at dusk yesterday and that was the last that I saw of him."

"Well, *Madame* Grimard, it seems that our mutinous priest has flown the coop, as well. No one in this entire village seems to know his whereabouts. He has abandoned his flock. Like your husband, he is another miraculous French fart that has vanished on the wind!"

She shook her head in shock. "I promise you, sir. I had no idea that Father Gibault was gone."

Hamilton plopped down into his chair. "Well, rest assured, *Madame*, that I will get to the bottom of this great mystery. I will find who is responsible. All parties in this conspiracy will swing from the gallows ... and that includes you! Now get out of my sight!"

Hamilton picked up his spectacles and began to examine the map of the Illinois Country that was spread across his desk. Captain Helm placed his glass on the mantle and moved to help Genevieve up from her chair. He escorted her to the door and opened it for her. He called to a British soldier outside, "Sergeant!"

The young man stepped through the door from the narrow porch outside. "Yes, sir?"

"Please escort Madame Grimard back to her home. And would you please extend to her every courtesy?"

"Of course, Captain Helm."

As the Virginian offered Genevieve's arm to the sergeant he made eye contact with her and silently mouthed the words, "I'm so sorry."

Genevieve offered no response.

❧

*January 1, 1779*
*The Cabin on Indian Creek - Illinois Country*

Rain pounded on the roof of the cabin. Water dripped haphazardly from over a half-dozen holes and cracks overhead. Pots and bowls scattered across the floor captured the invading moisture. Pierre was sitting up on his thin mattress of pine straw. He grimaced at the horrid smell that wafted from the bowl in Charles Rimbault's hand.

"What in God's name is in it?"

"You do not want to know," quipped Charles. "But, rest assured, it will loosen up that brown, bloody sludge that you have been coughing up out of your lungs for the past week."

Pierre continued his interrogation, "Who taught you how to make it?"

"A Kickapoo Indian woman that I once shared a lodge with. Now stop your whining and pull up your shirt."

Pierre grunted but complied with his friend's command. He pulled his green homespun shirt up until it was gathered around his neck. Rimbault immediately began to slap the thick, warm, mucoid concoction onto Pierre's chest and then smear it around with a wood paddle. Pierre gagged at the putrid odor. He was immediately convinced that, if Rimbault smeared that obscene goo onto his body, there was absolutely no way he would ever smell the same again.

"*Mon Dieu!* It smells like a mixture of rum, piss, and pine tar! I may vomit!"

"You have barely eaten anything for a week now, so you have nothing to vomit. And how did you guess my secret ingredients?" he teased with a wink.

Once Pierre's chest was sufficiently coated with the fragrant syrup Charles fetched a steaming pot from the fireplace. He sat the pot down on the floor beside Pierre's bed and then used a short stick to fish a piece of heavy linen out of the boiling water. He allowed it to drain into the pot and cool off just a bit before wringing the excess scalding water out of the cloth with his leathery hands.

"Pierre, this is going to be very hot. It has to be hot in order to release the medicine and vapors. Do you understand?"

"Yes, Charles. Just get it over with."

His friend shrugged. "As you wish."

He quickly unfurled the scalding hot cloth and slapped it onto Pierre's chest. The sick Frenchman wailed like a stuck pig. Rimbault slapped his hand over Pierre's mouth.

"Let us try not to summon any unwanted neighbors," he implored. Pierre kicked and thrashed at the bed. "Calm down, you big baby. It will cool off in a short while."

Pierre finally ceased his screaming, growling, and groaning. Charles pulled his friend's shirt down over the hot poultice and pulled the wool blankets back up to his neck. Pierre breathed deeply of the fragrant vapors of pine that hung like a fog over his chest. The sensation actually felt good in his lungs, but the smell remained repugnant.

Pierre was livid. The painful burn of the cloth had been somewhat unexpected. "You did not have to melt my skin off of me, Charles!"

"I told you. The heat is what makes the medicine work. Besides, you are still alive, are you not? I swear, you whine like a nanny goat. It is too bad you do not give milk like one. At least then you would be useful around here."

"Cretin!" spat Pierre, a huge smile on his face.

"Fart catcher!" responded Charles, smiling even broader.

"Rapscallion!" answered Pierre.

"Dilberry!" returned Charles.

Both men chuckled. They quite enjoyed their customary insult contests.

"How long have I been asleep?"

"Almost four days. Do you remember arriving here?"

Charles whipped out his skinning knife and began cutting tiny green pine needles and dropping them into a cup of hot water.

"Barely. I remember you helping me from the canoe and into the cabin. I remember you building a fire. But my memory becomes a little cloudy after that."

Charles nodded and smiled. "You were in and out of consciousness for most of the first three days. Your fever got so high that I finally had to dip you in the creek to cool you off. The fever broke the next morning, and then you slept soundly until this afternoon. You have coughed incessantly from the moment we arrived. The product was dark yellow and mixed with blood for those first few days. But lately it has been clearing up, with just a tinge of brown. Your lungs are improving, I think."

"So, we have been here a whole week, then?"

Charles nodded. "Exactly seven days."

"Then it is the new year today!" declared Pierre.

Rimbault's eyes widened. "I suppose it is. To be honest, I had not even thought of it. Welcome to the year of our Lord, 1779, Pierre. Now drink this, but be careful. It, too, is very hot."

"What is it?"

"A simple tea made from the needles of the white pine. It is very aromatic and full of nutrients. I have added some maple sugar. It will open up your nose and lungs and help you get back a little strength. We will try some turkey broth later. I shot a bird two days ago and have the bones boiling in the pot."

"What happened to the rest of the turkey?"

"It was delicious," teased Charles.

Pierre sipped the yellow-green pine tea. It actually tasted pretty good. Pierre had expected a flavor akin to the pine tar that was smeared across his chest. The cool sensation of the vapors chilled deeply into his lungs and burned his empty stomach.

"How long will we stay here, Charles?"

"Until you are well, Pierre, unless these waters continue to rise. Thank God, we have a canoe. The lowlands all around us are beginning to flood, but it will have to be a flood that would impress Noah to reach the base of this cabin. We are on a pretty high spot."

"And where will we go once I am fit for travel?"

"We will take Indian Creek and the backwaters as far west as they will carry us, then we will walk to Kaskaskia and join the Virginians."

*January 8, 1779*
*Fort Sackville - Vincennes*

Governor Hamilton locked his fingers together across his belly and rested his elbows on the arms of his crude chair. The Spaniard prisoner, Francis Vigo, sat in a similar chair on the opposite side of the fireplace. Vigo sipped from a glass of sweet red wine. The cheerful, dancing fire in the large fireplace cast a warm, orange glow throughout the room as a soaking rain pounded upon the wood shingles overhead.

The ever-present Captain Leonard Helm lounged in a chair on the far side of the room. He sat near a small table that was equipped with a chess board. He sipped wine and pretended to study the positions of the pieces in his ongoing game with Governor Hamilton, but his real interest was in the governor's conversation with his Spaniard friend and ally.

"Mr. Vigo, I can find no cause to hold you any longer. I am releasing you to return to your home and business in St. Louis. I sincerely apologize for the inconvenience that we have caused you. Please, sir, express my deepest apologies to the Spanish authorities there for your temporary incarceration here. Surely you understand the confusion that existed upon our return and reoccupation of the fort, as well as our need to confirm your neutrality in the war."

"It has, indeed, been an inconvenience, *Señor.* However, your men have demonstrated nothing but generosity and kindness to me during my stay. Your officers have seen to my every need and comfort. I have been treated as an honored guest, not at all like a prisoner. For that I am very grateful."

Hamilton nodded graciously. "I want to be honest and forthright with you. I fully understand your willingness to do business with the American rebels. You are a businessman in search of a profit, as are all entrepreneurs. However, as a representative of Great Britain I must insist that you abandon all future dealings with these murderous thugs. Any assistance that you give them could someday inflict harm upon the armies of the British Crown, and that would be considered a hostile act." He leaned forward toward the Spanish merchant to project authority and confidence. "Do you understand what I am saying to you, Mr. Vigo?"

"*Si, Señor* Hamilton. I understand you very clearly. I will take your demands under advisement and will consult with the other partners in my company."

"I can ask no more of you, save one thing, *Señor* Vigo."

"And what is that?"

"I humbly request that you do nothing to injure the British cause during your journey home. Do not detour to Cahokia or Kaskaskia and offer the Americans any intelligence regarding our situation here. As you well know, the size of my garrison is less than one hundred men. Most of the northern Indians and many of our French allies have returned to Detroit. If word of our current status were to reach our enemies to the west it could prove catastrophic to our cause. Will you give me your word as a gentleman?"

The Spaniard stared into the fire for a moment, offering no response. Finally, thoughtfully, he drew in a deep breath.

"*Señor* Hamilton, I give you my word. I will not detour to the French villages to the west. I will return straightway to my home in St. Louis. Though I must confess, it will be no joy to travel in this endless rain."

Both men chuckled. Hamilton raised his glass of brandy to Vigo.

"Then I accept your word, and I wish you safe travels, sir. You may depart at first light."

"Thank you, Governor."

Leonard Helm grinned mischievously in the shadows beyond the light of the fireplace.

*January 29, 1779*
*Kaskaskia, Illinois Country - 180 Miles to the West of Vincennes*
Colonel George Rogers Clark sat alone in his office and pondered his next move. Clark was a stunning young man, with long, golden hair and a rugged, handsome face. He sported a butternut colored outfit made entirely of fresh buckskin. He sipped from a mug of hot tea as he listened to the rain running off the roof and spattering in the puddle just outside his window.

Clark sighed. He was growing weary of negotiating agreements and offering incentives to pacify the endless parade of Indian leaders who sought his favor. He was fed up with the constant conflicts that erupted among the various tribes that had encampments around the French villages. And he was absolutely sick of the winter weather, the incessant rain, and the rising water.

Colonel Clark was also growing weary of calming the frayed nerves and flighty loyalties of his skittish French allies who occupied the Villages of Kaskaskia, Cahokia, and Prairie du Rocher. These locals were quite prone to fatalism, exaggeration, and abandonment of the cause of liberty. Earlier in the month an enemy patrol of thirty men had approached in the vicinity of Kaskaskia. By the time word reached Clark and his men at a gala they were attending in Prairie du Rocher, the size of the enemy had grown by rumor to over eight hundred ... in the minds of the terrified French. Believing the numbers of the enemy to be large, the local Frenchmen then declared their sudden neutrality in the war. After the threat disappeared, Colonel Clark disciplined them for their lack of fortitude and continued to remind them of their cowardice whenever it was to his advantage.

There was also the frustrating lack of funds for the ongoing operations in Illinois. Colonel Clark had already risked his entire personal fortune on the venture. He still had received no support worth mentioning from the legislature in Virginia. Amazingly, his most loyal financial supporters had been from among the Spaniards in New Orleans. Clark's ledger books and the cash boxes of businesses throughout the villages of Illinois were filled with vouchers and promises of payment at some unknown point of time in the future. It was a delicate financial circumstance.

The return of the British to Illinois and the recapture of Vincennes had been the veritable "feathers that broke the horse's back." Vincennes was a humiliating and demoralizing loss. Clark's hold on the Illinois County was tenuous, at best. He was beginning to wonder if his campaign in the Northwest might fail.

Yes, it was safe to say that Colonel George Rogers Clark was growing weary of his army's poverty, the desolation of this faraway place, the cowardly French citizenry, and the overall environment of Illinois. He longed to be back home in Virginia or in camp with his Kentucky friends at the Falls of the Ohio ... anywhere but Illinois.

A gentle tap at his door snatched him from his solitude and self-pity.

"Come."

Corporal Lewis, Clark's office clerk, opened the door and stuck his head into the commander's office. "Colonel Clark, sir, there is a gentleman requesting an audience with you. It is the Spaniard, Francis Vigo of St. Louis."

"Good Lord! He left for Vincennes over two months ago! Send him right in ... and go fetch the other officers. He may have critical intelligence for us."

"Yes, sir."

Moments later Francis Vigo entered the office. Colonel Clark stood and shook his hand with familiarity and enthusiasm.

"*Señor* Vigo! Welcome back! You have been gone for a very long time. I was afraid that some tragedy had befallen you."

"My delay was not of my own choice, Colonel Clark. I was detained by the British at Fort Sackville."

"I suspected as much. Were you mistreated?"

"Quite the contrary, Colonel. I was housed as a guest and treated quite well. I believe that Governor Hamilton was simply trying to consolidate his gains and assume control over the region. He has been quite busy pacifying the town and trying to bring the local Indians over to his side. It has been most difficult for him." The Spaniard smiled broadly. "The respect for your Long Knives of Virginia runs deep around Vincennes."

Clark grinned. "That is good news to hear. It should make our efforts much less strenuous when we attempt to retake the fort in the spring."

"You should not wait so long, Colonel. I have some information that may prove helpful to you."

There was another knock at the door.

"Come!"

Four men filed into the room, all captains in Clark's army from Virginia. They each shook the water from their coats and hats.

"Enter, gentlemen. Find a seat. *Señor* Vigo was just about to enlighten me on the disposition of Hamilton's forces at Vincennes." He paused as the men found their places. "Please continue, *Señor* Vigo."

The Spaniard nodded. "When I departed Vincennes three weeks ago it appeared to me that Hamilton had a tenuous hold, at best, on Vincennes and its environs."

"Three weeks ago?" asked Colonel Clark. "Why did it take so long for you to reach us here in Kaskaskia?"

Vigo grinned mischievously. "It is because of an oath that I made with Hamilton. He made me swear that I would go straight to my home in St. Louis and not detour here to give you information about his forces. I honored my oath. I went home to St. Louis, then promptly turned my boat around and headed for Kaskaskia."

Clark and his officers laughed uproariously.

"Are you being sincere, Francis, or just toying with us?" asked Clark.

Vigo smiled broadly. "I am most sincere, *Señor* Clark. I am nothing if I am not a man of my word. Therefore, I kept my word to the very letter. But I swore nothing to Hamilton regarding what I would do *after* I returned home."

The men laughed again and offered copious congratulations for the ingenuity and cleverness of the Spaniard.

"So," Colonel Clark interrupted the celebrating, "What can you tell us about Vincennes and the fort?"

"I can tell you, Colonel, that all of Hamilton's Indians from the north have returned upriver, along with the majority of his French allies. He has perhaps forty British soldiers and militiamen under his command, and less than one hundred men total defending the fort."

Clark's officers gasped in surprise.

"They have less men than we do!" exclaimed Captain Joseph Bowman, Clark's second-in-command.

The other officers began to chatter excitedly.

"Calm down, gentlemen! We need to hear Mr. Vigo's entire report. Now, *Señor*, what about the town and its inhabitants? What about the local Indians?"

"The French settlers are most unhappy and displeased, Colonel. Hamilton's treatment has been very oppressive. He forced them to make new oaths to the British Crown. He has restricted their freedom of movement and curtailed much of their activity and business. He was even planning to execute a local man named Grimard, but the fellow managed to escape. I believe that some of the locals, most likely elements of the militia, helped dig a tunnel to set him free."

"Really?" mused Clark. "It sounds like those Frenchmen have managed to hold on to a measure of gumption. I am quite surprised. That is not very 'French' of them."

"Indeed. I believe, with all sincerity, that they eagerly await your return, Colonel. And with the small size of Hamilton's forces, I believe they will join with you in combating him. That is my most humble opinion."

"And the Indians?" Clark asked again.

"They remain separated from the British. A few ventured into the fort and town on business while I was there, but none of them have joined Hamilton and his army. Like I said before, *Señor*, their fear of the Long Knives is great. They do not want to be found in collusion with the British when you return. I suspect that they will be willing to join you, as well."

George Rogers Clark looked at his captains. "Gentlemen, if we wait until springtime, the tides of fortune could change. As soon as the rivers to the north thaw in March, Hamilton will get fresh reinforcements from Detroit. Vincennes will become their head-quarters for a renewed offensive into Kentucky. All of our outposts there could fall before next winter. Do you agree?"

His captains all looked at one another and nodded in the affirmative. Their colonel's analysis was, most likely, a correct one.

"Well, there it is, then," stated the colonel. He breathed in deeply and then stood. "We move on Vincennes immediately. Captain Bowman, prepare the men. Send representatives to the authorities in the French villages. Tell them we need volunteer regiments and that we need them right now."

"Yes, sir," responded the captain.

The men sat in silence and pondered the travails of the coming days. Outside the office the rain increased its intensity until it became a downpour. Even Francis Vigo seemed awed by the enormity of the task that lay ahead of these intrepid men.

Colonel Clark interrupted the silence of their thoughts, "That is all, gentlemen. Let's get to it. We have work to do. See to your men."

The officers stood silently and proceeded single-file out into the pouring rain.

⅀

*January 30, 1779*
*The Cabin on Indian Creek - Illinois Country*
It was almost dark. Charles Rimbault was cleaning his rifle as he reclined beside the cozy, warm fireplace. Pierre was busy washing dishes in an ancient wood tub that Charles had located in the clearing behind the cabin. A soft, gentle rain fell from the low winter clouds. There were significantly fewer leaks in the roof than during their first few days in the cabin. The rains had ceased and the sun actually came out for three glorious days during their second week in remote refuge. Charles took advantage of the good weather and used a combination of forest moss and pine pitch to seal most of the leaks in the roof.

Pierre's condition improved slowly. He had no more signs of fever, but the deep pneumonia that infected his lungs during his imprisonment continued to sap his strength for weeks. He was coughing less and less, but he remained physically weak ... far too weak to travel in the winter cold to Kaskaskia. Charles knew that his friend needed a couple more weeks of recovery time before they could depart their comfortable refuge. But the time of that departure was drawing nigh. The waters continued to rise in every direction around them. There seemed to be little game left for hunting. Their food stores were running precariously low.

"How long are you going to polish that old slab of worthless iron, you niffynanny?" teased Pierre.

"Until you get finished washing your twiddle-diddles, *mademoiselle*. You make quite the washer-woman."

"Fartleberry!" responded Pierre.

"Lollypoop!" muttered Charles.

A loud knock on the door of the cabin interrupted their ongoing contest of insults and invaded the serenity of their hideout. Charles lunged for his pistol that hung on a nail near the door. Pierre wiped his wet hands and grabbed a musket from the corner.

The door vibrated as the intruder pounded it again.

Charles whispered, "You get ready to open the door. I will kneel behind the table and prepare to fire."

Pierre nodded and darted behind the door. It took only a few seconds for him to get into position.

The door vibrated even more violently as an invisible fist pounded against it. This time, however, the knocking was accompanied by a very familiar voice.

"*Bonjour mes amis!* Open the door! I am soaked to the bone and my arse is frozen to my breeches!"

Pierre instantly yanked the door open and tumbled into the embrace of a cold, waterlogged friend. He exclaimed with great surprise and joy, "Francois Turpin, whatever are you doing here?"

# 17

## AN EPIC MARCH BEGINS

Pierre hung his friend's drenched clothes on a makeshift clothesline near the fire. Francois was cocooned within two wool blankets and seated cross-legged on another blanket on the floor in front of the warm blaze. He sipped thick, rich broth from an old pewter mug. It had taken several minutes to accomplish, but his teeth had finally stopped chattering and his cheeks were a slightly lighter shade of gray-blue.

"Why did you set out alone into this weather, you fool?" scolded Charles.

"I had to come and check on you fellows. A Piankashaw warrior visited Vincennes last week. He mentioned that he saw smoke coming from a cabin along this creek several days ago, so I knew that you must still be here. I surmised that something must be wrong. You should have departed for Kaskaskia a long time ago. I thought you might need some help."

"I have been very ill, Francois. The infection in my lungs was severe. Charles says that I almost died during the first week. With all of the rain and cold, we have been unable to depart without the danger of risking another fever. But Charles says that we will leave and head west in one more week."

Charles exhaled a disgusted breath. "What is truly bad wrong, Francois, is the fact that there are Indians who know we are here.

If the Piankashaws are aware of our location, it is only a matter of time before a war party of Shawnee stumble upon us."

Francois shook his head vigorously. "No one is venturing out in this weather, Charles. The warrior that I mentioned traveled through here by canoe, and he was alone. Besides, this little knob of land is the only spot of dry ground for almost three miles. The only way anyone is getting in or out of here is by boat. There will not be any hunting parties venturing into this flooded land. The natives will be hunting buffalo to the northwest. You are still safe here. Very safe."

Charles grunted in affirmation. He was obviously pleased. The men sat quietly for a while and stared into the fire. They sipped hot drinks from their cups and mugs. Pierre finally broke the awkward silence with a battery of questions.

"Francois, how is my Genevieve? Is she well? Has she given birth yet? How are my boys?"

His friend laughed. "I was wondering when you were going to ask! You can rest assured that they are fine, Pierre. No, there is no baby yet. But when I left she was getting very close. I think she is quite miserable by now. Surely it will not be long. And your boys are all just fine. Genevieve went through a rough couple of days after you escaped. Hamilton was quite livid when you escaped. He accused everyone around him of a vast conspiracy. He brought Genevieve into his office and interrogated her at length." Francois' face darkened with a grim frown. "He hit her, Pierre."

Pierre's jaw clenched. The muscles in his cheeks fluttered. In the firelight, Francois could see his friend's pulse throbbing beneath the skin on his temples.

"He did what?" growled Pierre.

"He struck her viciously during the interrogation ... backhanded her across the face and almost knocked her out of her chair. It was hard enough to dislodge the comb from her hair. She carried a deep bruise on her right cheek for a week." He smiled through the grim look on his face. "She wore that bruise like a badge of honor. The people of Vincennes regarded it as such. She has become quite the local celebrity."

Pierre ignored Francois' commentary and glanced at Charles. He growled, "Now I will most definitely have to kill that hair-buying bastard."

Rimbault nodded. "You'll get your chance one of these days. The Virginians will be back in a few months, and then we will make him pay."

⚬

*February 4, 1779*
*Kaskaskia - Illinois Country*

It was mid-afternoon. Pale gray clouds hung low over the gloomy river town of Kaskaskia. A steady, gentle rain continued its ceaseless soaking of the region. Huge puddles of water and soupy mud filled the streets and side roads of the town. Neither man nor beast could escape the miserable wet and cold of the dreary Illinois winter.

The men of the Virginia Long Knives and their French compatriots from Kaskaskia and Cahokia gathered along the rain-drenched bank of the Kaskaskia River and stared at the strange naval vessel that was about to launch into the slow-moving, muddy current. It was a clumsy-looking riverboat that had been refitted into a semblance of a military gunboat. The odd craft bristled with two four-pound cannons and four mounted swivel guns. It also carried a nine-pound field cannon strapped to its center deck along with an enormous cargo of ammunition, powder, and rations for Clark's Virginia army. In the center of the boat there was a structure comprised of new wood and timber. It was the newly constructed galley that would serve to feed the crew of forty-five men.

The commander of the vessel was Captain John Rogers, a cousin to Colonel George Rogers Clark. He was also the man responsible for the design and refitting of the rugged riverboat. Colonel Clark had recently dubbed the vessel the *Willing* as an homage to James

Willing, an American boatsman who had in recent months wreaked havoc on British shipping along the Mississippi River.

Clark's overall plan for the *Willing* was quite simple, but the timing of his plan was absolutely critical. The boat was tasked to follow a water course along the Kaskaskia, Mississippi, Ohio, and Wabash Rivers until it reached the vicinity of Vincennes. Simultaneously, Colonel Clark would march his army overland toward the same objective. The two forces would converge upon the village and then the Americans and Frenchmen would crush the British and their allies inside the walls of Fort Sackville ... *if* everything worked out perfectly and according to plan. Colonel Clark's strategy of attack relied heavily on the large guns, artillery, and ammunition on board this awkward little boat.

The locals who lined the bank cheered as men untied the ropes that tethered the boat to small trees along the edge of the water. Two crewmen on board used long poles to push the *Willing* out into the gentle current of the Kaskaskia river. Captain John Rogers stood proudly along the rail of his unorthodox naval vessel. He waved enthusiastically to his cousin.

"George, I'll see you at the fort."

Colonel Clark grinned. "You'd better. We will likely have empty bellies and wet powder by the time we reach Vincennes. And I will need that nine-pounder to knock on a few doors. Good luck, cousin." He waved to the intrepid men of his tiny navy as the boat disappeared to the southwest in the frigid fog and mist that hung low over the water.

❧

*February 5, 1779*
*Vincennes - The Grimard Home*

The sun still lay hidden below the eastern horizon. It would be at least another full hour before dawn would bring the orb's life-sustaining light and warmth to the remote, slumbering village of Vincennes.

Genevieve wailed in horrific pain. She held on to the small headboard of her bed with a grip that caused her knuckles to turn completely white. Her labor had been short but intense. She was glad that it was almost over, and she was grateful that the ever-supportive Josephine was present to help her. The tenacious wife of Francois Turpin had grown into an excellent midwife over the past decade. Indeed, she had delivered most of the babies born in Vincennes since her arrival. She answered the call without complaint when young Pierre came and pounded on her door to fetch her in the middle of the frigid February night.

Josephine yelled with delight, "All right, little Mama, the head is out. Good Lord! Look at all of that hair! Is this a baby or a bear? Now ... one more push, Genevieve! This is it! Just one more push! Wait for it ... wait for the contraction ... all right, there it is! Now, Genevieve! Push, woman, push!"

Genevieve felt an excruciating wave of pain as the baby's shoulders forced their way through the center of her pelvis. That brief peak of searing pain was followed by instantaneous relief as Josephine eased the fluid and mucus-coated child out of her birth canal.

"It is a girl!" Josephine shrieked. "It is a perfect little girl!"

The newborn arched her back and kicked her legs, flinging droplets of fluid into the cold air around her. Steam rose from the baby's warm body into the cool air of the room. Josephine quickly used her finger to loosen the mucus plug in the back of the child's throat. Moments later Genevieve heard a gurgling sound as the infant attempted to breathe. Then came the high-pitched whack of Josephine's hand on the child's bottom. The baby coughed and sputtered for a moment and then emitted a high-pitched, powerful, piercing cry. Both Genevieve and Josephine joined in with their own cries of celebration and joy.

Josephine quickly tied and cut the cord and then wrapped the baby in a plush linen cloth. She placed the child on Genevieve's chest and then began to massage her soft, mushy belly. Genevieve cried tears of utter bliss as she cooed and talked to her little girl. The baby's crying soon subsided as she nestled comfortably and securely beneath her mother's neck. Moments later the placenta departed Genevieve's birth canal easily and painlessly.

"You did a wonderful job!" declared Josephine as she deposited the afterbirth into a large basin and proceeded to clean up the usual blood, mucus, fluid, and feces that always accompanied childbirth. "She was, by far, the easiest delivery of my midwifing career." Her eyes twinkled and she smiled broadly. "You should be very pleased with yourself."

"I simply cannot believe that I finally have a baby girl," Genevieve proclaimed through tears of joy. "I have wanted a little girl of my own for so very long." She gently kissed the newborn's eyes and nose and then held her tiny, pink cheek up to her own.

Josephine glanced toward the heavy privacy curtains that were drawn shut across the far end of the room. Several glowing eyes peeked through the narrow crack between the two drapes. She smiled.

"All right, boys. You can come out now. Come and meet your new sister. Gaspard, you can come out, as well. Come and greet the newest member of the Grimard household!"

The Grimard boys darted instantly from behind the curtain, scampered across the room, and surrounded their mother. She held the baby out for them to examine. Their faces beamed with wonder and joy. Gaspard, Josephine's son, stood behind them and looked at the baby in silent curiosity.

"Oh, Mama, she is so pretty!" declared Jean-Baptiste.

The rambunctious Charles, barely three years old and still something of a baby himself, was not much of a talker. He climbed up onto the bed beside his mother and, without invitation, planted a firm kiss on the baby girl's forehead. Genevieve's heart leapt.

"I think she looks like Papa," declared Pierre. "Look at her long, wavy hair. And she has Papa's eyes!"

Genevieve held the little girl up and examined her closely. "I do think you are right, Pierre. And if she looks like your Papa then she must also look like you, because you are his perfect image." She lay the baby back on her chest and reached out to cup her hand against her oldest son's cheek. Little Pierre turned his head and kissed his mother's hand with tender affection.

"Whatever shall you call her?" asked Josephine. "Your Pierre is not here to help you choose the name."

"We already selected names several months ago. If it were a boy he was to be called Nicolas."

"Well, you will just have to save that name for the next one, perhaps. But what name for a girl?"

Genevieve smiled. "Pierre insisted that a girl be named with the most beautiful name that he has ever heard or spoken from his lips." She paused.

"And?" Josephine asked impatiently. "Do not keep us in suspense. What is this most beautiful name?"

"Why, it is Genevieve, of course!"

Both women and the room full of little boys giggled with joy.

*February 6, 1779*
*Kaskaskia - Illinois Country*

Colonel George Rogers Clark beamed with pride at his small army of one hundred and seventy men. The flags of the different companies that formed the determined little army hung loosely on their hand-cut poles, soaked by the cold rain. He guided his handsome mount to a position in front of the lines of frontiersmen and French settlers.

"Gentlemen, I believe you know that the task before us is a daunting one. We have many miles to march in order to reach and engage our enemies in Vincennes. Rivers, streams, and great floodwaters await us. As you can well see, the rains continue to fall from darkened skies. But none of this will deter us from the cause! We will march over land, we will wade through water and flood, we will overcome hunger and want, we will run through the fires of Hell if we have to ... and we will vanquish our British foes!"

The formation of men erupted in celebration, "Huzzah! Huzzah! Huzzah!"

"I will now ask the esteemed Father Gibault, fresh from his own escape from the minions of King George, to come and offer his blessing over our victorious army. Father, if you please."

Rather than beginning his prayer, the Reverend Father quickly launched into a rather lengthy soliloquy, a sermonette of sorts, that urged the men to remain strong and steadfast in the face of adversity. He droned on for several minutes. Although the speech was well-intended, the men grew impatient as the rainwater filled their boots and moccasins and their feet became numb from standing still for such a lengthy period of time. They were greatly relieved when, at long last, he held his rosary high in the air in front of the formation and proclaimed the blessings of the Blessed Virgin as well as the Father, Son, and Holy Spirit.

The moment the priest declared, "Amen," Colonel Clark yelled out to his troops, "Column to the right!"

The men all pivoted into a right face, except for two or three of the more backwoods fellows who were not quite sure about the difference between left and right.

Colonel Clark smiled and chuckled. "Boys, we will not be satisfied until we take back our fort! Now, let us go and go swiftly! Forward! March!"

The men, muskets and rifles perched high on their left shoulders, waved their hats with their right hands and cheered. The villagers of Kaskaskia waved their own banners and a vast array of colorful flags as they cheered the column of proud warriors. The men soon left the road and entered the muddy field to the east of the town. Their feet immediately began to dig deeply and become mired in the thick, mucoid mud.

It was but a harbinger of the conditions that awaited them on their historic overland trek to Vincennes.

$$\mathcal{Q}$$

*February 10, 1779*
*The Cabin on Indian Creek*

The dull, blue glow of dawn was just beginning to fill the cloudy skies to the east and cast its eerie shadows over their cabin refuge. The crest of the muddy knoll on which the cabin sat now formed an island beside the flooded Indian Creek. Francois tucked a small bundle of rolled oilcloth into the tiny cavity at the bow of the canoe. He stood and stretched and then cast a final glance at their cabin retreat. His personal canoe was suspended upside-down about three feet above the ground on low limbs between two small trees. The sight of his abandoned boat elicited a hollow pang in his heart. He hated leaving his precious property behind.

Charles had insisted that they proceed westward in a single canoe. He also insisted that they leave Francois' canoe in a sheltered spot and serviceable condition for any wayward pilgrim or Indian who might have need for it at some point in the future. Charles espoused the unwritten code of the *voyageurs* when he declared, "We men of the wilderness must look out for one another. It is only good manners. Someday we may need the charity and generosity of an unseen stranger."

But still, Francois despised leaving his boat behind. He tried not to dwell on it as he sighed and declared, "That is the last of it, gentlemen. We can get nothing else in this canoe." Without even thinking he added, "And I still think we should take both of the canoes with us."

Charles grunted his displeasure. "We will never be able to carry all of the cargo we have in this one, anyway. And we will eventually have to abandon any and all canoes when we reach the end of the floodwaters. Once we are on foot we will carry nothing but our packs, blankets, and weapons. All the rest of this stuff will have to be left behind. I swear, you fellows pack like a bunch of women!"

"We will be in this canoe for days, Charles," responded Pierre. "Just look around us! Water ... as far as the eye can see."

"*Oui.* For now. But I know this land, Pierre. It rises to the west, and then levels off at the Bad Plain. We will be walking by sunset tomorrow. Mark my words."

"Well, if that is the case, then so be it. Once we hit high ground and dry land we will make our decisions regarding what we will or will not carry." He sighed and looked bitterly at the tiny cabin and the floodwaters that surrounded them. "I am simply glad to leave this desolate, lonely place that reminds me so much of my weakened condition and sickness."

"On that we shall agree," declared Charles. The burly man smiled warmly. "I am growing restless, to be certain. But most of all, I am happy that you are better, old friend."

"Thank you, Charles. I am better, indeed, and eager to travel. Now ... let us go and find the Long Knives."

"And perhaps some meat and a good fire," added Francois.

"A jug or two of rum would be nice," chimed Charles.

Francois climbed into the front of the canoe, Pierre sat on a pile of deer hides in the center, and Charles occupied the rear. Once everyone was in position Francois used his paddle to push off from the muddy bank. Charles guided the canoe into what he believed to be the channel of Indian Creek and then the men paddled slowly toward the west.

*February 12, 1779*
*The Bad Plain - Illinois Country*

"We shall camp here, gentlemen! Sergeants and officers, see to your men. Build your fires high and let's get our clothes dry."

The men of the waterlogged army cheered.

"Captain Bowman!"

"Yes, sir."

"I see signs of buffalo here, Captain, and a trail that leads off to the north."

"I noticed that as well, sir."

"Dispatch a hunting party immediately. I want a man on every horse. We need a mountain of meat to feed this mob."

"Right away, sir."

Captain Bowman disappeared into the crowd to gather and equip his hunting party as the men spread out along the trees on the western edge of the Bad Plain. A short time later eight men on horseback, two Long Knives and six Frenchmen from Cahokia, galloped northward and disappeared into the winter mist in search of delicious, greasy buffalo.

The Long Knives and Frenchmen of Illinois were thrilled that Colonel Clark had called an early halt. It was mid-afternoon and they were thoroughly miserable. They were only a week into their journey and were already greatly fatigued, but the sudden appearance of dry land and sign of ample game brought about an immediate boost in attitude and morale. They all set about the task of building fires with great focus and intensity. With all of the rain that had fallen for almost a month, fire starting had developed into an almost impossible task.

Colonel Clark stood beneath a large cedar tree and quietly surveyed his men. His heart warmed with pride even as it broke with compassion over the lowly estate of his valiant soldiers. He muttered a quick, fervent prayer for his army as he reflected upon their suffering of the past week.

The first three days' march toward Vincennes had been somewhat tolerable. The army slogged along on muddy, water-soaked roads and across wide fields and made solid eastward progress. Indeed, on the third day of the journey the hardy men marched over twenty-seven miles on the spongy fields and roadways. The men remained energetic and of good cheer.

But on the fourth day everything changed. They left the semi-navigable settled lands and cut cross-country in a direct line toward their objective. They quickly reached a broad plain that was covered by water that averaged two to three feet in depth. Still, the men marched on. They were very tired, their feet became soaked and shriveled, and their limbs grew numb from the cold. But Colonel Clark urged them on with great cheer and enthusiasm. He further inspired his army by ordering the officers to dismount from their horses and convert them into pack animals for supplies and for carrying the sick. The officers joined their men in the frigid water that, on average, reached mid-way up their thighs. The soldiers began to look upon their leaders with an ever-deeper measure of admiration and respect.

The greatest challenge of their trek in the beginning days came on the fifth day out of Kaskaskia. They almost lost several men in an invisible, deep river that lay hidden beneath the floodwaters of the plain. Three men attempted to ford the waters at different locations and all plunged in over their heads and almost drowned. Their only alternative was to cut down several large trees and drop them across the river to form a crude bridge of timber and limbs. The plan worked. Although it required almost an entire day of back-breaking work and a careful, deliberate crossing, all of the men and all of the horses made it safely across the little river.

They continued to march through the rain and floodwaters for another day and a half before their present discovery of the oasis of dry land that was known as the Bad Plain. Once the colonel called the halt the men constructed shelters as best they could.

There were no tents, so the men constructed crude lean-tos from the ample cedars that grew along the periphery of the Bad Plain. A few men had small oilcloths that they draped over the tops of their cedar bough shelters. In less than an hour there were several dozen of the tiny lean-tos packed tightly with men who were warming their feet beside smoky, slow-burning, frustrating fires.

Far in the distance there came the echoes of four rifle shots in quick succession. Colonel Clark's heart leapt with joy. He stepped quickly from beneath the cover of his tree and walked enthusiastically among his tired, hungry men.

"Let's get some more fuel on those fire, boys! Fresh meat is on the way! You'll sleep with a belly full of buffalo tonight!"

※

*On the Eastern Edge of the Bad Plain*

The dull cracks of rifles exploded close by. Entirely too close for comfort. The three refugees from Vincennes dropped low to the soggy ground and took cover in a shallow dip. Charles gagged and cursed, for the dip was filled with dirty water.

Pierre, Charles, and Francois had abandoned their canoe only two hours prior when they reached the westernmost edge of the floodwaters. Charles, as usual, had been right about their over-abundance of cargo. The men strapped on as many bags of supplies and blankets as they could and then marched off toward the west through the high-canopied woods. Their walking would have been easy had it not been for the soaked, muddy ground. The air and misty rain sapped the energy and warmth from their bodies. Pierre felt the toll of the harsh conditions very quickly. It reminded him of just how sick he had been over the past month.

"From which direction did the shots come?" asked Francois frantically.

"The southwest," muttered Charles, "but I do not think they were shooting at us."

Francois stared toward the southwest with wide, horrified eyes. "How do you know?"

"Because there was no sound of a projectile or impact, Francois. We simply heard an echo."

"What were they shooting at, then?" countered Pierre.

"*Boeufs*, most likely. The beasts congregate here on the Bad Plain." He spat to his left. "I would not mind a mouthful of *boeuf* fat, or a nice slab of tender tongue. How about you fellows?"

Pierre and Francois licked their lips. They had not had a hot, filling meal in a number of days. Their stomachs ached for meat. Both men rolled onto their sides and stared longingly toward Charles.

"*Oui.* That is what I thought." He grinned. "All right, then. Let us proceed toward the southwest, but we must remain vigilant. We do not know if these hunters are friend or foe."

All three men used their weapons for balance as they scrambled to their feet.

"If we encounter anyone, we must act with an abundance of caution," Charles stressed. "Do not do anything stupid. Do not point a weapon at them unless it is absolutely necessary."

Pierre and Francois nodded their understanding.

"Check your weapons now," Charles urged. "We have been through a lot of water and rain."

All three men checked the lashings on the leather "cow's knees" that were draped over the firelocks of their muskets and rifles. They appeared to be sufficiently secured. The simple oil-soaked leather wraps performed the essential function of keeping the iron mechanism protected from water and the powder dry in their pans.

"Let us go this way," Charles declared, pointing slightly left of the direction that they had been following prior to hearing the shots. "Pierre, you lead us and set the pace."

Pierre trudged off in the direction selected by Charles. The rain lightened slightly until it became little more than a dull mist.

Their visibility improved just a bit. They had been walking for almost a half-hour and were nearing the top of a low rise when Pierre suddenly dropped to one knee. Charles and Francois followed suit.

"What is it?" demanded Charles, straining to see what had triggered the alert.

Pierre whispered, "I thought I heard voices."

"Voices? Really?" asked Charles. "I haven't heard anything but Francois' guts since we left the canoe back in the woods."

A small ball of mud struck the back of Charles' floppy hat. He grinned.

"What did they sound like?" asked Charles.

"I may be losing my mind," responded Pierre. "But I could swear that I heard *langue Française*."

"Not at all unlikely," reasoned Charles. "It could be settlers, or a long-range hunting party. But I doubt they are any of Hamilton's men."

"Agreed," declared Pierre.

"Well, there's only one way to find out."

Charles rose to his feet and loped off into the mist. Pierre and Francois quickly followed suit. They had covered another fifty yards when they saw several dark forms in the distance. And there was movement. As they drew closer they confirmed that those dark forms were, indeed, men. The unsuspecting hunters were busy skinning and carving choice cuts of meat off of four downed buffalo. Steam rose thickly from the exposed flesh of the animals.

Charles cradled his rifle in his left arm and cupped his right hand to his mouth as he shouted, *"Bonjour, les amis!"*

The men butchering the buffalo all abandoned their work in surprised confusion and began to grab their weapons and take cover behind the carcasses.

"Hold your weapons high," Charles instructed his companions. The three men held their weapons over their heads to demonstrate their peaceful intentions.

Charles yelled, "It is all right, gentlemen!  We mean you no harm!  We heard your shots and came in search of meat and news of the world!"

"Walk toward us slowly!" commanded one of the hunters in French.  "Do not make any sudden moves.  We have you covered."

The three travelers complied willingly.  The hunters remained silent and kept a sharp eye on them until they were within twenty paces of the dead buffalo.

"Stop right there, fellers," came a command in English from behind the nearest animal.  "Keep your hands where I can see 'em.  I won't ask you to lay your weapons down in this confounded mud and water."

"And for that we are grateful," replied Charles.  "What brings you fellows out on the Bad Plain on such a soft, beautiful day as this?"

"I was just aimin' to ask you the same question," responded the man with the curious accent.  He stepped out from behind the dead animal.  He was a tall, rugged fellow dressed in buckskin.  He was an older gentleman, perhaps even older than Charles, and sported a short, sandy gray beard.  His eyes were a brilliant blue.  The fellow appeared nervous, but curious.

Pierre and Francois looked at one another, confused.  Francois whispered in French, "What is, 'aimin?'" Pierre shrugged his shoulders.  They had great trouble understanding the tall man's talk.  Neither of them had ever heard that particularly unusual English word or the accent with which the man pronounced it.

Charles seemed undaunted.  He nodded.  "Fair enough, sir.  I am Charles Rimbault, a river *voyageur* of this territory.  These are my friends Pierre Grimard and Francois Turpin.  We are residents of Vincennes, and only recently escaped from the British there in late December."

A distinctly French voice called from the rear of the hunting party.  It came from a man who had been concealed behind the most distant buffalo carcass.  The voice shouted a familiar name, "Pierre!  Pierre Grimard!  Is that really you?"

Pierre stepped forward and strained to see who it was that was calling his name. Then he recognized the man behind dirty, beard-covered face.

"Jean-Baptiste! I cannot believe it!"

The two men ran toward one another and then embraced in the muddy field in the center of the partially butchered buffalo. Pierre's old friend, Captain Jean-Baptiste Barbeau of the French militia at Fort des Chartres and godfather of his first son, picked Pierre up off of the ground as he hugged him tightly. The other men, who moments before had been locked in a standoff of suspicion, quickly lowered their weapons and began to gather around the reuniting friends. The two fellows laughed heartily and launched into an animated discussion in French.

Pierre howled, "What are you doing here, Jean-Baptiste?"

"I am in command of the company of troops from Cahokia and marching with the Long Knives to liberate Vincennes."

Pierre's eyes widened in disbelief. "The Virginians are here?"

"*Oui*. These are two of them right here." He pointed to the tall, older fellow, and switched to speaking in English. "Pierre, I would like for you to meet David Johnston of Virginia, and this is his young friend, John Cockrell."

The Virginians exchanged friendly handshakes and smiles with Pierre and his two companions.

Jean-Baptist converted back to French, "We are camped on the western edge of the plain about a mile to the south. Our men are attempting to dry out from all of the floodwaters that we have traversed. We were tasked as a hunting party, dispatched to bring back fresh meat."

"Then it is fortunate for us that we heard your shots," interjected Charles Rimbault. "You saved us much travel. We were headed for Kaskaskia so that we might join up with Colonel Clark and his Long Knives."

"Fortunate, indeed," responded the captain. He slapped Pierre enthusiastically on the arm. "Father Gibault told us all about Hamilton's plans to hang you and how Bousseron and his men dug you out of the fort! Where have you been since then? He said that it was way back on Christmas Day. He was shocked and heartbroken when he did not find you in Kaskaskia. We assumed that you must have been recaptured or killed."

"When I escaped, I was very ill with a horrible infection of the lungs. Charles paddled me deep into the wilderness by canoe and we remained hidden in a remote cabin. Francois joined us some weeks later. We remained there while I recuperated. We just left our cabin by canoe yesterday morning and began walking this afternoon when we found dry land." Pierre was confused. "How did you see Father Gibault?"

"He left before daylight on the same day that you escaped. He claimed that he had urgent business in Kaskaskia, but I quite imagine that he assumed that the British would hold him responsible for you." The captain winked. "I do not want to call the Reverend Father a coward, but none of us have yet discovered the nature of his mysterious 'urgent business.'"

The Frenchmen gathered around then chuckled knowingly. The two English-speaking men looked on in a state of awkward confusion.

Captain Barbeau switched back to English again. "Forgive us, gentlemen. Allow me to explain. This fellow, Pierre Grimard, is an old friend who served with me many years ago at Fort des Chartres. He relocated to Vincennes for his business almost ten years ago. He is the one who escaped from Hamilton's jail … the man who was sentenced to hang on Christmas Day!"

Private Johnston's eyes widened in admiration. "We have heard about you, *Monsieur* Grimard! The story has been told around our fires about the Frenchman who escaped from Fort Sackville through a tunnel in the ground."

Pierre grinned, "Well, sir, I did not accomplish it on my own. Many men worked diligently in order to set me free." He pointed at Rimbault. "Charles is the one who completed my escape downriver."

He redirected his finger toward Turpin. "Francois was one of the men who dug me out. I owe my life to these two men, and to at least twenty others back in Vincennes. I am anxious to get back there and see them set free from the tyranny of Governor Hamilton."

"And I am purty sure that Colonel Clark will be achin' to speak to you gents and find out some more about the goins'-on in Vincennes," responded Johnston.

Charles Rimbault leaned his rifle against the head of a nearby buffalo and grinned with determination as he whipped out his skinning knife. "We can sing songs and hold hands later, boys. How about we hurry up and get this meat prepared and loaded onto your animals? I, for one, am anxious to locate one of these fires of which you have spoken."

꩜

Colonel George Rogers Clark leaned against the trunk of a large cedar tree that hung as a canopy over his lean-to and campfire. He licked tasty buffalo grease off of his fingers and noisily sucked fibers of meat from between his teeth. Pierre, Charles, and Francois rested lazily on the other side of the large, bone-warming fire. The three men had just provided the colonel with a thorough, detailed briefing on the enemy's disposition at Fort Sackville.

The colonel belched loudly, grinned, and patted his satisfied stomach. "Gentlemen, I hope that you are as warm and filled as I."

"We are, indeed, Colonel," replied Pierre. "And we are so very happy that we happened upon your army in this vast wilderness. It was an amazing turn of fortune. I would have been heartbroken if we had traveled all the way to the Mississippi River and discovered that you were already gone."

"I do not believe in fortune or happenstance, Pierre. I believe that everything happens for a reason ... that God in His sovereignty orchestrates the matters of men in order to fulfill His will and purpose. Do you believe in such a notion, as well?"

"I have never really thought of such a thing, Colonel. I am a simple man. I follow the guidance of my priest and trust that he has the interests of my faith and soul in his good hands."

Clark chuckled. "I don't believe in placing my soul or my arse in anyone's hands, Pierre … not even a priest."

"That is your prerogative, Colonel."

"Indeed. Well, whatever your theology may be, Pierre, I am most appreciative of the intelligence that you and your compatriots have provided me. I am confident that it will prove invaluable when we reach Vincennes and launch our assault."

"*If* we reach Vincennes," mumbled Charles Rimbault.

"I beg your pardon, sir," retorted Colonel Clark.

"I said, 'if' we reach Vincennes, Colonel. And that is one hell of a big, 'if.'"

"Nothing will stop us from liberating Vincennes and retaking our fort," declared Clark.

Rimbault shrugged. "We shall see. There are miles of open water to the east, Colonel. Miles. Leagues. Sometimes it is ankle deep, sometimes it is chest deep, and occasionally it will be over our heads. We need boats, Colonel. How I wish to God we had both of the canoes that we abandoned during the past two days."

"We shall make it, *Monsieur* Rimbault. These intrepid men have already walked one hundred and fifty miles in six days, some of it through waters like those you describe! Do not doubt the fortitude of my men!"

"I have no doubts about their courage or desire, Colonel. I am merely pointing out that they may have to swim the last thirty miles … in the dead of winter. So far the season has been mild with only rain. But we are moving into the heart of the Illinois winter. Snow and ice may be upon us in days. The waters that surround us might freeze before our very eyes. Sir, the worst part of this journey lies in front of you, not behind you. Mark my words."

Clark closed his eyes and exhaled deeply. "I pray that you are wrong, *Monsieur.*"

"As do I, Colonel. But time and experience have taught me that I am usually right. Just ask Pierre and Francois."

Both of the Frenchmen rolled their eyes at their rough, backwoods friend. Colonel Clark burst into a hardy, contagious laughter that seemed to infect the entire camp. Choruses of laughter erupted around the many fires that dotted the tree line.

Charles stood and took two steps toward the colonel, interrupting his laughter. "But know this, Colonel, right or wrong, I will be right there with you. Whether marching, swimming, or crawling, I and my comrades will be by your side when we attack that British devil in Vincennes."

Colonel Clark rose, stared into Rimbault's eyes with a steely gaze, and then reached out and grabbed his hand with a vigorous shake and a broad smile.

⤳

*February 12, 1779*
*Vincennes - In the Back Room of Bousseron's Store*

Captain Francois Bousseron was frustrated. Though only a single candle illuminated their clandestine gathering, he was so irate he felt as though the heat of the tiny flame were about to melt the flesh from his angry face. Bousseron wanted desperately to do something to aid in the American cause, but he was incapacitated by a lack of courage and interest among his officers. He desired to launch guerrilla attacks and utilize partisan tactics, but no one else within the militia wanted to risk reprisals by the British soldiers inside the fort. This sentiment was doubly frustrating to Bousseron, since it was painfully obvious that the men of Vincennes outnumbered the British and their foreign French allies by a ratio of at least two to one.

Bousseron cracked his knuckles and exhaled in frustration. He attempted to disguise his disgust as he stared at the impotent lieutenants who surrounded the tiny table. He was reasonably sure that his efforts to conceal his disdain toward the junior officers were not working. He decided to change the subject.

"Gentlemen, is there any other news? Any other matters of intelligence of which we should be made aware?"

The men sat and stared blankly at the center of the table.

"So, that is it? You have nothing." He could hold it in no longer. He spat on the floor beside his ancient, rickety chair and declared, "I abhor ineptitude and cowardice!"

"Look, Francois," responded Lieutenant Oscar Hamelin. "You must understand our position. Hamilton threatened to kill a dozen men when we helped Pierre escape."

"But he did not do so," retorted Francois.

"No, by the grace of God, he did not. But he could have! Now, just imagine how he would respond if we began to sink his boats, or set fire to his supplies, or even ambush and murder his men. Our families and homes would pay the price, Francois."

Bousseron considered the man's words. He nodded slightly and grimly. He knew that Oscar spoke the truth.

"So we must wait, Francois. We must wait until the end of winter. That is when the Long Knives will return! And when they do, we will join them. We will join them with both our hearts and our muskets. And then we will drive the British out of our village and fort and we will live as American citizens! But until the Long Knives come back, we must wait. We are not strong enough on our own."

Bousseron swallowed his pride and nodded again. "Then we will wait for as long as it takes," he affirmed. "Let us pray that the warm weather comes early so that our friends will return. Perhaps April will be the month of our liberation and salvation."

He and his men had absolutely no idea that the army of the Long Knives was camped at the edge of the Bad Plain, a mere thirty miles to their southwest.

# 18

## SUCH BRAVE MEN

*February 13, 1779*
*Overlooking the Little Wabash River Valley*

"I have never seen anything like it," declared Captain Bowman.

The other officers standing near him did not respond. Their awed silence more than conveyed their affirmation of Bowman's simple statement. The spectacle that lay in front of them was the flooded valley of the Little Wabash River. There were actually two branches of the river at this location, situated a little over three miles apart. The area between the two ridges that marked the eastern and western peripheries of the valley was over five miles wide. The entire river valley now formed a shallow floodwater lake. The Long Knives and their allies had no choice. The had to cross it.

"How the hell are we supposed to get across that?" wailed one of the rugged, waterlogged frontiersmen.

"We have already been through more water than this, gentlemen. Once again, we will wade across," declared Colonel Clark. "Oh, and what an adventure it will be! A story that you will tell a thousand times to your children and grandchildren! But first we must find the best underwater pathway across the valley. Captain Bowman!"

"Yes, sir."

"I want a dugout canoe. A big damn dugout canoe. Drop a substantial tree and get to work at once hollowing it out. As soon as it is seaworthy I want men dispatched with probes to mark the shallowest route. Once they mark the trail we will use the canoe to transport our sick and what is left of our baggage."

"But how will they mark a trail, Colonel? Everything is under the water."

"Not everything," declared Clark, pointing at the trees. "Our boatsmen will mark the limbs of the trees to show us the way. Have the men use strips of light colored cloth and linen."

"Yes, sir. Right away, sir," responded Captain Bowman. He was somewhat less enthusiastic about the task than was his commanding officer.

The captain assigned a substantial crew for working on the dugout and dispatched hunting teams to the north and south along the ridge. He ordered the remainder of the men to make camp and build shelters and fires. As dusk neared the men settled into what had become their soggy overnight routine during the trek to Vincennes. And, as usual, they went to bed hungry when the hunting teams could not locate any game.

*February 15, 1779*

"This is not so bad," declared Francois as he waded through the shallow water. The men marched in a long, single-file line. Charles marched directly in front of Francois. Pierre followed close behind. Dawn was just breaking to the east. As usual there was no warm, orange glow of sunrise to greet the men on this particular morning, for once again it was cloudy and dreary. The column of over one hundred and fifty soldiers moved slowly and deliberately in the softening gray darkness through the muddy, foamy, debris-filled water. Each man was careful to follow in the footsteps of the fellow in front of him. The canoe soon floated past them, laden with piles of bags and six extremely ill men.

Thus far, the colonel's plan was working. Though the boat-building process had taken well over a day, the enormous dugout canoe had proven ideal for the task. Scouts took the canoe forward on the previous afternoon and located and marked a relatively shallow "trail" through the water, returning to camp just before sundown. They had located an island of dry land that measured a little over a half-acre. The scouts determined that the army could reach it in a single day's march. The colonel then ordered the men to cook a hot evening meal and to waterproof their baggage as best they could. There was no meat, so the men ate a thick gruel of boiled wheat flour and cornmeal.

That mouthful of gruel would have to hold them until the next evening, for there was no time to stoke fires and cook again the following morning. The army had too many miles of flooded land to cross.

So, the men walked, kicked, stumbled, and cursed their way through the chilly water. They looked out for one another and offered assistance and encouragement to their comrades. They were in amazingly jovial spirits. Some of the men even managed to tell stories and jokes to help keep their compatriots entertained … anything to help keep their minds off of the unimaginable task that lay in front of them. Dozens of animated, friendly conversations were ongoing up and down the wet-legged column.

"This water will get worse as we near the first fork of the river," growled Charles, ever his less-than-optimistic self. "It cannot remain knee-deep forever."

"Well, at least it is a more pleasant day than the past few we have endured," encouraged Pierre.

Though a soft rain continued to fall, it was, indeed, significantly warmer than the previous two days. The men were thankful for the small break from the cold air, which would have added greatly to the misery of the crossing. They prayed that the warm spell would hold out until they finished traversing the flooded plain.

Two hours into the march the column stopped. Men strained to see what was going on up ahead. A message soon made its way down the line. They had reached the first river crossing. Pierre, Charles, and Francois were close to the rear of the column, so they could not see far enough ahead to know what was going on along the invisible bank of the first fork of the Little Wabash River. Soon, however, the men began to inch forward very slowly. As they neared the crossing they could see that the army was being ferried across in groups of ten men in the huge canoe. They could also see a small elevated scaffold in the distance that held the sick men and the baggage, keeping both dry and safe from the reach of the murky water.

It took almost two hours to complete the crossing, but everyone made it over safely. The horses swam across, then the march continued. The depth of the water varied between two and four feet. It was not pleasant, but it was almost tolerable. The men were thrilled that the trail was well-marked and that the water seldom extended over belly-deep. By mid-day they had taken to singing. All up and down the line songs erupted that did much to lift the spirits of the tired, hungry travelers … most of them, anyway.

"How I wish they would shut up!" Charles complained. "These Virginians do not seem to know how or when to simply be quiet. They must always hear themselves talking, or bragging, or singing."

"They are merely attempting to distract themselves," responded Pierre. "Let them have their fun. This day is miserable enough as it is."

"I suppose," muttered Charles.

"What would it take to lift your spirits, Charles?" inquired Francois.

Without any hesitation he responded, "Four jugs of rum, a two-pound steak, two loaves of bread, and a Kickapoo girl around eighteen or nineteen years old … not, necessarily, in that order."

Francois laughed. Pierre shook his head in feigned disbelief. And they marched on.

The column halted again shortly after the sun reached its zenith at mid-day. They were, once again, preparing to cross a river. Colonel Clark took the same exact approach as with the first branch of the Little Wabash. He ordered the canoe to carry the sick men and baggage across and then ferry the remainder of the soldiers. The men patiently waited for their turn in the canoe, except for one ambitious lad.

"Look at that!" exclaimed Francois, pointing toward the river.

The men close to Francois craned their necks to see. The sight that greeted them caused them to launch into a chorus of laughter and yelling. Even the crusty old Charles Rimbault could not hold back his smile. The drummer for the Long Knives, a boy of no more than twelve or thirteen years of age, sat cross-legged on top of his perfectly balanced drum as he paddled across the deeper water of the river with a short, flat piece of wood. The makeshift raft worked out so well for him that he continued right along into the shallower waters on the other side. Indeed, he paddled along on his drum for the remainder of the day. That lighthearted diversion was all that the little army needed to lift its spirits and propel it forward toward their destination for the night.

The Long Knives and their French compatriots reached their small island destination two hours later. There was ample wood for fuel, though it took some time to stoke the fires high enough to burn with any intensity. By dark the light rain had ceased and the men were drying their clothes and feet beside toasty fires. Once again, a gruel comprised of coarse grains provided their only nourishment. The men were growing more and more disturbed as they watched their supply of grains dwindle to almost nothing. The game that they had been counting on for meat along the journey had long fled the region in search of higher ground. Despite the luxury of their tiny spot of dry land and the amazing warmth of their fires, it was still a depressing night for the cold, hungry men.

Pierre and his friends huddled in the damp darkness as close to their fire as they could get. Pierre had been coughing for several hours. It was not a deep, fluidic cough like the one he had suffered back in December, but it was enough to worry Charles.

"Are you feeling all right, Pierre? I noticed that little hack of a cough started up again earlier this afternoon. It seems to be bothering you a bit more this evening."

"I am fine, Charles. I just have a slight tickle in my throat."

"We must keep a close eye on your health," cautioned Francois. "We have come too far for you to get sick again."

Charles nodded grimly. "It is true, old friend. We need to keep you as warm and dry as possible. I will speak to Colonel Clark tomorrow and get you a spot in the canoe."

"That is not necessary, Charles. Like I told you ... I am just fine."

"We shall see. But I am still getting you placed in the canoe. The Colonel knows of your recent illness. I am quite certain that he will agree with me."

Pierre did not respond. Instead, he attempted to change the subject. "How far are we from Vincennes?"

"Under ordinary conditions we would be there in two days or less. But with all of this water, I cannot be sure. It may take us a week to finally cross the Wabash."

"We do not have enough food or supplies for another week," declared Francois. "What will we do?"

Charles tossed a large stick into the fire, then stated matter-of-factly, "We will get very cold and very hungry. And soon."

※

*February 23, 1779*
*Dawn - "Sugar Camp" in the Flooded Bottomlands of the Wabash*
Pierre jumped at the loud boom that echoed across the icy water. It was the cannon at Fort Sackville, sounding the morning wake-up call

for the British and French soldiers garrisoned there. They had heard the morning explosion without fail for the past six days. Pierre's heart lifted just a tiny bit knowing that he was so close to home.

But his moment of brightened spirit was very short-lived. He was lying on his right side, with his head resting on a large, flat stone. He tried to lift his head but his *voyageur's* cap, soaking wet when he lay down the previous evening, was now frozen beneath his head to the face of the rock. He wiggled his left arm and felt the brittle crunch of his capote. He could not believe it. His clothes were quite literally frozen on his body.

The Frenchmen and Long Knives of Clark's army were thoroughly exhausted, hungry, freezing, and desperate. They were less than six miles from Vincennes, but the village might as well have been a thousand miles away. The men were stranded on a tiny island on the eastern side of the Wabash River. They struggled to sleep, with their only rest coming in brief and fitful naps of exhaustion. Their only food in the past three days had been a single mouthful of venison. But the most oppressive force arrayed against them was the vicious onslaught of winter. The weather had turned bitterly cold overnight. Ice formed in a half-inch sheet on top of the floodwaters. The men languished in despair. Many became convinced that their cause was lost. Most seemed assured that they all would die of exposure to the cold.

The frozen army included two new guests. Two days prior a canoe of Frenchmen from Vincennes who had been duck hunting had stumbled upon the Patriot army. They were promptly captured and interrogated by Colonel Clark and his officers. These men brought a good report for the Patriots. Neither the British nor the townspeople had any idea of their approach. The men gave excellent intelligence regarding the state of defenses within the fort. They also reported that the locals would, indeed, welcome the return of the Long Knives.

Though it seemed clear that these Frenchmen were their allies, the gentlemen were still held in custody and forced to remain with the Long Knives. Also, their canoe was confiscated for use in scouting out possible routes of approach through the overwhelming floodwaters. The larger dugout canoe was long gone, having been dispatched downriver by Colonel Clark to link up with the *Willing* and order it to move northward with haste to replenish the army's depleted supplies.

The army of Colonel George Rogers Clark, over one hundred and fifty men, still had six miles of ice-coated floodwater to cross and only one small canoe to carry its baggage and sick men.

Pierre's teeth chattered so hard that the bones in his jaw and skull ached. Francois hugged closely against his back. Pierre, in turn, melted into Charles Rimbault's back. Pierre's coughing had increased, but he took solace in the fact that he felt no signs of fever. He, like all of the other men on that tiny knoll protruding from the floodwaters, was simply cold to his very bones. There was no shame among the soldiers as they labored to keep warm. They huddled together in tight piles, their bodies pressed and intertwined close together in an effort to find any possible measure of warmth. There was scant fuel for fires available on the desolate island.

Colonel Clark was growing despondent, as well, but he knew that could not let his men see it. He had to maintain his positive morale and project confidence and determination to his weakened, dejected little army. In the dull glow of the dawn he waded out into the ice-coated water on the northeast side of the tiny island in search of a decent path toward the next island of exposed land. He descended almost instantly into water up to his neck. No matter which direction he moved, all he found was deep water.

So, Colonel Clark decided to fake it. He trudged back up onto the frozen shore, let out a shrill Indian war whoop, and then bent down and began mixing cold water with mud in his hands. He used the thick concoction as a crude form of face paint to decorate his cold, wind-chapped cheeks. He smiled broadly throughout the entire process and chatted constantly with the men reclining near him. Most of them thought that he had lost his mind.

Soon he jumped to his feet, his face smeared with dark lines of mud, and exclaimed, "Enough of this lazing around, men! We have a fort to take! We will walk the streets of Vincennes before bedtime this very night!" He pointed across the water to a large hill known as 'Warrior's Island.' "I want the canoe to shuttle the sick and the supplies to yonder spot of land, and then I want the rest of you to get up off of your dead arses and get into this water. It's time to take a swim, boys!"

Then, without another word, he turned and loped off into the water at full speed, swimming in a direct line toward the tiny spot of dry ground that rose above the flooded plain.

The men lay still for a moment, stunned by the sight of their floating commander. Then, quite suddenly, the entire army rose to its feet and screeched in defiance and rage against the oppressive weather and seemingly endless water. They quickly loaded three sick men into the canoe, one of them Pierre, and then bravely plunged into the frigid, ice-covered water.

Charles called over to his shoulder, "We will see you on that island, Pierre. Try to have us a good fire going when we arrive." He winked and smiled.

Pierre was too cold and too tired to respond. He lay still for a moment as the oarsmen grabbed their tools and began the quick two-mile trek to the large island. It took only a few minutes for them to traverse the short distance in the sleek canoes. They unloaded the three ill men and then began their return trip to the previous night's island, which the men had humorously dubbed the 'Sugar Camp.' There were still six other men lying on that hilltop who needed to be transported to 'Warrior's Island.'

Once ashore Pierre did as Charles demanded. He gathered ample brush and wood to light a fire. He had a vigorous blaze going in just a matter of minutes. He sat with the other two sick men and allowed the warmth to penetrate his aching body. It did wonders for both his members and his spirit. The men sat and watched with profound pity and some measure of shame as the other valiant Frenchmen and Long Knives made their way across the deep water.

"We are going to need more fires," declared Pierre. "Quickly, gentlemen. Let us gather fuel and make fires all along the water's edge."

The men followed Pierre's lead. As they worked to stoke more campfires they kept careful watch of their compatriots as they approached. Since all that Pierre and the others could see were heads and hats protruding above the top of the water, the men curiously resembled a long line of bobbing ducks. The men on shore knew that some of the swimmers were beginning to flounder and were becoming at risk of drowning. The canoe, after it deposited the other two loads of sick men, began to make quick runs out to the stricken swimmers and then back to the refuge of Warrior's Island. Each time the tiny boat delivered two or three men who could neither walk nor swim any further. The water was beginning to become full of such hapless men. All along the submerged column of soldiers were exhausted fellows clinging to dead logs and whisper-thin tree tops, each waiting for salvation by canoe.

The men operating the rescue boat wasted little time. They rolled load after load of frozen men onto the shore and then immediately headed back out to rescue others. Pierre and the original sick men discovered that they had become among the healthiest and most vigorous soldiers in Clark's army. It remained up to them to help pull these frozen, almost dead souls from the muddy beach to within reach of the life-sustaining fires. They covered the poor fellows with blankets recovered from the pile of baggage and massaged the frozen soldiers' wrists and legs in an effort to get their blood flowing and speed the warming of their frozen flesh.

Almost four hours later the men who actually completed the trek through the frigid water began to stumble onto the island shore. Some of the stronger and healthier of the men dragged one or two other soldiers by their arms and deposited them onto the muddy bank, only to turn and dive back into the water to rescue other comrades.

Pierre witnessed the bravery and fortitude of the Virginians in complete awe and utter amazement. He wept openly at the courage and strength on display among these strange men. He watched eagerly for his two best friends and grew more and more worried when he did not see them among the first few groups of soldiers on the beach. But his heart lifted when, almost an hour later, he spotted a huge Virginian dragging both Francois and Charles through the water. His friends were thoroughly spent. When they reached the land they could not even move their arms, their bodies were so cold. Pierre jumped into action, pulling his companions closer to the warm fires and seeing to their needs.

Colonel Clark was the last man out of the water. He waited until every single one of his soldiers was deposited safely onto dry land. Ultimately, one of his young, hearty privates had to drag him onto the dry ground, as well.

The colonel, kneeling beside one of the fires, declared, "Never have such brave men accomplished such an impossible feat! Patriots of Virginia and Illinois, I salute you!"

The shivering men responded with an amazingly robust, "Huzzah! Huzzah! Huzzah!"

Quite suddenly a different chorus of excited yells emanated from among the men surrounding the fires. They pointed toward a distant speck skimming across the water. It was another canoe! Four men with rifles jumped into their small French canoe and took off in pursuit of the other boat. A half-hour later the four smiling men returned with not just one, but two canoes. The newer vessel was almost as twice the size of the original canoe taken from the Frenchmen.

The newly confiscated Indian canoe had been full of redskinned women and children. In addition, the vessel contained almost a quarter of a buffalo, a sizable pile of dry corn, and some beef tallow. There were even two large kettles for cooking. The

Virginians who captured the boat had courteously deposited the former owners at a safe place along the bank of the Wabash and returned victoriously with their war prize.

Colonel Clark beamed. "Let's get some water in those pots, men! Divvy up that beef fat and corn and start dicing that buffalo meat. I want hot stew for all of these valiant soldiers! We need some sustenance to make it across this final stretch of water. I want to enjoy some hot French bread in Vincennes tonight!"

Again, the men cheered.

𝒮

*February 23, 1779*
*Three Hours Before Sunset*
*On the High Ground - One Mile Southwest of Vincennes*

Clark's army made the final leg of the journey across the deep floodwaters without incident. They made use of their two canoes to shuttle all of the men across, first to another small island for a brief rest, and then onto the last leg of the journey toward the high ground that ringed the southern and western edges of the village.

While his men lay napping in the tall, brown grass, Colonel Clark scribbled a brief message for the townspeople of Vincennes. His succinct note read,

> *Gentlemen,*
> *Being now within two miles of your village with my army, determined to take your fort this night, and not being willing to surprise you, I take this method to request such of you as are true citizens and willing to enjoy the liberty I bring you, to remain still in your houses; and that those, if any there be, that are friends to the King of England, will instantly repair to the fort and join his troops and fight like men. And if any such as do not go to the fort should here- after be discovered that did not repair to the garrison, they*

*may depend on severe punishment. On the contrary, those who are true friends to liberty may expect to be well treated as such, and I once more request that they may keep out of the streets, for every person found under arms, on my arrival, will be treated as an enemy.*

G. R. CLARK

The colonel handed the finished note to Pierre. "Sergeant Grimard, I know you are not feeling well, but I need you to take this letter and deliver it to Captain Bousseron. Have him spread the word among the townspeople. I want the locals to stay inside and out of danger. I want as little confusion and interference as possible when we launch our attack. No men of Vincennes are to be on the streets or under arms. Understood?"

"Yes, sir. What will you do in the meantime?"

Colonel Clark grinned mischievously. "Do not worry about us, Pierre. We are going to put on a little show for all who may be watching. We are going to pull out all of those colorful flags that the women of Kaskaskia gave us, mount them on some poles, and then parade our men back and forth in that open draw between these two small hills." He pointed at the spot he had in mind. "If the British see us, I want them to think that we have a thousand men encamped out here." He winked. "And it wouldn't hurt for the Frenchmen of Vincennes to think the same thing ... so don't go into town and give any of our secrets away. Just deliver the message and then go home and check on your wife and family. Once you deliver your message you will be considered off-duty until morning. You have more than earned a night of rest in your own bed."

"Thank you, Colonel. Would it be possible to make a special request?"

"Certainly, Pierre. What do you need?"

"Might Francois Turpin and Charles Rimbault accompany me, as well? Besides your two captives, they are the only other men from Vincennes. I know for certain that my friends would like to go to their homes. Charles has not seen his wife and children since March when he departed for New Orleans."

"Of course, Pierre. Go and fetch your friends. They are furloughed until morning, as well. I will see you tomorrow."

"Thank you, sir."

Pierre tucked the dispatch inside his bright red *voyageur's* hat and then trotted off to tell Charles and Francois the good news.

Pierre, Francois, and Charles devised a quick plan. They would approach the village from different directions in an effort to avoid suspicion. They did not want townsfolk or friends to recognize them. The fact that their faces were covered with over two weeks' worth of thick whiskers would be a tremendous help. They pulled their hats down low over their brows and pulled the wool collars of their blanket coats high around their necks, perfectly concealing their faces from the sides. A few strategic smears of mud and grease on their cheeks completed their disguises. The three men each looked like one of the many backcountry frontiersmen who often strayed from the dense forests into the streets of Vincennes.

"So … we will each make our separate way to Bousseron's store, and do so as quickly as possible without arousing suspicion," declared Pierre.

The other two men nodded in agreement.

"Once we deliver the message and explain everything to the captain, we will wait for cover of darkness to return to our homes. Agreed?"

"*Oui,*" answered Charles. Francois merely nodded again.

"Very well, then. I will see you gentlemen at the store. Good luck."

The three men shook hands and then quickly entered the woods to the west of the village. They moved quickly and silently and soon lost sight of one another among the dense tree trunks of the virgin wood. Pierre uttered a silent prayer for his friends and continued on his path toward his grain mill. He knew of a partially concealed alley between the mill and Bousseron's store. He planned to take advantage of the cover afforded by this little-used pathway.

It took less than a half-hour to reach the outskirts of Vincennes. Pierre quickly made his way toward the stone structure of the mill. He quietly ducked inside to hide for a moment and catch his breath. His heart was pounding with excitement. As he looked around the inside of the mill he felt joy and encouragement. Nothing was changed or out of place. His horses snorted gently in their stalls outside. The animals seemed happy and well-fed. Little Pierre was obviously being conscientious with regard to his responsibilities to the family business. Pierre smiled proudly as he thought of his exceedingly mature little boy.

After a few minutes of rest Pierre eased into the alley and began to make his way toward Bousseron's store. As he neared the establishment he noticed a modest crowd of people gathering in the street out front. He made his way toward the back of the group. The people were staring beyond the town commons, the huge field where all of the livestock of the townspeople grazed, at a colorful spectacle beyond. Far in the distance to the southwest, a line of flags bobbed behind the low hilltops. There appeared to be at least a dozen of the brilliant banners soaring high in the cool winter breeze. They were dispersed at approximately fifty-yard intervals. Occasionally the heads of men appeared over the crests of the hills.

The people of the crowd chattered excitedly. Pierre heard the Frenchmen muttering, "Who are they? Where did they come from? How many must there be?"

He heard the excited voices of many women in the crowd. One of them exclaimed, "There must be a thousand or more! Do you think it is the Americans?"

Another man in the crowd inquired, "Americans? Should we notify the fort?"

The moment that he made his suggestion several men cursed and a few nearby hands slapped the sides of the would-be informant's head. Two rugged men quickly grabbed the fellow and dragged him into a narrow alley between two nearby buildings. They, apparently, had some disciplinary and educational matters to teach the stricken fellow.

Pierre hid his grin beneath the flap of his dark green blanket coat. He glanced to his left to see if there was any reaction from the fort. He could see no sign of alarm or alert. It appeared that the view enjoyed by the townspeople was blocked from the line of sight of the fort by the buildings of the town and several thickets of cedar and pine trees. Pierre scanned the crowd and soon caught sight of both Francois and Charles. The newly-christened spies were standing nonchalantly along the periphery of the group. Charles was leaning against a tree. Francois stood in front of the bakery. Pierre glanced back toward the general store and noticed a tall, handsome man standing beneath the low porch, peering with great interest at the flags and engaging in animated conversation with the men near him. It was Captain Francois Bousseron of the Vincennes militia.

Pierre nodded to his friends and gave a quick jerk of his chin in the direction of the store. Both men nodded subtly and then began to inch their way toward the front door of the establishment. Pierre pulled his collar up a little higher around his chin and ambled nonchalantly toward the militia commander. He approached the shopkeeper from behind and then reached out and gave a gentle tug on his apron.

He disguised his voice as best he could. *"Excusez-moi, Monsieur.* Might I have a moment of your time?"

Bousseron slapped Pierre's hand and continued to stare toward the parade of flags and men. He scolded disgustedly, "Can you not see that I am busy? Look at the spectacle in yon field! I will help you in just a moment."

Pierre gave the man's garment another, firmer tug. *"Monsieur.* I must insist. We really need to talk."

The man spun around and glared at Pierre with his hands on his hips. He seemed quite perturbed by the unwanted interruption. It was clear that he did not recognize his old friend.

"What do you want, you imbecile? The store is closed! Come back tomorrow!"

Pierre pulled his collar down slowly to expose his face. He grinned and then spoke softly in his normal voice, "Francois, are you sure you cannot make some time for a few old friends?"

At that exact moment, Francois Turpin and Charles Rimbault stepped onto the porch behind Pierre, each cradling his musket in his arms.

A look of realization washed across the man's entire countenance. Bousseron's eyes flew open wide and his jaw dropped. The ordinarily loud and boisterous shopkeeper stood for a moment in stunned silence, almost refusing to believe what his eyes were seeing.

"Well?" chirped Charles Rimbault. "Do you mind if we go inside, you big tightwad? My arse is frozen shut and I think that bite of buffalo that I ate four days ago has been resurrected and is starting to eat me from the inside."

Captain Francois Bousseron's face converted into an enormous smile. He grabbed Pierre by the arm and almost shoved him through the open door of the store. He hustled Charles and Francois through the opening in a similar manner and then slammed the door closed and bolted it from the inside.

♫

*Hamilton's Office - Fort Sackville*

Major Hay stormed into Hamilton's headquarters unannounced. His face was red and his expression registered consternation.

Governor Hamilton, obviously bothered and book in hand, peered at the officer over the top of his reading glasses. "Major, what is the purpose of this rude interruption?"

"Sir! We have just received a report from one of our Indian scouts! He reports that he discovered evidence that a large body of men had recently camped on a small island six miles to the southwest, in the midst of the flooded lands."

Hamilton closed his book and then removed his glasses and tossed them onto the desk.

"He said that it was a large body?"

"Indeed, sir. Remnants of multiple fires and a large camp site."

"Tell me, Major Hay, how could a large body of men be encamped on one of those tiny hilltops? And, for that matter, how could such a large body travel through the deep floodwaters that now cover this region? Does your Indian propose that we have an enemy out there that now possesses a naval presence on the Wabash River?"

Major Hay nodded in humility. "I am merely reporting the observations of one of our paid scouts, sir."

Hamilton stared at Major Hay for a moment and then reached for his glasses to resume his reading. "It must be a scouting party, nothing more. Most likely it is a forward group dispatched from the rebel base at the Falls of the Ohio. Order Captain Lamothe to take a detail and some canoes. He is quite adept at locating, killing, and scalping these rebels. Instruct him to locate, engage, and capture this force and return to the fort forthwith."

"How many men, sir?"

Hamilton exhaled, placing his contempt at the intrusion on full display. "Must I make every minuscule decision in this fort?" He glared at the major. "Twenty men should be more than sufficient. Make sure there are British troops intermixed among the French militiamen."

"As you wish, sir."

Major Hay bowed submissively and quickly exited the governor's office. Hamilton nonchalantly returned to his reading, totally oblivious to the attacking force that lay hidden less than a mile from his fort.

The four men concealed themselves in a small, dark storeroom in the rear of Bousseron's store. The three ravenous travelers wolfed down huge chunks of fresh, warm bread smeared with thick butter and drank deeply from large jugs of fresh milk. Captain Bousseron quickly read the note from Colonel Clark by the dim light of a single candle.

"So, he does not want our assistance," Bousseron growled in disgust as he removed his glasses.

Pierre shook his head reassuringly. He coughed and labored to clear his throat. "It is not that, Francois. He simply does not want confusion in the streets when the attack begins. First he wants to make sure all of Hamilton's men are inside the fort. Once he gets his army in position I am quite certain that he will welcome the involvement of our militia in the assault."

"When will he come?"

"This evening. His plan is to infiltrate the town at sunset and then begin the assault on the fort under cover of darkness."

"How many men does he have?"

Pierre paused. "I am not at liberty to say, Francois. I will only say that he has enough good, hard men to do the job."

Bousseron nodded. "Does he need anything?"

"Does he need anything?" Rimbault exclaimed. He chuckled sarcastically. "Francois, the man needs everything! His men are starved and freezing. I doubt there is a single horn of dry powder amongst the entire lot of them. His men need shelter, fresh clothing, provisions, powder, and lead."

Francois Turpin added, "There is a supply boat that departed Kaskaskia with all of their powder and provisions. It was scheduled to rendezvous with the army on the Wabash, but it has not yet arrived. I fear that it may be sunk or lost."

"No matter. Once he enters the town, he will suffer from such want no more," declared Bousseron. "The townspeople will feed and clothe his army. And I have enough powder and lead to blow that rickety fort to hell and back."

"What? How?" exclaimed Pierre.

"Captain Helm and I made an arrangement in the final hours before Hamilton arrived. He entrusted all of the munitions of the fort to me for concealment. The British did not get a single pan full of powder from our stores. Everything is buried in a safe, dry place. All we need to do is dig up the supplies and hand them over to Colonel Clark and his Long Knives."

"Well, I suppose you had better start digging," quipped Rimbault. He belched loudly as he stood to his feet.

"What will you fellows do?" asked Bousseron.

Francois Turpin responded as he stood, "It is dark now. We are going home. We are officially off duty until sunrise tomorrow."

Francois smiled warmly in the glow of the candlelight. "You fellows certainly deserve the rest. Go home and see your families. I will get to work preparing for the arrival of our American compatriots. I will see you boys in the morning."

He rose and hugged all three men. He escorted them to the back door and wished them luck as they stepped out into the waning glow of the winter dusk.

♐

The last whispers of sunlight had disappeared from the tiny window. The world outside the Grimard home was shrouded in the dark purples and grays of night. Genevieve wiped the sweat from her brow in desperation. Her children had become quite insufferable. The tired woman was almost at her wit's end. Her baby girl was suffering terribly from the colic. The infant cried and fussed almost without ceasing. Her rambunctious boys were of no help whatsoever. It was time for bed, yet all the lads wanted to do was pretend to shoot muskets and play war, fall out in the floor and "play dead," and cause an overall din of madness and confusion inside the tiny Grimard home.

Genevieve screeched in weary anger, "Jean-Baptiste, I want you and Charles to stop all of that screaming and unnecessary noise and get into bed! Right now! I am tired of your constant wrestling and rough play inside my house. Daylight will come early tomorrow, and both of you will have many chores to do. Now get behind that curtain right now and crawl beneath those covers!"

"*Oui, Mama,*" responded the older boy as he darted obediently toward his pallet in the corner. Charles followed suit, though he continued to poke and trip his older brother on the way to their destination.

Genevieve scolded the younger boy, "Charles! Stop it, immediately! Do not make me come in there and put you in that bed!"

The lad complied, though he continued to sport a mischievous grin as he disappeared behind the curtain. Genevieve covered her mouth to keep from laughing at the precocious boy.

"We named him properly. He is *exactly* like Charles Rimbault," she thought.

She saw the larger hand of her ever-responsible oldest son, Pierre, as he reached up to pull the curtain closed. The exhausted mother breathed a prayer of thanksgiving and then sat down in her rocking chair to attempt to nurse her fussy baby. She had just removed the pins from her jacket and spread open her shift in the front when a subtle, hollow knock emanated from the front door.

Genevieve froze in fear. Who could it possibly be? No one ventured out after dark. Hamilton had declared a sundown curfew on Christmas Day when it was discovered that her husband had escaped. Anyone caught moving around after dark was treated as a possible spy. There had been no one outdoors after dark since that day except for a handful of brave men of Vincennes who actually were doing the clandestine work of spies.

A deep, hollow cough emanated from beyond the door.

Little Pierre had heard the knock, as well. He darted from behind the bedroom curtain, clad in only a long indigo shirt and stocking feet, and grabbed the pistol that hung on a rack beside the fireplace. He cast a glance at his mother. She was quickly pulling the flaps of her jacket back over her bosom and covering herself. Her eyes met her son's as he stepped forward and placed his hand on the latch. She nodded to him.

Pierre placed his face close to the rough planks of the door and whispered, "Who is there?"

A familiar voice emanated from beyond the door, "It is I! The man of this house!"

"Papa!" squealed little Pierre.

He flung open the door and froze in horror at the sight of the filthy, hairy, smelly man who lurked in the shadows of their covered porch. Genevieve appeared instantly at her son's side. She, too, froze in utter disbelief.

Pierre coughed deeply and then spoke hoarsely, "Well ... must I stand here in the frigid night, or might I come inside and visit with my family for a while?" He grinned, revealing a gleaming row of pearly teeth behind the whiskers and grime.

Genevieve, clutching her infant daughter, tumbled into Pierre's arms.

# 19

## THE ATTACK ON FORT SACKVILLE

*Darkness - On the Outskirts of Vincennes*

Lieutenant John Bailey of the Virginia Long Knives knelt beside Colonel Clark. "You summoned me, sir?"

The colonel placed a hand on the young man's shoulder. "Yes, John. I have a most important mission for you."

"I am at your service, Colonel."

"Excellent." He slapped the fellow's shoulder. "The Frenchmen have had ample time to spread the word of my orders throughout the town. The local residents should be in hiding and well-sheltered in their homes. It is now sufficiently dark to begin our attack. I want you to select fourteen of your finest sharpshooters and then advance upon the fort. When you are under adequate cover I want you to open fire. Make as much noise as you can and sow confusion within their walls. I want your boys to screech and caw like a hundred wild Indians."

"What about the remainder of our army, sir?"

"Don't worry about us, Lieutenant. We will be right behind you. We will infiltrate the entire town and surround the fort. Once you commence your racket, the rest of us will follow suit. That should put a pucker in old Hamilton's uppity British arse."

The young man chuckled. "I should think so, sir."

"All right, then. Off with you, lad. See that the job is done. If a single face shows itself in a window or hole, I want your men to put a ball through it."

"Yes, sir!"

The lieutenant jumped to his feet and disappeared silently into the darkness.

♌

Genevieve wept openly. Young Pierre quickly closed the door behind his father and then jumped and shouted in celebration. The other children, curious as to the identity of their nighttime visitor, quickly spilled from behind the privacy curtain. When they saw their mother in the visitor's arms they realized that it could only be their father. They descended with childlike enthusiasm upon their long-absent papa. Pierre hugged and kissed each one of them.

Genevieve held the baby in front of her husband. "Pierre Grimard, I would like for you to meet your daughter, Genevieve." She smiled. The baby wailed from hunger.

Tears began to streak Pierre's filthy cheeks. He turned his head to the side and coughed. He looked lovingly at the baby and then into the eyes of his wife. "It is a girl?" he asked in disbelief.

"Yes, my love. We finally have a baby girl in the family."

He examined the child. "Is she well? Does she have all of her fingers and toes?"

Genevieve giggled. "She is perfect!"

Pierre took the infant in his arms. She cried even louder. He held the little girl's face close to his and kissed her gently on her tiny, pink nose. He cried from absolute joy.

Genevieve joined in his weeping, and then babbled through her tears, "I do not understand, Pierre. From whence did you come? Why are you here? You know how dangerous it is for you to be in Vincennes!"

Pierre, holding the baby in the crook of his right arm, pulled his wife closer with his left.

"I am not alone, my love. I have come back with the army of the Long Knives."

She pushed back from his chest and stared wide-eyed. "The Americans are here?" she hissed.

"*Oui.* Colonel Clark's army is on the outskirts of the village. They will soon infiltrate the town and launch their attack on the fort. I came under orders to deliver a message to Bousseron so that he might instruct the local families to remain concealed in their homes."

Genevieve lay her head against Pierre's shoulder. "How long will you stay?"

"I am released until dawn tomorrow, when I must report back to the Colonel and join in the fighting. Tonight, I am allowed to stay here in my own home." He smiled warmly. "But a truly philosophical answer to your question is, 'forever.' I am never leaving Vincennes or you or my children again."

Genevieve released herself from his embrace and marched very deliberately toward her rocking chair. She wiped her tears as she went. She declared, "Well, if that is the case, you are going to have to do a bit of cleaning up if you plan to sleep in my bed tonight." She plopped down into the chair with an air of authority and began to open her jacket and shift so that she might nurse the baby. "Bring me my hungry daughter, please."

Pierre complied, smiling from ear to ear. His eyes twinkled with delight.

"Junior!" she barked.

"*Oui, Mama?*"

"Hang a pot of water over the fire. Your papa must do some bathing. Once I am finished with Genevieve I will shave his shaggy face and dispose of those horrible, prickly whiskers."

"*Oui, Mama.*"

"And fetch your father some fresh clothes. We are going to have to burn these filthy rags he is wearing."

"All right, Mama," responded Pierre as he darted to the shelf to find a clean shirt and breeches for his father.

"Pierre, are you hungry?"

Once again Pierre coughed deeply. There was a hollow, resonating gurgle in his throat and lungs. "I ate some bread and milk at Bousseron's store just a little while ago. But I am still famished. We have been starving for over a week. We ran out of food during the trek."

"I suspected as much. You look like a malnourished ghost. There is some venison stew still in the warming pot. Help yourself to it and the bread. There is also half of a bottle of wine in the cupboard. But drink only one glass! I will not have you drunk in my house this night. And that cough sounds terrible. I will soak you with salve and mint after you are clean."

"*Oui, Madame General,*" replied Pierre sarcastically and with a quick wink. "It is so very good to be home."

Genevieve beamed with delight.

The Long Knives and their French allies were in position. They followed closely behind Lieutenant Bailey's attacking force and fanned out throughout the town. Men were hiding behind fences, inside alleyways, on rooftops, and behind earth berms. All of them had their weapons trained on the dark timbers of Fort Sackville. Every man watched for signs of movement from within the fort. They saw none.

"This just doesn't feel right," declared Captain Bowman. "The fort is dark and silent. And this town is way too quiet and deserted to suit me."

"The people are doing as I instructed them," responded Colonel Clark. "That is good. I am glad they had enough sense to stay indoors."

"But why hasn't Lieutenant Bailey opened fire yet?" wailed Bowman. "Do you reckon he ran into some Indians or went and got himself captured?"

His words of concern had just departed his lips when the silent night was shattered by a deafening volley of rifle shots outside the main gate of the fort. As soon as the echo of the shots faded into the night air Lieutenant Bailey's men began to scream, screech, and wail. Their voices were eerie and other-worldly.

Colonel Clark grinned in the darkness. He declared gaily, "That should awaken a few folks inside the fort."

The colonel then threw his own head back and howled like a wolf into the dark of the night. Throughout the streets and alleys of Vincennes the other members of the army of the Long Knives joined in the screeching, howling, thunderous yawp. Their wailing was obnoxious in volume and unnerving in its tone.

✺

Genevieve flinched and jerked her hand at the sudden and nearby blast of the rifles. Her razor nicked Pierre's chin, drawing blood. There were over a dozen thunderous shots in quick succession.

"I am so sorry, *mon ami!*" She reached for the small cloth that floated in the steaming hot shave water.

Pierre simply grinned and plugged the cut with his thumb. He was about to respond to her apology, but was interrupted by the chorus of screeches and howls from Lieutenant Bailey's men. Moments later it sounded as if hundreds of savage voices had joined in with the horrible, fearful chorus. At least two dozen howling, screaming men ran past the front gate of the Grimard house.

Genevieve's lip quivered. It appeared that she was on the verge of tears. "Is it the Indians? Are they attacking our village?"

Pierre placed a reassuring hand on her arm. "No, my darling. That would be our friends from Virginia. The attack has commenced."

Soon more shots thundered from throughout the village, all aimed at the walls of Fort Sackville.

⚘

Governor Hamilton moved his knight on the chessboard, captured and removed the opposing rook, then chuckled teasingly at his friend and prisoner from Virginia, Captain Leonard Helm. The two men were enjoying a quiet game in the governor's quarters.

"Check! Leonard, you always fall into that same old trap. I would have thought that you might learn your lesson by now. You are not, at all, a student of this particular game, are you?"

"No, Governor. We don't play much chess in my little corner of Virginia. I have always been more partial to cards, myself, and the occasional contest of dice. Perhaps one of these evenings we can attempt a game in which I have greater odds of enjoying victory."

"Perhaps, indeed," answered Hamilton as he sipped from his glass of brandy. "We shall have a few more opportunities before the weather breaks, I am quite certain. I must say … I do not look forward to your departure for our prison in Detroit. It seems like a great waste for a gentleman such as yourself to languish in such a terrible place."

"You could always parole and release me, Governor Hamilton," Helm teased.

"And you could always renounce your rebel ways, pledge your oath to the King, and join my staff," responded Hamilton.

"Not likely, Governor." Helm confidently moved his queen to what he thought was a respectable position on the board.

"Well, there it is, then. A stalemate." He moved his own queen in a dramatic diagonal sweep across the board. "And a check-mate."

Helm stared disbelievingly at the chess board and cursed under his breath.

Hamilton gloated, as always. He declared victoriously, "I suppose that we must remain friendly enemies until this nasty conflict is concluded."

"Yes, sir. That is the way of things," affirmed the American captain as he sipped from his own glass of brandy.

Suddenly a barrage of gunfire broke the sleepy silence of the evening. The shooting was followed immediately by a chorus of howls and screams. The wailing voices grew louder and seemed to come from all directions around the fort.

Governor Hamilton surmised, "It appears that some of our native friends have returned. And from the sound of it they are celebrating yet another victory. No doubt their belts are loaded with ample scalps from those nasty rebel bandits in Kentucky."

Leonard Helm seethed with anger and hate, but he controlled his emotions well. He hoped that the darkness of the candlelit room concealed his red face of rage and his pulsating temples. He decided to take the opportunity to tease and aggravate his captor, as was his custom. He peered toward the doorway with feigned concern.

"That didn't sound like Injun gunfire to me, sir. I heard some Virginia rifles in that volley. I do believe, Governor, that this post is under attack."

Hamilton threw back his head and cackled. "Good one, Leonard! Yes, that is it! The rebels have arrived!" He waved his hands in the air with a pretense of panic. "What shall we do? Colonel Long Knife has arrived!" He laughed uproariously.

༄

Corporal Randall Thomas of His Majesty's Army was enjoying a quiet game of cards in the upper room of the southeast blockhouse. He and five of his British and French Canadian comrades had just recently enjoyed a hot meal, and were imbibing from a very rare jug of ale. There was very little malt beverage to be located in Vincennes in the dead of winter. They celebrated the fact that Fort Sackville, as usual, was supremely quiet after dark. Most of the men of the garrison, long overcome with mind-numbing boredom, had already retired for the night.

The corporal yawned. He was about ready to crawl beneath his own wool blanket that lay prepared for him in a sheltered corner near the outer fort wall. The rear wall that faced the inside of the fort was wide open to the night air. The open side of the room was where the long artillery ramp connected to the ground below. Thomas shuddered at the memory of the day they labored to move the artillery pieces up the ramps and into position in the block-houses. It was no small task to move a large cannon up to an elevation of eleven feet above ground. He shook his head in disbelief at the memory of it all. He did not want to ever have to do anything like that again.

Corporal Thomas longed to be in the warm barracks and his semi-comfortable bunk with the other men of his company. But, as usual, it seemed that he had drawn guard and artillery duty on the very coldest of winter nights ... and there was, of course, no fireplace in the open upper chamber of the blockhouse. He took some solace in the fact that he was lucky enough to have the final watch before dawn. At least he would be able to enjoy several hours of undisturbed sleep before his friend, Daniel, would rouse him to keep another useless watch over the dead little town.

He tossed his cards onto the gray blanket that served as their makeshift table. "That is it for me, gentlemen. You have taken all of my money. All I have left is my lonely little blanket, and now I intend to give it some personal company. I bid you all a good night." As he rose from his cross-legged position he said, "Daniel, don't you dare fall asleep on duty. And don't wake me before it is my watch!"

His pal, Private Daniel Jarrett, giggled. "Do not worry, Corporal, Sir! I will be as punctual as Governor Hamilton's daily constitutional!"

The other soldiers in the small room burst into fraternal laughter. A sudden explosion of shots near the fort, followed by the chorus of war whoops and howls, brought a quick end to their jovial exchange. The screeching and howling grew disturbingly louder.

"It sounds like that some of Hamilton's Indian friends have returned from one of their gory missions," declared Daniel blandly.

Corporal Thomas grunted in disgust. "No doubt they will all be decorated with those horrible, bloody scalps. Nasty business, that. I don't understand why our government dares to encourage such barbarity."

"Hamilton will do just about anything to defeat the rebels," declared Daniel. "I can't say as I blame him. I just want to finish this nasty, cold business and go back home. I, for one, am sick and tired of army life and weary of America."

Grunts of agreement echoed his sentiments, while outside the screaming and screeching continued.

"I say!" complained Corporal Thomas. "I do hope they have no expectations of entering the fort this evening. The major will never allow the gate to be opened after dark."

The corporal walked over to the narrow porthole in front of the barrel of the cannon. He draped his left arm across the heavy barrel to balance his weight, raised the wooden flap that covered the hole, and leaned forward to peer through the ten-inch square opening. Though the godless screeching continued, he saw little in the darkness below other than a couple of a fleeting shadows. Then, quite unexpectedly, he saw a brilliant yellow flash from between two of the buildings in the town.

That flash was the very last thing that Corporal Randall Thomas ever saw. A .44 caliber rifle ball entered his face through the bony ridge of his nose and exited the rear of his skull in a mist of blood, pulverized bone, and brains. The man fell limply to his side and slumped against the large wheel of the cannon. Blood poured from his head and ran down the painted gray spokes of the wheel, pooling in a black puddle beneath him.

The men inside the room were speechless from the shock. Their faces were covered in blood spatter. They could taste the coppery flavor of the liquid in their open mouths. Finally, after several seconds of frozen delay, Private Jarrett ran to the top of the ramp and screamed, "To arms! To arms! Corporal Thomas is dead! We are under attack!"

Moments later in the courtyard below a loud bell began to peal the sound of Fort Sackville's alarm.

The loud, shrill din of the alarm bell startled Governor Hamilton. He jumped from his chair so quickly that he flipped the chess board from its perch atop the tiny end table, scattering the carved stone pieces across the rough floorboards.

"What in God's name?" he exclaimed. "What idiot is ringing the alarm bell?"

He darted to the door and threw it open. Throughout the courtyard of the fort he saw men running and darting to and fro. Armed soldiers scrambled up the ladders onto the elevated perches along the tops of the palisade walls. He heard the voice in the far corner screaming, "To arms! To arms!" Meanwhile, the screeching and celebration outside the walls continued to elevate in intensity. Moments later his men began to return sporadic fire toward the town.

Captain Leonard Helm joined the governor at the door. He peered over the British commander's shoulder just in time to see a red-coated soldier scream and fall from the top of the wall and land in a crumpled, lifeless heap on the ground below. As they watched the action along the walls two others tumbled wounded off of the high perch.

"Hmm," Helm mumbled. "Methinks that some of my Virginia friends have decided to pay a little visit."

Hamilton spun and stared in blind rage at the impetuous American. "It appears so, Captain Helm. Well, so be it then. Let's just see how your backwoods friends appreciate the taste of British artillery." He marched angrily to the place behind his desk where his black cocked hat hung loosely on a nail in the log wall. He grabbed the hat, fluffed its white ostrich feather, and placed it proudly on his head. "Captain Helm, you will return to your quarters immediately and remain confined there until further notice."

"As you wish, Governor. I am your servant and your prisoner."

"Yes, Captain, you are. And you would do well to remember that fact."

The governor stormed out of his office, leaving the door open behind him. Helm grinned broadly and grabbed his own hat as he exited the building. He pulled the collar of his coat tightly around his neck, thrust his hands into its deep, soft wool pockets, and whistled a happy tune on the way back to his comfortable cell.

*Three Hours into the Assault*

"I want consistent, endless, and deadly fire on that fort!" bellowed Colonel Clark. "We must keep their heads down while our men complete the earthworks and other defenses."

Captain Bowman responded, "Colonel, our defenses are pretty much complete. We have made ample use of the six-foot fencing around the village commons. All open areas now have a suitable breastwork comprised of debris and lumber from dilapidated buildings in the town. Our men are well-concealed and in excellent positions, and our fire is steady and true. Our boys are hitting every target they see. The enemy cannot get off a shot from their elevated cannon. Some of the boys have even made hits through the open chinks between the logs, such is their fine aim. The enemy has suffered losses, that is certain. But the men are tired, sir. There are some who have loaded and fired over thirty shots, which is no small task with a rifle. None of the men have had any sleep, and they were already exhausted from their ordeal in the water yesterday.

All of them are hungry, if not half-starved. Might we devise a rotation so that the men may have some brief periods of rest? There are, after all, only so many targets to hit in the darkness."

The colonel considered Bowman's words quickly and then nodded his consent. "Your words are wise, Captain. Organize the schedule immediately. A reduction in fire is warranted in light of our grave shortage of powder and lead." He slammed his fist on the table that served as his makeshift desk. "We need that boat, damn it! Where is Captain Rogers and his *Willing*?"

A distinctly French voice answered from behind Colonel Clark. "*Excusez-moi*, Colonel. Perhaps I might be of assistance."

Clark spun and stared at the unknown fellow who stood near the door of his temporary office. "Sergeant, who is this man, and why was he allowed into my headquarters?"

Sergeant Micah Albertson stepped forward, his floppy hat held in respect across his chest. "Beggin' your pardon, Colonel. But this here feller is a Cap'n in the local militia. He says he has supplies that we might be a needin' fer the fightin'. I figgered you might want to parley with him."

"Very well, Sergeant. You are dismissed." The young man turned quickly and departed. Clark peered suspiciously at the stranger. "You're a captain, you say?"

"*Oui, Monsieur* Colonel. Captain Francois Riday Bousseron, captain and commander of the American militia of Vincennes."

Colonel Clark's eyes lit up with delight. "Captain Bousseron!" He extended his hand for a warm handshake. "I am so pleased to finally meet you! Captain Helm spoke very favorably and warmly of you in his correspondences with me. He described you as a brave officer and a true Patriot. I am so glad that you sought me out."

"I was somewhat reluctant at first, Colonel. I wanted to obey your edict instructing our people to remain inside their homes. But Sergeant Grimard informed me earlier about the lack of provisions that you and your men are facing. I am here to inform you that your men will suffer such want no more."

Clark's face betrayed his confusion. "Please explain, Captain."

"Colonel, I am currently in possession of the lion's share of the American powder and lead supply from your stores inside the fort. They are buried in a safe location, and are available for your use."

Colonel George Rogers Clark was flabbergasted. He could scarcely speak. "How ... how did you come to possess our army's munitions?"

"Captain Helm entrusted them to me in the hours immediately before the surrender of the fort. Neither of us wanted the British to have possession or use of our American supplies." He smiled warmly. "A pleasant surprise, no?"

Colonel Clark beamed. "A pleasant surprise, yes! When can you produce these supplies?"

"I can take your men to them immediately. We will need four or five men for the digging. We should be able to distribute the powder and lead within the hour."

Clark shook his head in disbelief. "Captain Bousseron, you may have just saved this entire attack from collapse and failure. All of our munitions, foodstuffs, and artillery are on a gunboat that failed to rendezvous with us on the Wabash. We fear that is has been taken or sunk."

"I am proud to serve the cause of freedom, Colonel. I swore my oath to Virginia and accepted my American citizenship many months ago. Hamilton forced us to renege on our oaths with our mouths, but our hearts have remained true to the United States and to independence."

"I am most grateful for your assistance and your loyalty, Captain."

"It is my pleasure, sir. Might I make a single request for my men?"

"Of course, Captain. How might I serve you?"

"I need nothing from you, Colonel, except for the honor of my men joining yours on the firing line. I command several dozen Patriots who wish to take up their weapons and help you take back their fort."

Clark smiled with admiration and pride. "I will issue the order immediately. Muster your men down by the mill. Captain Bowman will assign you a position on the line."

"*Merci*, Colonel. And one more thing."

"Yes?"

"I want you to know that the women of Vincennes will soon be awake and hard at work in their kitchens. They are already planning a scrumptious, filling, and hot meal for your army. They will be prepared to serve at dawn. We will establish a station in the small yard behind my store. After the sunrise please instruct your men who are able to go there to find food. We will, of course, deliver a meal to those men who cannot leave their posts."

Tears of gratitude welled in the eyes of Colonel Clark. "*Vive les Vincennes*," he declared.

"*Vive la liberté*," responded Bousseron.

🦢

Genevieve lay awake in the darkness, nestled safely beneath Pierre's arm. Right at that very moment she was, without doubt, the happiest woman in the entire world. She listened to the soft breathing of the children on the far end of the cabin and giggled softly at little Charles' adorable, high-pitched snore. But the most amazing, comforting, and peaceful sound in the house was the deep breathing of her husband. Though the gurgle in his chest worried her, she took solace in that fact that she would be able to nurse her own husband back to health.

Poor Pierre had barely made it through his meal, shave, and basin bath before tumbling exhausted into their bed. He never moved, or turned over, or uttered a word. He simply slept where he lay. Genevieve had somehow managed to get a fresh shirt on him and tuck his heavy legs beneath the wool blankets, all without him moving or making a sound. The poor man was entirely dead to the world. At least four or five gunshots exploded every minute during the ongoing battle for Fort Sackville. But still, Pierre never stirred. Amazingly, Genevieve realized that she and the children had become oblivious to the gunfire, as well.

The happy wife turned onto her side and stared at her husband's face in the dim glow of the fireplace. She snuggled closer to his side despite the overwhelming odor of the menthol salve that she had rubbed so liberally all over his chest. She did not care about the smell or the pungent burn of the medicinal vapors in her eyes. She simply could not believe that her Pierre was home.

"Oh, how I love this precious man," she thought. "And he is home to stay!"

But then the war outside her door came to mind. And she knew, for certain, that her husband would join in the fray at first light. The overwhelming urge to pray came over her soul. She responded to the urge by rising quietly from her bed and fetching her rosary from a velvet box on the mantle. She carried the precious piece of holy jewelry to the bed beside Pierre, knelt down on the cold, hard floor, and began to pray to the Blessed Virgin for the life and health of her husband.

"Why is my artillery silent?" thundered Governor Hamilton.

"Sir, the enemy fire upon the gunports is deadly and accurate," reported Major Hay. "We have sustained considerable losses in both of the cannon towers. The moment one of our gunners approaches the port to aim their weapon he is either killed or wounded."

"Losses be damned!" retorted the governor. "I want fire to commence immediately. Do whatever it takes. I want our cannon to rain death down upon these invaders!"

Major Hay bowed obediently. "As you desire, Governor. I will see to it myself."

"Do so, and quickly!" ordered the governor.

Major Hay darted out of the British headquarters and made his way across the compound to the southeast tower. He cursed as he ran. He was a frustrated commander. His men could not return any effective fire against the enemy. They were completely over-whelmed by the accuracy and volume of rifle fire from the rebels. He had a dozen men or more who had been wounded through cracks in the chinking between the logs, such was the deadly ac-curacy of the Virginians and their long rifles. At last he reached the long ramp of logs that led up to the artillery platform. He climbed the ramp quickly. A dozen men huddled low against the log walls. None offered any resistance against the enemy. The body of Corporal Thomas lay in the corner, covered with his wool blanket.

"On your feet!" barked the major. "We must get this piece into action immediately!"

"But, sir, we have tried," wailed a lowly private. "We've had four men wounded while trying to get off a shot at their breastworks."

"I am not expecting accuracy right now, son. All I want is vol-ume of fire. If we can get off a few shots, it may be enough to dis-tract them and keep their heads down. Then we can adjust our fire for effect. Do you understand?"

"Yes, sir."

"Excellent. Are you loaded and primed?"

"Yes, sir."

"Then roll that beast up to the hole and fire it!"

The men responded quickly, all the while remaining low and out of the line of sight of the enemy marksmen below. They eased the cannon forward until the barrel was protruding through the firing hole.

Major Hay thundered, "Cannon crew ready?"

"Ready, sir!" the men answered.

"Fire!"

The rear left man on the crew lowered the glowing match and made contact with the firing quill. There was a brief delay and then the cannon belched fire and thunder toward the south, directly toward the village of Vincennes.

Major Hay nodded. "Good job, men! Now do it again! I will see to the other crew." He scampered down the ramp and ran in the direction of the southwest tower.

❧

The explosion of the cannon ripped Pierre from his deep slumber. He heard the crash and hollow explosion of the ball somewhere nearby. There was an odd sound of splintering wood. Genevieve sat up beside him.

"What was that?" she exclaimed.

He coughed. "Artillery. Aimed in this direction. A building in town was hit."

"The British are firing on the town?" she wailed.

"It appears so. We are not safe here, Genevieve. We need to wake the children and move to a safer location."

Little Pierre appeared quite suddenly at the foot of their bed. "Papa, was that thunder?"

"No, son. The British are firing their cannons. We are going to move. Go get dressed and help your mother to get your brothers ready."

"*Oui, Papa.*"

Another explosion jarred their home. This time dust fell from the rafters and shingles overhead.

Genevieve inquired frantically as she tied the cords of her skirt around her waist, "Where will we go? To the church?"

Pierre shook his head. "It is not safe there, either. The church is closer to the fort and the fighting. We must move east, out of the line of fire from their towers. Bousseron's store is far enough in that direction. Quickly, let us get the children dressed and go there. Perhaps he will give us shelter. But we need to make sure everyone is dressed warmly. We may be outside for quite a while."

He shouted at his sons behind their curtain, "Boys, wear your coats and caps! Dress as if you were going on a hunting trip with me."

A chorus of tiny voices responded, "*Oui, Papa!*"

Pierre stood facing the foot of the bed beside Genevieve as he slipped his fur-lined moccasins onto his feet. His back was toward the main living area of the house. Suddenly the deafening sound of shattering wood filled their home. The wall to his right seemed to disappear as it tumbled inward. Genevieve screamed as splinters exploded outward and shingles rained down onto them from above. Pierre felt a piercing fire below his right shoulder blade as a piece of wood shrapnel embedded into the soft flesh of his back. He yelped in pain as he reached for his wife and pulled her to the floor against the side of the bed. He jumped toward the small cradle at their bedside and threw his body across the top of it in an effort to shield the baby from the falling debris.

Pierre could hear his sons screaming on the far side of the room, but there was nothing that he could do to help them. The cannon ball impacted the side of the stone fireplace about five feet above the ground. It exploded with a deafening roar, tossing molten fire in every direction and igniting cloth and wood inside the house. The heavy stone of the flue absorbed most of the blow, but the concussion was enough to shake the remaining boards of the structure loose from one another. The walls and roof on the northern end of their home collapsed into a dusty pile of rubble.

Something heavy struck Pierre's back and head. He was dazed and disoriented. He could hear the tiny screams of his baby beneath him, the hollow wails of his wife in the floor by his side, and the muffled crying of his boys somewhere beyond or beneath the rubble. Then he heard nothing. He saw nothing as blackness consumed his eyes and mind.

Pierre was unconscious.

"Colonel, their artillery has been ineffective," reported Captain Bowman. "The elevated position of their cannon is actually to their detriment. They cannot obtain line of fire on our men. All they have accomplished is knocking down a few houses in the village ... nothing more. We have suffered no losses from their big guns."

"Excellent report, Captain," responded Colonel Clark. "Is there anything else?"

"Yes, sir. Our scouts to the south have seen an enemy force of almost two dozen men. They appear to have come from the direction of our previous night's encampment."

"A scouting party dispatched to investigate our fires, no doubt," commented Colonel Clark. "We do not need a harassing force in our rear, Captain Bowman."

"I quite agree, sir. What do you suggest?"

Colonel Clark took a drink of hot tea from his pewter mug. He looked down at his desk and studied a hand-drawn map of the area for a brief moment. He nodded thoughtfully and then declared, "We allow them back inside their fort."

"Sir?" exclaimed Bowman in disbelief.

"I want all enemy combatants inside those walls," declared the colonel. "Besides, we cannot afford the possibility of a British officer running around in the woods stirring up the natives against us. It will be dawn within the hour. Order our men to cease fire shortly before the sunrise. Have them lay low in their positions and take cover in the village. Let's see if we can lure this patrol out and allow them to rejoin their comrades inside the fort."

"As you wish, sir." Captain Bowman saluted crisply and exited the colonel's office.

꩜

Something slapped Pierre's face. The sharp tingle of the blow burned against his cold flesh. He felt something heavy pressing down against his body. He awoke with a start and stared into the pale face of his friend, Francois Turpin.

"Francois! What are you doing here? What has happened?"

Pierre struggled to rise, but a covering of heavy blankets and the firm, persistent hands of his friend kept him in place where he lay. He scanned the area in an effort to discern his surroundings. He was inside a structure of some sort, but it was definitely not his home. The air was very cold. He smelled the presence of livestock. He saw a warm glow and heard the gentle crackling of a fire nearby.

"Where am I?"

"We are at your grain mill, Pierre ... well away from the range of the cannons."

Pierre exclaimed, "My family!" He struggled again to rise.

Again, Francois pushed him back down onto the ground. "Stop, Pierre! Be still. You have been wounded."

"But my family!"

Francois pointed to Pierre's right. "Your family is fine. Look! Genevieve and the children are here."

Pierre's heart leapt with joy when he saw his wife and children huddled against the nearby wall. She was busy trying to calm the crying baby and console the two younger boys. All of them were wrapped tightly in blankets. A small campfire burned close by on the dirt floor of the mill. There were other familiar families from the village seated along the walls and lounging nearby.

He called out, "Genevieve! Are you all right? How are the children?"

"We are fine, my darling. Pierre received a pretty large cut on his leg and Charles has a bruise on his head. Other than that, we are uninjured."

"Where is Pierre?" he asked.

"He has gone to Bousseron's to fetch us some food. He will be back in a moment."

Pierre shifted his gaze toward Francois. "How bad are my injuries? How long was I unconscious?"

"You were out for less than an hour. An overhead rafter gave you a pretty hard blow to the back of your head, but there is no swelling. You also had a pretty decent splinter of wood sticking out of your back. I got it out with little trouble, and there was not much blood. I cleaned the wound and bandaged it. Now you just need to rest. We cannot know, for sure, the extent of the injury to your head. Are you feeling at all dizzy or disoriented?"

"No more disoriented than should be expected, I suppose. No, I am not dizzy."

"Well, just lie still for now. Genevieve will see to you as soon as she gets the children under control. Pierre will be back in a moment with some hot food and tea. That should help all of you feel better."

"What about my house, Francois?"

His friend shook his head and pursed his lips. "It is a total loss, Pierre ... a pile of rubble. It is a miracle that all of you survived. Your boys were in the one portion that did not collapse entirely. You and Genevieve were saved by the frame of your bed."

Pierre shook his head in disbelief. "What about the rest of the village?"

"There are five other homes that were either destroyed or damaged significantly, and many others with minor damage. There were several injuries, but, miraculously, no deaths. Do not worry, old friend. Houses can be rebuilt. Your home can be rebuilt. Just be glad that you and your family survived."

"I am, Francois. Believe me. I am very glad. What about your family, Francois? Where are Josephine and the children?"

His friend smiled. "They are fine. She is tending to the injured who sought refuge at the church. They will be moved here at the first possible opportunity."

Pierre suddenly realized that the village was silent. There were no more sounds of shooting from the direction of the fort.

"What happened to the guns? Why have the Long Knives stopped firing?"

"I do not know, Pierre. Their guns fell silent just a short time before you awakened."

"Why have the rebels ceased their firing?" demanded Governor Hamilton.

"I am not certain," responded Major Hay. "Perhaps our artillery had more effect upon them than we have supposed."

"They probably had to go and dip their rifle barrels into the Wabash to cool them off. I'm sure they're all glowing red by now," quipped the Patriot Captain Leonard Helm. "Or perhaps they are taking a break for some breakfast and tea."

Hamilton ignored the teasing of his affable adversary. "There is some nefarious cause for their pause, I am quite certain. Have the men remain on vigilant alert. The enemy is, no doubt, well-supplied and equipped. We should expect as much from an army fresh from the Falls of the Ohio."

"You still doubt that these are Clark's men?" challenged Helm.

"Leonard, there is no way that Clark moved an army across the miles of flooded lands between here and Kaskaskia." He shook his head. "No … these are Virginians from the Kentucky lands, delivered here by boat. And if they are attacking this garrison with such precision and vigor, I daresay there must be at least five hundred of them. There may be a thousand or more. Only such numbers could explain the volume and efficacy of their fire."

Helm chuckled. "You would be surprised at the number of slugs that a couple of Kentucky boys can send downrange."

The door to Hamilton's office burst open. "Sirs! Captain Lamothe and his men are at the gate!"

"Are you certain?" asked Major Hay.

"Yes, sir. They gave the call sign and answered the challenge."
Hay shot a glance at Hamilton.

Hamilton nodded. "Get them over the walls, Major. We need the men and guns."

Twenty frightened English soldiers and French militiamen huddled, bewildered, near the front gate of the fort. They could not understand the stark silence and utter absence of enemy soldiers after so many hours of continuous firing. Their hearts leapt with joy when two rope ladders appeared over the palisade walls. The French militiamen scrambled quickly up the ropes and climbed nimbly over the spiked logs. The British infantry followed closely behind, their muskets strapped loosely over their backs.

Just as the final handful of men neared the tops of the ladders, the Long Knives, who had been watching from the shadows and enjoying the entertainment provided by the terrified and confused soldiers, suddenly resumed their shrill howling and screaming. The two Englishmen who were crossing the top of the wall at that moment jumped in fear and tumbled over the fort wall, landing with loud, hollow thuds on the ground below. The poor fellow who had been last in line for his rope ladder, and was almost at the top, leapt in horror and lost his grip. He fell clumsily to the ground outside the gate, landing with a gigantic pop, and shattering the wood stock of his musket.

The Long Knives who had seen him fall laughed and howled with delight. A few of them threw hunting knives that embedded into the logs only a few feet from his head. They screamed teasing curses at him as he limped back to the rope ladder and somehow managed to haul himself up and over the wall. The moment that his leg cleared the pointed logs of the palisade tops the firing resumed with great vigor.

The eastern sky began to glow its dull gray as the sun prepared to make its appearance above the winter clouds of the Illinois Country. Throughout the village of Vincennes dozens of roosters crowed of the coming dawn.

# 20

---

## UNCONDITIONAL SURRENDER

---

*Sunrise - February 24, 1779*

The attack upon the fort continued throughout the night and into the dawn. Pierre awakened early. He moved slowly, silently, and carefully as he pulled on his heavy, dark green wool capote. He winced at the sharp pain caused by the wound in his back. It took every ounce of willpower within him to control his overwhelming urge to cough. He glanced at his wife and children as they dozed peacefully against the stone wall of the grain mill. The dancing flicker of a campfire cast an orange-yellow glow across their pale, smooth faces. Little Pierre was nowhere to be seen. The adventurous lad was, no doubt, performing some act of service somewhere in the tiny village of Vincennes.

The sick, wounded Frenchman conspired to depart the mill without waking his wife. Considering all of his medical maladies, that was the only way he might avoid the certain tongue-lashing that she would unleash upon him for even considering joining in the combat at Fort Sackville. And she would be right. Pierre's body was ravaged by disease and injury. He had a mild concussion, a bleeding puncture wound in his back, and an ongoing case of lingering pneumonia. He should have been resting and recuperating in a warm bed, not marching off to war. But Pierre had a duty to perform. His British enemies had occupied his village and destroyed his home, and he was going to have his vengeance. He intended to see Hamilton dislodged from that fort. Nothing would keep him from this day's fight.

Pierre pulled back the blanket that was tacked over the open door of the mill and stepped outside into the chill of the early morning. Francois Turpin and Charles Rimbault were lounging against a nearby tree. Charles was seated on the ground and puffing nonchalantly on his walnut pipe. Francois stood beside him with a musket in both of his hands, the stocks of each one resting on the ground. Pierre smiled warmly at his friends. He recognized the weapon in Francois' right hand as his very own Charleville musket that he purchased before departing New Orleans back in 1769 ... a lifetime ago.

"I dug around under the remnants of your house and found something for you," reported Francois. He handed Pierre the musket.

Pierre covered his mouth to muffle a cough. "*Merci*, Francois. How did you ever manage to find it, old friend?"

"Oh, it was not difficult. I merely had to move a few boards around. I knew you would need something to shoot at Hamilton and his friends today." He smiled warmly. "I surmised that you would prefer not to throw rocks."

Charles stood and reached for three leather bags and two powder horns hanging on a nearby limb of the tree. "Your bags are filled with .69 caliber cartridges that some of the boys in town have rolled for our militia. They also poured and molded the balls themselves."

Pierre's eyes filled with pride. "I assume that my little Pierre was one of those boys."

Charles gave a crooked grin. "Of course. He packed those shooting bags for you himself and filled two extra horns with powder. The third bag is all loose lead and paper wadding ... just in case you run out of cartridges."

Francois declared proudly, "Your son spent an entire hour showing my Gaspard how to roll the cartridges. Now even my own son is able to contribute to the cause. Your little Pierre is quite the Patriot."

"As well I know," responded the proud father.

Charles handed Pierre a canteen full of water. He hung the straps of the ammunition bags and powder horns over his neck and tucked them under his right arm. He secured the carrying rope of the heavy vessel of water around the other side of his neck and dangled it beneath the opposite arm.

Francois glanced down the street in the direction of the fort. "Shall we?"

"Yes, indeed we shall," responded Pierre.

The three proud Frenchmen ... the three proud Americans ... marched down the narrow street in the direction of the fighting.

Governor Hamilton had just received a thorough report on their grim situation. Now that the sun was up his officers were able to make a proper inspection of the forces arrayed against them. Breastworks of earth and lumber as high as six feet ringed the fort. Those defensive positions bristled with the guns of attackers. The endless pounding of lead slugs continued against the walls of the fort. Hamilton and his men were under heavy siege.

"My God," declared Hamilton. "Then it is certain. We are completely and utterly surrounded."

Major Hay nodded in shame. "And there can be little doubt, sir, that the Frenchmen have added their guns to those of our enemies."

"We still have no reckoning of their numbers?" inquired Hamilton.

"No, sir. But their force must be considerable in size, considering the rapid overnight construction of their defenses and firing positions."

The major paused.  He scanned the faces of the other men in the room.  All of them seemed sullen and devoid of hope … except for that damned Virginian, Leonard Helm, who sat in the corner, gloating and grinning like an ape.  How the major longed to pull his pistol and put a ball through that aggravating, fiendish cretin's skull.  He simply could not understand the governor's bizarre friendship with the horrid man.

"What shall we do, sir?" inquired Major Hay.

Hamilton slammed his palm on his desk.  "We fight, damn you! We fight to the last man!  I will not hand the King's fort over to this rabble of bandits!"

2

The firing upon Fort Sackville increased dramatically with the coming of daylight.  There was no more shortage of lead and powder thanks to the ample contribution from Captain Bousseron. The addition of the Vincennes militia on the firing line increased Clark's forces by over half.  The colonel could not be more pleased with his men or the disposition of the battle.

The assault and siege were progressing as Colonel Clark had hoped they might, but the issue of victory remained in question. He feared that some yet unseen reinforcements might soon arrive from Detroit.  He also learned that Hamilton was in possession of a significant number of his army's correspondences and dispatches taken from a captured courier headed toward the Falls of the Ohio. Those dispatches carried receipts and financial records of the indebtedness that he had incurred during this extended military operation, and he did not want those records destroyed.

Clark decided that it was time to make a move … and a bold bluff seemed in order.  He took quill in hand and wrote the first of several correspondences that he would exchange with Lieutenant Governor Hamilton on that fateful day.

*Sir, in order to save yourself from the impending storm that now threatens you I expect that you will immediately surrender yourself along with all of your garrison and stores. I forbid you to hurt any more buildings of the town. I forbid you to destroy stores of any kind, or any papers or letters that you now have in your possession. If I am obliged to storm the fort you may expect no mercy, for by Heavens, you shall be treated as a murderer.*

*G.R. Clark*

Colonel Clark handed Bowman the written dispatch. "Captain, I want you to order a temporary cease fire and deliver this message under flag of truce. Make sure that all of our men are fed and provided with hot drink during the break."

"Yes, sir. Right away, sir." Bowman saluted quickly and bolted from Clark's office. Less than five minutes later the firing stopped.

Hamilton's face and ears turned blood red as he read the demand for surrender from Clark. He threw the letter down on his desk in disgust and exclaimed, "Why, that insolent, uncouth, audacious twit!"

"Whatever is the matter, Governor?" teased Captain Leonard Helm.

"That Colonial commoner has the gall to call me a murderer? Me! An officer of the King and the governor of this district! And he thinks that he has the authority to order me in regards to what I can and cannot do with dispatches in my possession? What a pair of twiddle-diddles this man must have! Such impudent gall! Neither his message nor his tone were civil in the least. This Colonel Clark is no gentleman, I'll have you know."

"Oh!" responded Helm with feigned surprise. "So, then it is George Rogers Clark? But I thought it impossible for him to cross those flooded lands." His teasing tone dripped with sarcasm.

Hamilton attempted to ignore Helm's mocking commentary. He picked up his own quill and dipped it in his ink well. He scribbled the following response on Clark's surrender demand.

> *Governor Hamilton begs to acquaint Col. Clark that neither he nor his garrison are to be prevailed upon by threats to act in a manner unbecoming the character of British subjects.*
>
> *H. Hamilton*

He folded the note with a single crease down the center and extended it to the commander of his military forces. "Major Hay, see that this is delivered to the enemy courier posthaste."

The major bowed obediently, turned, and marched out of Hamilton's office.

Clark gnawed on a piece of tough bread and grinned as he read the brief, entertaining response from Hamilton. There was a generous dab of butter and jam decorating his smacking lips.

"Well, that was salvo number one," he declared, wiping his mouth with his hand. "It appears that the illustrious Governor Hamilton requires some more convincing. At least our men had a nice hour-long break." He handed the note back to Captain Bowman. "Have all of our soldiers been fed?"

"Yes, sir. And generously, sir. The people of Vincennes have been most hospitable. The men are all worked up and ready to get at the enemy. We're going to have to tie a few of them down, I'm afraid. They're pretty much ready to storm the fort, British be damned."

Clark threw back his head and chuckled heartily. "Excellent! Then resume the siege, Captain. Bring all weapons to bear upon the fort. Keep chipping away at those timbers. But maintain one-third of our forces in reserve. Let the Frenchmen carry most of the load this morning so that some of our men might get a little more rest."

"Yes, sir. I will see to it."

*Mid-Morning*

Pierre loaded and fired again, as did Francois. They were not firing at anything in particular. They simply performed as ordered and shot at the fort. They could, on occasion, see movement along the tops of the walls or through the wider holes in the chinking, but it was absurd to think that they could actually hit such difficult targets with their old muskets. Their fire was simply not accurate enough for such sharpshooting. Charles expended a few shots when they first joined the line, but quickly became bored with shooting at logs. He decided, instead, to find a soft spot in the loose dirt and lie down until, as he vocalized, "There was something to shoot at that might actually bleed." He was sound asleep in the midst of the thunder of gunfire.

The Long Knives, on the other hand, continued to register an occasional hit with their supremely accurate Pennsylvania and Virginia long rifles. Pierre had personally witnessed two men wounded through tiny gaps in the fort walls. The constant firing was, indeed, having a deleterious effect.

"Charles is right!" declared Francois. "This is a monumental waste of powder and lead!"

"It is all for a strategic purpose," answered Pierre. "At least the British are keeping their heads down. I have not seen a single shot from inside the fort since we arrived on the line."

"Surely it must be demoralizing for them," affirmed Francois, trying to convince himself of the fruitfulness of his seemingly pointless labor.

"I should think so. That has to be Colonel Clark's goal ... to break the will of the enemy troops and force a surrender." He paused. "Because it will be bloody, indeed, if we actually have to storm the walls of that fort."

Francois shuddered at the notion. "I want no part of that."

A high-pitched voice interrupted their conversation. "Do you need anything, Papa?"

Pierre spun around and saw his son, little Pierre, kneeling behind him and holding a large basket covered with a white linen napkin. He also carried two large leather bags under each arm. It was a wonder that the spunky nine-year-old was able to walk at all with such a heavy load of cargo.

"Pierre! Son! What are you doing wandering among the breastworks? Do you not understand how dangerous it is up here?"

"I was careful, Papa. Anyhow, no one has seen a shot come from inside the fort since the parley earlier this morning." The boy grinned triumphantly at his father.

Pierre growled in disgust. "How in God's name do you know about such military matters? You are but a lad!" He pointed to a small depression behind a large log. "Stay low and sit down right there."

The boy complied. His grin never left his face.

"What is in the basket?" asked Charles from beneath the hat that still covered his face. Young Pierre gave the man a puzzled look. He had no idea how the supposedly sleeping Frenchman even knew that he was carrying a basket.

"Just some food for the soldiers on the line, *Monsieur* Gibault. I have been making deliveries. There is bread and jam, and a little bit of smoked, dried buffalo."

"What is in the bags?" asked Francois.

Little Pierre grinned and patted the bags on his right side. ".69 Charleville balls on this side and .44 rifle on the other."

Francois chuckled and shook his head. "Where is my boy?"

"I left Gaspard with the other boys who were pouring lead and rolling cartridges. He seemed happy and content inside Bousseron's store. There is a warm fire in there."

"Have you seen your mother recently?" asked his father as he reloaded his musket.

Little Pierre nodded. "She is fine, and the children are well. They have actually returned home with *Madame* Turpin." He nodded toward Francois. "*Monsieur,* your wife said that the mill was no place for the little ones. Now that the town seems safe from the cannons, most of the women have returned to their homes and warm fires. She invited our family to share your home."

His father nodded. "That is good news. What about you, son? How are you holding up?"

"I am a bit tired, but I will be fine. I plan to go to *Monsieur* Turpin's house as soon as I finish my rounds and all of my bags are empty. I could use a nap."

A voice soon bellowed from a Virginia officer down the line, "Maintain suppressing fire on the fort! You can rest when the war is over!" They looked in the direction of the voice. It was clear that the man was talking directly to them.

Pierre winked at his son as he poured a touch of powder from his horn into his pan. "We need to get back to work, son. You can leave us some of that bread before you go."

Little Pierre nodded and grabbed a foot-long loaf of bread from the basket, along with a small crock of apple jam. He hesitated briefly and appeared to have something to say.

"What is the matter, son?"

"I was just wondering ..."

"Wondering what?"

"I was just wondering what it is like to actually fight ... you know ... to shoot at the fort." He looked longingly at his father. There was a moment of awkward silence and expectation.

"Let him fire your musket, Pierre," encouraged Francois. "Lord knows he deserves it. He has served as much as any other man of Vincennes throughout the night." Francois turned, aimed, and fired his weapon. A billowing cloud of white smoke swirled over the top of their concealed position.

"Francois is right," chimed Charles from beneath his hat. "Let the lad shoot a time or two. Hell, he can shoot lumber just as well as you two niffynannies."

Pierre pondered his friends' words for a moment and then grinned at his boy. "Put your basket down and come over here."

Little Pierre eagerly dropped his basket to the ground and crawled toward his father. He made sure to keep his head below the cover of the logs and boards.

"I have a perfect little hole over here that you can fire through. But I do not want you to raise your head above this berm. You can just aim at the logs of the fort and then shoot ... one time. All right?"

Little Pierre nodded.

"Get on your knees right here and hold the stock against your shoulder. I will help you."

Pierre ran the barrel of the musket through the firing hole. He helped his son get into position and then knelt behind him.

"Can you see the wall?"

"*Oui*, Papa."

"Try to pick a large crack between the logs and aim for it."

Little Pierre nodded.

"All right, I am pulling the lock back to full cock. Now, remember ... it is going to kick hard. It might hurt your shoulder." He tugged on the hammer until it locked with a hollow 'click.' "You can shoot whenever you are ready."

Little Pierre paused as he aimed at a small hole in the wall of the fort. He could almost swear that he saw movement through the hole. The boy was trembling with excitement and anticipation. He thought, "There must be a British soldier behind that wall!" He could scarcely breathe or even think. He yanked the trigger. The massive musket belched fire and smoke and kicked hard against his shoulder, knocking him backwards into his father's chest. He lowered the stock and rubbed his sore shoulder. Black powder soot streaked and stained his face.

Charles lifted his hat from his own face and grinned broadly. "Congratulations, Pierre. You killed a dead tree." He winked at the boy.

Francois looked at the lad and chuckled. "Well, just look at that! Little Pierre, musketeer and Patriot of the Vincennes Militia!"

The boy's face glowed with pride.

❧

*The Noon Hour - Hamilton's Office Inside Fort Sackville*
"Why are our guns silent?" demanded the governor. "I have not heard cannon fire for many hours, and I hear no sound of musketry, either."

Major Hay's head hung low. "Sir, the artillery is ineffective. The angle of fire is such that we cannot bring ordinance to bear upon the enemy defenses. We cannot get any men into position to return fire with small arms because of the deadly accuracy of their riflemen. And to be honest, sir, we have just lost over half of our fighting force."

"Whatever do you mean, Major?"

"It is the French militia, sir. They have laid down their arms. They refuse to fight against their countrymen of Vincennes who now stand with the rebels."

Hamilton fumed. "Those damned cowardly French! I should have known better. I should have retained the Indians and sent the Frenchmen home to Canada. I will hang them all!"

"I daresay that there are more of them than there are of us, Governor. If they should turn their weapons upon us we would be easily overwhelmed." He took a single, timid step toward Hamilton's desk. "I beseech you, Lord. The fort is lost. I implore you, for the sake of the men in our charge, to seek the terms of surrender."

❧

A temporary white flag flew over the gate of Fort Sackville. The village and fort were eerily silent. The reason for the pause was the delivery of a correspondence from Hamilton ... a proposal for Colonel Clark.

The colonel held his right hand thoughtfully over his mouth as he held the note in his left hand and read it aloud to his officers.

> *Lt. Governor Hamilton proposes that the forces engaged maintain a truce for a period of three days, during which time there will be no works of defense within the fort. This proposal is conditional upon Col. Clark's agreement to same. Lt. Governor Hamilton wishes to confer personally with Colonel Clark and conclude an honorable agreement between our two forces. If Col. Clark is apprehensive about entering the fort, Lt. Governor Hamilton will agree to speak to him in front of the gate.*
>
> *24th Feb'y 1779*

"That pompous brat couldn't even bear to author his own message. He had one of his lackeys do it for him," muttered Clark in disgust. He looked to his officers. "Impressions, gentlemen? Suggestions?"

"Three days would be nice, Colonel," chirped a young lieutenant. "That would give us some much-needed time to rest the men."

Clark nodded. "Indeed, it would."

"But I don't trust him, sir," countered Captain Bowman. "Something does not smell right. Why three days? What will that accomplish? He's plotting something. I am sure of it."

"I was thinking exactly the same thing, Captain," responded Clark. "Hamilton must be expecting reinforcements or supplies. The notion of a three-day lull and then a surrender is pointless. He must think that we are all idiots." Clark paused and took a deep breath. "I believe that we are in agreement that we shall accept nothing short of unconditional surrender. Does everyone concur?"

The officers and sergeants around his table grunted and nodded their agreement.

"Very well, then. Captain, you may record our response by your own hand, which you may deliver to Hamilton's man immediately. I'll not meet him in the open. If he wants to talk, tell him we can meet inside the church. That is a good, safe, neutral ground."

"Of course, Colonel."

Captain Bowman took the quill and ink from Clark's desk, along with the latest message from Hamilton, and retired to a small table in the corner of the room. He composed the response and then handed it to a nearby lieutenant for delivery. Clark winked and smiled proudly at the captain.

❧

Hamilton stared numbly at the note in his hand. It read:

> *Col. Clark sends his compliments to Mr. Hamilton and begs leave to inform him that his forces will not agree to any terms other than the unconditional surrender of himself and the garrison. If Mr. Hamilton desires a conference with Col. Clark, he will be happy to meet with Mr. Hamilton and with Captain Helms, his prisoner, for conference at the church.*
> *Joseph Bowman, Captain*

Hamilton took a deep breath and sighed. "Clark has rejected my offer. He demands unconditional surrender. He proposes that we meet for parley at the church."

"So, he didn't want to go along with your three-day hiatus, eh?" teased Captain Helm. "Pity. Those boys of his could use the rest, I'm sure. And you, no doubt could use the time to get some reinforcements from upriver."

Hamilton stared angrily at his increasingly obnoxious friend. "You should go get cleaned up a bit, Leonard. Clark has requested your presence at the church, as well."

"Indeed?" commented Helm, smiling and rubbing the bristly whiskers on his chin. "Perhaps I should go and shave. I want to put on my best look for my commander."

"Well, do it quickly. We depart within the half-hour."

♌

The guns around Vincennes had been silent for almost an hour. Every eye behind the American positions was fixed upon the three men walking from the gate of the fort toward the church. The man in front, Lieutenant Governor Henry Hamilton, was dressed in a fine black coat and breeches. The second man wore the bright red uniform of the British army. It was Major Jehu Hay. The humbly-dressed Captain Leonard Helm walked subserviently behind his captors.

Colonel George Rogers Clark and Captain Joseph Bowman stood on the steps in front of the church. They were accompanied by Captain John Williams, a pioneer settler from Kentucky. Each man was clad in rough, wilderness-scarred buckskins. They were unshaven, smelly, and dirty. They provided quite the contrast to the fancy Englishmen who approached them for a formal conference.

As the men neared the church Colonel Clark spoke first. "Governor Hamilton, I am pleased to finally make your acquaintance."

"Colonel Clark," was all Hamilton offered in response, with the slightest of nods.

"Leonard, you look none the worse for wear," commented Clark.

"I'm better off than these two fellows," quipped the lighthearted captain, smiling wryly.

"Gentlemen, shall we go inside?" invited Clark.

The men were just about to enter the church when a chorus of war whoops and shots erupted from the field on the southeast side of the village. Every head turned in that direction to see the source of the commotion.

"Is that our men?" asked Clark.

"We don't have any forces deployed in that area, sir," responded Captain Bowman.

"Sounds to me like some of Hamilton's Injuns," quipped Leonard Helm.

Clark shot a glance at Captain Bowman and nodded.

Bowman turned to Captain Williams. "John, take your company and go give those savages a proper greeting."

"Absolutely, sir!" Williams trotted off in the direction of his men.

Clark turned to the two British officials. "If you don't mind, gentlemen, I think we will wait just a bit to see how this turns out."

Hamilton started to speak, "Sir, I object ..."

Colonel Clark cut him off, "We wait! Or you can go back inside your fort if you wish, Hamilton."

The British governor fell silent. The men watched anxiously toward the southeast as Captain Williams' men moved in the direction of the incoming Indians. Minutes later they heard the sounds of gunfire, cursing, and screaming. Hamilton and Hay winced, their expressions betraying their chagrin. The British contingent pleaded to enter the church immediately and begin the parley, but Colonel Clark insisted that they wait. The interruption and delay were agonizing for Hamilton. Clark sensed the man's discomfort and growing frustration. But still they waited.

Finally, approximately fifteen minutes later, Captain Williams and his squad returned with seven disarmed men. The captives were bound with leather thongs around their wrists. The Virginians prodded them along with their rifle barrels.

"Report, Captain," barked Colonel Clark.

"Sir, we jumped about fifteen of 'em as they got to the edge of the town commons. They was all a whoopin' and a hollerin' and beatin' their chests." He frowned grimly. "And they was wavin' them thar nasty strangs of scalps." He spat on the ground. "They seemed to think that we was a welcomin' party, of sorts, until we opened fire on their red arses. We dropped six in the field, all dead or dyin'. Two runned oft, but they'll all likely die. They was trailin' blood sumpin' fierce. They had 'em two French hunters for prisoners. We cut them boys loose. This here is the rest. Two Frenchies, four growed Injuns, and one red lad."

Clark stepped down off of the step and walked near to the two Frenchmen who were allied with the Indians. "I'm quite certain that you gentlemen were scouts, and nothing more, correct? Surely you had no part in the taking of these American scalps."

"No, *Monsieur!*" proclaimed both men. "We only came upon the war party as they returned to the fort and we joined with them for the journey."

"Even though they had two of your countrymen as prisoners?" inquired a confused Clark.

"It was because of the prisoners, *Monsieur.* Our desire was benevolent. We wanted to testify and insure their release upon our return to the fort."

Clark eyed them suspiciously. "Not likely. But, nevertheless, you two are free to go. Cut them loose, Captain Williams."

"Yes, sir!" He whipped out his knife and cut the leather thongs that bound the wrists of both men. They thanked the colonel profusely as they scurried away toward the village.

Captain Bowman spoke up, "That boy can't be a day over eleven or twelve years old, Colonel. Could we not release him, as well?"

Clark nodded. "Absolutely, Captain. Unlike my opponents, I am not the least bit interested in executing women and children."

As the captain cut the cords around the boy's wrists Hamilton burst out, "Executing?"

Clark turned and faced him. "That's right, Hamilton. Executing. These savages are heartless murderers of women and children. They have hanging on their belts the scalps of innocent settlers from the Kentucky frontier." He pointed toward some of his men. "Those might be the scalps of some of the family members ... wives and children ... of the men in my army. Surely you did not think we were about to show mercy to those who disregard such notions toward our people."

"What do we do with 'em, sir?" asked Captain Williams.

Clarke pursed his lips and pointed toward the gate of the fort. "Take them over there in front of the gate ... right in front of the enemy soldiers ... and have them tomahawked to death. That is, after all, a punishment befitting such savagery as these heathens have unleashed upon our American brethren."

Captain Williams spat on the ground at the feet of the Indians. "Beggin' your pardon, sir, but might I have the privilege of carryin' out the sentence myself? Hell, that might even be the hair of my own brother or his wife and kids hangin' on their savage waists."

"Do as you wish, Captain. I just want them dead and their bodies thrown in the Wabash."

Captain Williams spun around toward his soldiers. "You heard him, men! In front of the gate!"

The bitter Virginians marched the sullen natives into the street in front of the fort. They forced them to get down on their knees in front of the watchful eyes of the enemy.

Captain Williams bellowed in the direction of the fort, "This is what happens to those who would murder Americans! Beware the wrath of the Long Knives!"

He walked casually around behind the Indians, removed his tomahawk from his belt, drew the weapon high over his head, and then plunged it with hate and fury into the top of the first Indian's skull. A geyser of blood erupted from the stricken warrior's head. The other soldiers standing guard over the captives took a step back to escape the spray. The blade was imbedded so deeply that the captain had to hold the thrashing, convulsing man down with his foot in order to remove the weapon from his ruptured head. A gasp of disgust and awe erupted from both the men inside the enemy fort as well as from the men concealed behind the American defensive positions.

Captain Williams then slowly and methodically worked his way down the line, mercilessly tomahawking each man in the skull. His fatigue and emotion became evident on the final Indian. The last condemned man required more than one blow of the tomahawk to accomplish the gruesome job. When Williams was done, he was covered from his forehead to his waist with blood spatter. He calmly wiped his tomahawk on the back of the last Indian. He turned to his men and commanded, "Toss them in the river."

The soldiers quickly fetched lengths of rope and recruited other volunteers from among the Long Knives to help them move the bodies. They fashioned rough nooses which they tied around the necks of the dead and then pulled them through the puddles of rainwater and mud toward the bank of the Wabash. Once at the water's edge, the men loosed the ropes and irreverently kicked the bodies into the river. Afterwards they knelt down to rinse the blood and tissue from their hands and faces in the mud-stained waters of the fast-flowing Wabash.

Back on the steps of the church Governor Hamilton and Major Hay stared through eyes swollen with disgust. Hay covered his mouth and fought his urge to vomit. Hamilton shook his head in judgment at the scene he had just witnessed.

Colonel Clark stared lividly at both men. "Don't stand there and act all self-righteous, you murderous sons of bitches. How do you think those pet Indians of yours come into the possession of the scalps that you seem to like so much? You are no more civilized or any less bloodthirsty than those savages. You just dress nicer and talk a little better. Now, unless you want to finish this fight, I suggest you get inside this church and let's come to an agreement."

The crimson-faced Lieutenant Governor Henry Hamilton tugged proudly on his lapel and ambled through the door in the most dignified manner that he could muster under the circumstances.

❦

Pierre, Francois, and Charles were less than fifty feet away from the gruesome display of bloody violence. They watched in disbelief as the execution and its aftermath unfolded before their very eyes. Francois could not stop gaping at the enormous volume of blood that stained the mud in front of the gate of Fort Sackville.

"*Mon Dieu!*" exclaimed Francois. "I have never seen anything such as that!" He shook his head and stared in disbelief. "It was such a wanton display of cold-hearted savagery! How can such action be warranted or carried out by civilized men?"

Pierre said nothing. Already sickened from the disease in his lungs, he had quickly become nauseated at the sight of the blood and gore. He vomited up his entire breakfast when he saw the first blow of the captain's tomahawk. He was still shaking from the convulsions in his digestive tract. He was busy gargling water from his canteen in an effort to rinse the acid and bile from his mouth.

Charles Rimbault took a long, deep drag on his clay pipe and then spat over the top of the protective mound of dirt and lumber. "They received what they deserved, Francois. These were the same Indians who murdered innocent settlers and sold their scalps to the British."

"But to execute them without process or trial is immoral!" Francois objected.

"Trial be damned," muttered Pierre through the foul taste in his mouth. He gagged and coughed up a mixture of phlegm and stomach acid. He spat the yellow gob onto the ground at his feet. "They were godless, murdering savages. Charles is right. They got what they deserved. Probably better than they deserved, considering what they have done to white men."

"Just look at the men inside the fort," urged Charles. "Look at their faces. Their will to fight is gone."

Francois and Pierre peered over the barricade and looked at the men along the top of the wall. Charles was right. They could see the despair on the faces of the soldiers who were staring over the tops of the palisades. They were completely disheartened. Many appeared to be terrified, especially among the Frenchmen.

"It was a stroke of genius on the part of Colonel Clark," added Charles. "A powerful display of theater intended to crush the will of the enemy. And it worked. Clark may have just spared the lives of every man inside and outside that fort. Well worth the lives of four murderous Indians, I would venture."

Francois did not respond. He just continued to stare in disbelief at the enormous puddles of dark blood and the crimson streaks that trailed off toward the river.

Colonel Clark read the written proposal handed him by Hamilton and then tossed it into the floor at his feet. Hamilton stared at the paper in wide-eyed shock.

"You must think that I am stupid, Mr. Hamilton. Parole for your officers and men? Ha! Do you seriously think that I would allow you all to walk out of this place with your flags waving in the breeze and your chins high in the air so that you might go forth and engage in your murderous pursuits somewhere else? Not likely, sir! I have given you my terms twice already, and need not do so again. I will accept nothing short of your unconditional surrender."

Captain Leonard Helm interjected, "Sir, I would encourage you to consider options other than a complete surrender at discretion."

"Captain Helm, you are a prisoner of the Crown, and it is not proper for you to interrupt or participate in these negotiations," scolded Clark.

Hamilton responded, "Colonel, if his input would be helpful, I will release the prisoner to your recognizance at this very moment."

Clark shook his head. "No. Captain Helm will return to his captivity inside the fort and allow fate to determine his condition." He stood up from the church bench and placed his hat on his head. "Since we are at a stalemate, I declare these negotiations closed. You may return to your fort. We will allow the fire and blood of battle to determine the outcome of this contest."

Clark turned and strode toward the door of the church. His officers followed close behind.

Hamilton called after him, "Colonel, would you be willing to explain to me your reason for accepting nothing short of unconditional surrender?"

Clark turned to face him. He growled, "Oh, I will be happy to explain that, Mr. Hamilton!" He paused and attempted to compose himself. "Most of your Indian partisans, those despicable white men who encourage the murder of American settlers on the frontier, are sheltering inside that fort right now." Clark fixed an evil gaze on Major Hay. "I would love any excuse to put a bullet in their heads or a sword through their gullets. The screams of the widows and fatherless children on the frontier call for their blood, and my hands are compelled to spill it!"

"Who, pray tell, do you profess to number among these so-called 'Indian partisans?'" inquired Hamilton.

Clark walked angrily toward the two men and poked a finger in the chest of Major Jehu Hay. "Right here is the chief among them, sir. This traitorous Pennsylvania skunk who hires savages to slay his own countrymen. He deserves to be floating down the Wabash with his dead playmates. It takes every ounce of my will to keep myself from spilling his blood right here inside this church!"

Major Hay's face turned pale with horror. Hamilton seemed dazed and unable to speak. Their fear was palpable. Colonel Clark knew that he had them exactly where he wanted them. He shifted his steely gaze toward the governor.

"I tell you what, Mr. Hamilton. I'm suddenly feeling very generous. I will consider some of your proposals and give you my response in one hour. If we soften our terms, I will send a messenger under flag of truce. If we choose not to change our demands, I will order my drummers to sound the resumption of hostilities."

Hamilton bowed slightly. "I accept your proposal, Colonel, and will await your reply in one hour."

Hamilton bolted for the door, with Major Hay close behind. Leonard Helm lingered just a bit and made eye contact with Colonel Clark, who winked at him subtly and fondly. Helm covered his mouth to conceal his grin. Clark was pulling off a major bluff, and Helm knew it. But would Hamilton take the bait?

The three men exited the church and marched quickly toward the gate of the fort.

※

*One Hour Later*

Captain Bowman delivered Clark's new terms under a flag of truce. The colonel did not reduce his demands significantly. The soldiers of the garrison were still expected to surrender and turn over all munitions, equipment, and stores. The officers would be allowed to keep their personal baggage and effects and take them along to their final destinations as prisoners of war. Since it was late in the day, Clark declared that the surrender would occur at ten o'clock on the following morning. The conquered soldiers were expected to march out in formation, surrender their arms and accouterments, and prepare for transport to an American prison camp.

Bowman handed the written proposal to a courier and then waited patiently near the gate. Less than a half hour later Captain Leonard Helm returned with the governor's response. He was smiling from ear to ear.

"Good news, I hope," said Captain Bowman.

"Very good news, John. I'll see you in the morning." He shook hands with his friend and then disappeared behind the large wooden gates.

Captain Bowman ran quickly to Clark's office and handed him the folded document. Clark broke the governor's wax seal and read the note aloud to his officers:

> *Agreed to for the following reasons ... the remoteness from succors, the state and quality of provisions, etc ... and the unanimity of officers and men on its expediency, the honorable terms allowed, and lastly the confidence in a generous enemy.*
>
> H. Hamilton
> *Lt. Governor & Superintendent*

Clark offered no comment. He displayed no open emotion. He simply folded the letter of surrender and placed it inside his journal for safekeeping.

*February 25, 1779*
*Near the Gates of Fort Sackville*

The Long Knives and their French compatriots stood at attention in two long columns outside the main gate of the fort. Pierre insisted on securing a position in the line as close to the gate as possible. Little Pierre stood proudly to his father's left. Charles Rimbault and Francois stood to his right. Pierre maintained a careful watch through the partially opened gate.

"What are you doing?" asked Charles. "Why do you keep staring into the fort?"

"I'm looking for someone," Pierre hissed.

"Who?"

"I do not know his name, but I will most definitely know him when I see him."

Charles gazed at Pierre with a bewildered stare. Moments later a drum sounded a slow march from behind the gate. The doors swung wide open as Lieutenant Governor Henry Hamilton and Major Jehu Hay led the procession of defeated defenders. The red-coated soldiers of Great Britain followed behind their commanders. The French militia and a handful of Indians brought up the rear.

Pierre spoke boldly and sarcastically as Henry Hamilton passed in front of him, "I hope you enjoy prison, Hamilton. Personally, I believe you should swing from a rope."

Hamilton paused and stared in wide-eyed disbelief at Pierre, his formerly condemned prisoner. "So, you run with this rabble, eh Grimard?"

Pierre growled, "This rabble whipped your arse, Hamilton. Now get the hell out of my village. If I ever see you again, I will kill you." Pierre glanced at Charles and Francois and then, acting on what was for him a very uncharacteristic impulse, removed his hat and waved it in the air, shouting, "*Vive les États-Unis d'Amérique! Vive la liberté!*"

The two rows of exhausted, filthy, proud Patriots erupted into a chorus of, "Huzzah! Huzzah! Huzzah!"

Hamilton thrust his chin and nose high into the air and turned proudly away from Pierre. He and Major Hay resumed their march toward the awaiting Colonel George Rogers Clark. After a long, humiliating walk they stopped two paces in front of the victorious frontiersman. The drum cadence ceased. The enemy soldiers halted as both Hamilton and Hay dutifully removed their swords and presented them to the American officer.

"The fort is yours, Colonel," stated Hamilton flatly.

"The fort is mine, sir," echoed Clark as he passed the two swords to Captain Bowman for safekeeping. "Mr. Hamilton, please escort your men to the clearing beside the river for processing. They will surrender their arms there."

"As you wish, Colonel." Hamilton bowed graciously.

The drum beat resumed. Just before Hay and Hamilton moved to lead their men toward the designated spot, a voice near the gate of the fort suddenly and loudly exclaimed, "There he is!"

It was Pierre Grimard who had, once again, interrupted the ceremony of surrender. He thrust his musket into his son's hands and bolted from the Patriot formation. He stormed brusquely and with determination toward one of the French militiamen in the enemy column. He had to cross through three other rows of soldiers to get to him. Pierre stopped the man in his tracks. The poor fellow's eyes widened in confusion and fear. The drummer stopped his cadence abruptly. Every soldier, both ally and enemy, stared in dismay at the stormy, pale Frenchman who had suddenly invaded the column of surrendering soldiers. Everyone fully expected an act of violence.

Pierre declared rather loudly, "*Monsieur*, you are currently in possession of my property. I will have it back immediately, please."

The enemy militiaman's face transformed from utter confusion to complete recognition and understanding, for he carried on his left shoulder Sergeant Pierre Grimard's beautiful Pennsylvania long rifle, confiscated two months prior when Pierre had been captured. The man nodded in humble defeat, unshouldered the weapon, and handed it to its demanding owner. The fellow even removed his *voyageur* cap and tipped it toward Pierre in a respectful salute.

"*Merci, Monsieur*," said Pierre. He coughed with a deep, raspy gurgle. "I paid a handsome price for this fine weapon … far too much for you to throw it onto a pile of rusty British muskets."

The Frenchmen of the Vincennes militia hooted and laughed as Pierre returned to his place in the Patriot formation. As he reclaimed his spot in line he lifted the stock of his precious rifle to his lips and kissed the smooth, striped, curly maple wood. His comrades cheered. Many of them broke formation to walk over and slap him on the shoulder and congratulate him for his brazenness and courage.

Colonel George Rogers Clark, standing at the far end of the formation of Frenchmen and Long Knives, watched helplessly as the gaggle of celebrating Frenchmen overshadowed his surrender ceremony. His officers pointed and chuckled lightheartedly. Clark merely smiled and shook his head.

# EPILOGUE

*February 24, 1784*

It was an amazingly brilliant, clear day. The sun hung low and bright in the dazzlingly blue winter sky. Genevieve Colomb Grimard and her children stood vigil over a mound of fresh earth in the large, open graveyard beside the tiny Catholic Church. It was the same church in which her husband and the other men of Vincennes had sworn their allegiance to Virginia and the United States in the summer of 1778. Fort Patrick Henry sat less than a hundred yards away. Its timbers and palisades were dilapidated and in a shameful state of disrepair. The post had been virtually abandoned, untouched, and unused for almost three years.

Genevieve sobbed quietly. Father Gibault stood with his arm around the sorrowful woman. He held his enormous Bible in his other hand. Thirteen-year-old Pierre, already a handsome and rugged young man, held little Nicholas loosely on his hip. A single tear inched its way down the lad's cheek. Genevieve cradled her newborn, Marie Victoria, close to her breast. The other children ... Jean-Baptiste, Charles, Genevieve, and Helene ... stood solemnly between their mother and the elongated mound. The pile of dark, freshly disturbed soil covered the unmarked grave of their beloved husband and father, Pierre Grimard.

Pierre had suffered from pneumonia, pleurisy of the lungs, and a horrible catarrh for the five years since his ordeal in the winter of 1778-1779. Each winter after, the pneumonia recurred when the cold air and snows invaded the low country around the Wabash River. And each year the disease grew progressively worse. Even during the warmer months Pierre had struggled to breathe, such was the damage to his lungs. He continuously labored to capture life-giving oxygen from the frontier air. Every night he coughed and gasped with apnea to the point that he could barely sleep. The weakened body of the brave Patriot of the American Revolution, Pierre Grimard of Vincennes, finally succumbed to the continuous onslaught of the never-ending, ravaging diseases of his lungs on a frigid night in the winter of 1784. He died in his bed, holding his wife's hand and surrounded by his adoring boys and girls. He was laid in his final resting place in the cold ground the following afternoon.

Genevieve wiped her eyes with the handkerchief in her right hand. She looked up at the sea of people that surrounded them. The entire village had turned out for Pierre's burial. There were so many familiar faces. Charles Rimbault stood immediately beside the grave of his dearest friend. Francois Turpin and Josephine, surrounded by their children, stood nearby. All of the men who had served in the militia with Pierre were there. Amazingly, there were even a few of the Long Knives of Virginia intermixed with the people of Vincennes. A handful of those rugged fellows had remained in the Illinois Country, taken French or Indian wives, and started families of their own.

In the distance, she heard the familiar voice of Captain Francois Riday Bousseron. He commanded a group of seven musketeers who stood at the ready beside the gate of the abandoned fort. They were preparing to fire a gun salute in Pierre's honor.

He barked commands to the firing team. "Prime your firelocks! Make ready! Take aim! Fire!"

Genevieve jumped at the loud report of the muskets. Father Gibault offered a final prayer over Pierre's grave. Then it was over. The people began to meander slowly from the graveyard, eager to return to the warmth of their homes. Some of Pierre's closest friends ventured over to speak to Genevieve and the children. They offered the customary condolences and awkward platitudes that were the usual fare at funerals and burials. Within a scant few minutes the graveyard was empty except for the Grimard family.

Genevieve took a single step forward, bringing her toes into contact with the freshly dug earth. She took a long, deep breath. "I will miss you, Pierre Grimard. You were a good man and a brave man. You are and will always be the love of my life. And one day ... someday ... I will join you and rest here beside you in this yard." She turned and looked at her children and then added, "But I still have some work to accomplish before that day."

The young, beautiful widowed woman turned toward the pathway to their home. As she fixed her eyes on the narrow road a subtle movement high and to her left caught her eye. It was something bright and colorful. She turned her head and fixed her gaze upon the brilliant red, white, and blue flag of the United States of America that flew proudly on the pole beside the dilapidated gate of Fort Patrick Henry. The thirteen white stars arranged in a circle danced gaily upon the canton of dark blue. The red and white stripes suspended at attention in the breeze.

Genevieve closed her eyes and smiled. That proud flag represented her new country and the nation that her husband fought for. It was the country that, ultimately, he died to help secure. It was the flag of the great experiment among the governments of men that would provide freedom and opportunity for countless generations of descendants of the brave Patriot, Pierre Grimard.

She memorized every sight and sensation of the moment ... the cool crispness of the air, the brilliant orange glow of the sun, the gloriously beautiful flag, the crunchy brown grass, and the pale green river that flowed nearby. She wanted to always remember the moment that she said her final goodbye to her best friend and mate.

She sighed and reached out her hand to young Pierre. "Come along boys and girls. Let us go home. We have supper to prepare."

The fatherless family turned and walked down the dirt road toward their hauntingly empty home.

# THE REAL PIERRE GRIMARD
# OF VINCENNES

P ierre Grimard was my wife's ancestor. He was her fifth great-
grandfather in the line of her direct surname and the first
immigrant of that family line in America. The name in
French does not fit our phonetic reading of the word in English. In
French, the word sounds like "Gree-more," with the accent on the
first syllable. Over time, that has become the "Americanized" spell-
ing of the name. Today you can find hundreds of households with
the names, "Gremore" and "Greemore" scattered throughout the
Midwest. Indeed, my wife's maiden name was Kimberly Gremore.

I have endeavored to portray the character and history of
Pierre Grimard in as authentic a manner as I possibly could. For
many years, his descendants have assumed that he was of French
Canadian origins. However, the discovery of his marriage record
in the Diocese of New Orleans a few years ago dispelled that old
family legend. The marriage document names his hometown and
diocese in France and identifies the names of his parents.

Interestingly, the marriage contract also named Charles
Rimbault and Antoine Alexis as signers of Pierre's marriage surety.
I was thrilled to memorialize both of those very real, historical men
in my story. Beyond the marriage document I can find absolutely
no other records of *Monsieur* Alexis. I did, however, find evidence

of Charles Rimbault living in Vincennes prior to 1765. His presence in New Orleans in the summer of 1769 led me to form the logical conjecture that he was a river man, or *voyageur*. I turned that possibility into an important element in my story.

This marriage document and its unique location in New Orleans, along with the identity of Genevieve Colomb and her family, opened up an entirely new opportunity for the story lines that focused on the adventures of travel through the Caribbean and on the Mississippi River. These accounts, I believe, will help modern readers to better understand the great difficulty and hardships that many of the French migrants endured in order to make a new home on the distant frontiers of America.

I included the names of all of Pierre's children in the book. I did, however, change the order of their births for the sake of drama within the story. Helene was actually the oldest daughter, and born only one year after Pierre. However, to portray a motherly longing for a first baby girl, I wrote the infant Genevieve into the story as the first daughter born in the winter of 1779 (which she was … right in the middle of the incredible events in Vincennes). I did, however, make sure that I included Helene in the final gathering of children in the epilogue.

We are not certain as to the cause of Pierre's untimely death. We do, however, know that he died at some time in 1784, since his burial was recorded that year in the documents of the Old Cathedral Catholic Church in Vincennes. He was still a young man and actively fathering children at the time of his death. Only a scant few of the graves in the old French and Indian graveyard beside the church are marked. There are claims that several thousand bodies are buried there.

Being a young woman and having responsibility for seven young children, Genevieve Colomb remarried relatively quickly. She wed a local man named Jean-Baptiste Ouelette on September 12, 1785. As far as I can tell, there are no other records of her life after that marriage.

Pierre Grimard is not the only Patriot ancestor of my wife mentioned in this story. She is also descended from Francois Turpin. In 1809 Rosalie Turpin, the daughter of Francois, married Charles Grimard, son of Pierre and Genevieve. Like Pierre Grimard, Francois Turpin is also recognized as a Patriot of the American Revolution by both the National Societies of the Sons and Daughters of the American Revolution.

Since Pierre's service in the army was verifiable, as well as the written record of his burial in that local cemetery, interested individuals were able to secure a Veteran's Administration headstone for Pierre Grimard a few decades ago. His stone is displayed in a special formation along with nine other Patriots of Vincennes, including that of Captain Francois Riday Bousseron. My wife and I visit the site each year on our annual trek to the *Spirit of Vincennes Rendezvous*. She is quite honored to know that her ancestor is memorialized within sight of the beautiful George Rogers Clark National Historic Park and Monument that stands on the exact site of the old Fort Sackville. She is most proud of a personal photograph of her beside his memorial stone that we took during our first visit there a few years ago.

It is my sincere hope that you have enjoyed my fictionalized account of the contribution of the French soldiers and citizens in the Illinois Country to the cause of liberty and the founding of the United States of America. Most Americans know little to nothing about this theater of the Revolutionary War. Fewer still know about the involvement of the local French citizens. In most history books the Frenchmen on the frontier are given little more than a footnote. Indeed, many treat them with a certain measure of disrespect or even disdain. For instance, during the brief battle, most reference books mention that the British cannon caused little damage other than "knocking down a few houses in the town." But those were the homes of Frenchmen and their families, and they contained people who were under orders to remain inside during the night. We do not know how many might have been killed or wounded by that cannon fire. That is the reason why I sought to make the event personal by fictitiously describing the suffering of a single family during the siege ... the Grimard family.

If you have never visited Vincennes and partaken of its rich heritage and history, I highly encourage you to go. The best time to visit, in my opinion, is during the annual *Spirit of Vincennes Rendezvous* that is held on Memorial Day weekend each May. Hundreds of Revolutionary War reenactors descend upon the little town and transform the area around the old Fort Sackville into an extensive 18th Century encampment. The weekend includes multiple battle reenactments, amazing food, wonderful shopping, and incredible hospitality. I hope to see you there next year! Come and visit my little "Book Shoppe!"

As I close, I feel compelled to answer a couple of interesting questions from readers.

The first was, "Why were the Virginia soldiers called 'Long Knives?'" As best I can discern, it was because of the amazingly accurate long rifles that the men carried. Their weapons could reach far beyond the muskets, blades, or bows of their Native American enemies ... thus they were nicknamed, "The Long Knives."

Another question was, "What happened to the *Willing*, the boat that Clark sent downriver with supplies?" Well, the *Willing* finally arrived at Vincennes, but did so two days after the battle ... far too late to make a contribution. Since I ended my story at the surrender of Fort Sackville, I never mentioned it again.

Now you know "the rest of the story."

Thank you for reading my novel. Though much of it is, indeed, fiction, it could very well have been the story of Pierre and Genevieve and the brave Grimard family. May they never be forgotten.

*Huzzah!*
*Geoff Baggett*

# ABOUT THE AUTHOR

 Geoff Baggett is a small-town pastor in rural Kentucky. Though his formal education and degrees are in the fields of chemistry, biology, and Christian theology, his hobbies and obsessions (according to his wife) are genealogy and Revolutionary War history. He is an active member of the Sons of the American Revolution and has discovered over twenty Patriot ancestors in his family tree from the states of Virginia, North and South Carolina, and Georgia.

Geoff is an avid living historian, appearing regularly in period uniform in classrooms, reenactments, and other Revolutionary War commemorative events throughout the southeastern United States. He lives on a small piece of land in rural Trigg County, Kentucky, with his amazing wife, Kim, a daughter and grandson, and a yard full of fruit trees and perpetually hungry chickens and goats.

# THANK YOU FOR READING MY STORY!

I hope that you enjoyed my work of fiction. It was a pleasure preparing and writing it for you. I am just a simple "part-time" author, and I am grateful that you chose to read my book.

I would humbly ask that you help me spread the word about the books of my two series on the Revolutionary War. It's not easy for an independent writer to "break through" and find success in the overly-saturated book market. But you can help me in a number of ways!

- **Tell your friends!** Word of mouth is always the best!
- **Mention my books on Facebook or in other social media.** This is just a "high tech" form of word of mouth.
- **Write a review for me on Amazon.com.** Reviews are so very important in marketing these days. I am grateful for every review that I receive and watch my titles daily in search of new reviews.
- **Connect with me and like my author page on Facebook @cockedhatpublishing, and follow me on Twitter @ GeoffBaggett.**
- **Use my student books in your school curriculum!** I currently have a teaching supplement for my first book for kids, *Little Hornet*, and similar products are under development

for my other children's titles. They are available for free (PDF downloads) on my web site. If you are interested in a "class set" for your school, please contact me directly. I make copies available for classrooms at a very low price.

- **Book me for a presentation!** I have several unique, engaging, and interesting Revolutionary War presentations available for groups or classes. I am a professional speaker and living historian. I will travel if I can have the opportunity to connect to readers and sell some books! Contact me through my web site, geoffbaggett.com, or through my Facebook author page, to arrange an event.

Thanks again! Please be on the lookout for my next novel in the series. This one will be about one of my North Carolina Revolutionary War ancestors. I'm already working on all of the research. The title will be *Soldiers and Martyrs.* Look for it in 2018!

*Geoff Baggett*

Made in the USA
Monee, IL
15 November 2020